The Elusive Language of Ducks

Judith White is a winner of the BNZ Katherine Mansfield Centenary Award, and twice-winner of the *Auckland Star* Short Story Competition. Her short-story collection, *Visiting Ghosts*, was shortlisted for the New Zealand Book Awards, and her first novel, *Across the Dreaming Night*, was shortlisted for the Montana New Zealand Book of the Year. She lives in Auckland, New Zealand.

The Elusive Language of Ducks

ONEWORLD

A Oneworld Book

First published in North America and Great Britain by
Oneworld Publications, 2014

First published in Australia and New Zealand by Random House
New Zealand Ltd, 2013

Copyright © Judith White 2013

The moral right of Judith White to be identified as the Author of this work
has been asserted by her in accordance with the Copyright, Designs, and
Patents Act 1988

ISBN 978-1-78074-400-1
ISBN 978-1-78074-401-8 (eBook)

Text design by Megan van Staden
Printed and bound in Denmark by Nørhaven A/S

This book is a work of fiction. Names, characters, businesses, organisations,
places and events are either the product of the author's imagination or are
used fictitiously. Any resemblance to actual persons, living or dead, events of
locales is entirely coincidental.

Oneworld Publications
10 Bloomsbury Street
London WC1B 3SR
England

Stay up to date with the latest books,
special offers, and exclusive content from
Oneworld with our monthly newsletter

Sign up on our website
www.oneworld-publications.com

For my mother, Beth Featherstone

Prologue

SALT

Drunk.

Yesterday, your mother died and now you are drunk.

You were both there and it was the salt that you had always refused her because you thought it was bad for her health, and now it was keeping her alive through the slow saline drip into her arm, and then the doctor said, No more salt.

It was time. You knew that.

The doctor insisting on plunging his oar into the deep, deep sea of your sorrow.

I'm going to have to turn this off now.

That's fine, we know what's going on. Now go away.

Already it had started. The breathing. The stopping and the starting of it.

The stopping and now not daring to look at each other. Then, as you sat by the bed, you read in the little handbook they gave you in that special hurried meeting in the office of the Primrose Hill Rest Home that, sometimes, towards the end, the period between breaths could be between ten and thirty seconds.

And yes, counting in your head, it was ten to thirty seconds, ten minutes to thirty years, as you waited for the next one.

And then the stopping and it was

Now.

And then the big heave so that you jumped, jumped out of your skin. And, only just, back again.

But . . . the silence and the waiting for the next one, the next breath. Mum.

Mummy?

The silence that was so silent, and afterwards your husband spoke to you about the great swirling wind, the great swirling

The great swirling outside and the leaves

And you didn't hear it, all you heard was the silence, your mother's breath stopped . . . the chatter stopped

And then

You put your hand on her chest and there was nothing there at all

Just the buttons of her nightie and no thump of a clock

Her breasts flattened into skin over bone

And then all the colour that was her life going away. Her lips white and her mouth open

And her cheeks whitening

And everything draining away.

The colour that she would have had a name for, in all its tones. Raw sienna, cobalt violet, ultramarine blue, Windsor yellow, cadmium orange, permanent mauve, etc, etc. You have no idea, really. The colours she squeezed from aluminium tubes, sloshed around with camel-hair brushes before she dabbed and made her magic.

All the colours that she absorbed through her eyes and interpreted and played with on canvas.

All the colour in her eyes.

Gone from her.

It's all so final, says old Joyce afterwards, in the lounge when you say goodbye to the others in their bucket seats who are waiting their turn.

But really it's all so now and everlasting, the life without her

The life without your mother.

And now you are drunk because you don't know what else to do with the thoughts in your head.

AFTERWARDS

And you bring out the boxes from under the house and go through her clothes and fill the car boot with them and take them to the Salvation Army. And you can't help yourself picking up objects that are too deeply connected to this time or that time and, inside your chest, a snake of pain grows too fat for the cavity it has found there; it has swallowed its own tail, and everything that follows is too big for its stomach. It has opened wide jaws and engulfed your life and down you flow into the tight darkness of the beginning and the end.

DOING THE TRICK

And as if it will make up for it all, they bring to you, as an offering, a baby duck.

Your husband's relations have a small farm in Te Awamutu. On one of his missions to the area, a business meeting in Hamilton, Simon had driven down to have lunch with his aunt and uncle. He told you that he'd had no say in the matter, but in fact he could have said no. That would have been the ultimate no say. His meeting was after the lunch in Te Awamutu and he had to stay in Hamilton overnight. He had excuses. But he explained to you that the duckling was waiting for him in the hard-based plastic carry-bag. All ready for the journey back to Auckland. A container of mucky mash for food, and a lid holding water.

They were well-meaning, and it could have done the trick. Every passing day had become a slushy footprint in mud. You were depressed, they said. You were not yourself. You seemed withdrawn. The duck was an orphan; it would die anyway. Everybody was worried about you. They thought a duckling would help. They thought a yellow fluffy duckling pooing and skittering around the wide well-worn seat of your mother's throne would give you something to think about. Is that the trick they had in mind? The one up the sleeve, the sleight of hand. From woe to go, just like that.

Chapter 1

THE GARDEN PATH

Sitting in the grass in the spring sunshine. Somewhere nearby a starling was munching on a song, savouring every whistley morsel before spitting it out for inspection in long chewing-gum threads.

The duckling was lying with its head resting on Hannah's ankle. Her other foot contained it in a safe haven. It appeared happy to be there. She wondered whether it thought it was a foot, or whether her feet were ducks.

It had been lumbered upon her; there was no doubt about that. When her husband had arrived home from Hamilton, several weeks ago now, he had hesitantly made his way down the garden path as she greeted him from the front door. He was carrying a bright orange carry-bag with a hard base, rather like a doctor's medical bag, full of quackery. He'd opened it, less than triumphantly, for her to see inside.

From the start she'd been aware of the whole projected scenario, the band-aid for the gaping wound. It did not stick. It somehow marginalised her grief.

And what are you going to do with this? she'd asked her husband. She closed herself tight against the chirruping fluff skittering in the straw.

It's for you. From Claire and Bob.

I don't want it. I don't want another creature to look after.

That's OK. I thought you might say that. Don't worry, it was going to die anyway, it's been abandoned. But what shall we do with it?

It smells revolting, she said.

I know, I . . . it's been running around in its mess since yesterday morning. And the water has sloshed everywhere.

Turning, she went inside. From the bedroom her mother called to her. No, she didn't, but always there was the echo of her voice lingering there, hovering in Hannah's head like wind chimes, waiting for the right breeze to knock a memory resonating into life.

She passed through the hall, through the sitting room and out to the deck where she leaned on the railing, staring across the valley. The magnolia tree beside her, winding across the deck, was just sneaking into leaf. They'd lived in this same house for twenty-two years, on the quarter-acre section in a hilly suburb near the centre of the city. The area used to be a patchwork of sections the same size as theirs, houses surrounded by daisy-dotted lawn stretching from fence to fence, with paths from the road to the houses framed by flowers. Over-laden plum trees had provided for sauce and jam, gorging kids, rows of preserving jars in wash-houses, and still there were plenty of plums for the birds. Lemon and grapefruit trees, heavy with balls of juice, grew in sunny corners. Neighbours talked over the fences and shared produce from their vegetable gardens, squared out at the bottom of the sections.

Now they were crammed in by apartments, town-houses and palatial new villas which, from time to time, sprouted a shroud of white plastic, like nursery-web spiders in a hedge, to allow workmen to repair leaks from poor construction. Video cameras surveyed properties. Alarms, like frightened birds, spasmodically startled the peace. Generally, there was no communication amongst the neighbours. Hannah and Simon used to be more than friendly with Eric, the man next door, but recently even he had withdrawn. And his music, which used to thread so enticingly from his house to theirs, had stopped.

Hannah.

An alarm, startling her. Simon had followed her to the deck, was standing beside her.

She'd placed her head into her cupped hands.

Hannah.

I don't want a duck. I don't want anything.

I know. I'm sorry. Come inside. I'll get rid of it.

How can you just get *rid* of it? I'm not pregnant. This creature has been born.

He'd stood there helplessly. He pitied her, she could see that. But she was pushing him, nudging him away from her, forcing him right up to the edge of the cliff. She was the last straw in a duckling's carry-bag.

Where did you put it?

On the front lawn.

On the *lawn?* Where the *cats* can get it?

Once again she'd turned from him, passing back through the house to the lawn, which was surrounded by trees and shrubs and ferns. She picked up the bag and returned inside, to the bathroom. She scooped the duckling into the bath. It ran skittering in panic on the shiny white porcelain. Simon stood at the door, watching. She took out the mash and the water dish.

Can you empty this into the compost, said Hannah, handing him the carry-bag. Have you got clean straw?

Oh yes, I think I have. Claire gave me some stuff. And fresh mash. The duckling will need a heat source, I believe.

When he returned with the carry-bag, she wiped it clean with paper towels and put it on a towel on the heated tiles in the bathroom, with the fresh straw that his aunt had provided. The carry-bag was made of strengthened plastic and its corners could be straightened rigidly to create a box. She leaned over the bath and cupped her hands around the noisy duckling, releasing it into the straw. Already there were two small heaps of mess in their bath. She brought out the disinfectant, turned on the tap and started swishing and scrubbing. She knew nothing, nothing at all, about ducklings. Nor about ducks of any description, except that they quacked and ate bread in parks.

Later, she'd googled 'ducklings' and found: They must always have water. They have no teeth and can choke on their food if they don't have water, as they can't chew. Ducklings are messy and will slop their water everywhere, will walk in it. Don't give them bread as they are not made for it. Ducklings might like the odd worm, but not too many. Too much protein and they will develop angel wings — wings that stick up. They eat greens and mash.

So she'd placed a bowl for water in its box. A green china jam dish from the cupboard, the size of about a third of an orange, in the shape of a flower. When the duckling stood in it, the bowl contained its fluffiness perfectly. The petals opened around its yellow form like an eggshell.

And that was several weeks ago. She had reluctantly agreed to look after the helpless creature until it was strong enough to fend for itself, before returning it to Te Awamutu or setting it free amongst other ducks in a park somewhere.

She leaned over and picked a dandelion leaf growing from the base of a rock. So tiny was the duckling that she had to rip up the leaf. She dangled the narrow strips in front of its beak so it could snap them up.

SOMETHING, SOMEONE, TO CARE FOR

When her mother came to live with them after she became ill, Hannah would lurch from sleep, wondering whether she might have passed away overnight. There were times when the anxiety was so insistent that she was forced to get out of bed and pad down the stairs to stand at her mother's door, listening for the soft snoring that filled the room.

Once, confronted by silence, she eased open the door, crept in and stood by the bed. Moonlight filtered in through the curtains and settled around the shapes of the motionless bedclothes, across her mother's face, the dark cavity of her open mouth, empty of breath. Hannah touched her cheek. Slapped her vigorously, calling. Suddenly her mother heaved and yelped, struggling in vain to sit up.

Oh, oh, I'm sorry Mum, I . . . was just looking for your teeth. She grabbed the first reason — however ludicrous — that came into her head.

Hannah, for heaven's sake, what's happening?

Nothing, I'm sorry. I just, I was just checking, that you were all right. Ssssh, it's OK. Go to sleep.

I *was* asleep. Where are my teeth?

They're in the glass. It's OK. I had a dream that you'd lost them.

Are they there?

Now, every morning, Hannah was awakened by her husband perfunctorily plodding around the house, his weight wrapped thickly around his middle, whereas hers returned to fill her head, unseen except for the pull of flesh from around her cheeks, her mouth. The weight of heavy deliberation.

Her first task was to check on the little duckling in the carry-box in the bathroom, to make sure he hadn't drowned in his water or died in his sleep from lack of whatever it was that ducklings needed that she hadn't been able to offer.

From the local pet shop she had bought supplies of straw to line his box, and special baby chook mash. Each day he ate a little more.

When he spotted her, the duckling peeped an urgent staccato code, for which she didn't have the key, but it soon threaded its way from its helplessness to the part of her that had become habituated to caring for the helpless. She only had to pick him up to soothe him. All he desired was to nestle into somebody, to sleep with his head pushed into a fold of arm or flesh. All he really wanted, of course she realised, was a mother duck.

Because of this, when she was at home the woman carried the duckling on her shoulder under her hair. If she was working at her desk, the ducking snuffled into her neck before settling to sleep. It was a strange companionable thing to have this downy ball rummaging through the blonde grassy shelter of her hair. At other times she spread a towel across her lap and he'd sleep there as well. Eventually, she noticed that, as long as she removed him from time to time, he didn't poo when he was upon her. She supposed that, in the wild, this was Nature's way of preventing mother ducks from being covered in the excrement of their brood.

VENTURING OUT

Gradually, as the weeks passed, the woman introduced the duckling to the outside world. She took him into the garden, looking for worms and pulling out weeds along the way. The duck kept close by her, almost dangerously so as she clambered on her knees around him while he pecked and skittered amongst the grass and plants. He wasn't strong enough yet to tear at leaves, so she continued to do this for him. As she didn't know which plants were poisonous for ducks, she guided him towards the dandelions and discouraged him from eating other vegetation. They discovered the fleas that erupted from the soil when she pulled away a brick or a piece of wood. He liked slaters and small cockroaches. The special purring chirrup he made when he ate rose in intensity whenever he made a bountiful find.

The garden had been neglected. Its parched soil felt malnourished, screaming with thirst. When they first moved here, twenty-two years before, they'd been surrounded by a low hedge, a lawn filled with daisies, and with plums, lemons, figs and mandarins on the lawn out the back.

She and Simon had laboured over the soil, digging in compost, and buying native trees, flaxes and ferns to attract birds. It was a project they'd enjoyed, quietly working alongside each other, often until dark when their tools and the weeds dissolved into shadows. In the early days, they'd kick off their shoes and fumble their way inside, laughing, without switching on electric lights. They'd fling off their grubby clothes to sink into a hot bath together, their skin stinging from the sun, the water muddying from their shared toils. They sipped wine or smoked a joint, ate previously prepared delicacies, and looked at each other in flickering candlelight from each end of the bath.

Over the years, the garden was developed to a point where it needed less attention. From time to time they'd revisit it with the same fervour, spending full weekends doing maintenance: weeding and pruning, planting and feeding the soil. But basically it looked after itself. The trees grew into a lush barrier from the rest of the world. It was only from the deck that they could look over and beyond to the neighbours' backyards, and over to the other side of the valley where houses and apartments were continually being crammed into any available space.

After her mother came to live with them, Hannah finished teaching and took on editing work that she mostly could do from home. Her mother's stay also coincided with Simon shifting from a solid day-job into semi-retirement. He took on engineering work that he could do from home, or which alternatively led him away for days or weeks at a time to other cities, sometimes other countries, on contract. Although they were spending more time in the house together, they spent less time nurturing each other. Hannah could see this clearly now. She'd been involved in the care for her mother. The garden became a shell that locked them against the world, into themselves. And their connection through their computers into separate domains left them trudging through different ethereal wastelands, and somewhere along the way they had become disconnected, their fingers seldom touching, moving onwards from a perspective that had once met, along parallel paths that steered them into an infinity apart.

And after her mother arrived, neither Hannah nor Simon had ventured into the undergrowth of the garden, neither of them pulled weeds or re-planted. Neither of them spent days or hours labouring until their muscles ached. On warmer days, Hannah had helped her mother outside onto the garden seat, with her handbag of course, bundled up in a bright crocheted blanket. She'd entertained her with readings from Shakespeare, absurdly shouting the Elizabethan language to be heard, not only by her mother, but all the neighbours and passersby, as well as triggering a nearby dog to soulfully howl the part of an unsolicited extra.

Meanwhile, the neighbourhood cats had moved in. Now Hannah anxiously shooed them away. She could spot their eyes glinting like malevolent creatures from a Rousseau jungle. Her own old cats skulked close by as well, displeased by this newcomer, a bird what's more, competing for her attention.

DREAMS

At night, the duckling slept in the bathroom, still in the same plastic carrier. Each morning she cleaned out the straw where his poos collected, all the plump worms of his dreams spurted from the night for her to see.

Her own dreams of late were to do with him. Foraging dreams. Losing dreams. And then, a truly distressing dream.

The day before, she'd heard a radio interview with a chef banging on about the exquisite flavour and texture of *pâté de foie gras*. He was exuberantly sharing a recipe for tender juicy duck breast, cooked slowly with juniper berries and brown sugar.

Later, an email from a listener was read on-air. Were people aware of the cruelty behind the production of *pâté de foie gras*? How ducks were force-fed five kilograms of mashed corn a day, pumped through long pipes thrust down their throats? The torture lasted over two to three weeks, swelling their livers up to ten times the normal size.

That night, she dreamt that she was pulling a roasting dish from the hot oven. Amongst a rocky landscape of potatoes, pumpkin and parsnips, the duckling lay sprawled, gazing up at her weakly. His crusty fluff was pressed against goosebumpy skin.

She quickly retrieved his little carcass from the roasting dish, pleading with him not to die. But his eyes were milky white. There was a hopeful shimmer of black in the centre, until even that closed, like the last bubble popping from quicksand. His head quivered then flopped onto the palm of her hand.

She woke, crying into her pillow in that peculiar condensed way of dreams. Simon's comforting hand was on her back.

Are you OK? he asked into the darkness.

The duck, she replied. I dreamt . . . that the duckling was . . . dead.

Oh, he muttered. The *duck!*

I . . . betrayed him.

For goodness' sake. I thought it must have been about your mother.

He rolled over, and already he was asleep again, his back a wall towering above her.

She lay with the ache of the dream still sitting like a brick on her chest.

She was thinking of those days of her childhood when all the breathing in and out was a stitching together of moments and moments and moments. Her fear of the night, and her fiercely beating heart as she stood shivering in the dark by her parents' bed until her mother eventually shifted over to let her in. She could still recall the sense of the delicious plunge into sleep once she felt safe.

And now her mind turned to the funeral parlour, with that organic smell hitting the back of her throat. An enormous wall clock whacked out the minutes, a clock from a busy railway station, where trains with no timetable arrived and departed on a whim. Her mother was already rotting on the board, though she wore lipstick, her cheeks were rouged and her hair was swept up as if her final journey had been on a motorbike. When Hannah curiously drew the blanket aside, she could see her mother's blood, black and pooling under her bones, only just held within her skin.

TALKING ABOUT LOVE

The woman's cats associated her with food. When they saw her, they sat upright with their ears pricked straight. Once they'd eaten their prime minced meat, they ignored her, unless it was cold or wet and they wanted to come inside. Their interest in her was self-serving.

When the duck saw her, all *he* wanted was to be with her. Whether or not his bowl was full of mash, his greens were piled around him or his water dish was replenished, he wanted only to sit on her lap or push his beak under the wing of her arm, or if not that, at least to sit contentedly at her feet.

She wondered whether this was a duck version of love.

One evening alone, before settling him down to sleep, she found herself sitting on the heated tiles of the bathroom with a glass of red wine by her side, musing out loud to him. She told him that the world was full of people who loved each other, or loved someone who didn't love them, or were loved by someone who was not the one they truly loved. Or worse, people who didn't love anyone, or who were loved by nobody at all. Everyone — she said, gulping more wine — could be defined by whom they loved, or didn't love, and whether that love was reciprocated. Everyone formed themselves around the quality of love they had within them. And that was who they were.

That's a bit obvious, the duckling replied. He said that he was sure his mother and father would have loved each other forever if tragedy had not intervened.

She told him that after *her* father died, so many years ago, her mother had tended to her own wizened mother, who clung to life as though it were a galloping horse, her white-haired head resting on its mane, fingers clasped into its gums like a bridle. Finally the horse had flung her off. After that, Hannah's mother had lived alone.

When she went on to mention, in a somewhat maudlin tone by now, that some people were very difficult to love, oh yes they were, the duck asked her why she'd bother loving them at all.

Surely you just love them, or not?

It's not that easy, she replied, spinning the tip of her finger around the rim of her glass. She told him that loving her sister, for example, was like loving a bee trapped in a jar, if he could imagine that.

You're frightened to take the lid off because you don't know whether she's going to sting you or fly away. On the other hand there's the honey side of her, but it's seldom experienced.

The woman recounted how her sister had arrived from Christchurch, straight from the plane, on the morning of their mother's funeral just a few months ago, dressed in black tights, short black skirt, professional jacket. Black sleek hair in a short bob, red lipstick. Heels that clipped noisily as she hurried about, apologising that her husband Toby couldn't come, kissing the cousins and Simon's relations and friends she'd met and never met, the hobbly uncle and the smelly old guy no one knew, and the celebrant — everyone — on the cheek. Everyone at the funeral was branded with a smudge of red along the continuum between ear and mouth: intimacy was determined according to the proximity of the lipstick to the lips. During the service she read a poem she had written. Even people who hadn't met her mother dabbed their eyes. At the reception in the hall afterwards, people came to Hannah and remarked about its poignancy.

While Hannah hung back, exhausted by the event of her mother's death and years of lack of sleep, Maggie spoke to everyone, her hand resting on arms, her eyes meeting theirs, babbling like a motor boat and pulling out their own stories as if she were sifting strings of weed from a lake. After the club sandwiches, asparagus rolls, little meat pies and cup cakes in the hall alongside the chapel, they traipsed back home, Hannah and Simon, and Maggie. Auntie Claire and Bob had a cup of tea and left soon after for Te Awamutu.

That night they lit a fire for the first time that winter. Maggie got stuck into the gin. Simon and Hannah opened a bottle of champagne. Hannah had a glass of bubbly and a leftover club sandwich and went to bed, leaving Simon still drinking. He had finished the bubbly, and Maggie had persuaded him to have a gin. The fire had settled down and was glowing like an angry fist.

A couple of hours later Hannah woke up. Simon wasn't in bed. She got up to go to the bathroom, and found Maggie lying on the couch, her arms and body curled around the framed photo of their mother, the one that had been propped against the coffin. Simon was squatting at her head, his hand on her shoulder. Hannah saw that he was holding a bucket. He looked up as Hannah peered around the door.

What's going on? she asked.

Your sister isn't feeling well. His voice was thick. Maggie turned her head in a delayed, jerky kind of way. Her face was as wet as winter. Her lips were pale. The ink pad had run out. The gin bottle was on the floor, nearly empty.

We're talking about *Mum*, said Maggie. Your mother and *my* mother. And your darling husband is telling me things. Aren't you, Simon, you sweet man? And she shoved her fingers backwards through his hair and over his face and into his beard, lingering over his mouth. He tugged away.

Maggie is upset, he explained to Hannah.

I know I am, and he's right, he's as right as rain, the dear man, but my mother has just expired. Dead. Would you believe it? My mother. And my whole life, trying to live up to expectorations, expectations, ex marks the spot and now she's gone, and I will never know whether I made it. She didn't give me the test results. Did I pass? All that time, and where is she now? I don't even know whether she liked me.

She did, said Hannah. She missed you terribly.

Maggie hoisted herself up from the couch, sat up, tore at her hair, then flopped back down again before continuing.

I rang her once at her place, before you kidnapped her, and she thought the *kids* were with her — the kids who have been in *London* with their father for *years*. She told me that she could see them, and she complained that she cooked for them and, not only would they not eat her food, but they didn't help with the dishes afterwards. She was away with the fairies.

That was the medication, said Hannah. She had episodes like that, hallucinations. You would have caught her on a bad day.

Yes, darling, but what was the point? In the end, what could we say that was real? Nothing.

She was proud of you, said Hannah. And Toby, she liked Toby, too. After all the divorce trouble, she was pleased you found someone who was more suited to you.

She never told me. Honestly. Would've been nice to hear it from the horse's mouth.

Her words mushy, running into each other, slow.

She ached for you. She'd tell everyone about you, your job, so important. *My daughter, in advertising . . .*

Everybody except me. You've no idea how hard it has been for me. Toby's all fun and games, you know. People think I'm strong, but it's all a mouth. A myth. Huh. It's all word of myth. You've no idea what my life's like. What I have to put up with. No idea. Nobody. Simon has though, now, don't you, sweetie? How tough it's been for me?

Simon by now was sitting back in his armchair, drumming his fingers, yawning and shuffling his feet over the carpet. He glanced at Hannah, then fixated on fiercely flicking at crumbs on the arm of the chair. Maggie attempted to sit up again, swinging her legs around to the floor, groaning, still clutching the photo.

I'm armour-plated because I've had to be, and if only you knew how heavy all that stuff is to carry around. Hauling it around, clanking and jangling in the dungeons, OK, OK, bucket, quick Simon, sweetie, give me the bucket, here here here.

Simon leapt over and pressed the bucket at her chest, under her chin.

She dropped the photo and threw her arms around the bucket.

God. Oh God.

Her voice echoing in the bucket. She retched and heaved violently and fruitlessly, before pushing the bucket away.

God. I'm gonna die on the day of my mother's funeral.

Come on, Maggie, said Simon. No, you're not.

Hannah was leaning against the door, amazed but not surprised that her sister could flip the occasion of her mother's death into a means to seek attention for herself. Simon stared at Hannah for help. She went over and helped prop Maggie's head onto a cushion. Together, they bundled her, moaning like a cow in labour, onto her side. Simon lifted her feet onto the couch again. He went to the linen cupboard and pulled out a crocheted blanket and a towel. He spread the blanket over Maggie, arranged the towel under her chin over the couch, and left the bucket within easy reach.

You're a good man, Simon, she murmured, her eyes blinking, her hand waving like seaweed in an attempt to grasp his.

By the time Hannah returned to bed, after making sure the fire was safe and picking up bottles and glasses, the good man was snoring on top of the duvet, still in his clothes, the eye of his navel winking at her between shirt buttons.

In the morning Maggie had left, her taxi arriving on schedule at six-thirty. Only a waft of her perfume floated in the room to suggest that she'd been there at all.

Hannah glanced down at the duck on her lap. He'd shoved his head up into her sleeve and by his breathing she could tell he was asleep. When she moved, though, his head was out and alert again.

Oh, I've been miles away, said the woman. Sorry.

It's been interesting, said the duck. That Maggie, she's a one all right. And the man. What about him?

What do you mean, what about him?

You love him?

And she realised that she felt awkward about answering this question. It seemed complicated. A little acidic spot of infidelity etching its way through the shiny paintwork. Guilt, like rust, never sleeps.

Of course I do, was the easiest thing to say, and that's what she did say, and of course she did, but she didn't like the feeling of discomfort that hovered.

Chapter 2

IN THE UNDERGROWTH

The duckling was becoming more gangly and straggly. An undergrowth of white down was sprouting amongst the yellow. Also, on top of his tail, hidden by fluff, there was a round plug of sunny yellow tufts. Hannah examined it with her fingertip; it was soft and sensual, resembling in appearance and touch the centre of a dandelion flower. And it felt significant, like a storehouse for a fountain of feathers, fizzing to burst into a fanned display.

Look at this, she said to Simon, who was sitting at the kitchen table, working on his computer. She held the duckling in the crux of her arm and rummaged through the tail fluff to display the golden plug. She knew Simon didn't care much for the duck, but he also had a tendency to be pedantic. He peered over his glasses and said, Hmmm. Looks like a gland of some sort.

Shortly afterwards he told her exactly what it was, as if he'd known all along.

It's a uropygial gland, he read from the screen of his computer. It produces oil to spread over the feathers to make them water-repellent. It's strongly developed in waterfowl such as ducks, and not all birds have them. Emus, ostriches and bustards don't. Hmmm, no, wait a minute . . . What you're looking at is the uropygial *wick*, under which is a single narrow nipple-like papilla, producing vitamin D precursors, extruded cells, ester waxes, fatty acids, fat and sudanophilic secretory granules.

What's a bustard, wondered Hannah, and what's a sudanophilic secretory granule? But she didn't dare ask.

Ducks are more buoyant than they would be if their feathers absorbed water, continued Simon. *And* they have hollow bones. If ducks die at sea, say after an oil spill, ninety per cent of them float for at least two weeks.

Hannah looked at the duckling with its hollow bones and uropygial wick.

Well, she said. Well, we have learnt something.

SOMETHING TO TELL HER

Simon had always relied on knowledge or information as a means of communication.

The first time he'd asked her out, rather casually, one cold Easter, to a university tramping club get-together, there'd been a bonfire. Baked potatoes encrusted with thick charcoal, sausages, white bread, tomato sauce, mulled wine, laughing camaraderie. After eating, everybody sat on logs around the fire and hollered out rude songs into the chilly night. *She'll be coming round the mountains when she comes. The hair on her dikydido hung down to her knees.*

Then, without any preamble, he'd grabbed her hand.

Come, I want to show you something, he said.

She'd clambered up from the log and followed, or rather was pulled behind him, along the grassy dunes, down to the beach and around a headland of rocks, their boots squelching through the wet sand left by the low tide. Around the next bay they stood against the rocks, sheltering from a keen wind cutting its way under their coats. The icy blue light of the full moon was shattered across the choppy sea. It's stunning, Hannah said, pushing herself against him, more for warmth than anything.

Diving into his coat pocket, he pulled out a large pair of binoculars. He moved behind her, resting his arms on her shoulders, breathing close to her ear as he held the binoculars to her eyes, directed towards the moon. His hand, she noted, was trembling. She took the binoculars from him, adjusting the focus as he pointed out the main craters and seas and mountains. He had names for them all. Unaccountably, she started to giggle, and the more she tried to stop the worse it became.

What's funny? he asked.

Nothing, she replied, but the more unsettled he became, the more the bubbles burst out from under the lid of the boiling kettle.

As he pulled away from her, she could feel his sense of rejection and this made her worse.

What's wrong? What did I do?

She stopped until the hysterics exploded from her again.

I'm sorry, she kept saying, I'm sorry.

He wound the strap around the binoculars and stuffed them roughly back into his pocket.

She pulled herself together.

I just don't get the joke, he said and, when she started giggling again, he grabbed her and placed his mouth over hers. He tasted of charcoal, sausages, tomato sauce, mulled wine. He tasted of teeth and tongue. He tasted of everything she had ever wanted, forever, in her whole life. Suddenly they were urgently making love, still bundled up against the cold in their layers of clothes, she with her back pressed against the rock face, and, above her, the unblinking eye of the moon, with all its craters, seas and mountains, shattering itself into every particle of her being.

Afterwards, as they ambled hand-in-hand back to the bonfire, he said, with an element of hurt lingering in his voice: I still don't get what it was that you were laughing at.

I'm sorry, she said again. I tend to giggle when I'm nervous.

But really, she'd been laughing at his premeditation, his obvious preparation, she was laughing because he had set up everything so that he could have the excuse to put his arms over her shoulders, and his cheek against her cheek to murmur craters and lakes in her ear. He could have muttered anything — the periodic table, his favourite ice-cream flavours, characters from *Animal Farm*; he could have been silent. And all these months at university he had given her no clue that he even liked her. They were both a few years older than the other students who were straight from school, and they'd enjoyed lengthy discussions in tutorials, in groups over coffee, sometimes sitting next to each other in lectures, in a contrived arbitrary sort of way. It had suddenly seemed ridiculously hilariously gloriously funny.

And then he'd said, There's something I need to tell you.

Oh?

I don't want to tell you now, but just remember that I told you this: that I need to tell you something.

You're married with three children?

No, he said.

Ten children?

Don't be silly.

I know you're Australian, she joked. And I don't mind.

I'm wishing I hadn't mentioned it. It's not funny.

You can tell me, she said.

I don't want to tell you now as there might be no point. I mean it's early days, I mean . . . I don't know what *this* means to you.

OK, she said. Sure, that's fine.

I mean, we've only been 'us' for five minutes. Well, maybe seven, he said.

OK, she said again, and nestled into his armoury of jerseys and coat. And she took from this that he was looking at a meaningful relationship, and, although this would normally scare her off so soon, for some reason she knew it was to be, and didn't mind at all.

THE DUCK AND THE MAN

Hannah was stressed, bogged down with a sudden overload of the editing work she did. Sometimes the duck felt like the breaking point and she had to call on Simon to help her. And it so turned out that Simon, who had played an instrumental part in the duck coming to stay, didn't like to touch it unless it was wrapped up in a towel and placed carefully in his lap. And even so, when this was forced upon him, he sat upright in a meditative pose with his eyes closed. The epitome of contrived tolerance.

The first time she handed him the duck, after the duck had been freshly bathed in warm water in the wash basin, both the man and the duck protested. The duck wriggled to be free.

He doesn't like me, Simon said to his wife.

He doesn't like me, the duck said to the woman.

Well, you'll have to get used to each other, said the woman to both of them. If you want me to cook your dinner, she said to the man. If you want me to clean out your box and give you fresh water and stir up your mash, she said to the duck. And smash up a snail or two, she added. And pudding for you, as well, and if you'd like me to be relaxed enough to have a wine with you later, she added to the man.

She eased the duck from Simon's big smooth hands. Held the duck against her stomach, rubbed his damp downy breast with the towel. He pressed against her and nuzzled into her shirt. He thought he had won. Simon, too, thought he had won. He yawned and stretched and scratched his ear. She chatted to each of them a little, and once they had both calmed down, she wrapped the duckling in the towel again and passed him over to the man. This time, both duck and man were resigned to each other.

The duck was outgrowing the carry-bag, so Hannah had bought a large plastic storage box which he slept in at night in the bathroom. But he needed to have more of a free run in the daytime. And it was Simon who, under some pressure from her, had built the makeshift hutch for the bottom of the garden. A third of it was a wooden covered shelter, and the rest was a run enclosed above and around with chicken-wire. It was makeshift because one day the duck would have to go.

At first the new hutch, about two metres long, seemed enormous, but already with his water dish and mash bowl and the towelling cloth in the shielded corner for nestling into when the wind was cold, it felt cramped. Hannah was thinking they should extend it. She'd imagined he would love his new abode, but once the duck realised that this was the place of confinement when she went away during the day, he would squeak unhappily every time she brought him near it. Now he threw himself insanely against the netting, over and over, trying to force his beak through the wire holes along the rows. This one and this one and this one. He was a persistent gambler, clinging to the vain hope that one of the wire holes was the magic one that would let him through.

While Hannah was there, he ate, or sat looking at her. But as soon as she turned her back, the cheeping started. He was like her fridge door, reminding her that she had left it open. He was the smoke alarm needing a new battery. He was the drier saying that the clothes were ready. The microwave saying the food was done. The phone calling for an answer. He was an electronic beeper, reminding her to be anxious, that she was leaving him alone and motherless, and that she was mean mean mean.

She thought of her mother in the Primrose Hill Rest Home. How, in the beginning, she would shuffle along the corridors — her handbag, now almost empty, over her arm — until the staff found her again. Sometimes she would set out with a wobbly friend, the two of them supporting each other, out for an adventure along the pastel-hued corridors that all looked the same. In the end, to stop her escaping, they'd crammed her bones into a bucket chair from which she couldn't get up. In the end she couldn't get up from anywhere. In the end she couldn't stand. In the end the only exercise she had was to bat with her right hand at a balloon thrown directly to her from the centre of the room.

TO BELIEVE OR NOT TO BELIEVE

The duck was about a month old when the woman placed him in his cage and went out to a long meeting about a book on adoption and its association with mental illness. All day she had to consider people who were isolated or depressed or manic around issues of adoption.

She couldn't help thinking of the duck in relation to all this. At the meeting she mentioned him to people she hadn't met before. She was told that ducklings didn't have a defined gender until later, according to how they fitted in with the dynamics of the rest of the flock. Hannah found this difficult to believe, but even so, wondered whether she was actually influencing the final gender of her duckling. Somewhere, quite early along the way, she had started assuming that he was a male, and for no other reason except that she *felt* that he was. Almost without doubt. But when she was also told that drakes in general were rapacious and aggressive, she just *knew* this wouldn't be the case with her gentle little duck, whatever gender he turned out to be.

As soon as she arrived home from the meeting, the duckling jumped up and ran at the wire netting.

The woman picked him up from the cage, her hands slipping under his belly to calm his clockwork legs. He was like a puppy, such was the intensity of joy as he snuggled into her. She was a dandelion leaf salad, the sun on his fluff after a bath, she was a paddock wriggling with worms, she was a wing, she was a mother duck.

I thought you would never come back, he whimpered. He told her how cats had slunk towards the cage, their whiskery noses investigating. How it had rained — the first time he had experienced water that hadn't been presented to him in a dish or a basin. Today it had fallen from the sky, and she hadn't been there. He dug his beak under her hair, delving into the skin of her neck. She sat down on the steps of the deck, and he laid his neck upon her stomach, burying his head into the crook of her arm, and finally the chirruping settled, and in the silence, in his silence, she thought she could feel his heart vibrating against her arm.

And she thought of his anxiety and isolation all day long, and wondered whether there would be issues in the future over his adoption.

FILLING UP HER LIFE

As the days passed, the duckling's shape pushed out further into the form of a duck. It looked as though a thumb had pressed its beak outwards. Its body was stronger and also longer, its neck snaking out from its body. It was a balloon being blown up in the night by a masterful street artist. One day, she thought, its tail might be tied into a knot and the duck released to float away into the sky, to join all the other fluffy white balloons that skidded high across the wide summer blue.

The woman wondered what would happen to the duck when he grew up. She visualised him filling up all the spaces she had to offer. She imagined going down to the bathroom one morning, to where he slept on straw in the large plastic box, only to find that the duck was a square thing occupying every corner of the box.

Chapter 3

And with every new day it seemed that he had learnt things overnight about being a duck.

The woman took him down to the tiny pond in the garden, surrounded by trees and lilies and tall reeds. Two life-size ducks — one a decoy and one a concrete sculpture — cluttered up the pond, along with a slimy plastic lily-pad, a plaster-of-Paris frog, an ugly spouting fountain, and a weathered wooden bridge. Pieces of driftwood sat at the edge. Several orange goldfish lurked in the shadows. It was a once-crafted pond, abandoned.

When the duck was still a pom-pom he floated on the water, wildly paddling his little legs until he started to sink. He'd then panic back into the hands of the woman, with his transparent fluff sticking to his naked pimply skin.

Now that he was bigger, he plodded around the edge, flicking his head under the water before wiping it over his back. The woman, sitting on the bridge, watched him as he lifted his body upright and flapped his winglets. Then he took himself across to the other side of the pond where there was a mini beach of stones. Standing in a patch of sunlight, he poked his beak into his downy breast, as if exploring new terrain, searching for a clue to his duckness.

It was a new development for him to be apart from her while they were together. They were separated by a muddy puddle of water. They were separated by a vast expanse of pond, where she as a woman and he as a duck were different beings. He stood up tall again, fluffing up, flapping. Every day he did this now.

The mysterious overnight educator had informed him that he would fly, and *every day* he checked to see whether this was the day.

LAYING OUT THE FOUNDATIONS

The woman looked at his stumpy wings fluttering uselessly. The design plan of his day-to-day evolution was impeccable. Even if he *could* fly now, it would be perilous for him, crashing into the walls of the world and careening into the mouths of cats and dogs and rats. Once he flew, where would he go? And how would he know to stop? She thought of thistle-down floating high in the sky and imagined that it was individual feathers on test flights, checking out the lie of the land, the sigh of the wind, the lift under the wing, and finally all returning to assemble on the duck for the first grand take-off.

DIFFICULT DAYS

Sometimes unpredictable events or expectations settled on a day before it had even started. They arrived by email, or phone. This day they'd arrived in a couriered box. The house shook with the early morning hammering on the door. Simon was in Sydney at a conference, and Hannah was still dozing in bed. When she opened the front door, there was the box on the doorstep, delivered by a guy in a uniform and a cap.

There wouldn't be time for the duck today. She cleaned his bathroom box and let him scurry behind her to his daytime cage on the back lawn. When she dropped him in, he chirruped in disbelief, demanding that she come with him to probe the catchments of dew in the bromeliads. He wanted her to peel back the long leaves of the agapanthus, so he could snaffle the cockroaches and wood lice leaping like people from a burning building.

He was too little to be released to forage alone — there were too many predators waiting for him. And he wanted to be with her.

She picked him out again and plonked herself down on the grass. He sat on her stomach.

That's better, he said.

I can't be with you today, Ducko, said the woman. I just can't.

What do you mean? You *are* with me. Everything is good.

But not for long. I have work. I have to go inside and work.

That's OK, I can come, too.

Ducko, she said. Listen. A box arrived today from the outside world. From the world outside *our* world. And when I opened the box, the whole house was filled with birds, dark flapping crows batting their wings against my face, their claws pulling at my hair. Squawking at me for attention. I screamed at them. Get out! Leave me in peace! I opened the window, releasing some of them, but they sat on the railing around the deck, or on the roof, or hid in leafy branches. Waiting for me.

That's terrible. I didn't see them. What did you do?

I flapped. Inside, one was drinking water from the kitchen sink, lifting its head as if about to gargle a song. Another paced on the kitchen table, its claws clattering like pins on the wood.

And then what?

Duckie, each crow is a task on a list. And I don't have energy for them today. I'm tired, Ducko. I have to catch the crows and tie coloured bands around their stiff-worm legs before they'll go away, labelled as done.

That's all very well, said the duck, but what's that got to do with me?

What it's got to do with you, Ducko, she said as she stood up and opened the lid to his cage, is that we're not going foraging today.

As she walked away she could hear the vibration of the wire netting as he threw himself against it. She wondered whether the feeling she had was anything like a mother might have, walking away from a crying baby.

And on top of that, this morning, when she'd been searching for a pencil sharpener, she'd opened the top drawer in her mother's bedroom cabinet, and there she was presented with all the non-descript knick-knacks left behind when her mother had gone to Primrose Hill. Spare glasses, magnifying glass, comb, birthday book, a writing pad with half-written letters, abandoned because her disease made it so difficult for her to write. Hannah picked up the pad and flicked through it. *I ask myself whether I will ever be happy again*, she read. And there it was again. The pain, swelling in her chest, in breech position, kicking its heel against her heart.

During the course of this day, the weather shifted. It seemed that the wind was filtered through ice. She went to the window. The sky had sucked up the shadows from the earth. The garden was misshapen, its edges gnawed into by its shivering self. Animals slunk by and tentatively sniffed at the wire netting. The duck had pulled himself under the wooden covering, into his own darkness, where Hannah had left a heap of soft towel. He'd backed into it, and tried to become a part of it, so that he was unseen. Hannah went once more down to the garden to put a tarpaulin over the cage to keep him warm, then left him again.

When she finally returned to the duck from her work, it was night. She took him inside and filled the bathroom basin with warm water. He stood there, letting the heat seep into his body as Hannah sat on the bath edge, her face level with the basin, talking to him softly. He flitted his beak at her mouth. It gave the impression of kissing her, but she knew that he was checking that her lips weren't two fat, lazy worms.

After the bath, Hannah dried him on a towel and held him for a while.

She had more work to do, another crow to deal with, so she put him to bed in his box. As soon as she left the bathroom he hurled himself out of the box. He'd managed to do this once yesterday, too, for the first time. She put him back and turned off the light. He clambered out again, waddling triumphantly into the kitchen where she'd just sat down at the table to work. Again she returned him to the box, but again he flung himself out onto the tiles. She could hear his flippers slap slap slapping on the floor as he crossed the hall and proudly waddled his way to her feet. She returned him to his box, but she hadn't even left the room before he was out again.

The woman yelled at him.

This is the last straw!

As she strode towards him she caught him accidentally on her foot, propelling him out into the hallway, where, to her astonishment, he spun a full circle, a feathery top spinning. He then stood motionless, his yellow feet splayed on the wooden floor, his eye black and piercing. He was measuring her, wondering whether she was a thing to be wary of. Until that moment, he had accepted her unquestioningly.

What did you do that for?

I'm tired.

What did I do?

You got out of your box. Over and over.

I wanted to be with you.

Well, she said, I don't want to be with you.

The duck let go of his legs and flopped into his nest of self. The woman plonked herself down on the bathroom stool. The duck in the hallway, the woman in the bathroom.

I'm tired. The crows. So much work to do. And now you. It is like having my mother here all over again.

Your mother is dead.

How do you know that?

You told me. But even if you hadn't told me, I would have known. It's in your eyes, in your blood.

The woman sighed. All I want is for you to be in your box. Now. Like a good duck. Please.

He cocked his head at her. Then he stood up, waddled into the bathroom and over to her feet. She scooped him up.

Bed, she said. Bed, or else.

Or else what?

Eat.

Eat?

Christmas dinner. Yum. Cranberry sauce. Drumsticks. Hmmmm . . .

The duck said nothing. She cradled him, feeling his warmth spread through her body. Even his feet on her arms were warm. Even her heart felt warmed by him. He was a warm machine. He was a hot-water duckle.

Be a good boy, she said.

I am, he said, uncomplaining now as she placed him back in his box.

NIGHT TERRORS

Later, Hannah thought about the duck's reluctance to go to bed. In the mornings he was quite content to sit in his box, greeting her with his mouth open, cheeping gratefully as he snapped up the strips of leaves she offered. He'd then wait patiently while she did her chores. If she popped into the bathroom they'd have a hello, but there was never any frenetic scrambling to escape. She was thankful that he gave her this precious time in the mornings before having to clean out his box and head outside.

Before her mother had moved into Primrose Hill, caregivers provided by the government would march into the house each morning to bathe her and prepare her for the day ahead. Hannah eventually resigned herself to the fact that strangers had the run of the house downstairs, strangers who would sneak her mother's make-up and perfume and creams for themselves. Although she didn't like this, she didn't complain; she was grateful for that small amount of time to herself. She also felt a nudge of guilt that she wasn't continuing to attend to her mother's ablutions herself.

When she questioned the duck the next day about this anomaly between his morning and night-time behaviour, he told her that in the mornings he was happy because he knew it was just a matter of waiting and that she would come because that was what happened. She would come and then together they'd go out into the garden and look for food. He would wait for her all day, he said.

So, why are you such a pain about going back to bed at the end of the day, then?

Because it's the night and you go away.

But you're safe here. Nothing can happen to you, truly. It's nice and cosy in our bathroom, with the heated tiles and the door that closes, and a curtain over the window. The worst thing that could happen is that you spill your water.

I know all that.

So what's your problem?

Well. You might not come back.

Me? Oh, Duckie, of course I'll come back.

Don't laugh, he said. There are slinking evil things out there. Sometimes I hear the front door close. I hear your footsteps up the path. You and the man go out and you don't come back until the night is half over.

Going to the movies or out for a meal occasionally hardly takes up half the night. But in any case, I *do* come back and I always will, she said.

But sometimes things happen, he said enigmatically. Bad things. In the night. Bad things that might stop you returning. When you leave me in the night, I'm left not knowing whether I'll ever see you again. Why don't you sleep with me?

I sleep with the man in a bed upstairs, she told him.

Can I sleep with you in your bed, then?

Hmmm, I wouldn't mind, but I don't think the man would like that, she said. But I could ask him.

The woman thought of her pillows and duvet stuffed with feathers. How many ducks had died to make them? How did they die? She pictured peasant fingers yanking at the breasts of limp or — worse still — squealing ducks. Should she ever bring her duck to her bed, she suspected that he might see her as a traitor.

TMI

The first plucking generally yields about sixty grams and the second, about six weeks later, a hundred to two hundred grams. Animal welfare groups find this repeated plucking cruel, as it is painful. Dead ducks can be plucked by scalding them in water at around sixty-five degrees centigrade for a couple of minutes. Down is removed by a plucking machine or by hand. The feathers are dried in a drier.

Sometimes information is too readily available, Hannah thought, as she closed her laptop.

DOWN TIME

That night Hannah was lying in bed with Simon, just back from his conference. He was reading his iPad, holding it propped upright on his chest. His other hand lay open alongside his body, and her hand, resting in his warm palm, felt like a contented duck in a summer pond. And, she couldn't help noticing, recently so many of her musings were skewed in relation to ducks.

Simon, she said.

Hmmm?

Do you ever feel uncomfortable about sleeping under a feather duvet and on feather pillows?

No, he replied dozily. I feel very comfy, thank you. It's nice to be back in my own bed. Hotel bedding is unwelcoming and sterile.

No, I mean, when you think about it. I was looking it up today. Some down feathers are actually plucked while the ducks are still alive, over and over, every six weeks or so, as soon as they've grown more. It'd be like some monster pulling out our hair.

That's not totally true, he said, and she knew he was going to give her a lecture. Not all, he continued. They're also plucked from the dead birds after they're killed for their meat. So don't worry. And the eider down is taken from the lining of the nests after the hatchlings have left. That's pretty well controlled these days.

So you *do* feel uneasy about it. You've obviously been doing some research yourself.

Only a couple of years ago, when we were choosing the new duvet. I was looking for the best down. And did you know, he added, that some dinosaurs grew down as well? In France they found down feathers from the dinosaur era, preserved in amber. And a decade or so ago, 124-million-year-old fossilised feathers from theropod dinosaurs were found in a place called Liaoning in China. We never think of dinosaurs as fluffy things, do we? Think of how many duvets *they'd* make.

I'm serious. It doesn't feel right.

I am, too. In actual fact, he added, it's commonly accepted in certain scientific circles that all birds have evolved from the aforementioned theropod dinosaurs, and are in fact dinosaurs themselves.

Don't twist everything I say into scientific twaddle. You're such a pedant. You're trying to avoid reality.

Speaking of which, he said, I've been thinking, too. It's four months since your mother died. For the first time in years, we are free. You're tired, truly — you need a break. Let's go somewhere. Somewhere nice, a cottage by a beach, or in the bush. Over to Waiheke. Or anywhere you choose. Hop on a ferry or a plane, and off we go.

She pulled her hand out from his, the old duck panicking, taking flight.

We can't. How can we? We can't.

Why not?

Well. Who would look after . . . ?

Who would look after . . . ?

He made her say it.

Who would look after the duck?

He hauled himself up from the sheets and stretched back against the wooden bed-head. He was doing those annoying neck exercises that prepared him for something difficult to say. She turned and peered up at him. His ruffled mix of grey-black hair. His conniving eyes squinting at her. His beard sleekly wrapped over his chin, every hair a silver strand feeding into the loom of his mouth. What thoughts were weaving through the words of this fabricated conversation?

And here it came:

That's another thing. I've got another meeting down in Hamilton next week. He pulled his bottom lip out and over his moustache. I'll take the duck down to Te Awamutu. Back to its pond, with other ducks, where it should be. You've done a very fine job of looking after it, but it needs to be rehabilitated with its own kind. And, he added, so do you.

She noticed his rumpled skin, and the soft flesh of his arms. In a few years he'd be sixty. One day, she thought, we will both die, and who will go first?

I can't have a break, she told him. With Christmas coming up. Everyone coming to stay. There's so much to do. And I've got another editing job coming up. It's not the time to go away.

Well, after Christmas then. There's a possibility of a contract in Christchurch for a while. We could both go.

Christchurch! What about the earthquake?

They've *had* the earthquake. It's over. OK, apart from a few aftershocks. We could stay with Maggie and Toby. But, anyway, the duck. I'll take the duck down to Te Awamutu next week.

The duck's not ready.

She climbed out of bed.

Where are you going?

Toilet, she said.

But down in the bathroom she sat on a stool in the dark by the duck, sleeping in his box. When she finally returned, the light was off and the man was asleep. If I die first, she thought as she lay floating aimlessly through the night, on and on with her hollow bones and her chest aching with grief, who will look after the duck?

But if the man died first, she at least would have the duck to look after her.

PREMONITION

A darkened room, a long time ago. Thick curtains pulled over the window by the bed.

She was staying at her grandmother's and had just awakened from an afternoon nap. Mad cries of seagulls outside. She was sitting up, surrounded by a whole country of double bed, with the rolling hills and valleys and fissures of a silk-covered eiderdown. Her chubby fingers picked at a tiny stalk protruding from one corner, tugging at it until it slid out of the hole to reveal . . . a feather! Unfurling itself to dance in her breath, like smoke on a stick.

Later, her grandmother came into the room and held her over the chamber pot from under the bed. She didn't manage to pee, but when she was removed, they both peered into the dry pot. A soft feather lay curled there.

'Look, Nana, I done a feather,' she said.

'Oh, you little poppet!' her grandmother had cried, hugging her tightly. And then the story moved from that room into other rooms, and other places. It was related over and over, and always the reaction was laughter. From this, Hannah as a child experienced and understood the pleasure of being funny.

And now, Hannah was thinking that it had taken a feather from a duck to give her this realisation, and how, many years later, a whole living shimmy of feathers on legs was still able to amuse her.

Chapter 4

THE WOMAN GETS ANALYTICAL

The duck was just a duck, just a bloomin' duck, a generic duck that began as a yellow pom-pom like every other duck of its type. Its fluff was gradually being replaced by down and feathers in a schedule that was pre-ordained. Even though she had never taught it anything of significance, it had learnt to snap at mosquitoes, preen itself, and to shiver its beak into the mud and earth looking for worms. She had been imprinted on it, just as any person or any animal would for any other duck that had become stranded without its own kind.

So the bond between them was nothing special at all: it was a common old garden one. The anxious cheeping whenever she went away, or came back into view, had provoked or triggered a response from her that made her feel protective towards it. Nature had set it up very nicely. As every grandmother or mother felt towards her grandchild or child, there was the ingrained sense of love, or whatever it was, to save the next generation from harm.

How *cute*, how *gorgeous*, each and every baby creature was for most normal mothers on the planet. So common, that those words had become clichés in that sense. Love was just a biochemical or electromagnetic response. It was probably measurable in all its differing intensities in the endocrine system. Or the blood. Or the air between them.

And so with her duckling. She had been duped by Nature, been pulled in, drawn deeply down into the sloppy sloshy scheme of things.

As measles ran its course (or the common cold, or a stomach bug, or Parkinson's disease), the signs and symptoms — the process of the onset, the duration, the aftermath, etc — were normally predictable, with varying degrees of severity and side effects according to the individual. The variation depended on the state of the victim at the time. All were ailments that progressed in more or less the same way. They all consisted of a list of stages, to one degree of intensity or another, dependent on the host.

She was the host to the duck, that was for sure. She'd been afflicted by a duck. It was an ailment that wasn't in her medical books, and she was uncertain as to what stage she was at with it now, or whether it was terminal. And the side-effects were unknown.

PARKINSON'S

Her mother was afflicted with Parkinson's disease. Over the years her body had lost its lively suppleness, her fingers stiffened, her handwriting became minuscule, and she couldn't do up her buttons. And she'd had more and more of a struggle to paint freely. At first, although they commiserated with her, neither Hannah nor her mother's friends had really understood the difficulty.

Their coaxing was well-meaning: Don't give yourself negative messages. Just do it.

But it won't happen, her mother would reply. I can put the paintbrush onto the canvas, but there's something happening between my brain and the paper. I simply *can't* paint the way I used to.

In the end it was the constant falling over that brought her reluctantly from living independently in her own home in Hawke's Bay to living in Auckland with Hannah and Simon. A night of lying on the floor of the bathroom, like a wounded gull with the tide rising, as the handbasin overflowed unceasingly through the night, spewing water around her and out into the living room carpet. Her head was resting on a sodden towel which she'd either fortuitously landed on or had managed to pull under her head. In the morning she was discovered by the caregiver arriving to give her a shower, and was taken to hospital in an ambulance, bruised and shivering, and later developing pneumonia. She never returned to live at her home, and resented this.

Take me to the sea, she'd say to Hannah. Just take me to the sea and let me walk and walk and walk out into it. I mean it. It will be better for everyone.

Or: Just take me to a nice place in the bush and leave me there. Truly, dear, I'll be happy to go, surrounded by Nature.

But instead she had to leave her friends from her hometown and live another three years, in a body battened down as it flailed to be free, like a stunned and trussed insect, packaged up for devouring later.

I just can't think properly, she would say. I think I'm going mad. You'd tell me, wouldn't you, Hannah? You would, wouldn't you?

Of course I would, Hannah would assure her with a hug, but you're not mad, not at all.

And she wasn't.

Sometimes, Hannah would arrive at Primrose Hill to see her mother's face hanging cocked, her mouth open and her eyes as dead as the flowers that wilted in the Agee jars on the locked piano. Or, at other times, her face was puffy with anxiety, her eyes searching for familiarity. Around her in the lounge, other old people sat in chairs and bucket seats, either resigned to isolation or, in an act of solidarity, their dry old voices quacking like hungry mallards across a pond. Help, help, heeeelp.

But when Hannah marched in, greeting them jovially one by one, all of those faces perked up as she called each one of them by name. That was the label around the handle of the suitcase of their own lives, and that was who they were, and they were happy to be reminded. That was the call they had responded to from the time they were babies, from their teachers, whispering lovers, enemies, roll calls, and this name would be the identifying tag around their toes. Only their own children didn't use their name. To their children, they were universally Mummy, Mama, Daddy, or Papa, but that, too, defined who they were beyond any given name, defined a status and connection that, above all, was unique and permanent.

And Hannah's own mother's face came alive when she saw her, because she was the link to all the known things. Her caregivers had no idea what she was talking about when she mentioned a person she had once known; or a spontaneous recounting of an incident from her past, as if assuming the caregiver had been privy to her train of thought leading up to it. When Hannah arrived, all the obscure off-beat comments that wafted like leaves from an old tree upon the people who'd never known her, now had value. These leaves became meaningful, because Hannah knew the twigs and branches from which they fell; she had embraced the now-bending trunk of her mother's life.

And each leaf held the code to enter conversation, the means to enter a room. All the doors squeaking open and there they were, together, discussing the people who had featured in her life. Until in the end the hallucinations caused by the drugs toyed with her mind, and eventually the disease spun a mesh through her thoughts, and they too were fastened down.

Who's Ted? one of the caregivers asked one day, as Hannah was feeding her mother. The caregiver was sitting at the dining room table on the other side, feeding another resident.

Ted's my father. Mum's husband. He's been dead for decades. Why?

Ah, I see. Her husband.

Why? Did she mention him?

Her mother was sitting between them, opening her mouth like a bird as Hannah spooned soup into her.

She was calling for him this morning. In bed, said the caregiver. It was just on dawn and she was calling from her bed, not in a panicky way, but softly, questioningly, as if she couldn't understand why he wasn't there. Just calling quietly, wondering where he was.

A DUCK BY ANY OTHER NAME

The woman was bathing the duck in the handbasin one night. She was perched on the side of the bath, ruffling the warm water around him.

Ducko, she said, I've been thinking. I haven't given you a name.

He paddled across to her hand. That's all right, he replied, I've already got one. His leathery maple-leaf feet slithered over the basin. She ladled him out with her cupped hand and wrapped him in the waiting towel.

What do you mean, you've already got one? She felt indignant. Had Simon's aunt, Claire, named him? I don't think you understand, she said.

Of course I understand.

So? And don't say it's 'Duck', because that's not who you are, it's *what* you are.

I am who I am, he said.

You are annoying, she said.

I might be annoying, but 'Annoying' is not my name.

Well, go on, tell me.

Why do you want to know?

I might need to call you. One day we might be apart from each other and I might need to call you.

We won't ever be apart from each other.

I would like to know your name. Please, Ducko. Tell me.

The duckling didn't answer. He was making himself comfortable amongst the folds of the towel, his beak bobbing, his eyes closing.

NOT KNOWN AT THIS ADDRESS

Hannah wanted to think that she would recognise her duck amongst others of his kind. But would she? And would he recognise that he was one of them? Would he feel less lonely if he were with her, or as an outsider in the flock?

Recognition of others and by others was surely the key to feeling a part of a community, part of the flock. Recognition was the reference as to who you were. How unfair it was to place her mother, at that late stage, amongst strangers. She had quickly become an 'old person', devoid of character or past. For the people who worked there, her life had begun when she was wheeled in from the ambulance on a stretcher. While no one from her past was with her, she was a stereotypical old woman. Sans everything.

The anonymity of old age was the transition towards, or preparation for, the annihilation that came with death.

Once Hannah had been visiting her mother in the Primrose Hill dining room when there was a sudden kerfuffle. A caregiver called out to Mina, the registered nurse on duty, to see to one of the old ladies having dinner.

Mina — the nurse who had once told Hannah how she hated her own mother back in Korea — peered at the old lady and quickly decided that there was nothing to worry about.

No, no, she all right. I saw her before, she all right. No problem.

The caregiver was left sitting with her, observing the old lady closely, obviously still worried.

Look at her! Look at her eyes, her lips, she said to no one in particular. Hannah made an excuse to wash her hands at the handbasin across the room, so she could observe for herself. It was the little bird, whose meek eyes peeked out at the world from her chair in the lounge. Hannah had often attempted to speak to her, but there was never much of a response, and for that reason couldn't remember her name. She'd rarely seen her with a visitor. When on occasion she'd played the balloon-patting game, the little bird had whacked the balloon with surprising fervour with her fist, her face still expressionless.

And now there she was, her tiny face still looking passively into the middle distance. She appeared to be her usual timid self. But the caregiver was anxious, upset that no one was taking heed of her concern.

Then the vomiting started. From where Hannah sat, back with her mother, the noise sounded more like drowning. The caregiver called for help again, and Mina was forced to intervene.

Take her to her bed, she ordered. So off she went, pushed off in her wheelchair across the dining room to her bedroom.

When Mina went by, Hannah asked her what had been the matter.

Oh, she just trembling, trembling, that's all, she replied.

For some unfathomable reason, Hannah was certain she was dying. And she was. The next morning Mina brought the news to Hannah as she was feeding her mother outside in the sunshine.

The death notice was in the paper the following day. Gertrude Ethel Williams. She was ninety years old, and the notice listed children, grandchildren, great-grandchildren. There were many. Hannah had never seen any of them. Perhaps they were all meek little birds scuttling quietly about in the back garden. A life was summed up in a death notice in the newspaper. Ninety years old and she'd hopped along to the end of a branch until there was nothing below her feet. No wind beneath her wings. And there she was, no more.

Like her mother, now, no more.

THE LONELY SEA AND THE SKY

Let's go to the beach, said her mother.

Hannah had been working at the kitchen table. Her mother sat in her easy chair, looking out the window. She'd been trying to fold the facecloths and tea towels from the washing basket at her feet, then attempting to place them neatly on the coffee table alongside her. She couldn't do it. She couldn't fold them squarely; she couldn't stack them in alignment with each other.

There'd been a storm overnight, and now the deck was shiny wet, littered with leaves and sticks and brown flesh from the last of the magnolia flowers. The trees were hardly moving now — as if the earth was just daring to breathe, loath to bring attention to itself for fear of another onslaught.

It was a Monday and Hannah thought of the whole busy week sprawling ahead of her, with so much to fit in around looking after her mother. It wasn't just a matter of jumping into the car and whizzing off to the beach; it was the preparation. The toileting, the hauling on of layers of clothes, the searching for the carefully hidden handbag, the slow ponderous walk up the path, the struggle into the car, and getting out again at the other end.

Are you sure it's not too cold? she said.

It's so still and steamy, I just feel like being by the sea.

Hannah closed her laptop. It wasn't often that her mother made any requests of her.

They drove into a small parking bay that served as a boat ramp and also led easily to a man-made rocky headland jutting out into the sea, still choppy after the storm. Hannah had prepared a thermos of tea with a couple of pieces of cake and was hoping her mother would be happy sitting in the car. The sea was like a fire on a cold night . . . a live, comforting thing to watch, triggering nostalgic thoughts and memories. She'd brought old bread for the gulls.

But they staggered out from the car, onto the rock. Her mother refused the walker.

I'll just hold on to you, dear.

Hannah helped her shuffle to a small concrete wall and suggested they sit there, but her mother insisted they go further, to the point where the rock dropped in a series of sharp ledges down to the sea. The tide was high, slurping around the rock. Her mother unravelled her arm from Hannah's and stepped away, flicking with irritation at Hannah's response to steady her.

Just let me breathe the sea air, she said. Look at those blues, and that sky . . .

She took another step forward, then toppled. Hannah, shrieking, seized her, enough to stop her tumbling into the sea but not to stop her crunching onto the rock, landing with a guttural grunt, lying there, blood already oozing from a gash in her head, her arm twisted beneath her.

Hannah threaded an arm along the rock under her mother's head, and tried to lift her, but she was a dead weight. A jogger came rushing to help.

When the ambulance arrived, her mother was just flickering back into awareness.

Am I dead yet? she said.

And after recuperating in hospital, it was decided by the doctors that she must move into the Primrose Hill Rest Home, where every day she asked that same question, in one way or another, until one day she got the answer she was looking for.

Chapter 5

THE HAND OF GOD

Hannah was propped against a tree in dappled shade, trawling through a manuscript resting against her knees. The heat was homogenising her thoughts. A couple of tui were making a fluttering clatter above. The duckling was lying nearby with one of his feet splayed out behind him, and the underside looked remarkably like the soft pink palm of a hand. Spongy. He was revealing to her that there were elements of him that were human in character. His sole was human. She thought of the Michelangelo painting of the creation of Adam — hand reaching out to hand — but when she touched the foot he quickly withdrew it.

Excuse me, he said. Why are you poking me?

I'm sorry, she said. It's just . . . your legs . . . and your feet. They used to be so tiny.

Now the legs looked like separate entities, big, reptilian. They were the foundation blocks for something much larger than he was now. Each web-cloaked finger a claw, a pin-sharp nail, although these were not as lethal as they had been, now that he was running around more.

Simon had told her about the flexor tendon in birds. He'd explained how it ran from the muscle in the thigh, over the knee (which she knew bent backwards, not forwards), down the leg, around the ankle and under the toes. When a bird was resting, its body weight made the knee bend, and this in turn drew the tendon taut and so closed the claws. He added that birds had been discovered dead with their claws still clamped around their perches, so effective it was.

Even though every day she stared closely into the terrain of the duck's body, the ongoing changes happened magically, a sleight of hand, no doubt with help from the overnight educator. It was difficult to remember what he'd once been like. For example, when did these transformations occur?

- the extravagant fresh ruff of feathers frothing up along his sides
- the real feathers growing in his fat and wobbling tail
- the tiny symmetrical shoots and the triangular borders before the fill-ins

- the dense down replacing the yellow body fluff
- his number-one blond crewcut
- the new tufts growing across the black holes that were his ears
- not to mention his legs.

It was a dissolving thing, the details of the past duck soon forgotten. She knew he used to be a little fluffy thing, but couldn't relate that form to the present duck. His baby self was a dream fading with the new day, the past swirling into oblivion. Over and out.

LEST WE FORGET

Yesterday, she discovered that one of his claws was cracked, and, when she examined it further, a tiny curl of claw fell off in her hand. A white comma, reminding her to have pause, for breath. A little comma of an unborn child swimming through underground pipes beneath the city, and into the sea, and for how long did it bob through the waves until it was reduced to its elements?

PITTER-PATTER OF LITTLE FEET

It was five weeks after the tramping club do. Hannah and Simon were lying in bed, a single bed with green sheets, three woollen blankets and an eiderdown he'd brought over from Australia, which used to belong to his grandmother. In the room was a desk under a steamy window that she knew looked out onto a wet wooden fence and the path that ran from the gate around the house to the landlord's entrance above. Today the curtains, also green, were drawn closed. At one end of the room was a sliding door to a built-in wardrobe. Hanging on a wall there was a square framed print of a tree on a hill (not his). Above the desk was pinned a clipped Leunig cartoon (his), and some complex engineering design (his). The toilet and bathroom were in the hallway outside the room, where carpeted stairs ran up to a locked door to the interior of the house. There was enough space in the room for two people to get undressed, but only just. Their clothes were thrown over the chair that stood out from the desk.

Hannah remembered this scene as if it were yesterday. She could still hear the dull thuds of running steps as the landlord's children played in the sitting room above. She could hear muffled voices and a distant radio or television. She could hear the rain against the window. Without getting out of bed, they were able to turn the light on and off by pulling a plastic bobble on a string that hung from the ceiling.

Simon was idly scratching her head as she lay in the crook of his arm. This time she had brought her own pillow. She could smell the sexy warmth rising from his body under the tent of blankets. They hadn't spoken for a while, but she was thinking of the statement he had made on that first night, about his having something to tell her. She was no longer curious about this. Whenever it came to mind, an irrational twinge of fear shot through her stomach. This morning it was hovering above them, and she could feel it was about to swoop. She moved from her back towards him, pressing her naked self against the length of his wiry body. Tugging the eiderdown over her head, she thought, This is where I live. I can go no deeper than this. I am never going to move from here. This is where I will live and where I will die. I will never eat or drink again, because everything I have in the way of nourishment is here in this moment. If I lift my head above the covers, I will be eaten.

Simon gently pulled the covers aside. He turned and kissed her forehead.

Hannah, he said, and she waited.

And then he said, Hannah, Hannah sweetheart, why are you crying?

DOWN BY THE BEDSIDE

From time to time Hannah would pick up her mother from Primrose Hill and take her for a drive. On this occasion she parked the car on a boat ramp facing out to the sea. She threw stale bread out the window to seagulls squawking around them. Next time she would bring a cushion to allow her mother to see from the car more comfortably. Without the energy to haul the collapsing infrastructure of her body upright, her mother was only just able to peer over the window sill towards the empty expanse of sand. She seemed oblivious to the birds.

After a while she muttered, almost inaudibly, It was dreadful, just dreadful about the baby.

When Hannah questioned her, she turned her head, a look of horror clamped on her face.

You don't *know* about the baby?

No, what are you talking about, Mum?

Your baby is dead.

I don't have a baby, Mum, she said, but even so a lump of ice melted in her chest. Seagulls fought and scratched the bonnet of the car, all feathers and wings and gaping gullets.

No, you don't, not anymore. It's dead now.

Mum, what are you talking about?

Before I saw it yesterday, this happened last night. She was drowned and it was my fault. You need to know this. My fault.

No, Mum, it was one of your dreams. This is nonsense. Stop it.

Look. You are Hannah. Your husband is Simon. I live in the Primrose Hotel with the Queen Mother. I have Parkinson's.

Well, yes, that's mainly true. Very good, Mum. But the other isn't.

But that proves it. If that is true, the other *is*. Your baby *is* dead and it's my fault.

Mum. Mum, ssssh. It's not true, I know.

Hannah was stroking her mother's hair, her temples, her forehead, trying to ease the enormity of her troubled thoughts, the ghastly confusion.

I heard them. Last night. They were all standing around my bed, discussing whether to shoot me or not, and in front of my very eyes, each one made their decision and said I should be shot. And then I went to sleep, while I was still alive.

But, Mum, you are still alive now.

Her mother looked at her, exasperated, her skin puce with anxiety. She shifted her gaze back out the window.

There's madness in this family. I think you should know that. I've been meaning to tell you for some time, she said.

And then she added, Just look at those seagulls.

SECRETS, PASSED ON

Her mother crying. Flumped over the sink, sobbing. The sink was filled with her tears, bracelets of froth around her arms, with teacups and saucers floating around like flotsam after a wreck. Hannah, just home from school, burst in upon her, causing her to jump upright, sucking all her strength from the day to pull herself together. Hannah wrapped her arm around the thick gatherings of her skirt.

Mum. What's the matter?

Nothing, said her mother. She'd sniffed, wiping her face with her arm, leaving a trail of lather across her cheek.

I'm sorry. She gulped the fortifying air. I'm fine.

Years later, Hannah had reminded her mother of the incident, and cautiously asked what had made her so unhappy. Her mother pretended to have no recollection of it. Hannah didn't believe her. She wondered about people and the secrets they harboured or endured, wrapped up and placed in darkened compartments of their memory in the name of privacy, or suffering, or protection from the consequences that might ripple from revelation or the breaking of a confidence, the releasing of its energy into a judging world.

As each of her mother's friends, associates and family died, so did branches of collective knowledge that contributed to her history snap away and fall to the debris of the past.

In the end, Hannah was the person who knew her mother and her history more intimately than anyone else alive on the planet. And this knowledge was selective, limited to her own bias. Her perception of her mother was relegated to her own increasingly questionable memory.

And so, even now, a whole lifetime of even the residue of her mother's *being* was eroding. The occasional memento or photo could be seen as markers, but without reference they would become meaningless. Soon she'd be nothing. Her biography, her personal information and data stuffed into the side-packs on a horse whose rump had been slapped, sending it careening through a desert until it was out of sight. Even the dust that marked the disappearance would settle.

Her grandchildren, Maggie's children, now in London, still had the opportunity to carry her genes forward. Otherwise, only her paintings, her vision captured in colour, would exist of her.

As Simon had mentioned not so long ago, there had been over three billion years of life on Earth.

About two hundred thousand years of modern man in the form of *Homo sapiens*.

The duration of any one particular human from their birth to death would not even qualify as a dot on a time-line. A mysterious bursting into tears one afternoon was as significant as a sparrow's tweet.

LOSING CONTROL

In the beginning she would know.

For example, a day's tally could be: one dandelion leaf, one worm, a small beetle and some hand-rearing mash. She was impressed the first time he finished the first full leaf, albeit broken into pieces. Gradually more things were added to his diet while they were foraging.

And now, today, she'd thrown him twelve to fifteen large snails. He waddled after them, a clown in sheep's clothing. Just *whoomph* down the hatch, the large lump of each snail sliding along his neck, like an elevator descending a high-rise building. He wolfed up his pellets and mash. Not to mention whatever he found as he wandered behind her, and all the leaves he munched along the way. And there it was, a few hours later, the evidence, the mush of it all dolloped behind him.

THE HAUGHTINESS OF DIGNITY

She had a whole day out of the house. A work meeting, other chores, then taking a wheelchair-bound friend of her mother, visiting from Hawke's Bay, to the aquarium at Kelly Tarlton's, where they dawdled past tanks of fish, sharks, crayfish, penguins.

When she finally arrived home, Hannah decided not to go down to the bottom of the garden to say hello to the duck. It would mean that she'd be engaged with him for the rest of the evening or, if not, giving him false hope before having to leave again to cook and write a report about the meeting. The thought of his slap slap slapping around her feet as she tried to cook dinner, leaving his little plops of the day's feeding on the floor, and his panicking squeaks whenever she disappeared around the island in the kitchen, was too much. She would be forever having to clean up after him. So she left him in his hutch while she prepared dinner for Simon and herself.

She thought she might make up for it by allowing the duckling on her knee as they ate, but when it came to it she couldn't be bothered. Even though Simon might not voice his displeasure, he would let it be known. And the crows had managed to find their way in again and were sitting around the place, shifting from one leg to the other. She was only just aware of them, but they were there. Deadlines lurking.

Finally, just before dark, she went down to the hutch, where the duck cheeped urgently as he sensed the vibration of her footsteps approaching. He'd tucked himself way back into the covered area. He had no food but plenty of water. She slipped her hand under his belly and lifted him out. He paddled uselessly mid-air until she adjusted his position to give his feet a landing on her hand. She went to the secret store she'd discovered amongst the agapanthus and pulled a few snails from the wall. He was starving.

Where've you been? he growled. All afternoon.

She told him about her visit to Kelly Tarlton's, where she'd seen the grey downy penguins packed between their parents' legs, as if the stuffing was falling out of them. She described the older penguins whose feathers were moulting and how they held themselves with such haughty dignity as their sleek sheen erupted into feathery ruffle, and how they too looked like soft toys that the moths had found their way into. She talked about some of the penguins lying on the snow with their flippers held out as if they were waiting for the next wave to take them back to Antarctica. And how she had watched through the glass wall of the tank as the penguins torpedoed backwards and forwards through the water.

The duck turned his head away from her, and she finally noticed that he was curiously silent.

Something wrong? she asked.

No, he squeaked.

Is something upsetting you?

I'm practising haughty dignity, he replied archly.

What do you mean?

You wander down as if nothing is amiss after ignoring me all day and I discover that you've been out admiring other birds and you expect me to be impressed.

Chapter 6

THROUGH THE HOLE AND BACK AGAIN

Hannah and the duckling were sitting on the steps at the bottom of the deck soaking in weak sunshine while Hannah had a break from her work. Suddenly there was an eruption of leaves in the hedge nearby. First a shaggy blond head, then a tangled mess of ponytail, and two pink smiling faces forced branches apart, and there they were. Eric's grandchildren. She hadn't seen them for six months.

Eric lived next door. They'd lived in the area for so long, and yet Eric was the only person they really knew. There used to be an easy camaraderie with him, but for months now he had just grunted at them, and then only if he had to. It was awkward living next door to someone who clearly harboured animosity towards them. About two months before her mother died, he'd pulled away. He wouldn't answer the door when she knocked, even though she knew he was inside. He made sure he wasn't out in the garden when she was, or, if he was already there, would saunter back inside. The questioning note she poked under his doormat was returned to her letterbox with *Return to Sender* scrawled on the folded paper. Whatever the rift was about, Hannah did not know, but she suspected Simon might have had words with him about her spending too much time over there, helping with new curtains in his fading sitting room. He'd been long divorced, but his daughter, Sheila, would often visit, sometimes leaving him to babysit her two children who were used to having easy access through the hedge with their grandfather.

We came to see you, said Max triumphantly. He was clutching a red plastic car.

Hello, my little monsters, she said. Look how you've grown!

She picked leaves out of Max's hair. It doesn't take long, she thought. For hedges to grow over, for memories to disappear, for friendships to fade to nothing.

Yes, we did, said Rosemary. We comed, and I had an ice-cream.

Where's your grandfather? said Hannah.

He's over there, said Max, pointing back through the fence.

Does he know you're here?

But the children spied the duckling nestled on her lap, and moved in close.

Rosemary already had her chubby fingers around his neck, and the duck was wriggling furiously. He was not used to anything other than reverent handling. Hannah unclasped the tiny boa constrictors and told her to be gentle. Max demonstrated how it was done, by patting the outer edges of the duck's down, as if testing a hedgehog.

Does Poppa know you're here?

He went to sleep. Can I hold the chicken?

No, I want to.

I said it first.

Just a minute. Tell me, Max. Just wait a minute and tell me. When did Poppa go to sleep?

Before. Before when we came to see you.

Hannah stood up and went to the hole in the hedge, hoisting aside branches to peer through to the lawn next door. Eric was sitting in a plastic garden chair, and indeed he was asleep, his chin buried in the chest hair frothing through his shirt. She darted to the cage and dumped the duck, ignoring his tantrum against the netting as she sprinted back to the hedge.

Come on, back we go, she said to the children, and they all crawled, bumping against each other through the opening that used to be an easy thoroughfare between the two houses. They stood up and she took their sticky hands, kissing first one and then the other. She had missed them.

Ssssh, she said, taking the children on exaggerated tiptoe over the grass to Eric. He looked unkempt, his hair lank and tousled, a few days' growth of grey bristle over his soft chin. He was wearing the brushed-cotton blue shirt that she — they — had given him for Christmas a couple of years ago, rolled up past his paint-splattered elbows. What could have destroyed the camaraderie that they'd had together, the jocular discussions over a glass of wine or two, the friendship?

Hannah's got a chicken, announced Rosemary. Eric snorted loudly. His eyes shot open. He blinked, then registered that she was there. She held her ground, even though her heart was pounding. Why was her heart pounding? He sat up, rubbing his eyes.

What? What's going on? he growled.

Eric, she said.

He threw his head into his hands, rubbed his face vigorously and shook his head.

The kids came over to see me. You were asleep.

Hannah's got a chicken, said Rosemary.

It's a duck, said Hannah.

Well, that's very good, said Eric. As if I didn't know. Most likely the whole bloomin' neighbourhood knows.

Eric, said Hannah.

Come on, kids, we need to go inside and have something to eat.

He didn't look at her as he rounded the children into his care, and she felt their fingers slipping from hers, her hands empty again, as she turned, her eyes welling with tears, to crawl without dignity back through the hole in the hedge.

BEAUTIFUL MUSIC

There was more to Eric, if she were to be honest. Eric was a self-employed house painter. He was also a musician. In his younger days he had played the fiddle and the cello. For a few years he was even a member of a country music band, The Eketa Hoons, which toured in the summer, doing gigs in country halls.

Hannah had never had much to do with his wife, but by Eric's account she couldn't stand his music and had left him for the man who mowed the lawns at his daughter's primary school.

There was something about music. If it be the food of love, play on. Play on, my lover. Simon had been in Uganda. She tried not to think about it. That Easter. She'd been hanging out the washing and he was digging in his garden. They often chatted over the hedge, which at that time was kept lower than it was now. It was a sunny day with a good breeze for drying clothes. She'd been grappling with a sheet. Eric had a gumboot balanced on the spade, his hands clutching the handle as they talked. His head shining through his hair. She'd mentioned casually, conversationally, that she'd like to hear his band one day.

Well . . . he'd said, looking fixedly at a bit of something he was scratching on the spade handle. Then he raised his eyes to hers. We've got a gig at a country music festival in the Coromandel tomorrow afternoon. Can't promise you'll like it, but, if you're willing to take a punt, you can drive down with me in the morning. But, he shrugged, it's probably late notice . . .

He flicked a flop of sandy hair behind his ear.

The Eketa Hoons consisted of four men. Singer and guitar, bass, fiddle and drums. All about fifty, all a bit weathered, all a bit sexy, dressed in black shirts and jeans. All constantly connected by seemingly mischievous glances, as if sharing some arcane joke. They all sang a bit. They knew how to have fun. That was it. She'd often heard Eric practising both his violin and his cello next door, but she'd never seen him play. His body lithe and alive, his bow sawing the fiddle so vigorously.

She'd positioned herself on a rug in the grass. There was something about the lilt of the music, so light, so uplifting that she wanted to get up and dance with the other picnickers bouncing uninhibitedly in their bare feet, their hair flinging, the sun glinting on smiling cheeks. The singer was gruff and seductive, the lyrics funny and romantic. Her heart was flying, fighting against the Lilliputian forces of shyness pinning her to the ground.

Afterwards Eric came and sat beside her on the rug.

That was great! she'd said and she'd astonished herself by flinging her arm around him, and kissing him briefly but enthusiastically on his perspiring cheek. The music had created a sense of intimacy.

Thanks, he'd muttered, lifting his cowboy hat as if to let out all the steam and energy of the music. He replaced the hat, fizzed open a can of cold beer from the chilly bin she had prepared, and drank, the afternoon light glowing on his tanned, closely shaved skin. His hat dropped off into the grass. His hair was pulled into a short pony tail. His nice sharp jawline just beginning to soften with age. She picked up his hat and handed it to him. It had an oily green feather poking from the hatband. Why was she remembering these small details? His delphinium blue eyes. Yes, delphinium blue. Or were they? Surely not. They certainly weren't now. Did eyes fade with time? Or with circumstance?

Eleven years ago, this was, when Simon was in Uganda on a contract for three months.

They'd booked separate units in a motel for the night before the drive back the following day. They'd had fish and chips on the beach and a bottle of wine. They'd laughed like idiots. She hadn't realised how funny he was, all those years of knowing him. Was he *really* so amusing? What had they talked about? Before she returned to her unit they had hugged goodnight. Then they kissed. They had melted together in a kiss. They were two ice-creams smashed together. She had pulled away. Aghast. Smirked at him self-consciously.

G'night, she'd said, backing away like a fool, crashing into a large pot plant. She could feel the crunching of the plant beneath her. She started to laugh, her knees up, her feet waving mid-air, her bottom wedged in the pot. He grabbed her hand. Have a good trip? he'd said, pulling her out. Pulling her out like an unidentified creature rescued from mud. She didn't recognise herself. The red geraniums were flattened. She tried in vain to pull them upright. Oh dear, she said, and she knew she couldn't look at him again, so she turned, scuffling through her bag searching for the key to her unit. She turned around. He was standing there. Waiting. Her hands were shaking. The key, she said. There it was, in her pocket. She opened the door. He was still standing there. Passively. Under a perfectly contained bowl of light under the soffit. Little black flies dancing, so excitedly. She gave him a childlike wave, her fingers playing notes on the keyboard of the night. And closed the door. And all night she thought of him.

The next day Eric had organised to give the bass player a ride back home. Hannah insisted on sitting in the back seat. She'd dozed, listening to their banter, their boys' chatter about music and musicians. Simon was much more serious, in general. Hannah and Eric were alone in the car for just ten minutes after Justin had been dropped off; Hannah back in the passenger seat, staring out the window. They were nervous, restrained, quiet. Back home, they stood on the footpath, their arms loaded with their overnight bags, and, in his case, his fiddle.

I had a lovely time, thank you, she said.

Yeah, me too, me too, he said nodding furiously. His hat fell onto the pavement. She bent, scooped her finger under the chinstrap he didn't use, and pushed it under his arm. Then they split; he into his house, she into hers.

Their attraction to each other boiled for a couple of weeks, lurking under their skin, waiting to be released. Hannah would lie in bed listening to the sombre threads of his cello or the bright enticing notes of his fiddle, and she knew he was playing for her. And all the windows of their houses breathed shared air, gaping to be fed. She imagined them both leaning across the sills, their elongated wavering tongues straining to touch.

There was no way Hannah wanted to be unfaithful to Simon. No way. But one afternoon, a couple of weeks later, there'd been a storm, one of those crazy furious storms. A flying branch had smashed the window of their basement. Rain was pelting into the laundry. She'd dragged a large piece of plywood from the basement and was trying to hammer it across the window, but the force of the wind was pulling the wood from her grasp. Then Eric was beside her. She held the plywood against the house as he hammered. They almost had to yell at each other to be heard above the gale. Thanks so much, she said and then they were drinking the water that fell from each other's face, into their shared ravenous — yes, ravenous — mouths. His cold hand slipping under the collar of her raincoat, over the skin of her shoulder onto her back. They couldn't deny it this time. He took her by the hand and led her through the shuddering hedge and up the path and into his house.

It had lasted a week. Well, eleven and a half days. It had stopped while it still had life. It had stopped because, if it hadn't, it would never have ended. It had stopped because they didn't want to hate each other. It had stopped because it had to stop because they would have consumed each other totally. It had stopped because his teenage daughter had arrived unexpectedly when Hannah was in bed with him in the early morning. Sheila just let herself in through the front door and they could hear her pounding towards them up the stairs. Hannah flung herself onto the carpet between the wall and the bed, lying under a tent of blanket. She didn't move for the next hour, as Eric sat in his dressing gown with Sheila drinking coffee downstairs at the kitchen table, talking about boyfriend trouble. Hannah was forced to evaluate her life and her marriage and the choices she had to make. She was forty years old.

Six weeks later she discovered for certain that she was pregnant.

FOETAL POSITION

When the cramps and the bleeding started, she knew what was happening. There wasn't enough room in this body for one more. Is that what it was? Not enough room in this marriage for an intruder?

It was a Friday afternoon and she'd just arrived home when the pain in her stomach started to take her breath. She welcomed it; willed against it; was relieved; longed for it not to be true.

She took herself to the shower, shuffling, kneeling on the floor of the shower as the pain intensified, leaning over the plastic stool she'd grabbed for support. The water soothingly hot on the small of her back. She started to bleed heavily, the liverish clots swirling by and slithering under the elevated plug cover, and down the drain. She was a concertina, wheezing out a long groan as her muscles determined to squeeze from her the darling little one. Then she was sure, almost sure, absolutely certain, that she saw him, or her. She saw the lump of different blob hesitate as it was caught for a second at the stainless steel plug cover. She dived to retrieve it, pulled the plug from its place, but he or she escaped, and down it went, down the drain. It was just having a wee pause to peek at her before it left. We could have had fun together, she thought it might have been saying.

And yes, she told it, I love you already.

Had she rejected it or had it rejected her? The little boy or the little girl, the little musician or ballerina, or writer or magician or brain surgeon. Already she'd started making plans, had been fantasising that Simon could be overjoyed. Unlikely. And still the cramps and the bleeding continued on and on, gradually diminishing until she was able to force herself to her feet. She turned the tap off. She dried herself, wrapped herself in pads and a towel and crawled into bed, and she had nobody to talk to about it. Nobody. That was the trouble with secrets. She wanted to tell Eric that she had lost their child. She remembered her desperate search for her keys at the door of the motel unit. They were in her pocket all along. And this wee one had been waiting all along, too. She wanted to rush next door and have another try, but of course she couldn't, and five days later Simon returned.

Chapter 7

OTHER DIMENSIONS

They lived near the sea. From her window, Hannah could see the mountain lazily swooping up from the ocean, beckoning her to walk through the streets and onto the sandy beach. On this particular day she watched a seagull floating on the water. It seemed content just to *be* there, bobbing on the swell of ruffled waves, succumbing to the action of the water. Like a duck.

The only water her duck had experienced, apart from occasional rain, was confined to a drinking bowl, handbasin, or a cluttered shallow pond.

That night, instead of bathing the duck in the handbasin, she put him in the bath. He eyed the white shiny enamel, and then looked at her, then at the froth of tepid water pelting from the tap. He tried to escape, but the sides were too high. The woman cooed reassuringly at him. He slurped some water. She fed him torn shreds of lettuce. He nibbled and gulped, then sucked up another drag of water. As the level rose, he started to walk around on tiptoes. Little dainty prances. Then he was afloat. He was incredulous. He gave the side of the bath an elegant push and there he was, gliding to the other side. She turned off the tap. Silence. He was weightless. He was an astronaut in a void of fluid space with the grinning face of the moon peering over the edge of the world. Pushing off again with such an air, his big yellow feet touched the bath as an old lady's fingers might nudge a friend's arm as a reminder of something shared. The duck was remembering that, of course, this was what ducks did. The woman felt as though she, too, was hanging there. The white bath, the white duck, the clear water, the silence. She was with the duck in his head, relieved of the gravity of all things. She had an immense sense of joy.

The duck started to wash himself then, his body undulating through the water which swooshed from one end of the bath to the other. He flipped himself upright and flapped his wings. Took himself to the other end of the bath, then back again, surges of water spilling onto the woman's T-shirt and the floor. Finally he'd had enough. He stretched his neck up to the edge of the bath. The woman took a towel and wrapped him up. The duck flitted his beak over her lips.

I liked that, he said.

Of course you did.

And then at that moment Simon walked in and stood by the door. He saw the leaves floating in the bath water, saw the residue of splats settling on the bottom, saw the bathroom floor flooded and Hannah holding the duckling, closer now, to her chest.

I'm going to clear it up, she said. Look, the disinfectant, the cloth. All ready to clean. Don't worry.

It's not *that* I'm worried about, he said, pulling at his beard. He went away saying no more.

SPLIT DECISION

The next morning she woke up to Simon sitting alongside her on the bed, his hand resting on her shoulder. Her heart jolted. The duck! Something had happened to the duck!

What? What's wrong?

Ssssh. Nothing's wrong. Hannah, your nerves are frazzled.

Oh, sorry. But—

It's a corker day. Have a shower and hop in the car. We're going for a little tramp . . . to the waterfall, I thought would be nice . . . Then dinner at our restaurant on the way home. I've been waiting for you to wake up, but we mustn't waste the day. It's already after nine. I've made the picnic. It's all in the car.

He gave her rump a friendly whack.

Come on. Like we used to.

Hannah yawned. *Like we used to.* It must have been five or six years. This had always been a special outing for them; they'd seen it as an injection of vitality when they'd sensed their lives becoming staid. They'd be invigorated by the wild dangerous sea, the sharp air of the west coast, just being in Nature. The dinner at the end of the day was always intimate, happy.

I'm sorry, Simon, I can't. I've got work to do.

It's Sunday.

I know, but I have deadlines, if I get behind . . . And I've got to sort out the duck for the day . . .

The duck is sorted . . . all clean and in his cage.

What? You put the duck in his cage? Anyway, he needs food.

He *never* touched the duck. She sat up, reaching for her clothes.

He's eaten. His box is clean. There's food in his cage. Everything is organised. I found a couple of snails even. He couldn't help the self-satisfaction leak from his voice. No excuses.

I can't, I just can't. I'm sorry, Simon. You can't just land this on me.

Whyever not? It's called spontaneity, Hannah. Remember?

I'm tired and I've got work to do. You know what it's like. *You* have contracts you have to finish sometimes. She was dressing now, hurriedly.

The duck would be fretting, worried that something had happened to her.

She pushed past him, but he took her arm, grasping it tightly.

Look at me, Hannah.

She glanced at him, at his intense earnest face. The wall was more comfortable.

I had a dream last night, he said. Look at me, Hannah.

She looked at his chin, his lips within the grey sleek beard. She could smell the dampness of fresh shampoo.

I dreamt that I was looking for you. We were in the mountains, and you raced on ahead, disappearing around a bend. I couldn't reach you. I was calling to you, but I couldn't catch up. When I came to the bend you'd gone. The sky was black, so black. Ahead of me was a track winding through snow, leading down into dense bush. I'd lost you . . . Then I woke up, and there you were, lying beside me.

He moved her so that she was facing him, put his arms around her, pulled her to his chest.

She dropped her head onto his clean crisp shirt. Why? Why, why was it so hard to dissolve into him?

If she let go, she would fall into his dream.

He lifted his hand to her neck, twisted her hair around his fingers, pressed her head closer to his chest.

Slowly she eased away from him. Her hair fell back to her shoulders, he released his arms. She moved away, stealthily, as if she might awaken somebody left sleeping in their bed.

She crept down the stairs, through the kitchen, hurrying now across the deck, down the garden to the duck.

There he was, chirruping at her as normal.

I'm sorry, Ducko, she said, lifting him out of the cage.

Once inside again, finally, she found a note on the kitchen table. *I'm off. Can't waste a good picnic. Can't waste a good day. Can't waste a good life.*

Chapter 8

HOMECOMING

My mother came home today, the woman said to the duck.

Hannah was supposed to be working, but she'd taken her laptop outside, to the chair that cut under her legs, and the glass-topped table covered with a wintering of green that she could scrape runnels into with her fingernail. She'd decided to work outside so that the duck could run around on the lawn, out of the prison of his cage.

She'd always hated the cruelty of battery hens. She didn't want him to become a battery duck, although sometimes she worried that he was living like one. Or a wind-up toy, with a switch that made him walk like a clown, slapping his flippers on the wooden floor inside, or on any flat surface like the paths and deck. When he ran, it was as if the switch was set to a pace too fast for the machine, his whole body flailing out of kilter, one leg almost crossing over the other. Yet there was a gracefulness in his gracelessness, and he never failed to make her laugh. He could make her laugh from a deep happy part of herself, a part of herself she hadn't accessed for a long time. She'd been like a piano accordion from which the last wheeze had been squeezed, to be clipped up and stored away in a cobwebby cupboard.

And now she was holding him. She'd hoped that he would run through the grass, pleased to be free, poking his beak amongst the leaves and stones. Instead he'd dumped himself at her feet under the chair. She wondered whether she had trained him to be dependent upon her, whether every morsel he ate from now on would have to come from her hand, whether he might die from starvation should they ever be parted.

The wind was fresh and the shadows of the late afternoon were beginning to creep under her skin. The duck nestled against her stomach, edging his head beneath her breast. He let his eyes close, although they shot open again at any sudden noise — a car door somewhere, a nail-gun across the valley.

The computer sat untouched as she studied the changing terrain of the duck. He was half feathers and half fluff now. His back looked like a carefully landscaped triangle of toetoe planted from his tail and halfway up his spine, yellow tufts that stood up amongst the white fluff when he was preening himself, as if a wind was gusting across a tussocky headland. His naked chicken wings were almost concealed beneath a curve of new white feathers. His fat dog-waggy tail was a grubby brown.

Didn't you hear me? said the woman. She was playing with the remaining yellow fluff on his head, licking her fingertips to sculpt it into a ridge of mohawk. Punk duck.

What? said the duck.

My mother came home today.

Ah yes, he said. I heard that. You're testing me. I know your mother is dead.

Yes, said the woman. That's true. But she came home. A woman dressed in black arrived on the doorstep holding an orange rose and my mother in a box in a brown paper carry-bag. She came inside and placed the bag on the kitchen floor. The woman had a cup of tea and a gingernut and we talked about Christmas and then she went away. And there Mum was. A bit like you. You arrived in a bag and there you were.

But I wasn't dead.

No. But you were in a carry-bag and you smelt as though you were.

Why did I smell?

You'd come a long way in a car. And stayed overnight in Hamilton. Old poos. But I gave you a bath and cleaned out your straw and stuff, and you were soon as fresh as a daisy.

Does your mother smell?

No. You'll have to meet her. She would have liked you. She always said that after she died she'd like to come back as a seagull.

I'm not a seagull.

I know, but you're a duck.

I don't see the connection.

Well, a seagull is feathery like you, with webbed feet and the same shape, more or less. They fly over the sea.

Why did she like seagulls?

She had this idea that they were free. She wanted to be free. She loved the idea of soaring high on a current of wind and just hanging above the world.

The woman looked at the duck. His head was now cocked to one side, with that inquiring eye. It occurred to her that her mother might have been reincarnated as a duck. And this duck. There would be an irony in that. Her mother's essential self still held prisoner. Free in a way but bound to her. Her wings still undeveloped. Perhaps it was true that death was not a release but a stopping for a moment until the next time. And then a carrying on from where you left off. And perhaps you were always as you had been then, in an essential way, before you died.

Are you my mother? she asked the duck.

Don't be ridiculous, what are you talking about? I'm a duck. Was your mother a duck, too?

No. She quite liked ducks, though. Yes, she did. We'd go to the park and feed them.

Them?

Yes, lots of them.

Lots? What did you feed them? Snails?

No, bread.

Are there lots of ducks?

Yes, lots.

Like me?

Some like you. Some different but the same. But you're an individual. You're one duck. *They* are lots of ducks . . .

The duck was thoughtful for a moment, before he said, Yes. I remember now. Lots of ducks.

ONE OUT OF THE EGG

And Hannah was taken back in time as well, and she can feel rocks under her feet and hands, the gentle warmth of a cloudy summer's day, and her mother close by with tanned arms and legs, wearing shorts and a flowing blouse. Clambering over boulders. To one side, the sea sloshing around the rock edges; and to the other, grassy cliffs rising to the mottled sky. Back at the campsite on the private farmland, her father is taking care of her baby sister.

They wander on and on, investigating pools and shells and bones until they stumble upon a plump creature with gaping beak crouching amongst the rocks. Her mother is just as puzzled as she is as to what it might be, which compounds the mystery. Her mother, who has the answers to everything, except who made the world and when did the world begin and when will it end. And where does the sky end and what's on the other side. And . . .

But this earth-bound creature is an enigma. It has black webbed feet and its fluff is speckled with colours of the rocks and sand and driftwood around it. It could be a bird but it is too fat. It's a mouldy pumpkin. Nothing in their experience relates to it. As they peer at it, seagulls wheel around them, whining and squealing. Fretfully. Aggressively. Some swoop unnervingly at their heads.

They both move away uneasily, pulled onwards by curiosity and absolute contentment, and a whimsical inquisitiveness as to what might lie around each rocky bend. When they finally come to a small bay, they sit on the beach sharing a piece of chocolate — the only food they have. Dainty terns scamper in front of them, leaving footprints in the sand like arrows pointing the way for the journey home. And her mother is suddenly aware that during their oblivion the day has moved on. They scramble the long obstacle-course back to camp, noting the fluffy creature again as they pass, still amidst the cacophonic vigilance of the seagulls. They arrive just as the day is beginning to fade, and there's her father with ten-month-old Maggie in his arms as he paces the sand by the rocks, his gaze fixed anxiously in their direction.

They've been away several hours, lost in reverie, not so much as mother and daughter but as two spirits moving alongside each other in the trueness of their being, in awe of the world in which they live.

WHERE TO GO

And for a little while, Hannah forgot that her mother was sitting there in the box, in the paper bag with the string handle, by the fridge. And then she passed and said hello and wondered where to put her. It was only when she picked up the box and felt the weight of it that she had any sense of it being *her*. She thought of the times she'd helped her mother up from a chair, or the bath, or a fall onto the floor or in the street — all that weight was there in the box. The lightness that was her laughter, her sense of fun when she had that, all of the lightness that held her upright, all that lightness was gone.

Hannah carried the paper bag with her mother in it to the other end of the room. She considered putting her under the couch, but it seemed disrespectful. Now her mother was here, she just didn't know what to do with her. It was pretty much how it had been in life, after her mother came to stay when she became ill. She found a strip of sun on the window sill that looked warm, so she placed her there, for the time being, in the box, in the paper carry-bag, looking very much like a dumped shopping bag.

When Simon came home that evening, she waited for him to notice the bag on the window sill, but he was preoccupied with his work. Or seemingly so. Nothing was said. Nothing had been said, either, about his outing to the west coast, about her not accompanying him, though his dream about her had seeped into her mind, as if that barren terrain had been territory they had experienced together, as if his dreaming vision had been true.

After dinner, and when he'd gone to bed, Hannah took her mother to her old bedroom and slid her into an empty drawer. She found herself leaving it open a little, for air. She stood back. Then she took her out again. It didn't seem right to put her in a drawer. She pulled back the covers of the bed where her mother had spent her time of transition between her independent life and her ensnared life at Primrose Hill, and placed the bag and the box between the clean sheets. She made the bed again, arranging the duvet so that her mother's presence was a barely distinguishable bump in the covers, a life over and done with, and tucked away.

THINGS HER MOTHER TOLD HER

Don't talk with your mouth full, don't be silly, don't use safety pins if your buttons fall off, don't squeeze your pimples, how can we expect world peace if we can't have it at home, don't lie, don't answer back, don't be cheeky, be nice to your grandmother, don't stare, don't read with a torch under the blankets, be nice to everyone, don't pick your teeth in public, don't cut your nails in public, tidy your room, don't pull your cheek like that, if a job's worth doing it's worth doing well, a little lipstick would do wonders, if you keep your glass full they can't fill it up again, don't frown, kiss on the doorstep and then say goodbye, sex is wonderful after marriage, don't, you must know when enough is enough, don't be silly, get a haircut or tie it up, mend your holes, keep in touch, be kind, don't be silly. Be nice.

THINGS HER MOTHER TAUGHT HER

As an example, in the way she lived, her mother taught her about love, about beauty, about colour, about compassion, about commitment, about loyalty, about courage, about selflessness, about kindness, about modesty, about generosity. About gentleness and dignity. About humility. About selfless service. About honesty and respect. About friendship. All the good things. All the other things had gone and the good things were left.

And she wished now that she could talk to her mother about all those virtues, about everything, with hindsight, as an overview; she wished she could express her appreciation to her mother as the person she was before her demise. Before the illness. She wished she had been nicer. She had so much understanding, now, that she didn't have before, and the reason why her mother did this and that, which at the time seemed . . . ridiculous, or unnecessary. If only she'd been more grateful. But it was over, and all she wanted to say to people who had mothers was: Take the chance while you have it.

But now she had the duck, and there was something about this duck that felt like a second chance.

NOT A BABY

Hannah's work was interrupted by a text from Simon. Two of his engineering colleagues and their wives were coming to dinner.

Sorry, Ducko, she said as she sprinkled poultry pellets into a cabbage leaf. This is *it* for us today. Not only the crows but I've got the house to tidy, supermarket, cook dinner, and then attempt to pretty myself up. Panic stations, I'm afraid.

What about me? You're so mean. You don't care. Come back. Come back. Come back back baaaaack.

As it turned out, the evening was awkward; she hardly knew the guests and she felt like a dowdy waitress. The two wives discussed books she'd never even heard of. Hannah attempted to bring in some light and witty anecdotes about the duck, but she felt Simon's foot pressing upon hers, grinding it heavily to the floor. She stopped mid-sentence and no one seemed to notice. A budgie pausing mid-chirp. As they left, saying their goodbyes, one of the women called her Harriet, and the husband insincerely apologised to Hannah for 'talking shop'.

And then, when they'd all gone, the duck.

The hutch stank. Usually Hannah kept it clean, but tonight the cabbage leaves were pearly bowls of poo. Flies, disturbed by the torchlight, ping-ponged above the grass, pinging in the pong. She picked up the duck, adjusting him so that he was lying with his belly against her chest, his neck lying across her shoulder. He was becoming too big to comfortably rest his feet on her arms. He greeted her desperately, nibbling gently at the soft skin under her chin. He smelt like a wet cow yard. He reeked of neglect, her neglect.

Inside the house, Simon was clearing up the dinner dishes. He turned his head from the sink.

Honestly, he said. Look at you with that thing. It's not a baby. Really.

Hannah struggled not to cry. It was the last straw. Her relationship with the duck was attracting some snide comments. Jokes at her expense, barely disguised mockery. She pushed past him, wanting to say so much but saying nothing. In the bathroom she caught her image in the mirror. How pathetic, wild, lonely, old, she looked. She was fading away. Her reflection revealed a deranged woman who should be pacing the moors on a bleak, mist-swirling afternoon. And indeed, the duck could be a swaddled baby with an elastic neck and a deformed pinhead resting under her chin.

She just wanted to plonk the duck away in his plastic box. Instead she placed him in the bath and set the water running. He was used to having baths now. She always started out with the bath empty so she could relish the transition from clumsy old waddler to elegant floater. He started to coo as he lifted with the rising water. He turned upside-down and dived for the poultry pellets she threw in, snorting softly as he cleared his nostrils. He was as happy as a duck in water. Her depression rolled off her like water off a duck's back. He was a sitting duck, a paddling duck, a much cleaner duck. Tonight she was not laughing but was absorbed by the watching of him. She could watch him forever. She wondered what it was about, all this. She hated being forced to think about it.

He floated on a boat of thick feathers. When had *they* arrived? If she dipped her fingers into his chest, the tips of her fingers disappeared to the first joint. Her fingers were like old legs trudging through snow.

The man called out to her.

She hoisted herself from her knees and backed out of the bathroom, careful to keep in sight of the duck, his black watching eye intense.

What did you say?

I said, I'm sorry. I shouldn't have been mean.

She faced him, and all the fury that had stopped her responding to his first comment surged back again.

If it weren't for you, I'd have my own babies.

The duck stopped chirruping. The man became motionless at the bench. The moment was sucking in air. She was between the two in the hallway, stepping from the sight of the duck to confront Simon. She waited, but he said nothing. He had received her words and had turned to stone.

Meanwhile, the duck was going mad over her disappearance. She could hear the heaving turbulence of the water, the thump as he threw himself against the side of the bath. When she re-entered the bathroom, his head was poking above the bath rim like a periscope, gliding up and down, up and down along the rim of the bath, searching for her.

Their moment of peace had been destroyed. It took a while before the duck stopped panicking, before her own heart had settled. She knelt beside him, letting her hand gently ruffle the water, while she concentrated on breathing, on harnessing her breath back to a regular pace.

Then Simon came to the door and hovered there, watching. She didn't turn around. She didn't hear him go, but she became aware of her shoulders, gradually releasing themselves from her ears.

TIPPING POINT

In 1966, Hannah had her very own baby. She'd arrived home from school and found her mother and father holding hands in the sitting room, gazing into a cane bassinet nestled in an oval wooden stand. In the bassinet, a mustardy red creature, mewling in vibrato, punched miniature fists at the air. Her parents pulled her back tenderly. Careful you don't tip her over, sweetie.

But Hannah was the one who had already tipped over. She'd tumbled headfirst into the needy eyes, the imploring eyes of her new sister. Her one-armed Teddy and her hairless doll, Pamela, with the blue eyes that opened and shut, were instantly forgotten.

Even though her mother expertly unbuttoned her blouse and kept a discreet blanket across her chest, Hannah could sometimes spy the swollen nipple eased from her sister's milky mouth as her mother's breast was delivered back to its rightful place, like a tongue pulled in after eating ice-cream. Hannah knew her own role was secondary, but nonetheless she'd make sure to be there to help wash the baby in the plastic bath on the kitchen table, splashing warm water on the naked wrinkled skin. She'd poke her nose over the bassinet and watch her sister's ugly beautiful face soften into sleep. For a time, she was sure that Maggie was going to grow into one of those perky-eyed monkeys she'd seen in pictures, and she wouldn't have cared.

But then the creases filled up with their mother's milk, and the ruddy skin whitened and the eyes deepened. And when Hannah discovered she was able to make her baby sister laugh, this became her sole intention in life. It was so simple. Hiding behind a tea towel and going *Boo*. Throwing tissue balls into the air and going *Wheeeee*. Putting a red stuffed cat on her head and letting it fall off. Maggie's plump face would split into a fissure of laughter, her body cramping and jiggling, her mouth open to let the joy pour out and swirl around the room.

Before Maggie took her first tottering steps alone, Hannah would take her by the hand and lead her wobbling to her mother and father's open arms. When Maggie was able to walk, Hannah led her around the house and down into the garden and down the street and into town and up the long straight streets to the end of the road, and along the footpaths to school where she watched for her in the playground. After a year at school together, Hannah biked to intermediate, and then to high school and, by the time Maggie was at high school, Hannah was writing copy for the local radio station.

Where Hannah's hair was blonde, Maggie's was jet black. Where Hannah was pale and tiny, contentedly dreamy, Maggie was strong and sporty, with long froggy legs and burnished skin and inquiring dark eyes. They were Snow White and Rose Red. Maggie grew into pretty dresses, then sharp punky dresses, into independence, into a wild defiant thing, a thing who would be more likely to bite than hold anybody's finger, who knew everything, who was quick, cheeky, disobedient, who slammed doors and rocked the house with retort. She had so many friends that Hannah had to close her own bedroom door in search of peace. It felt as though the house was overrun with young devils. Hannah withdrew into books or sat in the willow tree by the back fence in her jeans and listened to the birds.

By the time Hannah was thinking of leaving her job in Hawke's Bay to go to university, Maggie was sneaking out of her window at night to meet her feral mates to smoke cigarettes and ride as pillion passengers on motorbikes with youths in black leather jackets. In the small hours one morning, her parents were awakened by a knock at the door. Two policemen on the doorstep informed them that their daughter was in hospital after being flung off a bike by the river. No, you have the wrong person, she's in bed, they assured the police.

It was just grazes and broken ribs and burns from the exhaust, and shattered trust. They could feel their thirteen-year-old daughter slipping from their control. Notoriously, she was the daughter of a school teacher. Their father. Everyone knew who the bad girl was. Hannah had been so good. Hannah had been no trouble at all. What had they done in the ensuing years for it all to go so badly wrong?

A year later, after a tip-off one Saturday night, Hannah drove with her father out of town and off a country road, through a gate across paddocks to the river. Teenagers were scattered about, or sitting around a bonfire. A ghetto-blaster was shrieking manic music at the night.

What's all this? their father had said as they climbed from the car.

A boy was vomiting against a tree. Another two boys were hauling a branch through the grass to replenish the fire.

Where's Maggie? Who are these people? They're drunk. Drunk!

Indeed they were. Bottles scattered everywhere. No one knew or was telling where Maggie was.

Other parents arrived in cars behind them. Some of the boys ran into the bushes. Somewhere by the trees a couple of cars vroomed into throaty action. A motorbike wove across the paddock. The girls who could stand up were busy helping their friends who couldn't. But once they stood they didn't know where to go, looking stupidly into the glare of the headlights. Others were asleep in sleeping bags.

Hannah's father tugged at his coat under his throat, his mouth open as if to make an announcement. Half the kids there knew him from school. What had he been about to say? They never found out. He took a step backwards, then staggered to the stony ground. At that moment the music stopped or was turned off. The fire was crackling and the river was rushing by and the light from the fire was flicking over her father's contorted face. His hand was pulling at the buttons of his coat. Some distance away, a girl was chattering obliviously. Car doors were slamming.

Not long after, Maggie appeared in a dishevelled state, hiccoughing uncontrollably.

Hannah looked up at her from where their father lay.

Look! she screamed. Look what you've bloody done now.

Chapter 9

NO FIXED ABODE

They had visitors coming to stay, so Hannah had to unearth her mother from the cosy grave of bedclothes and once again face the issue of where to put her. She walked around the house with the carry-bag, eyeing this sunny corner, or this window sill with a pleasant view over the valley, or the old glory box, still smelling of camphor balls, that her mother had used for storing collected items such as sheets, towels and nightdresses before her marriage.

She was trying to imagine where her mother would most be comfortable. Somewhere picturesque, inspirational. Somewhere in Nature, maybe. She stood staring pensively out the window. Her father's ashes had been tossed into waves from jagged rocks in Hawke's Bay, amidst cracking thunder and driving rain, amongst swirling rose petals and beneath wheeling keening seagulls.

Seagulls.

Recently, Hannah had been taking more notice of the seagulls at the beach. Their huge wings. Unlike the scruffy old duckling, every feather was locked into place on their sleek thick necks to give the appearance of smooth porcelain.

She'd watched them strutting around in the sand, squealing for crusts, their skinny red legs with old-man knobble-knees.

The duck's legs in comparison were like fence posts, his knees barely visible under a ruffle of feathers. His legs were yellow with fishnet stockings pulled up into the suspenders under his fancy feather pants. They were serious legs designed for a big clown. How tall was he going to become, how big? His beak looked as if it were growing mouldy, a black symmetrical smudge smeared halfway up from the curve of his smile. She had experimented by scraping her fingernail across the black to see whether it would come off. It didn't. There were pink lumps now framing his beak, and these also had mottles of black. Perhaps he was rotting from all the puddling around in filth?

She wondered what would happen if she brought him to the sea, with all that sky above and the depth and spread of ocean below. He might just bob along on a soft summer's day, getting smaller and smaller as he drifted away from her, the steady gaze from his black eye like a peep-hole into loneliness.

At that moment there was a knock at the door. Their visitors already!

Hannah shoved her mother into the very back of a pot cupboard and raced to open the door.

PEER PRESSURE

Night-time. The duck was still in his cage. Hannah could hardly stand it. She went out with a clean towel for him to nestle in. He emerged from his cubby hole blearily, expecting her to pick him up. She felt like a traitor. She felt lily-livered.

The reason she wasn't bringing him inside was simple: fear of censure. Their farmer friends, two burly brothers from Puketitiri in Hawke's Bay, had come to stay for a few days. She knew without doubt that they would have something to say about a duck sleeping in the bathroom. They'd think she was nothing but a foolish middle-aged woman. They would scoff: Hah! Poultry inside! You'll be sorry! It's an animal for Christ's sake!

As it was, when they'd spotted the duck outside in the cage they'd eyed him up as a meal prospect.

Yeah, great eating, Barbary duck, not as fatty as other ducks. He'll be just right for Christmas dinner. If we'd known you liked duck we coulda got a couple out of the freezer.

ONCE SHE HELD A HEART IN THE PALM OF HER HAND

When she was about thirteen, Hannah's father pulled his flat-bottomed boat with an outboard motor from the garage. He was now selling it for something bigger. A couple of rugged, tanned duck shooters arrived to look at it. They were wearing shorts and khaki shirts, and every sentence was splattered with swear words. Bloody this and bloody that and I'll be buggered and we got the bastard. The day was sunny and hot and they all stood negotiating for the boat in the driveway, while Hannah as a young girl watched from the back steps. The deal was done and the men went off with the boat.

A few weeks later, one of the men arrived at the back door with a couple of ducks hanging from his hand, his big finger separating the two woeful heads. In gratitude for the boat.

When he'd gone, her parents discussed the ducks. They'd been uncertain; it was the plucking and the gutting they weren't sure about, and, really, duck meat was a bit rich. Hannah was interested in the inner workings of things — dissecting frogs and sheep's eyes at school was a real curiosity for her. So she offered to prepare the ducks for eating.

Her recollection of it all was a haze now, but she could still recall the sensation of yanking the feathers from the flesh, the naked skin ashiver with goose bumps which were actually duck bumps, and the last few insistent ones plucked individually. And then the gushing spill of intestines, a slimy visceral mass of innards and her fingers squishing through it all as she tried to identify each of the parts. The heart amongst it all, sitting in the palm of her hand. Then, it had been just a meaty heart. Now, when she thought this in relation to *her* duck, with that engine pumping to all the machinery of her living duck, she felt sick. Back then, she'd felt sick because of the stench. She remembered dry-retching violently as she worked. And by this stage, what had happened to the heads? She recalled the concrete double tub and her mother's preserving jars filled with fruit on the shelves alongside her. She remembered her parents bemused by her curiosity that gave her a detachment from it all. And after all that, the meal not such a treat. All she could remember now was her parents complaining about the gamey flavour.

But of course, she had no intention of talking to the duck about this.

GENTLEMEN'S CLUB

The farmers told them a story of a woman from the country who collected unwanted male ducks because she knew they were destined for the roasting dish. She now had a flock of eighteen male ducks all rivering on her rural property, dipping and diving and splashing in a gang, all coming to eat the handfuls of maize she sprinkled out for them, all thinking she was their mother duck.

Hannah wondered how a person could love eighteen ducks when she barely had the capacity to love one.

Anyway, there was a shift in the intensity between her and the duck. She hadn't had the same time for him of late. They hadn't had the hours to garden together, to forage and weed. And when they did, he wasn't quite so clingy. He'd be content to sit apart from her. Just the other day, she'd climbed a steep bank to attend to plants and there hadn't been the same cheeping call. *She'd* been the one with the moment's concern. She stood up from the foliage, her eyes flitting over the garden for him and . . . there he was. Concealed from her, but he had placed himself so that his eye was upon her. That intense beacon beaming through the panic of separation. It was a posture of independence as if he were practising for the eventuality.

It felt like something akin to resignation. He was a ball being spun from a fraying rope which was stretching further and further until one day he'd be flung off and away from her, into the sky — his new wings flapping.

VISITING TIMES

It was the third evening of the farmers' stay and they'd all just arrived home from a party. Hannah went to the bathroom to wash her hands. There was no chirruping welcome. The room was full of the absence of him. There was only the absolute stillness of something gone.

The farmers and Simon sat around the table drinking whiskey. Hannah sat down and listened to the things that men talked about. They were having an animated discussion about an experiment, based in Moscow, in which five men, encapsulated in a make-believe spaceship, were well on their way into a simulated journey to Mars. There were three Russians, a Frenchman, an Italian and a Chinese man. They had eighteen months in which to understand their cultural differences. The man from China taught them Chinese. Their emails and conversations to their loved ones and colleagues back home were given a twenty-minute delay to reflect the time it took for signals from Mars to reach Earth.

Simon knew all about it, had something to say about it. The journey was going to culminate in three of the cosmonauts bouncing around a sandpit in a module connected to the spaceship. This was to be regarded as a virtual landing on the planet.

Well, said Hannah, isn't that what we're all doing? Travelling on a simulated journey to the end of our lives?

The men stopped their discussion, and they all looked at her for a moment.

Crikey, Hannah, said Bruce. You've got me there.

Roy, his brother, clamped his warm, rough hand on her shoulder. You've always been a bit of a philosopher, Hann, he said kindly.

Hannah left the trio. She took the torch and crept into the night, crunching over stones, past the pond to the hutch. She was careful to keep the torchlight subtle, not to shine it in the duck's eyes as she had the night before, making him fling himself in panic at the cage wall. Tonight he rose from his towel in the corner, snaking his neck forward into the darkness, with just the tiniest hesitant gurgle of cheep. He was a white shadow in the dark. He was a ghost.

She sat in the grass and cooed at him. He was the ghost of her mother who wanted to be a seagull but had found the body of a duck in the night and thought, That'll do. He was the ghost of her mother, blinking from that half-dead place, wandering from the back corner of her mind, to see whether the only person in the world she could trust had anything to offer her.

And then that person left, left her mother alone in the rest home, to go back over the lawn to the light and laughter in the house above.

And in her heart Hannah was aware of the disappointment she had created through her brief, unfulfilling visit.

LIVINGSTONE

She was in love again. They were free to be in love again, she and her duck. The farmers left without her having to divulge any behaviour that could be categorised as obsessive or eccentric by those who didn't understand. He was her secret, her bit on the side.

Now, armed with a vicious bread knife, secateurs and a red-handled weeder, they made their way to the bottom of the section. Out of sight from the house, beyond a stone wall with a rotting wooden gate, this portion had been abandoned for years. There had been a vegetable garden here once, flourishing with beans and lettuces, tomatoes and corn. Now it was a spongy mattress of kikuyu grass. There was a small bush area where tui used to sup nectar from flax flowers, but the long woody stems were now rotting amongst other tangled foliage. Tree ferns spouted a fountain of dead fronds. Cabbage tree leaves lay thickly-woven underfoot, with fibrous borer-hollowed branches scattered amongst them.

They could be in safari suits, the woman and her trusty duck, slashing through undergrowth, pulling at layers and layers of desiccated leaves and branches, disturbing wetas that aggressively lifted their thorny legs, ready to attack.

The duck was uncertain of the new terrain. As she hacked away, he sat patiently, jumping up to gobble shiny black spiders and wood lice. Mercurial lizards slid into nowhere. Occasionally they came across a pooling of rancid rainwater caught in the base of palm fronds, holding a brew of worms and mucousy slugs.

The woman's face and arms itched as she surged forward, a pile of branches and leaves growing behind her. Finally, they burst through to a small clearing around the old wooden shed, the man's workshop.

Well, here we are, said the woman to the duck. Civilisation at last.

She turned the metal doorknob and tugged. The wooden door was either stuck or locked. She peered through the cobwebby window. She hadn't been down here for years. The shed was crude but neat, with high shelves stacked with books and notebooks. A workbench spanned one wall to the other. There was also a bench seat that ran almost the length of the shed. On the floor were bags of blood and bone, lime and gypsum stacked against the wall, some spewing their stuff onto the floor. The unlined walls had exposed four by twos, and a few garden tools hung from nails, with various tins along the beams. Cobwebs hung in clouds from the ceiling.

Well, she said to the duck. With a bit of work this could be a nice cosy duck hotel one day.

The duck waddled wistfully behind her as she turned and started back to the house. At the deck, she picked him up. She kicked off her gumboots and stepped inside. Simon was working at his computer. He looked up, his fist wrapped around his beard, his eyebrows dipping to the bridge of his glasses. His eyes resting on the duck.

Hi, she said brightly.

What's going on?

Oh, I was just coming in for a cup of tea. It's so hot out there.

I mean, why are you bringing that thing inside? You are both extremely dirty.

We've been gardening. Oh well — she backed, her enthusiasm imploding — can you pass me out a drink then? Water'll do. Actually, you're right. I'll clean up and come in for lunch. I've got work to do.

Simon's chair scraped loudly across the floor as he stood up to pour her a glass of water. Hannah drank and handed the glass back. She turned and took the duck back to his cage.

The man is coming between us, said the duck.

Don't be silly, said the woman. He's a bit fussy, that's all. He's not used to ducks. Never mind. We've had a lovely morning together, and really, I do have work to do.

But that night in bed she moved across the sheets towards Simon, resting her body against his back. She folded her legs into his legs, wrapped her arm around his plump stomach. She always loved the way his skin softened after a bath, and the fragrant hint of soap. Pulling herself against him, she sank gently into the comforting position of familiarity. And suddenly he twitched. Violently. His whole body in a dream-sinking spasm, rejecting her. He was a shanghai and she was a stone, flung away from him, from the bed, out the window, a stone with flailing arms and legs, thrashing madly through the night sky, then plummeting back to Earth, back to bed, where she yanked the bedclothes across her shoulders, spinning over and over and over away from, far far away from him, into sleep.

Chapter 10

THE UNBEARABLE POLITENESS OF POOING

This evening Hannah had attended a dinner party with a group of women. The conversation had turned to pets: stories of puppies, old dogs, old cats, kittens, and thrushes in a nest outside a window.

And I have a duck, she'd announced.

Oh, a duck! they'd chorused awkwardly. Where did you get a duck from?

She found herself holding her cupped palm across the table. When he arrived he could sit in my palm, she said. A ball of yellow fluff. An orphan. Ostracised by the flock.

Cute! they cried.

And now he's bigger than a football. He's a fatball. He's ugly and grubby-looking. He follows me everywhere.

She'd felt like a turncoat.

But doesn't he *poo?* somebody, of course, had to say.

Well, yes, she said, thinking of the conversation that she'd once had with Max, Eric's grandson, as he sat on the potty. Yes, everyone and everything poos. Mummy poos, Daddy poos, Auntie Jane poos, and Poppa. Yes, and me as well. And Simon? Yes, and Simon. And birds poo and cats poo and dogs poo and elephants too. And baby elephants? Yes, baby elephants and caterpillars. And ducks.

Somebody else said, as a loud aside and with particular emphasis: They do. They certainly do. Everywhere. *Actually*, they don't stop.

Hannah was wishing, how she was wishing she hadn't started this. She didn't mention how she cleaned his hutch out each morning, now that he slept outside, relocated the hutch across the lawn every two or three days, had spent a fortune on rubber gloves, hosed the lawn, scooped up any stray dollop on the deck. Had paper towels and a mop and bucket within ready reach inside. She hadn't mentioned that, after years of looking after her mother, a little duck's plop was like pesto in comparison.

Then, in an effort to rescue her, another woman said, I bet it has character, does it?

Oh *yes*, said Hannah. Oh yes, he *does*.

In what way? asked the same woman, who had just talked about her cat as being resilient, determined, intelligent, haughty, resourceful.

Umm, he's umm . . .

She was stumped. Did he, in fact, have any character at all?

He's *clingy*, was all she'd been able to find to say.

Yes, but what sort of characteristics does it have, *specifically*. Clingy, yes, but its personality. Does it have any particular personality trait you enjoy?

Hannah had stopped herself saying that he was a loving duck, who needed her to hold him, nestling his beak under her hair and under her chin, or wangling his neck beneath her shirt and under her arm after she'd been away for a while. She was viewing the middle distance above the candle in the centre of the table as she thought. Somebody passed the salad, offered the wine around, somebody else clattered her chair back to go to the bathroom. The stuttering silence that had been stumbling from Hannah's head was filled again by chatter.

And now she was driving home and the question was haunting her. His personality. Any redeeming characteristics. How well did she know her duck? What was the attraction to him? Was it because he made her laugh? The questions were disconcerting. Her mother had drained any nurturing tendencies until she felt she had nothing left. She didn't need another dependent creature. So, what was going on? Perhaps the love between them was an ongoing love between her mother and herself, transferring itself from body to body as each one died.

When she died she might become a snail, and, should the duck eat her, what would happen to the love then?

But. Personality?

DARLING ONE

Now that she was spending more time in the garden, the neighbourhood cats regarded this as reclaiming her territory, so the threat of cats was lessening. Her roar at the white long-haired lion slinking in the bushes, watching the cage, must have been heard across the valley. However, there had been some alarming incidents over the past couple of weeks.

She was always amused at how adept and quick the duck was in finding a short-cut to her, should they become separated, winding through passages in the undergrowth to appear at her feet. One day, though, she was behind the stone wall, still dealing with the jungle by the shed. With his short-cut logic, he pushed himself through an opening in the hedge to reach her on the other side of the wall, landing in the public right-of-way that ran alongside their property. His pleading cries alerted her as he realised there was no throughway to her on the other side of the wall. She, too, panicked, racing along the dividing wall and back again to the gap in the hedge. She imagined having to tear up to the top of the section, out the gate and down the path to retrieve him, and by then . . . the possibilities already gripped her. Neighbours seeing the opportunity for Christmas dinner. Cars. Mauling dogs. Just plain old disappearance. Meanwhile, she stood under the trees with wet leaves around her toes, calling desperately.

Ducko! Duckie!

He paced frantically on the other side of the hedge, his eye on her. She cried out to Simon.

Help! Help, Simon. Help!

Her heart beating crazily. Ducko, come on. All the endearments, embarrassing even to herself. Darling one. Come on, come to Mummy.

And, of course, he found the gap, pushed through again, into her arms. And there was Simon running down from the house, his face taut with anxiety.

Hannah? What's wrong?

She was still breathless, holding the duck's feet still.

The duck, the duck escaped. Into the right-of-way.

He stopped abruptly. Oh, he said, the bloody duck. I heard you calling.

I was worried. I thought you cried 'Wolf'. I should have known better.

She watched him go. He kicked a plastic bottle flying across the section.

And now, today, Max and Rosemary arriving unexpectedly through the hedge, and Max taking it upon himself to terrorise the duck. The duck escaping around the house, through the bromeliads, darting around the clivias, over the lawn, under the trees into the open front doorway, through the foyer slap slap slap, into the hallway, the kitchen slap slap slap slap, the living room, the deck and squeezing through a narrow corner and halt.

Max also halted. Hannah caught up. The duck had managed to find a haven away from Max, behind a post onto a wee ledge without a railing, with a drop of five metres to the ground. He was petrified, lifting one foot then the other, over and over, staring into the space below.

Where's your little sister? You should be looking after her. Go and get Rosemary now! cried Hannah.

The boy rushed off to find his sister. The duck tried to back through the gap he'd slipped through so readily, but the feathers that had eased the smooth passage now prevented it. Hannah slipped her hands between the post and the house to squeeze him out. She tucked him under her arm and took off to find the children. Rosemary.

Rosemary had found the tadpoles that Hannah had been acclimatising in a large bowl by the pond, with the intention of giving the pond more life. The little girl had, with Max's blessing, five of the tadpoles lined in a row on the bridge over the pond, and was dipping into the bowl for more. And was experimenting with one of them between her fingers and thumb, examining its sloppy slimy texture. Hannah threw the tadpoles back, but that particular one floated to the top.

She fished it out and displayed it on her palm.

Look. Look at this poor tadpole. It's going to die now.

Don't worry, said Max. It can die into a frog.

The duck, suddenly there beside her, snapped the tadpole from her hand, squishing it in his greedy beak, a bulbous head one side and the tail the other before gobbling it altogether.

The children's nonchalance turned to disbelief.

The duck ate the tadpole. He ate it. He ate it all up.

Max. Rosemary. What are you doing over here, anyway? Where's Poppa?

In the garden.

Well, I think he'd like to see you. I'm sure I heard him calling you.

She guided them back through the hedge. Eric was digging in the garden.

I thought you might be worried about your grandchildren, she called.

I knew exactly where they were, he said. I've had my ear out.

Well, you didn't hear them squelching my tadpoles.

She turned to the duck at her feet.

You're disgusting, she said.

What?

Eating that tadpole, and in front of the children like that.

The boy's a monster, chasing me the way he did. And what was I supposed to do with that thing? *Look* at it? It was delicious. Are there more?

All this consumption, she said, exasperated. What sort of example are you setting the children? All the little creatures in the garden, and here you are, gobbling them up.

I'm teaching them about all the little creatures in the garden, said the duck. And all the big ones that like to eat them.

Like duck for Christmas dinner, said the woman.

And the cruelty of people who pretend to be kind, said the duck, and she heard the voice of her mother repeating, *You have a cruel streak, you really do.* He waddled down to the back of the garden into the obscurity of dusk, and didn't come when she called him. Before she put him in his cage for the night, she had to hunt for him as he crouched, hiding, sulking, amongst the clivias.

SITTING UNDER A TREE

Sometimes the woman became a heavy thing, her arms and legs filled with stone, her heart squeezing thick mud through the tendrils of her veins. Her cheeks were packed with gravel, pulling her mouth down towards the earth.

And on this particular day, the duck scrambled onto the dusty old pond of her lap and wrapped his developing fevered wings around her and together they lifted into the air, a whiff of fairy-down rising. He placed his winglets over her eyes so that her vision turned inwards. Far below she could see a muddy puddle and an empty nest of white fluff. In a paddock nearby, its juices already sinking into the earth, the carcass of a duck lay sprawled amongst a wreath of white feathers, its neck twisted back and a wing splayed across the grass.

The woman saw a swirling of dry clattering leaves rising to meet them. She and the duck were sucked into the eddy, whirling through space. And now, beneath them, there was her mother, laid out on a bed with a towel rolled under her chin, pink make-up brushed on bloodless cheeks, her hair swept from her forehead onto the pillow, and a carnation lying on the sheet over her chest.

She watched as her mother unclasped her hands and raised high her thin bony arms, her thin feathered arms, her thin feathered wings, her immense white wings beating, taking her upward to join them, enfolding the woman and her duck within the deeply downy underside of her wings. They glided back down to where they had been sitting, the woman leaning against a tree, her feet in soft green grass, the duckling on her lap, and something else wrestling in her chest.

COLOURING IN

Hannah wished now that she had taken more interest in the process of painting.

All through the house there were framed watercolours on the walls. They'd been painted by her mother who had been a respected artist in Hawke's Bay — people often wanting to commission her to paint their favourite landscapes or homesteads in the country. This task was usually a painstaking chore for her; her modesty and lack of faith in her own work tying her flowing lines into stiff knots. To say she had a natural flare, rather than flair, for painting would describe her intuitive creativity accurately. She constantly observed the world around her in relation to its palette, to composition, to aesthetics. In a few minutes she'd be able to capture a scene or a face with a few free lines and a flourish of colour. She'd dismiss this ability with a nonchalant, *Oh no, that's just a sketch*.

Not long before she moved from Hawke's Bay, the painting society she belonged to had staged an exhibition of her work. She resisted fervently, embarrassed that she should be the centre of attention. By then her hand–eye co-ordination had been ruined by Parkinson's disease, so she was feeling especially vulnerable and unworthy of her artist's status. She refused to make a selection, until her friends barged upon her and pulled out their favourites from the boxes and suitcases of work gathered through the years. She succumbed to the inevitability of the event, and participated in the final decision as to which paintings should be exhibited. The paintings were mounted and framed. Everyone rallied together and helped with the hanging.

Hannah and Simon flew down for the opening. Her mother looked stunning in a new cherry-pink dress, with her wavy silver hair, her still-expressive eyes and engaging smile welcoming people as they arrived. The gallery owner buzzed patronisingly around the older guests, while fawning over the local artist, nationally acclaimed, who gave the opening address. After his speech, her mother's friends and fellow artists came forward one by one to acknowledge her talent. Her mother listened, mortified, unwittingly backing from the crowd, smiling humbly, blinking, pressing into the wall, framed and set up, her modesty refusing the praise. Hannah noticed her face draining as she wobbled on her stick, and bound forward to grab her arm as she finally collapsed, fainting into a chair pushed hurriedly forward. The gallery owner fanned her with the exhibition price list. Shortly after, her mother emerged from her retreat into oblivion. She looked up at the circle of concerned faces surrounding her. Hannah offered her a glass of water.

For heaven's sake, Hannah, what's the matter? Whatever are you doing with that? Her whisper was sharp and audible.

You had one of your turns, Mum.

For goodness' sake. I did nothing of the sort. There's nothing wrong with me, she said, pushing the water away.

Everybody chuckled warmly but uneasily and returned to looking at the paintings, sipping their wine and nibbling the cheese straws and club sandwiches. By the end of the evening, almost all the paintings had a red sticker next to them. All except one: a single seagull gliding against a wild sky above a stormy sea. And that picture was still Hannah's favourite, hanging on the wall at the end of the table where she worked.

When her mother moved to Primrose Hill, Hannah explained to the supervisor that her mother had once been a fine artist and asked if there might be some opportunity for her to pursue her interest. It was organised for her to attend an art and craft session once a week, and Hannah was given permission to sit in on the sessions. When the time came, they were directed to the art room — a small room with a table and a trolley cluttered with cardboard, scissors, paintbrushes and children's plastic squeeze bottles filled with brazen colours.

Four other women straggled in on their walkers, and were helped around the table. The activities tutor bustled around, squirting paint into pottles, handing out card and a paintbrush and crude stencils of fir trees, stars, flower petals and leaves. They each had their own little pottles. The task was to fill in the stencils — the trees and leaves with green, the stars with bright yellow, and the flowers with blue or red. Paper towels were used to dab at any stray paint.

Hannah's mother said nothing, but looked at the card and other paraphernalia in front of her. Then she turned to Hannah and asked for water.

Anyone else like a drink? asked Hannah. No one replied, so she went out to the kitchen and came back with a glass of water. Her mother took it in her bony hand, leaned over and emptied the glass haphazardly over all her pottles, water flooding everywhere.

Mum, what are you doing?! cried Hannah, uncertain as to whether this was an act of defiance or an accident. The tutor fussed around, yanking over and over at the paper towels as Hannah apologised, moving jars and pottles to allow her to soak up the mess.

Don't worry, mouthed the tutor at Hannah with an exaggerated wink. When everyone had settled again, her mother reached for a clean paper towel and spread it on the table in front of her. With intense deliberation she dipped her paintbrush into the now diluted blue and held it against the edge of the paper towel. The colour swam into the paper. She repeated the action, ignoring everyone else as they held their own paintbrushes mid-air to watch this crazy performance. Then she dipped her brush into the watery yellow paint and did the same further along the towel, watching with satisfaction as the colours bled together, the blue and the yellow merging into a wash of green.

Hannah suddenly understood. She felt like weeping with empathy for her mother and anger with herself that she should have been judgmental over her mother's unorthodox behaviour. Her mother was stubbornly but calmly resisting the kindergarten activity and was doing what she loved best of all: playing with colour.

NEW BLOOD

Although the duckling was allowed more time to run freely while she was around, Hannah kept him caged when she left the property, even if Simon was home. She couldn't depend on him to keep an eye on the duck while she wasn't there.

She had liberated the duck for a run this morning as she cleaned his cage, throwing in a bolted lettuce from the garden, concealing slugs and snails amongst the leaves. Once back inside, though, he found every one and snapped them up. By the time she'd replaced the lid of the hutch, he'd eaten them all. Eleven snails and five slugs. They were supposed to be his entertainment, little surprises to be discovered from time to time during the course of the day.

When she returned home, just before dusk, he was starving. The covered end of his house was heaped with bubbles of green poo. There wasn't much on the exposed lawn; she assumed he must have hidden away all day. She pulled him out and he hung into her, nuzzling her neck. Then they had a run around the garden, she jogging, laughing, while he waddled to keep up with her. She eventually led him to the pond, which she and Simon had cleaned and tidied up over the past couple of weekends, despite Simon's reluctance to do anything towards making the duck more comfortable during his stay.

She stood on the wooden bridge and the duck held back, staring at her questioningly. There was a nip in the evening. He took a few steps over the stones, joined her on the bridge, and peered down into the water. He shuffled uncertainly to the edge; he was Mr Bean trying to summon courage to dive from a high board, except that his jump was less than quarter of a metre. Finally he took the plunge, over the cord binding woman and duck, and into his automatic self, splashing around and washing his feathers.

Once done, he hauled himself onto the stones, then stood erect, flapping his wings. He surprised himself by toppling off-balance. She was shocked. His wings were beginning to have an effect on the air. The day spent cooped up in the hutch had been put to good use. All his energy had been pouring into his wings.

She felt a pang of grief. Soon he would have the strength to fly. She scooped him up and probed around his wings, those once naked morsels protected under their neatly designed feathered covers.

They'd been fluffing up, as if growing mildew. She'd been aware of that. But now the two rows of darts sprouting along the rims were flushed with nourishing blood. They were tender, alive, pumping with growth. They looked like two rows of pink birthday candles, with spindly feathery flames. They felt hot. He allowed her to place her hands beneath them, to spread them out to examine them, but it was as a favour and she had to treat them delicately. The power and energy that had been held back from these silly stunted flappers, while developing and maintaining the carefully planned planting on the rest of his body, was now shooting into the wings. The overnight educator was preparing him to fly. Had one of his ungainly practice flaps passed a test?

Her mother's words floated through her head. *All I want to do is soar high above the world.*

And then Hannah thought of Yuri Gagarin, the first man in space all those decades ago, *his* words to the world just on take-off: *Good-bye, see you soon, my dear friends. The vibration becomes more frequent, the noise increases.* And later, *I can see the Earth's horizon. It has a beautiful blue halo. The sky is black. I can see stars.* And then, *It is possible to determine the motion of the sea.*

Goodbye, my friend, her duckling might say to her, before lift-off, before finding himself in the infinity of it all, a lonely speck in the blue, flapping and flapping and flapping his new wings with no idea of where to go or how to stop, the vibration becoming more frequent, the silence increasing, determining the motion of the sea and not knowing what the ocean was, nor even that he was a duck.

SIMON SAYS

The spine of the feathers is called a rachis, and during the formation of feathers is filled with blood. Feathers in the wings and tails are the largest so they have the greatest blood supply, which is why they are called blood feathers. They grow from a follicle in the skin, in the same way as human hair does. They are like channels to a bird's blood supply, similar to veins. There are stories of birds bleeding to death through damaged blood feathers where the rachis acts like an artery. Once the feather is fully developed, the blood is absorbed back into the duck and this creates a hollow and therefore much lighter feather. Leading from the rachis there are branches called barbs, then running from the barbs are the barbicels. Barbicels hold the vane of the feather together, similar to Velcro or zips. They interweave with each other. Rubbing the feather the 'wrong' way unhooks the barbicels, and rubbing the 'right' way reconnects them again. The barbicels are very fine and almost need a magnifying glass to distinguish them.

If a blood feather is damaged and bleeding, the feather can be pulled out and the follicle plugged with cornflour until it seals.

Chapter 11

CUPBOARD LOVE

That night Hannah woke up strait-jacketed with horror. Her mother was still in the back of the pot cupboard. She had entirely forgotten. She sat up and switched the light on, aghast.

Whaaaa? Simon, lifting his head, blinked at her. What's going on?

I'm sorry, I just had a realisation.

He dropped his head down and threw his arm over his eyes against the light.

Good, he muttered. About time. We need to talk. But not now.

MOTHER DUCK

At the bottom of the urn was a screw. It wasn't easy to undo but she managed finally to twist it open, only to find a plastic bag within. This was the membrane between her and the last remaining elements of her mother. This was all the cups of tea and roast dinners and butter and cream and even her own mother's milk, all the breath she had breathed, all the words she had read, the beauty she had soaked up, the emotions that had coursed through her body — the love, the disappointment, the grief, the anger, the acceptance, the joy, the laughter — all reduced to this. Hannah winced as she stabbed a steak knife through the skin of the plastic bag. She allowed just a little of her mother — no more than a toe — to trickle into a ceramic dish. And how grey and colourless, so dry, thought Hannah sadly, as she tipped the urn upright again and twisted the screw closed. She returned the urn to the box and tucked it for the time being in the bathroom cupboard.

Now she was adding a sprinkling of mash and drops of water to the ceramic dish, stirring with a spoon. A miniature caldron. The witches from Macbeth came to mind. *Fair is fowl and fowl is fair.*

Her bare feet brushed through the dewy grass to the duck's cage. Her mother had always enjoyed the sensuality of wet grass on her soles. And she would have had a name for the specific golden hues that drenched every leaf with the light of new morning. Lemon yellow, burnt sienna, yellow ochre, ultra-marine blue. Whatever, she had no idea.

Hannah released the duck onto the grass. Before him she placed the dish with the mash. Her heart leaden, uncertain, she watched while he gobbled her all up.

There you go, Mum, she said. Pack your bags. One day you will fly on a high wind, to be free forever.

VIOLETS

So that she didn't have to open the urn each time, she tipped a portion of the ashes into a china sugar bowl with a lid, painted with violets. Her mother loved violets and loved fine china. Each morning she spooned some of the ashes into the duck's mash and watched as he slurped them up, making sure every single bit was gone. She placed the bowl on the sunny window sill in the spare bedroom. The urn she tucked back up into the bed where her mother used to sleep.

TICKING OFF

You left me for such a long time yesterday, the duck complained to her one morning. *And* the day before.

She had just pulled him from his cage but he was scrambling restlessly from her arms, his claws scratching her skin through her jacket.

I know I know, she said, juggling with his fidgety body until she had to let him go. I'm sorry. She couldn't say it wouldn't happen again. A big editing deadline for work, and Christmas in seventeen days. People coming to stay. Her sister Maggie, and Toby, her husband. Simon's brother from Australia. Things to buy, things to do. Preparations. Not much time for quiet contemplation with a duck, for foraging languidly in the undergrowth.

He looked up at her from the grass. The grass that needed mowing, she noted.

All day, I just sit. I know you clean my cage. I know you leave a nice plastic cushion covered with a clean white towel every day. You leave me freshly mixed mash and pellets. You shove bolted spinach and lettuce under the cage wall, so that it is secured when I tear at the leaves. You hide slugs and snails amongst the lettuces for me to find, and leave fresh water in my bowl.

You don't have to say any more, she said.

Yes I do, I do, I want to say it. It's not that I don't appreciate what you do for me. I also want to ask what is happening between us. You're not spending the time with me anymore. Like you used to.

The woman moved to sit on a rock by the grass, careful not to get her good clothes grubby. She had a meeting to go to. Across her lap she spread the clean towel she'd brought down, then scooped him onto it.

She was running late. She made a mental calculation. Five minutes. She'd give him five minutes. Her make-up could be done in the car.

Did you hear me? asked the duck, cocking that black eye at her.

Yes, yes. Look, nothing has changed between us, she told him. I still go to bed thinking about you. And when I wake up. This morning, just on dawn, a noise woke me up. I sprang out of bed, still half-asleep, and rushed out of the house and down to the garden to see if you were safe.

Can you believe that? I thought . . . it might have been an animal trying to get into your cage.

I *saw* you, said the duck. I saw you in the half-light out here, when the birds, the birds that are *free* in the trees, were just beginning to whistle up a song. But you didn't even say hello.

I didn't because it was just after five. I saw that your cage was intact and I went back to bed, to sleep. But I'm just telling you this: I *do* really care about you.

Well. Anyway, there's another thing.

What?

Five minutes was nearly up.

The man.

What about the man?

He frightens me.

Don't be silly. Why would he frighten you? He's not going to hurt you.

You don't know. You don't know what happens when you are not around.

The woman knew that the man wasn't so fond of the duck, even though he accommodated it. But really he wasn't so fond of flying things in general. She thought of him panicking in the night when a moth caught in his hair. She recalled the rough manner in which he shooed the birds that surrounded them when they ate fish and chips on the beach. How increasingly he referred to the duck as 'that thing'. In fact, she refused to look up to the house now, but she had a feeling he was broodily watching them from his desk, judging her for being obsessive. He was aware that she was pressed for time.

Don't worry, he's fine, she said, scratching the duck's neck. He wouldn't hurt you, that I do know.

There's something . . . unnerving . . . about him.

I'm sorry, Ducko, you'll have to be more specific than that. Look, he's probably just jealous. You're probably jealous of each other. There. That's it.

That's preposterous! What would I have to be jealous of?

She heard this but chose to ignore it.

Let's run away together, said the duck suddenly. Just you and me.

Ducko, she said. We can't do that. Anyway, where would we go? But honestly, I have to head off, now. I'm late.

I see. So this discussion means nothing to you?

It does, truly. I'll come back to it. Remember, I told you about the crows? I have to go.

Remember what *I* told *you*, the duck huffed after her as she made her way up the grass back to the house. All is not as it seems.

And as much as the rational side of her dismissed this, his words, like feathers from an exploded pillow, floated throughout her day.

Chapter 12

CURE BY DEMYSTIFICATION

Hannah would wake up in the night battling with her logical self. She had always considered herself a reasonable, contemplative person. She imagined the possibility of the overnight educator infiltrating her mind as well as the duck's.

She remembered the stories of ducks vacating lakes that they'd inhabited during the year in preparation for the duck-shooting season, and, what's more, flying to duck sanctuaries where they would be safe. How could they possibly be aware in advance of this man-made licence to kill, the permit to wipe ducks off the face of the Earth? The overnight educator had a finger on the pulse of duck flocks in general. There was something going on, something that defied education or explanation, and she was being vacuumed into it.

Her mother's words also haunted her: *There's madness in this family. I think you should know that. I've been meaning to tell you for some time.*

Eventually, after a night of skidding on the surface of sleep, she crept out of bed at dawn and settled at the kitchen table with pen and paper to write a letter to Claire, who did not have a computer, let alone email. She felt the occasion warranted a fountain pen and an ink well, but she had to make do with a biro.

Dear Claire,

I've been meaning for a while to write to you about the duck. And [she hesitates here] to thank you. I have a few questions. It looked like he was going to be a pristine white duck, but he is developing a lumpy red frame around his beak. Is this normal? I'm hoping it's not cancer. I'm thinking of the Hans Christian Andersen story about the ugly duckling. He's looking rather scruffy. His head has a furry mohawk of yellow fluff.

I need to know how much he should eat in a day. Can I overfeed him or will he know when to stop?

I'm also wondering what happened to his mother and the other ducklings. Simon said you didn't know for sure, but do you have any idea? Also, what sort of pond do you have? Where do your ducks sleep at night? Do they all huddle together? Do you farm them or are they wild ducks that arrive and leave when the whim takes them?

Every time I pose a question about the duck, Simon says: well why don't you just ask Auntie Claire, so here I am, doing just that!

Best wishes, Hannah

A few days later the reply arrived in the post.

Dear Hannah,

I am so glad to hear that our duck has helped you come to terms with your dear mother's demise. After all, she'd had a good innings and you did what you could when the quality of her life was compromised by failing health. Simon admitted to me that he was concerned about your emotional well-being. I know how these things take their toll, and really, dear, sometimes it takes a little distraction to see things as they really are. If your duck ever gets a bit much for you, you know we have a good roasting dish we can send up next time Simon calls in!!!!! And, a fabulous recipe!

Anyway, dear, your duckling is not a swan but a muscovy duck. Probably a male, from your description of the lumpy red around the beak. Muscovies in general come in a mixture of white, grey, grubby beige, and black. They graze on grass, and ours have a feeder of kibbled corn and pellets which last several days, so no, they don't just gorge until there's none left.

The ducks are really Bob's territory. He rounds them up at dusk into the covered duck-run — sometimes they escape and potter about at night. Possibly looking for snails or bugs in the moonlight. Apparently they keep together when they sleep, so Bob tells me, and the ones on the outer edge of the group tend to keep an eye open. They keep half their brains awake when they sleep so they're ready to detect predators. Isn't that interesting! I didn't know that until now.

We don't have a large pond, but it keeps them happy. Muscovy ducks mate with mallards, but their offspring is infertile. Still good for eating, though. People call them mullards, like a mule to a horse and donkey, I suppose. As long as your duck is getting food it won't wander.

I'm afraid your duck's mother was killed by a predator. Bob came across the remains by the water trough. After she disappeared she left six chicks behind, but your duck was the sole survivor after a few days.

We do farm them here and sell the progeny for food. Muscovy drakes are much sought-after because of their size.

As I sit here looking out the window, I can see Bob coming out of the shed with his axe. One of the roosters has been causing a bit of trouble and needs a bit of a seeing to. As long as Bob does the plucking and the gutting, I'm happy to deal with the rest. Bob's getting a bit fat, I'm afraid I have to say. Never mind. At least he has a good head of hair.

[Claire's own hair hung close to her head, thin and grey, like damp cotton.]

All the best, dear. We're looking forward to coming up to you for Christmas, and there was some talk that we take your duck back with us if you've had enough of it. We're looking forward to seeing how it has fared. Do let us know what we can bring. Roast duck? Just joking, dear. From Claire and Bob

Hannah screwed the letter into her fist, pressed her hips against the kitchen island, fighting for balance. The midday sun poured into the room, stirring leafy shadows around the walls. At that moment Simon walked in, noticed her face.

What's wrong? he said.

Nothing.

You seem upset. What's that you're holding?

I've just received a letter from Claire.

Oh? What's she got to say?

The duck. It's a muscovy.

But we knew that.

No, we didn't. Well, I didn't. You didn't tell me.

You didn't ask. I thought you knew. I thought you knew they kept muscovies.

I knew they kept ducks.

But anyway, what's wrong with muscovies? Does it make any difference?

I don't know anything about muscovy ducks. As it so happens.

Well, why are you upset?

I'm not.

He eased the letter from her hand and took it over to the kitchen bench where he pressed it flat with the heel of his hand. She watched his face as he read. At one point he lifted his eyes; she met his gaze and he pulled away to continue reading. She could see the busy movement beneath his lids as he absorbed the words. The busy, shifty side-step of his focus.

He folded the letter. I can't see why you'd be upset that your duck is a muscovy. What did you expect? You thought it was a swan?

. . . *sometimes it takes a little distraction*, Hannah quoted archly, *to see things as they really are.*

Yes, that was a bit flippant. Yes, a bit . . . well, not very thoughtful. But she was well-meaning. If a bit clumsy.

Oh well, she said.

What? he said. Is that what you're upset about?

What do you think? All this plotting behind my back to take the duck away.

What do you mean — behind your back? It was *mentioned*, that's all. They expressed a willingness, should you want this to happen.

He stepped towards her, his arm outstretched.

Don't be too sensitive, Hannah. People just want to help. Truly. You push everyone away. I don't know what to do anymore.

His hand floated aimlessly as she darted from his reach. I don't need help, she told him as she left the room to do some gardening with the duck. With the muscovy duck.

DUCK EXTRAORDINAIRE

The thing was, if she were honest, the thing was Hannah hated *knowing* that he was a muscovy duck or *any* sort of duck. She resisted the thought of his being part of a flock or a paddling or a raft or an anything of other ducks. She didn't want him categorised. She didn't want to know whether he was a male or a female. She assumed that he was a male instinctively, and she didn't know or care why. She didn't want to know what he mated with. She didn't want to know anything about him from any other source except her own observation. She didn't want her duck to be anything except the extraordinary creature that he was, whatever or whoever he was. Claire's letter upset her because there was some demystification that she had called for when she had written her own letter, but resisted now that it was here in the crumpled paper on the bench.

MUSINGS BY WILLIAM DRAKE

Ducko, Ducko, burning bright
In the shadows of the night
What immortal hand or eye
Could frame thy fearful symmetry?
In what distant deeps or skies
Burnt the fire around thine eyes?
Did He smile His work to see?
Did He who made the lamb make thee?

Chapter 13

WAR

The crows were beginning to shuffle back, placing themselves on ledges, in corners, squawking in sombre undertones to each other. To make matters worse, they'd coerced their way into her sleep, greedily pecking at the juicy morsels of her dreams.

And the day was hot and sticky. She sat outside with the computer on the table, with the duck at her feet, trying to work.

The duck was hungry. Not for the maize or the pellets readily available for him in bowls in the grass. He wanted her to go foraging with him. He wanted snails and slugs and cockroaches. To make his point, he started to nibble at her toes, not painfully but annoyingly. Then the nibbling became harder. She moved her leg, but he bit at her calf, viciously.

Oi! Stop it!

He came in again, this time with a hiss, biting hard. Pulling and twisting her skin. It was as if he'd decided to eat her.

Stop it! she shouted. She shoved him away. He hissed again and went for her leg. She batted his chest with the back of her hand — not too hard, but more firmly than before. He stopped, then backed, eyeing her.

This is silly, she said, picking him up. He sat passively on her knee.

What was that all about?

He didn't answer, but settled quietly into her lap while she worked.

Later, she followed silvery trails across the path and collected a handful of snails which she planted around the edge of the pond. The duck wolfed them all up except for a large one he couldn't swallow that subsequently dropped into the water. She dipped her hand in, to retrieve it. He turned on her, hissing and yanking masterfully at the skin on her hand. She tugged away, yelling at him.

Get out! Get out, go away! Go and find your own food in future.

She marched away and up the steps to the deck and into the house.

He made no attempt to pursue her, as he usually would. Quite a while afterwards, when she peered down from the window, she saw him still sloshing around the pond, contentedly slurping around the edges. Normally he'd be sitting under the deck, waiting for her like a dog, wagging his tail when she approached.

It was as if the attack had severed a tie between them. He had chewed his leash and was free. She was free. They were free from each other. Just like that. She imagined the overnight educator had mocked him for being so clingy. He'd finally taken note, taken the plunge, the twenty-five-centimetre jump from the bridge into the sloppy waters of independence. Well, that was fine by her!

She showed Simon the three blood blisters on the back of her hand. She was turning into a boysenberry. It's all over, she told him. The duck and me. We're finished.

Simon looked at her slyly. It just happened to be their wedding anniversary.

About time, he said. Welcome back. And then he added, To the real world.

There'd been a period of a few days at Primrose Hill when her mother had unaccountably turned against her, greeting her coldly when she visited. At first Hannah assumed it would pass, but the following day she was worse.

Go home! Be gone with you! her mother had said dramatically, flicking her purple hand as if Hannah might be a blowfly. Be off with you! Go home.

She decided not to visit over the weekend, but on the Monday her mother was still furious.

Mum, are you angry with me about something?

Indeed I am.

But . . . why? What have I done?

All her mother would say was, as haughtily as she could muster, You know very well.

I think if that is the way you feel, I'd better go home.

Yes, you'd better.

The following day, though, when she arrived at the rest home her mother's face was shiny pink with fear that she might not return. Her eyes sparked with relief to see her. Even now, Hannah wondered what it was she'd heard, or thought she'd heard, that had made her so angry.

Although she'd been aware that the pathways in the darkening mind of her mother did not always make rational turnings or often arrived at cul de sacs of confusion, and even though she knew that the duck was just a hungry animal expecting food from her and that was that, in both cases their attacks had made her flinch, as if they had each found tender places to pick at, normally concealed.

She kept away from the duck for the rest of the day and he eventually moved back to his place of vigil under the deck. By the time she trudged down to put him in his hutch for the night, he was peaceful. Neither said anything to the other. It was a grumpy truce.

I DO, BUT NOW I DON'T KNOW

It had been an almost casual decision to marry. They'd been running through busy streets, caught in a warm cloudburst after watching a movie in the city. When they arrived at the car, soaked through, breathless and laughing, they stopped to kiss. Let's get married, said Simon. OK, she said.

They had the wedding a month later on Rangitoto Island. They'd taken the ferry over, Simon in his suit and red bow tie attracting a few bemused glances, not to mention twenty-year-old Maggie who'd shaved her head for the occasion. She'd worn her deliberately-torn black jeans, black jacket with overhanging burnt-orange shoulder pads. Her sulky lips were purple, her eyes rimmed with fat black eye liner. Her boyfriend of the time was bare-armed, in a waistcoat adorned with safety pins, strutting in jeans and newly spiked black hair with a spiral through an eyebrow.

They were an eclectic group clambering through the meandering scoria path to the top of the volcano. Hannah wore shorts and T-shirt for the climb, but threw on a simple white dress when she arrived at the crater's rim. Neither Simon's parents nor his brother had been able to make it from Australia, but her mother and Claire and Bob had braved the ascent in semi-formal attire, grumbling good-naturedly, while all insisting on wearing sensible shoes, 'wedding or not'. Her mother wore a fuchsia hat with a flimsy wide brim. Hannah could still envisage it fluttering below her like a giant butterfly as she watched her mother make the last leg of the ascent.

They'd invited only six good friends. Their commitment to each other had felt so natural that they believed it was destined to be. It had seemed unreasonable to make a fuss, though they'd written their own words for the ceremony, which was officiated by a fresh-faced university chaplain. The weather had been spectacular. Blue skies, blue sea, and a view of the ocean and islands and city all around.

Hannah had just finished her studies and Simon took time off work. They'd rushed away three days later for five weeks' bone-numbing trekking in Nepal.

So now, twenty-five years later, they were out for dinner to celebrate their anniversary.

You look nice, Simon said. Is that new?

She didn't answer. She would rather not admit that she was wearing an elegant black dress that used to belong to her mother.

And as they contemplated the menu, of course she was confronted by duck. A crispy duckling on a kumara mash with a jus de plum.

Go on, said Simon. Go on.

Duckling, she said. It's not even duck. *Duckling*, it says.

She thought back to the yellow pom-pom on her shoulder, nestling itself into her hair. It wasn't so long ago.

Meat, said Simon. Go on. I know you want to.

No, she didn't. She pressed the blister on the back of her hand with her thumb. It was actually bruised, quite sore.

The waiter was French. She questioned him about the duck. Whether it was a big duck or a baby duck. He told her that eet eeza drumstick, comme une poire, a pear, Madame. Oui. The size of. The shape of. A pear. Oui.

A pear? It says *duckling* on the menu. Is it a duck or duck-*ling?* she repeated.

Oui, Madame, he said. Eet eeza duck leg, oui.

She looked at Simon. Why did he care whether she had duck or not?

I'll have the duck, she said. Her heart flipped. She quaffed a gulp of champagne.

Good girl, he said. Happy anniversary.

Indeed the meat was the shape and size of a pear. It was also the shape and size of a little fat duckling. The bone poked perkily from the meat. Decapitated. It was positioned on the plate in a pool of dark juice. Blood.

How is it? asked Simon, chewing his lamb, a trickle of fat wending its way through his beard and down his chin.

Fine, she lied. In fact, it was overcooked, falling into sinews like tiny worms.

Can I try it?

Sure. Have as much as you like. She stabbed half the meat from the bone and transferred it from her fork across the table to Simon's plate.

Hmmm, he said. Hmm, that's delicious. Isn't it, hmmm.

Yes, she said flatly, at that moment hating him. How many years had they been married? No one was married that long these days. Surely, enough was enough.

The next day she went down early and lifted the duck from his cage, cradling him against her chest. He pressed his head against her cheek, into her neck. She sat on a rock in the sun, and shifted him onto her lap. She examined him for change. The blood quills on his wings were bursting into tufts of feather. His wings were now extending into the ruff of stomach feathers.

I truly love you, Duckie.

And I love you, he said.

Why did you peck me like that?

He was silent. She stroked his back, dipped her hand into the burning hollow under a wing. Then, on an impulse, she rummaged deep into the feathers above his leg. She was shocked to make out a round lump of meaty drumstick.

MORE DINNER CONVERSATION

When her mother was alive, Hannah had often found herself talking with other people who had ill and aged parents. It was as if they were all agonisingly digging into sand on a large cold beach, using ineffectual toy spades, searching for the hidden boxes that might hold the answers to the questions they couldn't even articulate. In the end, their conversations would finish in a mess pitted with holes too deep for them to cover again.

And now that her mother was dead, she had no idea what it was they'd ever discussed, what could have occupied her thoughts so thoroughly.

But this night she and Simon were invited out to dinner with old friends — Woody and Fritha. Fritha was a duck fancier and had constructed a pond in her back yard to attract ducks. Her partner, Woody, was a hunter. A hunter of wild boar, deer, rabbits and ducks. Another friend, who used to live on a property with a lake inhabited by many ducks and frogs, was also invited. The conversation, all evening, had been dominated by ducks.

Why didn't you bring your duck? Fritha asked Hannah. Indeed, now, she had to ask herself, why hadn't she?

And so *this* conversational beach, in comparison with the worn territory of aged care, was warm and silky. Hannah and the duck fancier flung themselves into the sand, moulding castles decorated with feathers, eggshells and bones. Hannah was ecstatic. She had never quite appreciated Fritha's interests in ducks before.

Fritha gave her an umbrella and took her outside in pelting rain to proudly show off the pond. It had real duckweed, knots of green with loose threads dangling.

You *must* have some, she insisted, kneeling to scoop the water. Rain was pouring off the back of her coat. She shoved a plastic pot into Hannah's hands, full of weedy slop, the weed knitting the surface like a lid.

Gratefully, Hannah placed the pot in the car, before returning inside to join the others who were drinking wine and eating nibbles.

They were mothers sharing baby loot. Fritha shared stories of rapacious ducks, hungry ducks, lesbian ducks, dominant ducks, bereft ducks and ponds. Hannah told stories of sprouting feathers and astonishment and friendship and loneliness.

Oh, you love him! said Fritha.

Well, I like having him around, watching him, Hannah replied sheepishly.

You do, you do! You love him!

One day he'll fly away and look for a mate, said the friend who used to live by the lake.

I know, said Hannah.

Do they mate for life?

Some ducks do, but not muscovies, said Hannah. Any old duck, apparently. She'd been exploring online.

You might be sorry, in the end, said Fritha.

Some people cut their wings, Woody said as he moved around the coffee table, filling their wine glasses. You can cut their wings so they can't fly. If you don't want them to leave you. If you cut the wing feathers they grow back again, but if you cut the wings themselves . . .

Hannah had a vision of the pulsating wing, blood squirting from the quill feathers in a crimson fountain. She flinched, her stomach tightening.

How do you know it's a *he*, anyway? asked Woody.

I don't really, it's just that he's always been a boy. It could be that he's not. I suppose.

Mothers have a sixth sense, said Fritha. Anyway, do ducks have penises?

There was a silence. In the end, the woman who'd lived near a lake said she thought they did but she could be wrong. In all the time she'd lived near ducks, she'd never seen a duck's penis.

Fritha said, Well, what are they doing then, when they're doing all that mating kerfuffle? Something must be going somewhere.

Whatever it is, it's over in a jiffy, said the hunter, because they're at their most vulnerable. It has to be quick because of predators.

This is all very interesting, but enough is enough, said Simon, who had been quiet up until now. Really. If you don't mind my saying so, I was hoping for a little escape from it all. No more ducks. Please.

Seconded, said Woody. Quack quack quack quack quack.

Muscovies don't quack, actually, retorted Hannah.

Well, shut the duck up, whatever sound it makes. The hunter softened his jibe with a charming smile, but Hannah felt like hissing at him.

THE DAY THAT BIRDS FELL
TUMBLING FROM THE SKY

The rain continued. It was raining enough to soak the parched, dusty earth. Windy enough to fling branches and palm leaves from side to side; the backyard was now a shaggy dog shaking off every flea from its hide, howling around the corners of the house because it had been left outside in the wet.

Across Europe snow was falling. The world over there was icing up. Even the Danube was a mosaic of crunchy ice and snow. And Korea was having to postpone its war because of the weather. Planes in London were unable to venture into the skies; they gathered on the tarmac, like frozen birds congregating on a beach in a gale.

And here, too, the sky was spitting out dead birds.

On her walk that morning, Hannah found evidence.

1. A little green wax-eye lying amongst red and bruised camellia petals on the pavement, ants busying themselves around its head.
2. A seagull laid out on the high-tide mark in the sand, already pecked at, its rib bones like the hull of a boat in the making, resting in a dock of seaweedy driftwood.
3. The body of a penguin floating on its back in the sea, like a lazy swimmer enjoying the bobbing chop of the waves, the frantic movement of the sea giving it a semblance of life, a cruel unrelenting dance.
4. A floppy-headed young thrush snagged by a pile of brown leaves in a gutter, water gushing past towards the nearby drain.
5. An empty nest flung from lofty branches.

When the rain stopped, the earth steamed in the summer heat. In the moist aftermath, things bred. Mosquitoes clung like magnets to exposed flesh. Delicate tiny praying mantises burst from their zippers to sway on shiny leaves.

The rain was good for snails. After dark, Hannah took a plastic bag and trawled the streets glistening with rain under the yellow light of street lamps. Snails grazed peacefully like sheep on grassy verges, in family clusters, or the occasional large bull loner. She felt like a wolf on the fold as she plucked them from under hedges and bushes, over roadside lawns, in damp rotting vegetation alongside driveways. She was a shady, lurking predator. Her bag became heavy with frothy slimy prey.

Back home, she tipped them all into a disused aquarium. She probably had a hundred of them. The next day she fed them with leaves and clippings and closed the lid.

At times during the following days she threw them to the duck and he waddled after them. He was fat, ungainly, funny. He was a dog playing catch, except he ate the ball.

A HARD ONE TO SWALLOW

As Christmas approached, Hannah was distracted with things to do. She noted that the duck didn't seem to know how to act when she wasn't with him. From the top deck she watched him surreptitiously as he waddled about the lawn. He appeared forlorn. She imagined that the overnight educator had been taking the chance to tell him bothersome things. He pecked miserably at a leaf, or a stone or a branch, and then drifted around with a bewildered air, as if he was truly baffled as to what to do next.

On Christmas Eve there was the shopping to finish, and the cooking, and the organising for visitors. And now Hannah had her feet parked by the kitchen bench, slipping the knife under the rind of the ham, tugging the skin away to reveal the terrain of succulent white fat. She sliced a grid of diamonds into the lard, then pierced it with cloves. All around the world people were preparing dead animals in a similar fashion. It might be time for her to become a vegetarian.

Simon came in from mowing the lawn and weed-eating, chucking off his gumboots at the door. His jeans were wet up to his calves, furry with cut grass.

Hmmm, yum, he said, leaning across her to pour a glass of water. The sleeves of his checked brown shirt were rolled up to his elbows, and a bloody scratch smudged across his arm. As he drank, she could smell his familiar body odour, warmly herbaceous and sweaty.

He put the glass down, lifted her hair and gave her neck a quick kiss.

The duck's all plucked and gutted, he said. Where do you want it?

Up your bum, she snapped, flicking him away. She was sick of jokes about eating the duck.

Later she sat by the pond shelling fresh peas, while the duck vacuumed up the dandelion leaves she'd scattered there, darting impotently at the goldfish and randomly pecking at the stones around the water's edge.

Suddenly she noticed that he was selecting particular stones to swallow.

No! No, Ducko, no! She grabbed him, tipped him head down, knocking over the bowl of precious shelled peas, which spilled into cracks or rolled to join the new duckweed in the sludgy pond.

He clawed and writhed and flapped until he managed to escape into the water, fluffing himself up and repeatedly dipping his head under the surface. She wondered whether stone-eating was a neurotic action, in the same way that people obsessively pulled out their hair, or washed their hands, or cut themselves. She imagined him eating and eating stones to fill a void, until he *became* stone, to join the concrete statue of the duck already half-submerged there, like a headstone over a submerged grave.

THE SEARCH FOR MEANING

She dreamt that she was holding the duck upside-down by his legs. His beak was wide open and he was still. Dull grey stones plopped from his mouth one by one, landing in a pile at her feet. Each stone had written upon it a foreign word she couldn't understand. Finally the cascade stopped. She gave a shake and one more dropped out. This one was a green pea. She shook him again and more peas fell. She turned him upright again, but he was empty. He was a floppy feathered handbag, and she couldn't find his head. She was turning him over and over looking for his head. She found a zip in the handbag and inside a leather purse, and inside that . . . nothing. There had to be something. She scrabbled around in the purse and found a comb with a few white hairs curling from it. There was also a powder puff and a lipstick. In a side pocket she found a well-worn piece of paper folded into four. Inside a tiny thin scrawl. *Happy Christmas, dear.*

Chapter 14

PAPARAZZI

Christmas Day. Before lunch, Rosemary and Max arrived through the hedge with a box of snails. Rosemary was wearing a pink dress and a pink bow in her hair. Her bare arms were fat and downy. Max looked the real little man in clean shorts and a checked shirt with sleeves folded up his arms and secured by a button. His hair had been slicked from his forehead with water. She wondered whether Eric had done this before they came over. Normally, Eric would be over here himself. She squatted with each child balanced against a knee on the lawn as the duck devoured their offering.

Now we have to go, said Max.

We're going to have ice-cream, said Rosemary. Hannah placed her nose in their hair, first this one's head and then the other.

You smell delicious, she said.

But you can't eat me, said Max, wriggling to escape.

And you can't eat *me*, said Rosemary the parrot.

When they left to go back to Eric, she gave them a box of chocolates. To share, she told them. She also gave them a large walnut.

This is for Poppa, she said. Make sure you give it to him, otherwise there'll be no chocolates for you. She had already prised open the shell and replaced the nut with a note. She'd read a short story once of a mother who had done something similar with a walnut at her daughter's birthday party — made the walnut with something inside as the prize in Pass the Parcel. She'd liked the idea and had always wanted to use it herself but, as she had no children, she'd never had the opportunity.

In this case, she'd made several attempts at the choice of words for Eric. Some were meaningful, some cheeky, some bitter, some profound and obscure. In the end she wrote: *Is that our friendship, in a nutshell? Happy Christmas, Eric, from Hannah.* Then she resealed it with glue.

Claire and Bob from Te Awamutu arrived with a tray of asparagus rolls and savoury eggs. Bob with his fitting red shirt and his healthy head of hair, an electrified mop sliced in two with a straight parting. Hannah's cousin and husband from Titirangi came with a chick pea salad and their ruddy-faced teenage twin boys, who slouched into the house resentfully, and she knew they'd barely bring themselves to speak or look up from their cell phones the whole day. A younger cousin and her new boyfriend came, late and radiant with their hair still wet from showering. Simon's brother from Australia, Dennis, had arrived the night before. And Maggie and Toby came direct from the airport, dragging into the guest room the two bulging suitcases for the week that they were to stay. Maggie brought with her a burst of energy, greeting everyone loudly, laughing and joking, yanking the cheeks of both twins to induce a sneery smile from each. Well, that was something. Toby was nervy, thin, his elegant jacket hanging from the bones in his back, and when Hannah tiptoed to kiss his freckled cheek, he reeked of smoke.

Sorry about your mother, he said, his body jiggling uneasily. I liked her. We got along well.

This was the first she had heard from him since her mother died.

Thanks, she replied. That's OK.

Maggie told me that she had a great farewell.

Oh, did she? Yes, I think Mum would have liked it.

So, this was the Christmas package. This was the blast-off that the countdown of the past few weeks had been leading up to.

And all anyone wanted to do was to see the duck.

First of all Claire and Bob trudged down the deck stairs to the lawn, where they gathered around him in the sunshine. He stood, legs splayed, looking beseechingly at Hannah.

Oh, he's big, they said.

But he's gentle and he doesn't have a drake's tail.

And he doesn't have a mohawk. And not much of a caruncle. But he does have some. You might find, they said, that he'll lay eggs.

But then again, he's very big so he might not.

Then the rest of the party trundled down the steps, glasses of bubbly in hands. Even the twins bumbled along, bumping into each other as they went. Hannah picked up the duck as she normally would, cupping her hands behind his wings and swivelling him around so that he was upright against her chest. It was a practised motion that, as long as they prepared themselves calmly, they manoeuvred with grace. As he usually did, the duck touched his beak under her chin, at this cheek and the other. This time he was bashful, hiding for longer under her chin.

Suddenly she realised she was surrounded by shiny black eyes, duck eyes, single dark eyes blinking. Everybody had a camera trained on her and the duck.

She was aware of Simon standing back from it all, his arms folded tightly, muttering to Maggie.

I might be married to her, but *I'm* not a blood relative. And there's some consolation in that.

Hannah couldn't hear Maggie's actual reply, but she didn't like the way her sister laughed so conspiratorially at her expense.

IT WAS THE DAY AFTER CHRISTMAS

One day after Christmas Day. The duck had avoided the roasting dish, the fantasies around the ideal Christmas dinner when ham had become passé, the envy of those bored with thoughts of one more year of pig. No one had snuck through the fence and stolen him.

It was the first Christmas without her mother having to endure her decrepit body — the cracked old vessel that, over the last few years, had only just managed to contain her soul.

And there was another earthquake in Christchurch, a 4.9 aftershock. Maggie and Toby rang neighbours, ascertained that once again their house had escaped practically unscathed. A few things on the floor, some broken crockery.

Thank bloody goodness for that, said Maggie.

Toby brushed his hand over her shoulder.

I'm going for a walk, he said. His normally pale face was ashen. His freckles scattered under the surface like tiny autumn leaves trapped in ice.

Hannah didn't know Toby well, even though he had been married to her sister for ten years. He and Maggie both worked hard, drank a lot, partied hard. They each had children from first marriages, all now living overseas. He worked into the small hours as a chef in an upmarket restaurant in Christchurch. Hannah's infrequent conversations with him over the years made her think of twin water-skiers skimming and bouncing along the surface of a choppy lake, hauled behind the master controller at the wheel — Maggie.

Chapter 15

CRUISE CONTROL

And now all the long days travelling from Christmas towards New Year.

A year or so before she met Simon, Hannah and a friend had travelled to Sydney on the cruise ship *Achille Lauro*. As it pulled out from the terminal in Auckland, passengers were throwing streamers and unravelling toilet paper as a link to those waving from the wharf. She'd been able to distinguish the face of her mother amongst the pixelated sea of the crowd far below, but what astonished her more than anything was that she could determine whether her mother was looking at her or whether her gaze, rather than her head, was turned askance. Amongst those dotted faces below, the link between her mother's eyes and hers was discernible. It wasn't that she could see her eyes, but she knew when her mother was looking at her.

For at least two days she'd been encapsulated on the ship with hundreds of passengers as they moved from one destination to the other. There was no escape. The ocean and the sky surrounded them. Internally, they were entertained with drink and food and music and dancing and pursuing men. They were on an island, a spaceship, a floating seed capsule. They were parasites living in the gut of a floating duck. Some passengers were continuing to South Africa, some to England, back home or to start new lives. Everyone was in the same boat. If it had sunk mid-ocean they would have all gone into the soup together.

In many ways, the time between Christmas and New Year was like this. They were passengers on a boat moving through time between Christmas and New Year. At the other end, they would disembark and continue with their lives. Hannah only had to hope that there'd be no storms. Even more worryingly, that they wouldn't sink. She was aware that there were rocks lurking just beneath the surface.

HEAT WAVE

They were immersed in a heat wave. Their ship had slipped its mooring, was drifting from shore. Every morning Simon would dive into the sea for a swim but could never persuade anyone else to join him.

And now Toby was asleep on the couch in his beanpole jeans and black T-shirt, his lean white feet twitching spasmodically, his gingery hair wilting over his forehead as if it, too, was affected by the heat. Everyone else, muttering that they had overeaten, took themselves into the garden, searching for respite from the cloying humidity.

Simon's brother, Dennis, perched miserably on the wooden bridge with his feet on either side, cooling in the pond. Two divorces, and he'd just been made redundant. His whole demeanour was heavy, as if he had grown too round for himself and was sagging, only just supporting himself, his chin in his palms, his forearms resting on his thighs. His back was curved and his stomach drooped wearily over his belt. A goldfish, enticed by his motionless body, investigated the hairs on his leg.

Maggie, on the other hand, had filled a plastic bucket with Belgian beer packed in ice and was sitting on a rug in the shade alongside Simon, their backs against a cabbage tree. Even the duck was droopy, seeking refuge in leafy shade. Flies buzzed and darted in the sun. Birds hung around on the lawn with their beaks hanging open, their wings spread out from their bodies as if broken.

It was only when Hannah brought out the hose to wash away his droppings from under the deck that the duck sprang to life. When she shot the jet at his feet, he parked his legs apart on the tiles, like a dazed old man who had just wet himself. However, when she lifted the spray into the air above him, he was gone, crashing across the lawn around the pond. She couldn't resist giving his tail a sprong — he ran like the same old man rushing for a bus. She laughed. Whoever heard of a duck scared of water?

The others were lazily watching her. She was their entertainment, and it wasn't because they were sharing her delight. Instead, they were united in their disdain. Simon was pleased to have an ally; he had seen it before, after all. But Maggie was a keen spectator, her chin propped on her bare knees, swigging from a bottle. Hannah had an urge to give her tail a sprong as well.

The duck was watching her from behind a bush. She turned the hose off at the nozzle and dropped it by the pond.

Dennis, still on the bridge, lifted his head from his murky gaze and gave her a forced, embarrassed grin.

Are you OK? she asked.

Yep, yep. Yep. Thanks, he said, stepping up onto the bridge, shaking water from his legs before moving over to dump himself beside Simon and Maggie on the rug. He, too, was now drinking the beer that Maggie had handed him.

Hannah joined them, sat down on the edge of the rug, her toes in the cool grass. The duck placed himself beside her feet. There was an awkward silence. Maggie offered her a beer. She opened it herself and took a swig. No one said anything as the heat shimmered around them and the boat floated further and further from shore.

HALFWAY

Four days later and they were still afloat. Each morning Hannah stealthily mixed up the special mash for her duck and watched as he gobbled it up, along with a few members of an extended family of snails she'd found stuck to the concrete wall behind the agapanthus.

FINALLY, THE ROCKS

It had been a languid sloppy day with their destination only two days ahead. The sun belted upon them. If they'd been passengers in a yacht, its sails would have been drooping flaccidly. Toby took himself to his room to sleep, after promising to prepare the evening meal. The others left the house for a walk, ambling down the street and over the rolling buttocks of grass to the point.

Hannah could hear a skylark, a tiny bell jingling in the blue. She stopped, shielding her eyes as they followed the wavering dot climbing to the heavens. She imagined her duck one day accompanying the lark, his enormous wings batting against the air to swing from one end of the sky to the other, as if a pendulum suspended from the small bird, pinned to the sky.

Maggie and Simon had moved on ahead, out of earshot, with Dennis lumbering a short way behind them. He gave the impression of being such a lonely man. Maggie was laughing at something Simon had said, had thumped him on the arm and had her head back, her straight black hair bouncing on her shoulders. Then, abruptly, they both turned and looked directly at Hannah. She waved and moved to catch up, but they turned again and continued to walk, increasing their pace.

Dennis hung back for her, and they all straggled down and over the hills to the road and strolled along the waterfront to a restaurant. They sat at a table under a Norfolk pine and lethargically watched kids dash around slides and swings and up ladders and through tubes. Hannah could never come to terms with the screams and shrieks of children as they played — it always gave her an unnerving sense of underlying panic.

Maggie ordered a bottle of sauvignon blanc. Hannah waved her glass aside. It was too hot to drink wine in the middle of the day.

Of course you can't drink, you're in charge of a duck, said Maggie. I'm surprised you managed to leave it behind for so long. Or resist bringing it with you.

Does your duck have a name? asked Dennis gently.

Oh, let me guess, said Maggie. It would *have* to be Gabriel. No? Oh I know. Duckie-wuckie. Or maybe Quackie-wackie? Or is that *you*?

You realise, don't you, said Simon, that for one, Hannah's duck is not a duck, but is probably a drake? And secondly, it's not a true duck, as such, genetically.

Maggie rolled her eyes. What do you mean, not a *true* duck?

Well, it is and it isn't. It doesn't have the same DNA as a common duck, like a mallard. It's a *Cairina moschata momelanotus*. It's not a duck and not a goose. It's a perching duck, one of the greater wood ducks. It seems that they — scientists — had difficulty placing it in the order of things. Dabbling ducks and perching ducks and shelducks. Family Anatidae, genus *Cairina*. There are two species in the *Cairina* genus, but the other, the endangered *Cairina scutulata*, the white-winged wood duck, is not related in external morphology.

There was a silence. Everyone looked at him.

Fuck it's hot, said Maggie. Let's eat and start walking back before we quack up.

Back at the house, Toby was out. There was no sign of food preparation. Maggie grabbed a bucket of ice and beer, a book and a rug and went out to the lawn. Simon sat down at his computer, and Dennis went to his room and shut the door.

Hannah stood in the kitchen. Simon was peering at his screen. She moved over to the table and watched as he worked, but he didn't look up.

She said: I can't stand it.

His eyes flickered and he bit his lip, but still he continued his gaze at the screen.

You'll be right, he said.

I'm going mad.

You'll come right.

She left him and went outside to where the duck was waiting under the deck. She picked him up. Avoiding Maggie — who was involved in her book and didn't stir anyway — she went down to the very back of the garden, perching on the steps of the shed with the duck on her lap. He was so big now that he spilled over her lap from one side to the other.

Are we going foraging? said the duck.

Ssssh, she whispered. We have to be quiet.

What's going on?

Nobody likes me. Everything is closing in and I'm feeling sad.

You know I like you.

Ssssh, I told you. Not so loud. Anyway, you're a duck. And I don't even know your name.

I'm hungry.

What's your name, Ducko? They want to know your name.

By any other name, I'd smell as sweet.

Don't be stupid. Let's just sit here together and be very, very quiet.

OK. Together is fine. And after that? Snails?

Everything is going a bit weird, Ducko, in Peopleland. I'm not sure what it is, but I don't like it.

Snails? Cockroaches? Slugs?

Leaning from the step, she tugged at a few tufts of grass, directing the duck to a scattering of tiny cockroaches. She poked around with a stick looking for more. She hit a stone, and prised it up. Underneath was a small ziplock plastic bag, pressed flat by the stone. She peeled it from the soil. Inside was a key. The key to the shed.

Look at this, Ducko, she said. The key to your future hotel. We won't mention it just yet; we might need to do a bit of subtle negotiation.

She didn't bother to try the key, but eased the bag back into its earthy grave.

When the air temperature dropped, everyone made their way back to the kitchen where Toby, surrounded by a cluster of supermarket bags, chopped and scooped and darted and stirred. Maggie opened a bottle of bubbly and poured a glass for everyone.

Cheers, she said, insisting that everyone catch her eye as they clinked glasses. Come on now, make eye contact. Look at moi. That's the rules. No clinking without linking. In Europe it's considered boorish if you don't. Dennis, Dennis, lift up thine eyes. Looks don't kill.

She brayed like a donkey.

And with each eye connection there was a statement, thought Hannah. Each person revealed something of themselves. Toby was preoccupied, Dennis was depressed for some ungodly reason, as he always had been forever, Maggie was scathing, and Simon was so far away she almost didn't recognise him. She would need binoculars to cover the distance, to find the craters and seas and mountains of his orbiting thoughts.

They ate olives and delectable canapés that kept appearing, and by the time dinner was ready they'd already drunk two bottles of bubbly. Toby was a whirlwind, his shoulders up around his ears, prancing from the bench to the oven, ignoring them all as he worked. Soon there was a steaming creamy concoction of green-lipped mussels, prawns and schnapper in a bowl, with a salad of greens. And then Hannah realised it was almost dark.

Oooops, the duck, she gasped.

But the food is ready. Leave the duck for once.

She rushed outside, grabbed the duck, his legs air-cycling for the Tour de France. Fortunately she'd already set up his water and pellets. She peeled a couple of snails from behind the agapanthus, threw some bolted lettuce into his cage and tossed him, complaining, inside.

By the time she returned, everyone was eating.

You could've waited for once, said Maggie, her cheeks bulging.

There was a silence for a while as everyone tucked in to the meal. Another bottle of wine was opened and poured.

Toby, you're not eating? This is superb, said Hannah. He was pushing his fork at a mussel with disinterest.

Yeah, I am, I am. I'm never particularly hungry after cooking.

Leave him alone, snapped Maggie, reaching for her wine.

Remember how Mum would always have to have salt on the table, said Hannah. Whether the food needed it or not.

That's right, said Maggie. She used to complain bitterly about how you refused to let her have salt when she stayed with you. Told us how she used to sneak some wrapped in a tissue and surreptitiously sprinkle her food when your eagle eye was turned.

I thought it was bad for her, said Hannah ruefully. We were always told . . . arteriosclerosis . . .

Well yes, so much for a little knowledge being a dangerous thing. With her low blood pressure it turned out she needed it. I have to say that she felt vindicated after that was diagnosed.

Actually, said Hannah, actually, I'd like to propose a toast. She shot a glance at Maggie. We haven't given her much of a mention over the past few days and, rather than fight about her, I think it's time we acknowledge her. So, here's to dear Mum.

Here's to a gracious lady, said Toby.

To Mum, said Simon.

Dennis raised his glass.

Maggie lifted her glass half-heartedly.

Well, yes, all right then, to Mum. Poor old Mum. But I'd like to add this. She hated it here. Did you know that? She was miserable. Away from everyone she knew, her friends, her life. It was cruel to haul her up here away from her memories . . . of Dad . . . her whole married life down there. I couldn't believe, honestly, couldn't believe that you would do that to her.

Every cell within Hannah's body collapsed.

Her friends and neighbours were ringing me, imploring me to help, she said. There was no other choice. What else could she have done?

Lived at her home. As she wanted to.

But she was always falling over, fainting, hallucinating — as you noticed yourself. Did you see the scars on her hands and arms, and legs and head from her falls? Her skin peeled away like cling-film. Her skin was an old suit perished, left too long in the sun.

So what? What if she'd died on the floor? She wouldn't have had to endure what she did over the next few years. It was cruel. It was a travesty. And she hated it.

I didn't notice you having any say in the matter at the time.

I wasn't asked.

That's not exactly true. I kept you informed. I told you everything. Anyway, you have no hesitation in saying your piece now. It wasn't easy, you know. Looking after her. It wasn't exactly roses. Hannah sighed. But what's the point in bringing it up now?

Maggie dabbed at each corner of her mouth with a manicured finger. She tossed her Japanese-doll hair and blinked slowly. Lifting her cruel eyes to pierce right through Hannah from her heart to her back.

Actually. What I'd really like to know, while we're finally having a real conversation, is this: what is it about the bloody duck? Everyone thinks you're crazy. Everyone. It's just a filthy bird. It's absolutely filthy. And the way you handle it. And talk to the bloody thing. I don't know how Simon puts up with you. He has the patience of Job.

Hannah glanced at Simon who was zealously managing his knife and fork to extricate flesh from the shell of a prawn. She placed her glass on the table and left the room. Left the house and went into the garden. The night was clicking with insects, and somewhere the snuffling of a hedgehog. Over the road, loud music and mirthless laughter. She walked up the garden path, up the steps and out the gate and down the street. Footsteps hurrying behind her. Who? Maggie to apologise? Simon, to see if she was all right? The local mugger?

No, it was Toby. She was so surprised she forgot to be devastated, forgot to be angry.

He linked his arm through hers and joined her step as she marched. The smell of cigarette smoke leaked from his clothes, his skin. She could feel the hard rib cage of his skinny body against her arm as they strode in unison through the night. She hardly knew Toby, and for this reason she warily pulled herself together. They passed an old man leaning against his letter box under the spotlight of a street lamp while his obese dog trembled a poo into the grass. Further along, a gaggle of kids lounging on steps were snorting and giggling like kookaburras.

Neither Toby nor Hannah said anything until they arrived at the beach. People were sitting in couples or clusters on the stone wall. Behind them, a fountain sprayed rainbows from the mouths of serpents. Toby directed her to a place apart from others and they sat down, the hard cool stone cutting into her legs. Soft swathes of light swept the beach from the lamps above. Toby dived into his jacket and brought out his cigarettes. She watched as he flick-flick-flicked at his lighter, his face aglow as he inhaled deeply, cupping the flame like a secret.

Do you ever think of giving up? she asked him.

Do you ever think of getting rid of the duck? he replied.

Her heart sank.

Oh. You as well. Being mean.

Not at all. We've all got our obsessions and addictions. Our vices and devices. Sometimes we want to let them go and then we realise we can't, or we don't want to just yet, because we're afraid of the hole.

You think the duck's an obsession?

She felt him looking at her, but she took her gaze out over the sand to the small ripples at the ragged frill of shoreline, the black expanse of the sea pitching Rangitoto darkly against the sky.

Not in a bad way, he said carefully. It might be affecting your marriage, but it's probably not affecting your health. Probably a relatively common case of anthropomorphism. It won't give you cancer and it seems to make you happy. Doesn't it?

She nodded. I don't know. I suppose so. Why do you say it's affecting my marriage?

No, I didn't say that. Just that it might be. Might, I said. Marriage is a complex and varied institution that only the members of each branch who are privy to the subset of rules and conditions, determined either consciously or implicitly at some stage by both parties, can answer to.

You sound like a lawyer.

No. Just someone who has moved from one branch to another. Look. This is beside the point. Don't listen to your sister. She's got her own issues. She'll have forgotten everything in the morning. Everyone, including Maggie, knows you did what you could with your mother.

He flung his legs out and leapt onto the sand, then sat beside her again.

And Simon, too. He was right there beside you, the whole way. Your mother appreciated that.

His words hit her in the chest.

Yes, it wasn't always easy for him, she said lamely.

Bubbles of light fizzed along the horizon. Other solitary red, green and yellow sparks stuttered in the darkness, like an electronic display panel on the blink.

Are you aware, Toby said suddenly, that the universe is 13.7 billion years old? In a hundred billion years we will see no stars or galaxies outside the Milky Way, as no light will reach us, as the expansion of the universe, driven by dark matter or energy, will have accelerated away from us, over the cosmic horizon.

She laughed.

It's true, he said, inhaling.

No, she said. Come to think of it, I don't think I did know that.

Then, inexplicably, she felt anxious. She stood up, scraping her fingers through her hair.

It's too much, I'm sorry, it's all too much. I actually don't know anything, Toby.

Still seated, he eased her hand from her head, holding his cigarette out to the side, the smoke hanging listlessly.

Hey, he said. Don't fret, pet. It's all right. We won't be around at the time, so don't worry. In fact, the Earth won't even exist.

Scuffing the sand with her shoe, she muttered, So. What happens when we die?

We die. Kaput. Finito. Dead. It's all over now, Baby Blue.

You think so?

I have absolutely no doubt. So make the most of it.

Plonking herself back next to him, she said, Fuck.

He plunged his hand back into his inner coat pocket and brought out a thin joint. As he lit it, he dragged the smoke in short shallow gasps before passing it to her, still sucking between his teeth.

You thought differently?

I've been thinking many things about death since my mother died.

Perhaps it's time, then, to start thinking about life, he said. The precious things you have now, rather than those you've lost.

She hesitated, taking the point, before taking the joint.

I haven't had one of these for years and years and years. But, bugger it, why not?

She inhaled and choked, composed herself then inhaled again. She sat in the silence as the night gathered itself around her, pulled itself around her and her sister's husband sitting on the stone wall at the beach.

Toby, I've actually done an appalling thing.

Have you, now?

Yes, truly. A dreadful thing.

Don't tell me anything. I don't want to know. Don't want to know anything, OK?

He scratched his arm, deeply and earnestly.

But I'd like to tell you. You don't have to do anything.

I'm impervious. I'm not the one to tell anything. Please, Hannah, no. OK? Don't.

Why not?

Stop it. No. Stop it, *right now*.

She sighed. All right then. You're probably a wise man.

Thank you. I can tell *you* things, though. Birds. Let me tell you about birds in relation to the afterlife. Your duck will have told you about birds, no doubt.

What do you mean?

When they die.

He shoved his body companionably up against hers. Scratched his knee.

The sky, Auntie Hannah. Now. You know where the sky ends, don't you?

As a matter of a fact, that's always been one of the big questions for me.

Of course it is. I recognise a sky-questioner when I see one.

He passed the joint back to her, saying, Where does the sky end, where do birds go when they die, and how do worms begin? Are you interested?

Is this another science lecture?

It depends on how you look at it. It's just the way things are. The sky gathers at the edge of the world. You see it sometimes, that billowing of cloud spewing up over the horizon. I know, don't tell me, the world is round, but just accept that there is an outer edge at the join in the roundness and that's where the sky gathers on a windy day. It all collects there with nowhere else to go, waiting for the wind to shift it back on its journey again.

Oh yeah? She held the soggy end of paper between her fingers. Their fingertips met as he took it and sucked, then flicked the butt at the sand, swivelling it under his foot.

Well, it's simple, that's where the birds go. To die. Well, there's a few unlucky ones that get grounded or eaten by a cat or shot by a hunter before they get there, but the others . . . that's where they gather . . . Look, if you think of it, there's all those birds in trees and in the sky all over the place and you hardly ever see dead ones apart from one or two after a storm, and yet there's birds dying all the time. Well, that's where they go, when the time comes. They fly and fly and hopefully they have the wind behind them, and eventually they're caught in that waiting place. It's a type of bird Heaven. You can imagine the noise. It's the whole bird-world in a tree just before sunset. When there's enough of them, there'll be a night storm, sucking them into the gurgler, which is really a strainer a bit like a mincer. It's very pleasant for them. Your duck will know all about it.

It sounds horrendous, said Hannah.

Think of the rotting mess if it didn't exist. We'd be slipping and sliding over dead birds underfoot everywhere. It's like a black hole but there's an outcome. They don't just disappear. Out of the other end of the mincer: what do you think?

Worms.

Exactly. You're with me. Yes. Well done. Worms. And when it rains . . . well, you know how you see worms all over the place when it rains? I've found worms halfway up banana palms, and in guttering. How do they get there? They're brought by the wind, newly sieved, and dropped by the rain.

You're a funny man.

He put his arm around her and gave her a quick squeeze. She was aware that this outing was orchestrated to make her feel better and she appreciated it.

It's a nice story, she said.

Story? It's the truth. Why do birds like worms? They're replenishing themselves.

Oh yes. And what happens to the feathers?

Clouds, of course. Ducks like yours and geese, etc, do the white and grey clouds, birds like ravens and crows do the black clouds, and parrots and peacocks, the sunsets of course.

Of course, she said.

He lifted his legs from the sand, swivelled himself around on his bottom and swung around onto the footpath, brushing his pants fastidiously.

We'd better be getting back. Look at those water serpents, spewing out that colour.

Hannah was still picking herself off the wall. He grabbed her hand. Come on, off we go.

And as they walked, arm-in-arm now, he suddenly said, Your mother was a fine woman. I liked her a lot. We had some good conversations.

Did you? Really? What about?

Oh, this and that. Art. Music. The world. She was a good listener. And she thought carefully about things. She had an appreciation for the finer aspects of life.

Thank you, Toby, for telling me that. It's easy to take people for granted. To dismiss older people as insignificant. You didn't know her for long.

For some years. She stayed with us from time to time, before she went downhill. She was great company.

Do you believe in reincarnation?

As I said to you before, no. I don't. But the mind plays tricks. After my father died, there was a guy who suddenly started coming to the restaurant. Always alone, two or three times a week, and always at lunchtime. I'd never seen him before. He always ordered fish — a favourite of my father's — and he looked the image of Dad. Same mannerisms. I'd watch him, mesmerised, through a one-way mirror from the kitchen into the restaurant. I'd make sure he had a particularly juicy and fresh piece of fish, or I'd slip him an extra entrée or delicate dessert. I'd find myself locked, motionless, staring at him. Then one day towards the end of lunch, when the restaurant was pretty-well empty, he brought in this blousy woman. She was much younger than he was. She had big blonde dry hair, red lipstick, painted eyebrows and a huge yellow kangaroo pendant sitting in her cleavage. I couldn't believe it. She wasn't my father's type. Except, I didn't know what my father's type was. My mother died when I was young, in a skiing accident, and, although I knew he'd had a few women friends, they had all been rather conservative and intellectual.

Anyway, I went into the dining room, wiping my hands on my apron, and stood by their table. I was shaking, heart going like the clappers. They looked up from the menu. I had no idea what I was doing there. Can I suggest you try the *coq au vin*? I found myself saying. The guy looked at me still twisting the apron in my hands, and said, What's wrong with the fish? I *always* have the fish. I said something like, Right sir, I'll look into it. I left and let the waitress take over. His voice had totally shattered the illusion. A brick smashing a mirror. Just those few words. American. Gravelly. Twangy. Snivelling. Not Dad. And up close he didn't even look like him. The rims of his eyes were red, and there was a sneer around his mouth that Dad never had. And funnily enough, he didn't return. I never saw him again.

They paused under a street light as Toby lit another cigarette. The streets were empty now, silent. All the lowly people tucked up in their beds.

Hannah said, So, for a while you *really* thought he was your father?

Logically, no. Of course. But in a deep primitive way, I guess I wanted to believe he wasn't dead. I missed him. And after that incident, I started to feel better, started accepting it. That wasn't long before I met Maggie, actually.

They were at the gate, and stopped as Hannah fiddled with the latch.

Thank you, Toby, she said. She lifted onto her toes to kiss him on the cheek. I don't feel so . . . I don't know, well, thank you, anyway.

He squeezed her shoulder, and took a deep drag of smoke before flicking the rest of the cigarette into the gutter.

They entered the house in good spirits, to the others still sitting at the table, drinking. Hannah could see them all searching her face, checking her demeanour.

There was that air of conversation abruptly ceased as they walked in; Maggie was looking sour and strained. Hannah noticed Simon moving away from her as they arrived. Dennis was broodily fiddling with his iPhone.

So, the absconders have deigned to join us. Where the fuck have you been?

Looking for worms and dead birds, said Hannah.

Toby went to the sink and poured a glass of water. Nobody else spoke, though Simon was studying her, too impassively, too coldly, to give her comfort.

Later, as Simon and Hannah undressed, they avoided looking at each other. They climbed under the sheets, two reluctant swimmers clinging to the edge of their own side of the bed, afraid of the deep, of being pulled under.

He lifted his hand and switched off the light.

She said into the empty bedroom, You and Maggie are getting along nicely together?

He said to the wall, You and Toby are getting along nicely together?

His voice was bitter.

She kicked at him, an awkward backward shove of her foot into the spongy flesh of his calf.

He said nothing. He didn't move.

And so they lay rigidly as they travelled onwards through the night. Finally she heard his gargled snoring. Downstairs there were other noises, someone moving around, bumping into furniture.

Her duck was in his cage, his head tucked into his wing, and she didn't know where her mother was anymore.

NEW YEAR'S EVE

They were having a New Year's party of about fifteen close friends and relations. They'd eaten dinner and drunk bubbly, and now it was nearly midnight. Hannah hovered alone, leaning from the balcony on the deck, looking over into the black garden where the duck slept. She could just make out the dense shape of cage in the darkness. Then she became aware of an almost inaudible crunching of gravel. She peered through the night into the foliage, expecting to see a lurking cat. But she suddenly made out the form of a person sitting on the rocks by the pond. Just before she called a greeting, she stopped herself. The light from the house provided some substance to the shadows and, as her eyes become accustomed to the gloom, she realised the person was intently occupied. She saw the white stick of arm, the brief glisten of the needle, a thumb pressing into flesh. She felt as if she was watching a play on a stage from the gods. Then the black shirt-sleeve was pulled down over the arm, and only his white hand was visible now, like a mime's glove. He stood up. She clapped. He paused, and they caught each other's eye before he made his way up to the house.

And then it was midnight. They all swung hands so gaily as they sang 'Auld Lang Syne', then crossed arms to continue — *and here's a hand my trusty friend and here's a hand in thine*. In the house next door, a window slammed as Eric shut them out. She saw the sky flicker as fireworks erupted behind the hill. There was a moment of uncertainty as the old year slipped the baton to the new. Everybody hugged everybody else, and she looked for Simon who had been next to her as they sang, but he was hugging her friends, his auntie and uncle from Te Awamutu, his brother, her sister. She watched him then, and no, he wasn't looking for her. She fronted up to him and said, Happy New Year.

He looked startled.

Haven't I done you? he said, and the lips he flitted upon hers were the lips of a stranger. There were unspoken words hiding underneath the skin of this mouth. The duck would have a field day with these writhing maggots. When did this happen?

Toby whispered into her hair that he was never going to touch it again, this was the turning point for him, the last time ever, and he allowed himself to slump onto the deck with his head against the wall, the dark rings under his eyes like wells for his eyes to slip into when the time came. He was a rake, pale, stereotypical, and, as Hannah looked at him, she decided that the world was a sad place and that there was so much she didn't know about the people in it.

She found three cushions, put two behind his spine, and sat on the other alongside him while everyone partied around them. He forced his eyes open and smiled at her wistfully. Thanks kiddo, he whispered.

She grabbed his hand, his fridge-cold hand, and tucked it against her body under her arm. He was staring at her fixedly, his lips moving in an attempt to speak, his tongue dry and foreign in its own home. Why . . . ? he was saying, why . . . ? And while she searched for the answer across the whole abstract plain of possibilities — why are you sitting here? why am I here? why is the world spinning so out of control? — she realised that, in fact, he was trying to ask for water.

Chapter 16

THE SHIP SWINGS INTO PORT

On New Year's Day, after a big clean-up, Maggie and Toby flew back to Christchurch. Dennis left with them, as he was going to rent a car from the airport and travel around the country for a couple of weeks' sightseeing. Simon was taking them to the airport.

I'll come, too, said Hannah.

That's OK, said Simon. No need. It'll be a squeeze with all the luggage. I've got stuff to do out that way, so you stay with your duck.

What sort of stuff? It's New Year's Day.

There's a good hardware store near the airport. Not your cup of tea.

And no, it was not. So she stood on the footpath and hugged them goodbye, Simon included. Her sister brushed her powdered cheek against hers, giving a haughty hug before she climbed in the passenger seat, next to Simon. Then Toby. She felt a surge of affection and concern for him. Look after yourself, she said, as he pressed his bony chest against her cheek and kissed her on the head. He looked ghastly, ashen. He folded himself up into the back seat next to Dennis. What a funny lot they all are, thought Hannah as the car drove up the hill and around the corner. She waved to the white hand and the smudge of face in the back window until they were out of sight. Then she walked down the path to the house.

She decided that while no one was home she'd allow the duck to have a bath, while she ironed Simon's shirts in the bathroom. Really, the duck had grown too big for the bath, flooding the bathroom with his enthusiastic swimming. But it would end up with a clean and happy duck and the ironing done. She went upstairs to their bedroom to gather the shirts. The room was a mess. Clothes and books and magazines. Christmas wrapping. The dust of preoccupied neglect. It was the last room in the house she gave her attention to when it came to housework.

On their unmade bed, poking up from the crumpled duvet, was an envelope. She thought nothing of it. She assumed it was a New Year's card, with conciliatory words. She was not in the mood for any kindness from Simon and nearly left it. The envelope was sealed. She tore it open.

The message informed her that he was going away for a while because he felt they needed a break from each other and that she needed to sort out her priorities and that he needed to think about things. What a cliché! The note was written on a blank card. On the front was a picture of Beatrix Potter's Jemima Puddle-Duck in a nest of feathers, spied upon by an evil-looking fox behind the door.

Lovely.

Happy New Year to you, too, sweetie.

She went outside and plonked herself down on the grass by the duck.

The man's gone, she told the duck. And I don't know where and I don't know when he's coming back.

Oh well, said the duck. He never liked me very much.

He used to like *me*, she replied.

I like you.

The weird thing is that he was mysterious about it. Why didn't he tell me? Why did he just go, why didn't he let me know?

The duck flitted his beak over her leg, then down to her foot, tugging gently at first, then roughly at her toes. The woman shifted her foot.

That hurts, she said. You know my toes aren't edible. You would eat me, though, wouldn't you, if you could?

She stood up, feeling consumed already. The duck cocked his eye at her.

Any snails?

You don't care. Nobody cares.

I do. I'm just hungry.

Everybody's hungry, she told him. And I'm the one they want to eat.

The duck stood up, too, and flapped his wings. She couldn't believe how large they'd grown. He was prancing around on tiptoes in his fishnet stockings and managed to fly-hop up one step.

One day you'll discover that the sky is very big, she said, and she intended the statement to sound unkind. What do you plan to do when you get up there?

I don't know what you're talking about. I'm not planning anything.

Every morning, as soon as I let you out of your cage, you test your wings. You're practising. One day *you're* going to leave me, too.

Don't be ridiculous. Where would I go?

It was true. He hadn't been anywhere. And his place of birth was a tragic place. He was delivered to her in a plastic carry-bag. Where *would* he go? He knew nothing of the world. She hadn't taught him anything. But then she remembered the overnight educator. What secret knowledge had been imparted behind her back? And where did her mother go? She had flown from her body with a magical ease, as if the hoisting from her physical old self was deliberate and planned.

And where was Simon?

JUST THE SHIRT ON HIS BACK

Before she went to bed that night, she opened Simon's drawers one by one, checking to see how much he had taken. As far as she could ascertain, everything was as it always had been, but she started hauling all his clothes out into a heap on the floor, then vacuuming and wiping the gritty detritus from each drawer. She knelt on the floor where she folded his T-shirts and singlets into a pile to return to a clean drawer. One of the singlets had a faded stain from a red biro that had leaked in the pocket of a favourite creamy olive shirt. It had happened at a barbeque. They'd both rushed to the hosts' bathroom, where he'd removed his shirt so she could scrub soap into the ink under the running tap, red juice flooding the handbasin. When he put the shirt on again, a red wet patch flowered across his chest. Oh well, he said, kissing her, and they laughed. Crikey, did she shoot you in the heart? some joker had said when they eventually emerged from the bathroom.

Now Hannah held the singlet to her face, breathing in the residue of forgotten intimacy. Stupid, stupid, stupid. Shoving it back, she closed that drawer, and went on with the task of folding his underwear and tucking his socks into pairs before tidying them away. She stood up then, and opened the wardrobe with the intention of culling some of his old shirts, but these were the ones he used to wear tramping, or in the garden, when they'd spent their happiest times with each other. And look, here was the creamy olive one with its splodge of red. These shirts he loved the best, the comfortable ones he would miss most if she disposed of them. She held them out one by one, then hung them up again, brushing them down as she slid each shirt amongst the others, feeling the emptiness of them.

NEW SKIN

The next day she drove to the hardware shop and bought paint. As Simon had pointed out, it was not her cup of tea, but she spoke to the retailer, an Indian man who guided her in a matter-of-fact manner, with none of the derision she anticipated, as to what to do and what to buy. Sugar soap. Filler, undercoat. A roller and tray. Sandpaper, several grades. Paintbrushes. And satin acrylic paint. White. She didn't know there were so many shades of white. She chose the whitest. Arctic fox.

Back home, she dragged the ladder from the basement and up to their bedroom. It was a project they had been talking about for years as they lay together in bed, idly chatting, their eyes darting around the tired walls with chipped and marked corners. It was a bedraggled bedroom, shedding skin. It had absorbed too much of their dreary life together and had had enough.

For the next few days she climbed up and down and up and down the ladder, peering at instructions on tins before washing, filling dents, sanding, painting, painting and painting. She grew a membrane of paint up to her elbow, over her clothes, in her hair, on her face. She stopped only when she was incapable of working anymore because she'd forgotten to eat. And while she worked, she thought. She thought until her head was bursting. She thought about her husband, and she thought about her mother, and she thought about her sister, and she thought about Toby and all the things they might have talked about, should they have had longer together. She thought about Eric, the man next door who used to be her friend, and she thought about his grandchildren. And she thought about the duck.

As she rolled the sticky paint over the walls, and the chest of drawers and the wardrobe doors, it seemed as though her life was becoming a blank empty thing and it was all of her doing.

Each evening she put the duck, complaining, into his cage with a cob of corn and a bunch of lettuce leaves just in case he hadn't found enough greens for himself during the day. Then she laboured late into the night, in the relentless heat and humidity. Outside the open window, the dark fused with the electric light that spilt from her bedroom. Beetles and mosquitoes flew in, clambering through the wet paint. She plucked them out with tweezers and painted over the damage.

Finally the job was done. She pulled up the sheet from the polished wooden floor and hauled all the tins and equipment outside. The walls and ceiling were a dazzle of white.

She made herself tea and toast and gulped them down as she sat on the bottom step under the deck. The duck waddled across the grass towards her. She ripped up a piece of toast and threw the bits to him. He gobbled them up and tapped the ground, his motley beak like the demanding forefinger of an old matron.

This is the fourth day without a snail, he informed her.

This is the fourth day without my husband, she replied.

SLEEP IN

The following day Hannah slept in. She was aching all over. She pulled the duvet over her head. It felt as though the new paint was too harsh for her eyes. But she hadn't finished yet.

She soaked in a bath, scrubbing at the paint engrained in her skin, lathering up her hair, picking out scabs of paint. She dried herself and dressed in clean clothes. It was only then that she remembered the duck. She rushed down to the bottom of the garden and lifted the cage door upward to release him.

He marched out and strutted around the pond, his tail feathers splayed in a stiff fan.

Sorry, Ducko, she said, chuckling at his haughty demeanour. I have other things on my mind.

She shifted the cage, turned on the hose and squirted down the night's poo from the grass, leaving the hose still gushing to water the garden. She bent down to sprinkle dried maize into his dish. Suddenly there was a loud whacking of wings and he was upon her back, clenching a lump of flesh in his beak. She jumped to her feet and shook herself, but for a moment he clung to her, his claws scratching through her shirt, before tumbling to the ground. He rushed towards her again, but she grabbed the hose and directed the water at his chest. The force knocked him back, but he braced his feet and stood ogling her for a second. Then he scurried away.

What did you do that for? she yelled after him.

She turned off the hose and raced inside.

Twisting her back at the bathroom mirror, she lifted her shirt. Already there was the heavy imprint of purple bruise.

DINOSAUR

He was enormous. His head was as big as the duckling that had first arrived. He was a dinosaur with an eye at the end of his thin neck, and a beak pulled out from the end of it. He was a mush of snails and half her mother cloaked in feathers all balanced on tree-trunk legs. Did He who made the lamb make thee? Did He who made the tiger make thee? Her cats certainly were asking themselves the same question, giving him a wide and respectful berth as they passed.

While the duck was preening, his wings hung like lopsided doors dangling from loose hinges as he dipped his beak into the secret downy-lined cupboard beneath them. They were almost as long as he was. Sometimes he lolloped around the pond, the raceway around which she used to run as he waddled in pursuit when he was a little clown duckling. He still ran the same course, in the same direction, his wings flapping, those little chicken wing delicacies now the magnificent wings of an angel, whether Gabriel or Lucifer she had no idea.

He was one of the Wright Brothers, or Richard Pearse, cranking up a large machine and trying to make it airborne.

BLANK CANVAS

Once again she headed out in the car. She bought white sheets. She bought a new white duvet cover. She bought a white woollen rug for beside the bed. She bought white cotton fabric, a white wooden picture frame. She bought a white cotton nightdress.

At home she washed the new sheets and duvet cover, threw them in the drier, put them on the stripped bed. She tucked the new nightdress under the pillow. Meanwhile she'd dusted off the sewing machine. She sewed curtains.

It used to be that she made all the curtains for the house, until her enthusiasm for any renovations waned. Although she and Simon had worked hard on their home when they were young, they'd decorated the house to a certain point of satisfaction and then, blinkered to its natural decline, neglected it.

Finally she hammered a picture hook into the pristine wall above the bed. Her intention had been to place in the frame a favourite photo of herself and Simon together, but she also experimented with a particularly charming and seductively quizzical photo of the duck. It looked fitting there on the white wall above their bed. In the end, she chose to leave the frame around a blank white canvas.

She hadn't heard from Simon since he left, nor had she tried to contact him.

GETTING UNDER HER SKIN

That night she collected a few of her clothes from their bedroom and closed the door. Downstairs, she stuffed them into the empty drawers of the spare room, her mother's old bedroom. She undressed and climbed between the cold sheets, lying on her back, her head upon the same pillows that had cushioned her mother's dreams. She looked around the flesh-pink room with its misty floral wallpaper, and at the door. This had been her mother's territory, her outlook, before moving to Primrose Hill.

Hannah pulled the sheet over her face and closed her eyes. She could hear her mother's voice saying to her, *You know, your blood flows gently through your body and then it comes to . . . it comes to . . .* The following words were elusive, but she knew Hannah understood.

How still she had become and how peculiar not to have the steady course of breath in and out of her body. Her blood was seeping from its customary highways and byways, drawn by gravity to the grave, collecting like ballast beneath her. She was aware of Hannah moving in the surrounding space. She could feel the presence of Simon there, too. One or the other touched her head, fiddled with her hair. But mainly it was the walking around her head, backwards and forwards. Her daughter, her little girl, Hannah. Simon standing back. He had been a caring, patient son-in-law. He was a good man. For that she had been lucky. Where was Margaret? Busy? She always had such important things to do.

There was no emotion anymore. No sadness. No fear. No anger. Just awareness. Aware that her life had been spent and that she had loved and had been loved. Aware of time squeezing itself into itself as she left them. Aware of the colour gone.

Chapter 17

FLIGHT

From the stairs to the bottom of the garden, heaving himself along a few feet from the ground, the duck flew, his wings thwacking the air. He came to a halt alongside her, his neck craning, his feet skidding in the stones by the pond.

Wow, Ducko, you clever boy!

She was so proud of him.

You did it!

He cocked his head at her as if to say, So what? She picked him up for a congratulatory cuddle, but he wriggled wildly, his feet clawing at her arm, until he landed heavily on the grass.

Baby's first steps, and it felt as though he was moving away from her.

DREAMS OF THE AFTERLIFE

And her mother was undeniably a part of him now. The residue of her body was in the process of infusing with the elements of his own composition. Each day a couple of teaspoons gobbled up with his mash. And one day he would take her soaring, high above the world, free, as a bird, just as she longed for in her living dreams.

FIGHT

One morning Hannah was in the garden dreamily picking up cabbage tree leaves when a feathered monster ambushed her, intent on eating her toes, her ankles, her legs. She fled, springing over the pond and onto the bridge, through plants to the other side. In vain. It was still tearing at her feet, a pterodactyl with wings spread.

She darted behind a chair on the lawn, using it to shield herself. Her pursuer changed tack. She dropped the chair. Lunged to catch the snapping beast, but it twisted its serpent neck and ripped at her hand. She hurled the thing off.

It gathered itself. Gripped the hem of her jeans. They spun. Whirling dervishes. Feathers, white blur. Dancing, fighting, courting. Whatever. She didn't know.

They froze for a second, staring at each other before it rushed in for the kill again. She dived, grabbing its beak shut, but it tugged away. The strength of it! It flew at her, chomped at her hopping feet. And then suddenly it stopped and sidled away.

She watched him, panting.

It was over.

Ducko.

She gingerly picked him up and, sure enough, he allowed her to place him on her knee. They sat passively on the grass as her heart and breathing settled. She examined her wounds. Her arms and feet marked with red and purple welts. Her hand bleeding.

Was this something ducks did? Were all waddly old plodders host to nasty nimble ninjas? Was he a Trojan duck? She rubbed her fingers deep into the feathers over his chest. Flakes of duck dandruff floated to her clothes, to the grass. He craned his neck, pulled his head back.

She gently placed her hand around his beak. It was feverishly hot. The minuscule feathers around his face were moulting, to reveal a red wartiness, a thumping raw skin of blush.

Ducko. What's going on? We could have really hurt each other.

Even amidst the ferocity of it all, she'd been anxious that she might step on his head, or any part of him.

It happened again a few days later. She had just covered his hutch with the tarpaulin as she did now each evening, and was preparing his food. Once again he went for her feet, his wings flattened. She grabbed his beak shut and yelled at him. NO! He yanked his head away, snatching at the skin of her hand. She picked him up and threw him into the cage, but he was out before she could swing the door closed. Again she managed to get him in, and this time closed the door, but the next second he'd barged through and was upon her. He was a wing-beating devil. She flung him with force to the end of the cage and thrust the door down with a spade shoved against it, then a large stone. All was still. She stood gasping, listening until she heard a movement. He was eating.

Back up at the house, she inspected the new bruises. She tried to analyse what might be triggering these attacks. Not enough snails? Not enough foraging? Lack of attention? Did he hate her? Was she feeding him the ashes of a maniac, and not her mother at all?

All the following day she kept away from him, apart from cautiously letting him out of his cage in the morning. For a while she watched him silently from the top deck as he listlessly pecked at a piece of straw on the lawn. Then he cocked his head and stared at her. Neither said a thing, but she felt he was unfriendly. She was relieved when she was able to put him to bed without a hitch.

The next day he appeared cordial and calm, darting at beetles and crickets exposed as she pulled a few weeds from the garden.

This is better, Ducko, said the woman. We're friends again.

What are you talking about? We've always been friends.

Come on, she said. Those attacks. What's going on in your head?

He tapped his chest several times with his beak. He wasn't going to answer the question. She didn't expect him to. It was unfathomable. The answer lay in the treatises of animal behaviourists. It was nothing to do with love or betrayal. This, at least, was the counsel she gave herself. He plodded away from her, scooping his beak into the loose soil, sucking up water collected on a large yellow leaf.

The next time it occurred, just as she was beginning to relax with him, he was even more determined. She was bringing in the washing and he made his way towards her from under the deck. He pecked in a casual manner around the clothes in the wash basket. Then he leapt up to perch cockily upon the pile of clothes.

King of the castle, eh Ducko? she said. But I'd rather you got off my clean washing.

She was unpegging a white towel. He flew from the clothes and started to have a go at the towel that hung from her hands. She dipped the towel to cover her legs, but he pushed through to her feet, tugging at the sandals she was wearing. Then he struck her toes. Viciously.

NO!

She flicked the towel at him.

NO! Stop it!

He paused. His wings were extended ominously. Then he charged again. She thrashed the towel in the air towards his face, but this only made him more furious, attacking her feet, her legs, flying at her arms. They were two wild things.

He stopped, his feet apart, and eyed her.

Ducko, she panted. No, no, not this. Let's stop. Good boy.

At last he'd come to his senses. She was his kind and loving foster mother, his fellow forager, his soul-mate.

He sprang upwards and flew at her face, his claws scratching at her neck. She could smell the hot muskiness of his body as a wing whacked her temple, bone on bone. She reeled, shoving him away with her forearm. When he came at her again she flung the towel over him, felt for his wings folded against his body and held him down, struggling, on the grass. She couldn't believe his strength. His head was motoring maniacally beneath the towel. She tucked the cloth beneath his belly, wrapping him up loosely. She grasped him firmly against the ground, careful not to injure him, and then released her grip and ran. Looking back, she could see him still dealing with the towel before she escaped into the house.

She was a battered thing. Her arms and feet were like an old woman's, her skin covering patches of tamarillo flesh. There was already a painful lump by her eye. She dabbed disinfectant then antibiotic cream over the deep scratch down the side of her throat. If the duck was her mother, she wanted her dead, there was no doubt about that. If the duck was just a duck, it was not the duck she used to know. The tadpole was metamorphosing into Mr Hyde. The kitten was now a tiger.

She sat dejectedly on the couch with her phone and wrote a text. *Hi. Missing you. Where are you? x*

Delete.

Then: *I presume all is well with you. I hope you are enjoying your thinking.*

Delete.

Hi. How's thinks?

Send.

GOING TOGETHER

Could her mother really want her dead? There had been an incident at Primrose Hill that was squatting broodily in her thoughts, even though she had tried to laugh it off, to shoo it away whenever it emerged. The whole scene from that morning visit was still vivid with the several layers of revelations it presented.

The head nurse was giving attention to her mother's arm as she sat propped up in bed. A thick piece of her skin had been folded back from the bloody interior — bones and ligament. She couldn't say flesh because there wasn't any. Hannah had perched herself by the bed as the nurse dressed the wound, pulling the skin closed and taping it together with tiny strips. Alongside were the raised scars of many such tears, a criss-crossing of mending in a threadbare fabric, too thin to tolerate the rough and tumble of life.

When the nurse left, Hannah opened a box of chocolates from the bedside table. Only three left. It had been full a few days before. The box was lined with glitzy gold plastic, pocked with compartments for each individual chocolate. She placed the box on the bedspread and her mother, who normally hated kitschy glitter, gasped in awe.

Oh, oh, oh, that's so beautiful. So beautiful.

She held the box, tutting in amazement, holding her head this way and that to catch different angles of light. Hannah plucked a chocolate from the box, stripped the chewy centre away from the exterior shell, and popped the rest in her mother's mouth.

Hannah went to the communal kitchen and made a cup of tea. Back in the room, she'd then fed her mother a knob of cheese on a portion of savoury biscuit — a tiny little nibble of her favourite titbit. She'd chewed it eagerly. It was only later that Hannah discovered it gathered in a pulp at the front of her mother's mouth, along with the chocolate. She encouraged her to spit it out, which she did readily. She had two mouthfuls of tea and then stopped.

Hannah realised that her mother had no will or energy to swallow. Basically, she was starving herself. Food sat in her mouth and pooled there, eventually festering into the stench that Hannah had been aware of recently. On top of this, they stuffed medication crushed up with insipid stewed fruit into her mouth and it lingered between her teeth and cheeks until they shoved something else in, followed by a rich sickly-smelling fortified drink that came in a carton with a straw. If her teeth weren't cleaned properly, everything rotted there, like a dead rat in a gutter.

It was palliative care now, this had to be the case.

She took her mother's passive hand and held it to her cheek, then placed it back on the blankets. Then she stood up and paced around the room. She stopped to look at the memorabilia on the notice-board. She unpinned a photo of the family: her mother and father, Hannah in her early teens, and Maggie — Margaret — all in their night clothes, squeezed together against pillows in her parents' double bed. Their faces were mellow from sleep and their tanned arms bare. The weather was probably hot, a Hawke's Bay summer. The camera must have been set up — propped on a small tripod on the window sill in front of them — but there was an unrehearsed air as if everyone had relaxed after they'd assumed the photo had been taken or had failed to work. Her father had his arm behind Maggie with his hand holding her mother's neck, his fingers under her hair, and they were looking at each other fondly, perhaps after a comment, as Hannah too was looking across at her father. Only Maggie still faced the camera, her gaze direct, confronting, enigmatic. She held a blue teddy bear in the crutch of her arm.

Hannah took the photo to her mother and watched as she stared and stared, her eyes drinking in the faces one by one.

There's you, and Dad and me and Margaret, Hannah told her, pointing at each person.

Her mother gave her a dismissive glance, then went back to studying the photo. Hannah would have loved to peep into the reel of images running through her head. Were her thought processes intact enough to be able to enter the past, to recall all the nuances of the relationships that had been entangled through her life? As if she'd read her thoughts, her mother suddenly lifted her head and looked directly at Hannah: Hannah, dear, you have been the most wonderful daughter I could ever have had, you truly have, and that's not just words.

Hannah, overwhelmed, bent to press her lips on her cool cheek. She had the urge to say that she loved her, but the words had the ring of a cheap retort. They smiled at each other then. It seemed she was surfacing from some sort of sludge in her mind to become lucid again. The splendour of that nearly empty box of chocolates. What had she actually seen? What was that glistening gold translating itself into?

And then her mother said, He is not your father, you know.

What do you mean? Don't be silly, Mum.

He is not your father. Have I not told you that before?

Of course he is. What makes you say that?

Because I know. I was there. I am telling you this.

And Maggie?

Yes, Margaret; but not you.

So who *is* my father, then?

At that moment the rest-home chaplain came into the room. Ah, he was *so* delighted to catch her mother awake, *and* in her room.

Hannah had wanted to turn him around and march him out again, especially as her mother had never had much time for him. In Hawke's Bay she would go to church, and later, when she couldn't, the minister would come to her to give her communion. But not here. She'd either lost her faith, or she just did not like this minister, a cherry-faced man of about sixty with rheumy eyes magnified behind crooked yellowing glasses. His ever-ready smile was full of teeth . . . The wolf who already had eaten the grandmother and was now looking for another one.

But her mother, always the lady, introduced Hannah to him as her wonderful daughter.

He said, No doubt you have been a wonderful mother, too. Isn't it good to have your daughter by your side?

Then her mother had announced quite meaningfully: It won't be long now.

The minister pulled at his shirt collar and glanced at Hannah, checking to see how she was taking this. He was a man accustomed to moulding his words to fit the occasion.

She repeated her statement. I said, it won't be long now.

He then said, No. No, but you'll be going to that lovely place where Jesus is waiting for you, and you will never be alone and your daughter will always carry you in her heart.

Then he asked if he could say a prayer, and Hannah, who was still spinning from her mother's revelation, whether true or false, reluctantly agreed, thinking of her mother kneeling at her bedside every night when she was a child to recite their prayer. *God bless Mummy and Daddy and Hannah and wee Margaret and save us from illness and accidents and fires and earthquakes and death, and may we love each other forever and ever. Amen.*

The minister had his own words up his sleeve, and he pulled them out like an unravelling old sock. He rambled on about passing to that other place and how Jesus Christ Our Lord would be with her forever more and how she had been a wonderful mother, for Jesus Christ's sake, amen. He had his hand, bloated and crusty, on her mother's forehead, and held Hannah's hand with the other. His spherical face held the all-teeth smile he wore all day long as he sidled up to vulnerable people and told them that they would be passing into the hands of Jesus. For Christ's sake. And that he, only he, could do the deed if they opened their hearts to him, as he was the desperate one, the one snivelling around in search of forgiveness and deference from half-wits who thought he was their father or brother or the long-dead grocer from up the road and who nodded to anything he told them, and if he dropped the ball it had nothing to do with him. Amen.

When he had finished, he unfolded a woman's cotton handkerchief from his shirt pocket, wiping his hands, dabbing his brow. The handkerchief had a rose, like a droplet of blood, embroidered in the corner. He looked at it uncertainly, his eyes down as if still in prayer. Then Hannah's mother surprised them both.

I'm not going to go alone, you know.

The minister looked puzzled and Hannah laughed uncomfortably.

Oh, is this a private thing between the two of you? he said, glancing at Hannah, stuffing the handkerchief into his trouser pocket. He lifted his hand and placed a fingertip at a corner of his lips, where a rogue nerve had started its busy dance. Her mother then repeated that she wasn't going to go alone and that she was going to take Hannah with her.

Oh yes, Hannah's coming too.

Am I, Mum? Hannah had said. I'm not so sure about that, actually.

And you, too, she said to the minister. It won't be long for you, either.

This was too much for him. He closed his twitching mouth over his teeth and left the room. After he'd gone, her mother said, He shouldn't have done that. I didn't want him to do that, Hannah.

I'm sorry, Mum, she said. I didn't realise that.

Oh well, her mother said resignedly. We'll look out for him next time.

But you were telling me about Dad?

Her mother searched her face earnestly. She had the wide-eyed look of a child at a fairground, overwhelmed by the complexity of life. Within her tiny body, there was still the person who was aware and knowing. When she surfaced, these gems, or fossils, emerged.

Outside, the cicadas were singing after all those years of being white fat grubs in the earth. Maybe her mother had had a little sing that morning as she crawled to a top branch before lift-off?

Mum? Dad. You were telling me about Dad.

But her mother had slumped back into her silent, slumbering, distant self.

At the time, as she stood watching by the bed before leaving her mother, now asleep, Hannah's mind had twirled around the helix of memories and shared genes. Although she would try to broach the question of her father again, her mother seemed unable or disinclined to enlighten her. There was no one else to ask. She had to assume that it was untrue, but, even so, a bothersome stone lurked under her foot.

She'd walked from the room, and down the pastel corridor, past the rooms where other waiting people sat in armchairs, or in their beds, alone. Except for one. There was the wolf, leaning over a grey-skinned cadaverous woman, her mouth open like a cave. He raised his head as Hannah went by, and their eyes locked. He was chewing, his smile temporarily clamped shut by stolen toffee.

She felt confident that her mother would never have a visit from him again.

IN MODERATION

Her father had been a moderate man. He'd been a moderate gambler. He'd buy a weekly ticket in the Golden Kiwi Lottery. He'd put money on the horses. Sometimes he won and sometimes he lost. If he won he'd arrive home with presents and flowers and laughter. If he lost he'd go straight to his study and close the door and they weren't allowed to disturb him. Her parents didn't fight often, but on these days her mother would be tight-lipped and grim. He'd died before casinos came to New Zealand, otherwise he probably would have tipped a moderate amount of money down that drain.

He drank moderately and smoked half a packet a day and had a moderate respect for God.

He was a high-school English teacher. He wrote poetry that he'd read out to whoever was there at Christmas.

When she was little, Hannah would sit on his knee while he told her stories of magic and malice, wrapping his deep resonating voice like a cloak around her. And then when Maggie was old enough, Hannah would balance on the fat arm of the easy chair and savour the stories in their different versions all over again.

He would sing old songs with his own lyrics. He had black sweeping hair and a dimple in his chin.

He'd fantasise about setting off and sailing alone around the coast of New Zealand. He'd build boats in the garage which he would launch but never take far out to sea, building another, always bigger, model, as if the pursuit of the dream was more satisfying than the playing out of the waking reality.

This was the man she'd always regarded, without question, as her father.

Chapter 16

Chapter 18

SOMEWHERE IN THE MIDST OF
THESE CHANGES . . .

Hannah received a text from Simon: *Hi. Good to hear from you. Thinking deeply and searchingly. Have a contract in Christchurch . . . with aftershocks. You OK?*

She told him she was OK, thank you. She didn't ask when he was coming back, but she had to admit to herself that she was relieved to hear from him, despite feeling betrayed. Had he allowed himself to be swallowed up by her sister? She considered that they might be having an affair, but dismissed it. Simon wasn't cool enough. He was an engineer, a pedant, wore tweed jackets and black skivvies, beige woollen jerseys pulled over the pockets of baggy trousers. He liked to bike and walk along bushy tracks. He didn't smoke, but if he did choose anything these days, it would probably be a sweet tobacco pipe, and he'd gnaw it contemplatively down to the bone. But no. He was far too kind and deep and ponderous for Maggie. She was attracted to musicians, artists, wordsmiths and wayward adventurers. People on cliff-tops, searching the horizon for the mast of a foreign ship.

Hannah packed away her doubts like putty into the jagged cracks of her reasoning.

SHIFT

Time passed. So many things had happened and yet nothing had happened at all. The world must have swung with the New Year into a different playground. The duck no longer made the woman laugh. The tufty feathers around his head had been falling out and his skin was now exposed, a crimson shiny hide, growing malignantly until it was too big for itself, cracking into a mosaic of bulges. A black stain spread almost symmetrically through the redness. From the top of his beak, the glossy knobble that had been sprouting there was swelling into a cherry tomato. He looked furious, embarrassed.

Ugly.

And his behaviour towards her was continuing to change. She was wary of him. If she went to the garden she'd carry a wide leaf rake for protection.

The urgent baby-duckling cheeping had stopped. When had it stopped? He now made a variety of other noises, as if, finally questioning what he might be, he was experimenting with a range of animal expressions to see which one suited him best. He was a tui, picking up all sounds of the world around him, even though the tui was black and sleek and elegant with its curly ruffle of beard, flitting through high branches and gorging itself on kahikatea berries; the duck in comparison was whitish, shaggy and cumbersome, with his angry face and warty growth, waddling around like a bewildered old man. Sometimes he stood alert and whinnied like a head-tossing horse. He could hiss like a snake. He made an attempt at a coo, like a grizzly pigeon. And when she came near him, he shuddered like a swimmer emerging from an icy pond. He wagged his tail and whined or panted like a dog. He also had a guttural strangled grunt, not unlike the noise her mother made when she was close to death.

Along these lines, something more alarming had happened. The duck had changed his eating habits. Snails had become abhorrent to him. He might take one in his beak, but would spit it out as if it were poison. She thought at first that the particular snails she offered had been eating something which rendered them unappetising, or that their shells were difficult to crack (so she smashed them, shuddering with repulsion, with a brick). He'd eagerly pick up the mashed viscera, but then would drop them, tossing his head vigorously to rid himself of the very memory of them. Even tiny soft-shelled baby snails had the same effect.

Not only that, he no longer would eat his mash. He'd touch it with his beak and move away. She'd hold it under his beak, this way and that, as he turned away, that way and this. Finally he'd hiss and give her an admonishing nip, a warning.

Ducko, she said, you can't just eat half my mother. You can't just take half of her soaring high above the world. What about the other half, left behind, yearning for freedom. Yearning for the other part of herself. Please. Just a little bit each day.

But no. Day after day, she would coax him but the duck would eat no more snails, no more mash, with or without her mother. Crickets, cockroaches, worms, baby slugs, wheat and fresh corn on the cob, thank you very much.

A drop of sauvignon blanc with that, Ducko? she asked sarcastically, leaning on the leaf rake. Oh? Only champagne? We'll see what we can do.

The duck had a deliberate, haughty way of ignoring her when he wanted to. She was sure his demeanour was intended to be infuriating.

WHERE THE WILD THINGS ARE

One day the duck was resting on the deck when a white-faced heron dropped from the sky and landed on the railing. Hannah was working at the table inside. She hardly dared to breathe as the two birds examined each other. The duck lifted one leg after the other, in a deliberate hesitant way, cocking his head towards the heron. And the heron was angling its head to look at the duck. The heron in contrast to the duck was tall and grey, elegant and slim with yellow stilt-like legs, a thin curling neck and a sharp black beak. They were each fascinated by the other and, apart from the duck's on-the-spot stepping, both held themselves rigidly as they stared. After a while, the heron's curiosity seemed to be satisfied. He was just a fat cumbersome duck after all. It launched itself into the air, making a graunching cry of farewell. The duck lifted his eye heavenward.

Hannah went outside. It was the first time in all the years they had lived there that she had seen a heron on their property. How many times had it flown by, observing the strange duck below, reminding itself that it must pop down for a visit some time?

Well! she sang. Mr and Mrs Muscovy-Heron, huh?

Mind your own business, said the duck, and with that he started to preen every feather.

They never saw the heron again, but there was other feathered company. The duck often had a scattering of birds around him, mainly sparrows and a blackbird or two. There was also a turtle dove, dressed in hues of powder-pink and purple with a collar of brown spots. Her wings were a cloak of soft browns overlapping, the scales of a fish on a sky-swimmer.

The turtle dove would be perched on the fence waiting for the duck when Hannah let him out of his cage in the mornings. The attraction was food, wheat or maize left in his cage from the night before. But there was some sort of camaraderie between the duck and the dove. Perhaps they loved each other. Turtle doves were monogamous and paired for life. He certainly tolerated her as she strutted and cooed around him during the course of the day. She'd rush at the marauding sparrows until they lifted into the air out of her way, dropping again as she turned her back.

The sparrows increased in number and the turtle dove grew round and fat. Hannah was sure that if she patted the bird, it would bounce up and down like a ball.

Each day Hannah would leave a corn cob in the water bowl under the deck; the duck would tear at it hungrily, slurping and tossing it around until most of the kernels were gone. The sparrows and dove would finish it off, efficiently pecking into the cavities where he'd left juicy titbits.

Then the cobs started to mysteriously disappear. Hannah tied them onto a decking post with string cutting deeply through the kernels. Still the cobs were moved, dangling at the far reaches of the string. The duck now avoided the corn. Something was frightening him.

She brought out an electronic trap from the basement and left it under the deck. For three days nothing happened. Then within two days she had two plump shiny-coated electrocuted rats. Once upon a time, her cats would have done this job.

The following day, a sparrow lay dead in the trap. Another day, another rat. And then the turtle dove.

Hannah felt sick. She turned her back on the duck and held the limp dove in her cupped hands, studying the perfect symmetry of the markings of its feathers. It lay so peacefully, so unaccusingly. She put the trap away. The creatures she killed these days, either directly or indirectly, on behalf of her duck.

Finally, she forced herself to go for a reconnoitre to the man-made lake in the city where she knew other ducks would be. She parked the car and ambled over the grassy hillocks and down to the water's edge. She pulled the plastic bag full of bread from her bag and sat on the rocky bank, her feet hanging over the side. From across the lake, swarms of birds streaked towards her.

Hannah hadn't been near ducks since the arrival of her duckling. Now she was surrounded by black swans, honking and squeaking, with their supercilious necks and crimson faces spreading into scarlet beaks, their wings a fluster of ruffles and frills. They looked as if they'd been sitting at a mirror with lipstick and hairspray, preparing themselves for a ball. The lake was chopped up from paddling feet. Busy little black ducks — with short white beaks, white legs and feet — flipped upside-down to disappear disconcertingly under the water, until they popped up some distance away. Eels lurked around the rocks. Sparrows fluttered like leaves from the trees onto the grass behind her. Haughty geese waddled around a planting of flax to join the crowd. Pigeons strutted their stuff. They all joined in the feeding frenzy around her torn-up bread. None showed any interest whatsoever in her toes dabbling over the side.

She stared at the quacking mallards, so tiny in comparison to the draught horse of a duck that waited for her at home. There were no muscovy ducks. None of the ducks were shaking and shuddering as her own duck had been greeting her recently. It must use so much energy to do this. He was an overgrown humming bird grounded in a muddy paddock. He was a mangrove humming dog.

How would he fare if she brought him here, walked away, and never came back?

But how could she? What about dogs? Traffic? Other aggressive ducks?

And what about this warning she had read somewhere: Do not set a tame bird free. It can only lead to death or trouble or misunderstanding.

And then there was the most compelling reason. How could she release the duck anywhere now? How could she, now that her mother was irrefutably a part of him? A part of her mother at least. There were moments when she had to ask herself: What have I done? As her mother would say, whatever in the name of Heaven had got into her head?

Chapter 11

Chapter 19

NIGHT VISITOR

Sometimes the night is a different place. For a person alone in a house, the night becomes another territory, teeming with all the secrets and lies and fears and regrets that have accumulated in that person's life up until that moment. The night can whisper and thump, whack against windows, scratch and skitter above the ceiling. Depending on how you are at the time, you can listen, take note, be influenced. Or you can ignore the busy conference of the dark, let it chatter on without your attention.

On this particular evening, Hannah was ignoring the night as she worked, editing at the table by the heater where normally Simon would be working convivially nearby. The cold had forced all the outside noises into shelter, all the birds looped into knots, and the trees holding themselves motionless for fear that a shiver might start their leaves dropping one by one to the ground and so risk exposure to the approaching autumn.

Alongside the table, the blind over the narrow window was up. When she heard the crunching of twigs on the ground outside and glanced over without concern, all she could see was her own reflection. She returned to her work. The sound surfaced again, so she stood up from her chair and pressed her nose and forehead against the cold pane, just in time to see Eric standing there. The light from the window fell over his hairy chest, his milky white stomach and, as he turned, the folds of his back, his buttocks, his thin ballerina legs. He was an albino chimpanzee, escaped from the zoo of his mind, lumbering through the foliage of the garden. She unlatched the window and whispered into the still air.

Hey, Eric! Eric, are you all right?

She grabbed a blanket from the back of the couch and rushed through the house to open the front door. Light from the hallway spilled into the garden beyond.

Eric?

Jungle smashing. A thud, then silence.

Tentatively she ventured outside, towards the crash.

Eric.

She picked her way through the bromeliads, the ferns, the trees to where lay the tangled white mound of him, tugging to free his foot from the root that had brought him down. She knelt alongside him, placed her hand on his cold damp shoulder. As he picked his head up from the mud, she caught a white flash of swivelling eye, an animal rearing from its tether.

Ssssh, she said to the father of the little worm that had made its way underground to sea, so long ago now.

She plonked herself down and draped the blanket over his back.

Eric. What's wrong? Please stop this. Talk to me. What is going on? Where are your clothes, for starters?

She was tiring of pleading so stupidly. Lifting her nose in the air, she sniffed for evidence of alcohol. There was none.

He finally extricated his foot from the root and hoisted himself onto his hands and knees to crawl away from her, crushing ferns and mashing delicate groundcover with his ploughing shins. The chimp had become a caveman with his deerskins trawling each side of him through the undergrowth.

I would like an explanation.

How arch this sounded to her ears, but she needed to feel less helpless.

Then he stopped, collapsed himself into a noisy heap of blue blanket. Was he crying or laughing? He was a heaving, snorting buffoon and he didn't belong in her garden. He was destroying her plants, crashing uninvited through her evening. After all this time of bewildering silence, to arrive like this! She was shivering now, and angry. She had work to do. She wanted him off her territory.

Nonetheless, she tried one more time.

Would you like a milky Milo? I could bring one out to you, or you could come inside if you prefer?

He sat up, clutching the blanket under his chin, his face a pathetic mask of hopelessness.

All right, he said.

Oh? Oh good. OK then. Outside or inside?

Out here'll be fine, thanks. Sorry, sorry, he mumbled.

She jumped up and sprang through the foliage onto the lawn and inside. Quickly she prepared the Milo. Four heaped teaspoons in a large cup with sugar, and up to the top with milk. Two minutes in the microwave. She tested it. Just right. She took it out to him. He was gone.

She called. No answer. From his house, his bathroom window flooded with light. Off again. Then the room next door on. Off. Then upstairs to his bedroom. Bugger him.

Trembling, she took the Milo inside, drank a mouthful, then filled it to the top with a good dollop of brandy. She sipped as she continued her work.

OBSESSION, ATTACHMENT AND ADDICTION

The following day was infiltrated with images of Eric lumbering about in her garden. She couldn't concentrate on her work. His behaviour was irrational. If she'd known the contact details for his daughter, Sheila, she might have rung her. Why was he naked and had he been spying on her through the window as she worked? If he had only knocked on the door, she would have invited him inside.

But now, as she was walking along the waterfront, she felt that this pretty day held a message for her. The sea was sucking out to expose normally submerged rocks, a deeply inhaled tidal breath revealing the craggy bones of the Earth. She was flooded with questions and this day was trying to reveal something to her.

It had started with spotting a mother with a baby, in the company of an older couple all sitting in the sun on the stone wall by the path. The young woman had fat florid cheeks. Her eyes were big and moist, her lips thick and flaccid as they slurped kisses onto the bald head of the baby she clutched against her chest. She was tender with her devotion and more than generous with her kisses. And then Hannah realised with a degree of discomfort that the floppy baby was a life-sized doll.

As she continued to walk, she passed a woman with long grey wispy hair pushing a pram. Children and their parents had gathered around the pram, and Hannah peeped past them to see a perky lap-dog tucked under a grubby knitted blanket.

Looking around, she saw all the families lazily strolling by the beach. Parents clutching chubby hands, hugging babies, anxiously chasing toddlers as they wobbled through the sand towards the sea. Lovers pressed into each other. A teenage girl leaned over a stylish old lady in a wheelchair who curled a purple sea slug tongue around an ice cream. The girl gently readjusted a towel across the old lady's chest, dabbing at a milky drool hanging from her chin.

And again Hannah couldn't help but wonder about the chemistry, supplied by Nature, which made for attachment between one person and another, a person and another object, a person and a dog. A man and another man's wife. A man and his cello. A person and her mother,

her dead mother. An alcoholic and drink, a drug addict and his drug. A woman and her duck.

All these people clearly were attached in one degree or another to the object of their affections. But love. What *was* love and what was it all about? Was it all interconnected? Was it the same chemistry? Was love just chemistry, was addiction love? What was the nature of it all?

She thought of Simon and the intensity of feeling between them when they first met. And the long years they had lived alongside each other, their skin loosening into miniature folds around their eyes. She wondered where he was now and what he was doing.

And last night. Was that chemistry or chaos?

Hannah was mystified as to what might have burned so fiercely between herself and Eric so many years ago. She couldn't evoke the man she knew then from the Eric of now. Did age bring its own brand of metamorphosis, from hot dog to curmudgeonly, heavy, slobbery old dog?

Then she recalled the time she'd lifted Max into her arms.

Oooof, she'd groaned, you are getting so heavy!

Max replied: Poppa's stronger than you. Poppa's a gorilla.

Well, she thought now, there you go.

REASONS (EXCUSES) FOR INFIDELITY

Because he had pushed her off the tight-rope. Because he'd made her laugh. Because he'd strung a love song through her heart. Because his chest felt like a landing place for her weary head. Because she didn't have to stand on tiptoes to kiss him. Because the storm made her do it. Because he made her suddenly feel lonely. Because the smooth skin of her life had bulged like a cherry balloon. Because he looked sexy in black. Because it felt like fun. Because it was fun. Because he teased her. Because he was there. Because he told her that if she let him fiddle, he'd be her beau. Because her husband was so far away it didn't seem to matter. Because once she opened the door and there he was, holding an empty picture frame around his head. You're driving me up the wall, he'd said. Would you like to come to my place and hang around with me?

And then it was over. They avoided each other. She wanted to close all the windows in her house, pull all the curtains and sew them securely with rope, shift furniture against them to block out any sound, any stray sigh of his that might be floating by. But she didn't, of course. And she needn't have worried. There was no more music from the house next door. Just like that. It was as if a tree full of birds had been cut down.

When Simon arrived home from Uganda, that first night in bed she was paralysed. The world was silent as it strained to listen for every sound, every breath she took. Simon held her in his arms and waited for her. Finally she wept. She wept because she had missed him, and because she was missing Eric. She wept because she had lost a baby. She wept because she felt like a traitor. Simon held her gently and asked her why she was weeping. She cried more. He held her until eventually she was able to turn to him. He presumed it had been just because she'd missed him. But all the birds in that chopped-down tree knew there was more to it than that.

Quite a few months later, Eric met a woman who moved in with him. Suzie.

One day Simon said, We haven't seen Eric for a while. Why don't we invite them over for a drink?

Hannah said, Oh, I think he's pretty involved with his new girlfriend. We should let them be.

But he invited them anyway. Suzie shoved aside all awkwardness with relentless cheery chatter. Gradually all the taut cords of longing between the two houses began to sag, then shed their scabby crusts before falling to the ground. The music started up again for a while. Hannah could hear Suzie's strident singing along with his fiddle and she didn't care. The woman couldn't sing in tune anyway.

Not long after Suzie returned to her old boyfriend in Darwin, The Eketa Hoons went on their last tour. The singer developed nodules on his larynx and called it a day, and the drummer beat it to Nelson. By this time the hedge had grown, but until recently they'd always kept a natural gap as they popped backwards and forwards.

Chapter 20

SENTINEL

Now that the duck could fly, he spent quite a bit of time on the fat limbs of the magnolia tree winding across the deck. On the wide wooden railing, she'd left a water dish that was really a plastic cat-litter tray — one of several she'd bought and placed here and there around the place. As she worked she could watch through the window when he washed. She loved to see him slapping around in the water, beating his wings, his feathers shimmying and shivering, his body surrounded by an aura of mist against the sky. He'd dive his beak into his uropygial gland, plastering dobs of yellow through his feathers. Or he'd pace up and down along the tree limbs, moving from the shade of the magnolia leaves to the open railing, where the whole world lay before him.

She was amazed at his sense of balance . . . he was a poem whose multiple components each shifted and flowed in accordance with the position of the others as they vied for equilibrium, as he wrapped his rubber feet round the edge of his water tray, or stood on the deck railing, or a shaking branch. On a squally day, he was a ship with an ugly red prow and a sail full of gusto, adjusting to every blast of wind buffeting around him. His tail would lift and drop to meet each wave, his body modifying its stance in micro-twitches to shift up down, up down.

Whenever she came into his view, his crest would lift in a stiff mohawk, his whole body charged with excitement. He'd turn to stand and stare at her as she moved inside the house, always searching for that eye-to-eye connection.

If she kept still as she worked, as long as she was within his line of vision, he'd pull up one leg deep into his feathers under his wing, and balance on the other, like a stork, ostensibly asleep with his white furry eyelids folded over his eyes — two fluffy mounds looking out of place in the boiling red of his face. Occasionally he would drop himself onto his belly and tuck his head into the feathers of his wing, and this was the stance she loved the best, because it suggested he was relaxed and at peace, and, despite his recent unnerving behaviour, that was all she wanted for him.

WHITE RAG TO A DUCK

Reasons. If only she could understand the *reasons* for the unprovoked attacks against her. She sifted through all the incidents she could remember, searching for a common theme or clues or triggers that might unravel the mystery.

She was thinking of the time, a while ago now, when she left a heap of leftover rice on the grass, with the idea that the duck might like to nibble at it, and should he not, she knew that other birds would wolf it up. But the duck acted warily, waddling sideways past the mound. She persisted, picking him up and placing him by the rice with his beak hovering over the top of it, but still he shied away, whining fearfully.

Then she noticed how he liked to attack the white plastic-covered cushions used for his night-time roosting in the cage. There was a pattern to the way he pecked at them, grabbing a piece in his beak and thrusting, before jumping on top to repeat the pecking once more.

There was the white towel he flew at while she was putting out the washing, and the white washing basket he jumped onto before he went for her.

And the attacks were more likely if she had bare feet or, especially, if she was wearing her red sandals. Her white duck feet with the flash of bright red face, from his point of view. She had surmised that her exposed flesh was an obvious target, but now it was looking as though colour might be the trigger for his aggression. White, primarily, with red, or sometimes black, added to it. She wondered whether the predator that killed his mother had been white. She wondered whether he had a sense of his own whiteness. The overnight educator had been hissing in his ear: What are you? Man or duck? Get her, get her. Go on, go! Show her what you're made of.

But she was still bemused. Was this normal duck play or was it serious?

When she investigated through the internet, Hannah discovered a couple of videos on YouTube showing fighting muscovies. Wings batting, necks curling round necks, beaks clamping. She knew the instant bruises those sucking beaks caused. A panicking voice-over was screaming: Look at all the blood. There's blood everywhere. Are they trying to kill each other?

231

She read that muscovies could fight to the death. Territory. She watched video footage of muscovy ducks mating, the male trampling the back of the female, tail furiously sweeping from side to side, beak wedged in her neck. The pair didn't look much different from the muscovies fighting.

And then she found the *New Scientist* slow-motion video of the copulating muscovies. *Coitus interruptus. Coitus interruptus scientifica.* A scientist was holding a ruler measuring the penis which was coiled like a corkscrew, a corkscrew from the $2 Shop, an uncertain rocket spiralling its skewed and rambling way to its destination. According to the scientist, the penis was twenty centimetres long. The burst from erection to ejaculation took .36 of a second. A third of a second. The cloaca of the female spiralled in the opposite direction of the male, apparently in an attempt by Nature to save the female from forced copulation.

Why didn't Nature create a less aggressive creature? How could it be that Nature designed the male and female organs to be so diametrically opposed to each other? Did He who made the he, make she?

The woman played the video again. She was astonished. This eruption of activity emerging so swiftly from such a depth of feathers? A third of a second! If 'one hickledypickledy' was the measure for one second, then it was all over in a hickle. And so many ducklings owed their lives to this!

The woman laughed.

Look at this! she said out loud. But of course, the man, who would have had something to say about all this, was not there.

LANGUAGE

When she ventured out on her regular walks, Hannah passed strangers who smiled at her. She smiled back. She smiled at others, they smiled back.

Even when her mother was locked into herself with the disease, her face usually lit up when Hannah walked into the lounge of the rest home.

And then there was the foreign couple facing each other at the beach who'd been engaged in furious debate. She couldn't understand their language, or guess the subject of the discussion, but the hostility of the eyes, the curling lips, the jutting chin and their gesticulation made it obvious to her that this was not a friendly conversation.

She thought of Simon and all the non-contact mannerisms and expressions and micro-expressions she was able to interpret without the need for words. From the insignificant — such as itching his nose, or stroking his beard or tugging his ear — to a more thoughtful frown, or pursing of lips, or craning his neck. The face a rubbery canvas constantly giving out signals which left little doubt as to their meaning. A glance or an expressive hand that was able to stop her, show disapproval, question her whimsically, soften her with love.

But the duck. The duck hissed, trilled, snorted, whined, panted and made raspy grunts. He rhythmically dipped and bobbed his head this way and that; swayed his head horizontally; tapped the ground or his foot with his beak; faced her alarmingly; shuffled sideways. The crest of his head feathers would shoot up, his wings would flatten, and at times he'd suddenly sit upright, head high, his whole body erect, while an eerie high-pitched quiver of sound leaked from within. He'd silently snap his beak rapidly into the air as if he'd reverted to his babyhood and was begging for food, or was gulping at invisible mosquitoes just out of reach, or was blind and mad, or was trying to tell her something but couldn't find the words. As if as if as if. Her interpretation of his language was all relative to her terms. Conjecture. The only sound she understood for certain was the happy soft feeding cheep he made when they were out foraging together.

The overnight educator who formed and informed him had always shoved her aside. Even though she and her duck had lived alongside each other almost from the time he was born, they were unable to reliably communicate. Even though she had observed him so intimately. His language had formed and his range of expression was complex and diverse, even though he had never encountered other ducks of any description to relate to. They were worlds apart.

TELLING HIM

We are worlds apart, she said to the duck when she was out digging in the garden, juggling with fat worms (curling and twisting like the penis she now knew he had) which he snatched from her fingers.

I wouldn't put it that way, he said. We get along quite well most of the time, sharing the same world quite compatibly.

I never have any idea of what you are thinking, she said. I don't know anything about you. I don't know what your intentions are. I don't know whether you're happy or not.

Does *anyone* know whether anyone is happy or not? Do you know what other *people* are thinking?

I suppose you're referring to the man? she replied grumpily.

Not at all, he said slyly. You read too much into everything.

But nonetheless, he'd hit a raw nerve, and she knew it was intentional.

THE WOMAN TRIES TO GET PHILOSOPHICAL

There were moments when Hannah deceived herself into thinking that Simon's absence was just one of his normal contracts. She was not unused to being alone. He'd had periods away for longer, although usually they kept in touch through phone calls or texts, the odd emails. The frequency of contact had lessened over the years, but when they were apart, their communication, however brief, was like a reassuring touch of a foot under a table.

Their friends also were accustomed to his trips away, so she didn't have to offer any explanation. Using her work as an excuse, she avoided invitations out. She didn't want to see anyone. It had been easy to start nudging the world away, and now it had taken on its own momentum, flowing further and further from the diminishing existence of herself and the duck within the boundaries of the garden.

But there was the nagging concern, growing as time passed, that Simon's leaving was more serious than a temporary fanciful tiff. She had no doubt that her sister would have been feeding discontent into his veins over the Christmas break. The Christmas to New Year's cruise had left her beached, while the others had carried on without her. Had they all been in consultation with each other? Had Toby known when they had walked together so companionably that evening?

Loneliness is a strange thing, Hannah said to the duck as he poked his beak into the small stones around the pond. She was sitting in the grass watching him. We're all stranded creatures, stuck on our own little islands of sticks and straw, dealing with life as best we can. Some of us don't do very well, I'm afraid. We peck around at our feet and worry about the water around us rising and ebbing, and we do things that we sometimes later regret.

What are you talking about? said the duck. The only water I know is the pond here, and the dishes that barely have enough water to clear my beak, and the rain, and the hose water you squirt all over the place. And how can you regret anything? Whatever is done is done.

It's simpler for you. You're a duck.

But why is it simpler? You're a you. What's the difference? Every day was tomorrow or will be yesterday eventually.

You're down the chain, duckie. You're not responsible. You don't have to make decisions. It's not so simple. Beyond the garden. Or even *in* the garden.

You keep saying 'simple', 'simpler'. What does that mean? You are not so different from me, actually. What is there to regret?

Regret is a stomach ache after you've eaten too many worms or corn or cockroaches.

How could you *ever* eat too many? You eat and then you stop when you are full.

All right, then. Biting the hand that feeds you. You might regret *that*, one day.

I don't regret anything. Though I wouldn't mind a worm, now that you mention it. Right now would be good.

Right now. Right now, he was busily probing his chest feathers with his beak. Right now, she could screw his thin neck.

Actually Ducko, to get back to my original subject.

Original? I didn't notice anything original?

Loneliness. It's a strange thing. You think you just want to be by yourself. You don't realise that you're becoming lonely until you suddenly are. And then it's too late.

Pardon? Are you riddling again? I *never* want to be by myself.

One minute you're just drifting along and then your mother dies and you know it's not a bad thing because her body has been disintegrating for some time and you can see it happening in front of your very eyes over years and years. It's all in the order of things. So there're no surprises there. You're sad and you think about her a lot, but you're not lonely. When she was alive, the two of you just got along with *being*. Your lives weren't particularly entangled. Her life and your life. And then when she needed you, you looked after her and then she died and then you miss her and that's normal. And then there's a duck in your life and everyone hates you and, and, your husband leaves you suddenly, and that's strange but your lives weren't particularly entangled, but then, suddenly, suddenly you're alone. With a duck that attacks you. And it feels like *life* attacking you. And you miss him, your husband, and you don't know why. You miss everything and everybody and you feel so confused. And it feels like everything you ever knew is backing away from you. And that you're becoming a tiny shrinking dot. And that you have no capacity for love anymore.

Well. That was an outburst if ever there was one. But I'd like to point out that at least we have each other. We will never be alone while we have each other.

We might not be alone, Ducko, but we still might feel utterly lonely.

I'll never be lonely if I have you, he said.

Duckie, she said. It's time you told me your name.

She reached down and picked him up, arranged his feet upon her thighs. She cupped her hand across his full feathery breast. She wanted to drop her head gently upon his back and close her eyes, but he snorted and hissed, then started to whine pitifully, his feet scrambling over her jeans as he eyed the ground for escape.

You see, Ducko, she called as he waddled away from her across the lawn. That's what I mean. You have the capacity to make me feel more wretched than I was even before I knew you.

The duck stopped and turned around, facing her.

Well, as we're getting to the nitty gritty, he houghed in that raspy throaty way of his, why do you always end up handling me inappropriately?

What do you mean?

You *know* I don't like to be picked up.

Really? So, you tell me now?

Yes. I'm telling you now.

Chapter 21

EXPERIMENT ON PLANET EARTH

Across the world, in Moscow, the six men who had been acting out a simulated mission to Mars in a hotchpotch of windowless isolation chambers had arrived. On the fourteenth of February, two crew members clambered into bulky spacesuits and, with a robot rover, they'd made their glorious entrance onto the powdery terrain of the red planet. They carried out virtual experiments, took samples, and planted three flags — one for Russia, one for China and one for the European Space Agency. Now, a week later, before being faced with the tedious eight-month journey back home, they were in the process of conducting the third of these forays onto the surface of the planet, which in fact was another module a few metres away from the so-called orbiting tube. In fact, Mars was just a dusty old sandpit. Afterwards, after the earthquake, Hannah couldn't help wondering about the power of the imagination. Whether the fantasising cosmonauts, bounding around the improvised faraway planet, without being subjected to any simulation of weightlessness, had had any influence on the monstrous repercussions on the other side of planet Earth.

There'd been a discussion about the experiment on the radio. Strangely, it was particulars like this that made her miss Simon most of all. Should he be listening, he would revel in the details, she knew, and he'd be investigating the scientific data, would be marvelling at the possibility that one day in the distant future men might make the actual voyage to that planet. She, on the other hand, could only see it in relation to their own lives, a bewildering and farcical mission to nowhere.

With the radio still accompanying her, she prepared to do some gardening with the duck.

She didn't feel like lunch but chewed on a couple of dates and a few almonds, had a drink of water, then filled a plastic bottle with more. It was a sunny day. Outside, she shoved her feet into gumboots in case the duck took it upon himself to attack her feet. She gathered her gloves, trowel, weeder and a bucket. The day was chirruping with crickets and cicadas, and the tui was chattering noisily in the kahikatea tree. The duck jumped off his perch under the deck and plodded languidly onto the lawn after her, down to the pond area where she was preparing to do some weeding. She dumped her stuff in the shade.

The news was on.

Breaking news.

Another earthquake in Christchurch. It had only just happened. Bigger than the last one.

It wasn't only the information but the panic in the announcer's voice that was alarming.

Christchurch.

Hannah grabbed the radio and rushed back to the house. She rang Simon's cell phone but was taken straight to his answer phone. She left a message: Ring me. Are you all right?

She rang again. Still the same. Nothing. She paced around the house. Please, please. She sent a text: *Just send me a 'yes' if you're OK.*

She tried to ring Maggie. The same. Then she texted her:

Are you and Toby OK? Do you know where Simon is?

She didn't know Toby's mobile number. Back to the news, and yes it was a bad earthquake. The city centre crumbling, the cathedral. People hurt. Blood, bodies. A bus crushed. 6.3. Not as bad in magnitude as the last one, but closer to the surface and to the city centre. Roads damaged, and that new word again: liquefaction.

Hannah was praying, for heaven's sake. She stood, bumping her forehead against the wall. She pulled at her hair. The radio was now flooded with stories, bad stories. Bricks falling, everywhere bricks falling. And her husband was there. And her heart was clamped in a vice.

Don't ring, they said. The system was overloaded. Only ring for emergencies.

She switched on every radio in the house. The whole house was reverberating with bad news and no news. Helpless, she felt so helpless. The windows. The windows were splattered and cloudy. She hurried down to the laundry and filled a bucket with hot water and white vinegar and detergent. Back in the living area, she started to wipe the windows clean, drying them with crumpled up newspaper until they were sparkling clear. They were nothing but an invisible barrier to the world outside. Then she took a cloth and went around the walls and ceiling, cleaning away smudges and fly spots.

And then she heard from him. A text. *Chaos. Tried to ring you but can't get thru. I'm OK. Maggie and Toby too. Will keep in touch. Love.*

Love?

Then a text from her sister. *Hi. Mercifully we've all escaped injury and major damage. But once again Christchurch is in ruins. Thanks for asking. xxx*

Thank you thank you thank you. She went outside, sat on the bottom step. The duck was back on his perch.

It's all right, she said. Well, it's not all right — it's horrendous — but he's OK.

What's not all right? he replied. I thought you were going to come foraging with me.

She started to cry. She cried and cried, her head buried in the salty warmth of her fingers. Then she stood up.

Fuck you, she said to the duck. This is all because of you.

What? he said. What have I done this time?

FLYING INTO THE SUNSET

She was on the lawn, in the back garden, with the duck. It was just on sunset — the garden was framed with clouds, tinged with luminescent oranges, pinks and gold.

Look at that, she said to the duck. My mother would have loved those clouds. She would have painted them.

The duck flexed his feet onto the tip of his claws and flapped his enormous wings, lifting himself skyward. As he rose, the garden was enveloped in shade. The draft from his wings created a chilling wind that stirred dry leaves about her. And then she realised the dark shadow that was his own had become the night, and he had gone. No signal, no circling, no call of goodbye.

She fell back onto the grass and waited, watching the steady drift of stars. She was pinned through the heart into the ground. And then the stars peeled from the sky, at first one by one, then in showering clusters to land upon her, burying her in a growing heap of crumbled bricks. The seconds marked by her heart-beat either tumbled over-eagerly against each other, or waited in a silence that rushed like the ocean through her ears. She hadn't realised that the process of dying would feel so cold.

The dream was so powerful that she was surprised when she woke up to the cool breeze wafting with the early morning light through the open window. Her bedding had fallen to the floor, and she'd knocked a glass of water from the window sill; the fallen tumbler lay beside the wet patch, soaking the sheet beneath her.

She dressed hurriedly and clomped outside in her gumboots, armed with the leaf rake, to let the duck out. The garden had absorbed the dream from the night before, so much so that she looked to the place where it had occurred, expecting a flattening of the grass or some leftover crumbs from the bricks. She felt uncertain whether the duck would still be there. But he was.

He strutted out from his cage, his tail feathers fanned. Then he stopped. He looked at her, rubbing the back of his neck into the flat heart-shaped terrain between his wings. All she wanted was to pick him up and nurse him comfortingly, as she used to. But she didn't. She offered him a couple of crickets and a cicada, then plodded up the lawn and went inside to ring Simon.

CLAMBERING AWKWARDLY OFF HER HIGH HORSE AND INTO THE FIRE

Why was she so nervous after all those long years of being together?

When he answered, there was a weary wariness in his voice, and when she asked him how he was, he confirmed that, indeed, he was tired. His contract was on hold while the city concentrated on cleaning up.

Where were you when it happened?

In a café, having lunch.

Were you alone?

There was a group of us.

She felt a lunge through her heart as she asked, Is there someone else?

Yes, there was a group of us.

Don't play with me, Simon. Have you found someone else?

You mean, have I found a duck?

Don't be stupid, you know what I mean.

No, tell me what you mean.

Do you love someone else?

The back of her throat was closing, her breath caught like a fly in the web of her chest.

I'm not going to answer that, he said calmly.

Why not? You mean there is — there is, isn't there? Just tell me, Simon.

No, he said. No, I'm not going to tell you, because I want you to know what it feels like to doubt whether the person you love most in the world reciprocates that love. I want you to think about things, as I've been forced to think about things.

That's cruel.

Yes. It does feel cruel, doesn't it? It hurts. Oh, yes.

So I think about things and then what?

Don't know. Depends what conclusion you come to.

I've been thinking all the time, and I miss you.

Do you have any idea what it's like here? How's your duck?

Come back home, Simon.

This conversation is becoming more and more insignificant by the minute. Everything is in ruins here.

Everything is in ruins here, too.

You have no idea. No drinking water, no sewerage. The ground bubbling with putrid liquefaction. Mud everywhere. Rubble everywhere. Dust, filth. Roads twisted and cracked open.

So, come back home.

I can't. There's too much to do here. Shovelling mud, looking for people who *really* need help. There was a man, a man screaming, and no one could get to him under tonnes of rubble, no one. All of us trying, scrabbling through broken concrete, but it was impossible, and he screamed on and on and then he was whimpering and then it stopped. Mercifully. But then, that meant . . . I don't know who he was, but I wonder, I think about him . . .

She could hear him crying. There was a gulp of breath and then there was nothing.

Simon?

She waited.

Anyway, he said. Anyway.

I'm sorry, she said.

Well, yes.

I truly am.

Eventually we all get to an age when we are forced to re-evaluate our lives. It's probably not a bad thing.

Please . . . Simon. His name stuck in her throat.

So . . . It's nice to be needed. But anyway, I've got to go.

She heard him sigh.

Yes, of course, of course, she said.

There was a silence. She knew he was still there, and then, she knew, he wasn't.

GAGARIN

The duck was on the deck looking at her sitting on the sofa with the phone still on her lap. His beak tapping at the window, bap bap bap. Bippity bap bap bap. He sidled away and wandered over to pick up a twig, his feet slap slap slapping at the boards, like an old woman uncertain as to what to do with the long day ahead. He was dependent upon her, as her mother had been. He was waiting for her to go down to the garden and pull out weeds and all she wanted to do was shoot him. Without her, he felt useless. He *was* useless. She was the foil through which he had a misguided sense of his own value in the world. Just like her old mother when she came to stay, with that sense of still being the mother and she the child, when in fact the relationship had shifted to the reverse. And she, she was the mother of nobody. How on earth did she get into this predicament? Without the duck, her husband would still be here with her. Though of course, without her husband, she wouldn't have had the duck.

And what would Yuri Gagarin think of this? This pathetic dance of love and hate and yearning that, from the heavens, would not even have the significance of moths rising towards the moon.

The Earth has a beautiful blue halo. The sky is black. I can see stars. Oh yes, but wait. Oh, there's a woman with a duck, and they seem to be looking for crickets and worms.

The Earth plates shift and a man cries and cries and no one comes. A duck cries and she comes, and the man goes away.

And now no one can hear her own cries, and it just so happens that the Earth is cracking apart and the man is standing in ruins.

DECISION

The next day she rang again.

Simon, she said. I'm coming down. I've decided.

The relief, the flooding of relief, as she told him this. She had to hold herself back from tears because it was so simple, so obvious. Now that she'd decided, she was impatient to head on her way. She would drive down, bring her work with her, leave the duck in Te Awamutu, and continue onwards.

No, Hannah, he said carefully. I don't think so. Things aren't good here.

That's OK, I can help. Just tell me what to bring, what's needed down there. I'll load up the car.

What we need, what we really need, is for things to be as stable as possible amidst the chaos. It's not the right time for marriage counselling. Anyway, he added, and again that tone of voice: you have your duck.

It's all organised. Claire and Bob. I haven't asked them yet, but—

I'm sorry, Hannah. I don't know how else to say this: I don't want you down here right now. Don't come. No surprises. Please.

Hannah felt winded. She rubbed her bare arm. She was suddenly cold.

Hannah?

Finally, she said, So . . . are you planning to come back at all?

Of course. We need to talk, I know that. I just can't give *us* much attention as things are at the moment. What's happened here has brought everything into a sharpened focus. It's messy in more ways than one.

What do you mean?

I can't say, but I'll tell you everything.

Are you staying with Maggie and Toby?

Yes, I am.

Is Toby well?

Why do you ask?

Is he?

He's better than he was.

Simon. What's happening there? Apart from the earthquake. You could offer me an explanation at least.

I'm exhausted, he said. Please, Hannah. Can you please be patient?

I presume you have your car.

Yes. Dennis drove it down. I flew with Maggie and Toby.

Oh? So Dennis was in on this, too? Well, that's great. The whole bloody family. The whole extended scheming lot of you. And I thought this was about you and me, but it seems I don't even figure. I apologise for bothering you when you are so tired. I'm sorry for trying to make amends in the middle of an earthquake. Give my love to everybody, and goodbye — I'll get on with my own life.

Love? he said. Oh, Hannah, that's nice to hear you say the word. I haven't heard it from you for a while.

It takes two, you know.

Do you have any idea what it is like down here?

No, Simon, and that's because you're not communicating. You're trying to make me feel selfish.

I can't cope with that sort of talk right now. I have to go, Hannah. Let's just chew things over, shall we, and talk when we're more centred.

How can I chew things over when you haven't given me any meat?

Goodbye for now, Hannah.

He hung up. She was mad with herself for not disconnecting first. She thought about bundling the duck into a box and getting into the car and driving down there anyway. But he was right; she couldn't arrive in Christchurch with all her pitiful emotional baggage stuffed in the boot of her car while Christchurch was suffering in such a real way.

Chapter 22

IF THE SHOE FITS

Hannah had a yearning to scrub and scrub and scrub, with her hands immersed in warm, frothy water. She gathered a jersey that needed hand-washing and carefully snuck to the laundry around the side of the house to avoid the duck, who was strutting and posturing along the railing of the deck. On the path outside the laundry, she'd left a couple of white towels for the washing machine. The taps were running to fill the tub.

But suddenly he was there, at her feet. Not Dr Duckell, but Mr Hyde, the wolverine in duck's clothing. Her feet, in black leather shoes with toes covered but with a mound of skin exposed, were the prey. He was consumed by that unstoppable madness. She knew that look in his eye. He was tearing at her feet, the shoes, and, then, he stopped. Focusing on her face, positioning his feet. He was preparing to fly up at her. She grabbed a large blue plastic bucket and popped it over the top of him. Just like that.

His craziness was contained apart from a wildly wagging tail outside the bucket. The bucket was jiggling under her hand, but she swivelled her body around it and sped out from the laundry, up the side path to the front door and inside. She locked the door. And then she remembered the taps, hot and cold, gushing into the tub.

She rushed out the back way through the ranch sliders, grabbing the leaf rake. Over the deck and down to the laundry where the duck was skulking, now liberated from the bucket. Shielded behind the leaf rake, she sidled around him to reach the taps. But again he threw himself at her, under the rake, over the rake, under the rake, with unwavering focus. Keep calm, she reminded herself. She was cornered. She used the bucket trick again, to make an escape to the front door as before, but of course it was locked.

And there he was.

She sped back down again to the back, kicking off her shoes as a red herring, and darted into the laundry. The shoes were no red herring: he had what he wanted. She was now relegated to onlooker as he pecked and pecked at the little black shoes. His beak within the toe piece, his feet clasping the heel as if he was urgently struggling to clamber inside them, the whole quivering feathery tail-wagging duck of himself, desperate, so desperately intent on *being in* her shoes, and she felt he would turn himself inside out if he could. Then he tossed the shoes high into the air several times, willing the two dead useless black birds to move, to fly, to *move* why don't you? He grabbed them again. And then it was the towel. One shoe and the towel. The shoe one end and the towel the other, his neck outstretched, his tail wiggling, and then she saw it. She saw the little lump. Just a wee peep, whether before or after the .36 seconds she didn't know. Just a pink and shiny lump peeping from behind the belly feathers, no twenty centimetres of wayward corkscrew. He lay there, quieter now, grasping the shoes, the towel; the towel the nearest thing he could find that resembled the ravishing white duck that the overnight educator told him would be waiting for him one day.

So, the woman thought, he definitely is a boy, then. She'd always known, but now she knew.

An overwhelming sense of despair settled upon her. She felt responsible for this creature's isolation, his inability to be a fully operational duck, separated from his own kind. The only nourishment she could offer him was a few handfuls of corn. She was crushed by the dysfunctional nature of it all. Once again she'd found herself in the situation of rendering food and shelter to extend the life of another creature that was so lonely and out of kilter with its true self that it might be better off dead.

Afterwards, he gave the impression of being embarrassed, as she made her way past him to the deck. He plodded laboriously up the steps. His demeanour was one of utter despondency. For once, he wouldn't look at her.

Duckie? she said.

He ignored her. On the railing, he attempted a full wash in his water tray. Then he flew down to the pond. She could hear the savage batting of wings against water as he performed his ablutions. Then he stood on the stones preening every feather, as if in an effort to cleanse himself of the whole grubby episode.

JUSTIFICATION: A THOUGHT IN THE NIGHT

Was sex with a towel and a shoe any less meaningful than making love with no hope of procreation? At least it was sparing some poor muscovy female duck the indignity of being conquered by a ferocious brute having his way with her as well as all the others he could jump. There didn't seem to be any satisfaction in it for the female duck, especially if you considered that even Nature was on her side, designing her bits to counter the twirling dervish components of her assailant.

Hannah turned over, thumped her pillow, and drifted back to her fitful sleep, still not reassured.

BLOW-UP DOLL

Hannah surprised the duck by appearing around the corner of the house. She'd been out in the car and she was carrying a huge plastic bag. The duck flew onto the magnolia branch, pacing backwards and forwards, shuddering and huffing, his crest erect.

Ducko, she called. I have something for you. The duck bent his knees and ejected himself from the branch to fly down to greet her, almost toppling as he landed. She had her little black shoes on and he dived for her feet.

Wait, wait, wait, she cried. She dipped into the bag and brought out a fresh, white and fluffy Dacron pillow. She dangled it at his head, then tossed it down in front of him. He jumped on top of it, his beak clamped on a corner, his tail waggling desperately, his eyes glazed.

Ducko, she said, I'd like you to meet Annabel. Your new best friend.

MEETING THE NEIGHBOURS

As he soared down from the deck railing, the duck looked as though he could go anywhere. There was nothing stopping him. He'd launch himself from the railing and twirl around the magnolia tree, on his way to South America, or back to his birthplace of Te Awamutu. He'd hear the call of the wild, feel the forces of the changing seasons and join a V-shaped convoy of huffing muscovies heading south. Or north. Or east or west. Wherever.

But in fact it wasn't like that at all.

He'd take off and head towards her in the garden. There was an air of panic about him as he came in to land beside her, his feet tumbling over themselves to prevent his chest and neck hitting the ground. He'd grown into a feathery lump with wings, big hard wings with elbows that clouted her on the side of the head. And he didn't *go* anywhere. He was able to recognise her boundaries, and trusted them as his own.

On the odd occasion, though, he had crashed across the borders in error. Once she was weeding under the feijoa tree by the shed. He flew from the pond towards her and over the tree. There was nowhere to land but in the yard of their back neighbour. She had to rush out of the gate and down the right-of-way and up the path to her neighbours' house. Knocking on the door, with the leaf rake in one hand, she felt that she'd landed inside that Grant Wood Gothic painting, except the pitchfork was a leaf rake and the man wasn't there beside her.

Excuse me, I'm your neighbour and I think my duck is in your backyard.

Oh how cute, you have a duck?! said the woman, with three kids of various heights peering at her in their dressing gowns, freshly bathed and bundled up behind their friendly mother.

Would you like to come in? We were just saying the other day we need to know our neighbours.

Thanks, I'm sorry I'd love to, but . . . he needs to go to bed, before it's dark.

Oh? Of course, said the mother with her brood of children as if that all made perfect sense.

Hannah went around the back of the house and there he was, stomping through a precious vegie patch towards her, grunting and huffing, into the towel she had brought to wrap around him in case he panicked.

The neighbour opened a window and called out.

Ooh, is he safe? He's enormous. What's wrong with his face? It looks like a monkey's bottom. He looks like a vulture.

He's a duck, a muscovy duck. Hannah tried not to be too arch.

A what?

Muscovy. Muscovy duck. Well, a drake, in fact. They're from Mexico.

Oh really, did you bring him over specially?

Hannah escaped with the wrapped-up duck tucked against her body, clutching his wriggling feet through the towel until they quietened — the hands of a frightened child in her grasp. The leaf rake swivelled under her other arm.

What if he strayed again? And what if one of those children had been playing in the backyard with red sandals and soft white feet and bare arms. Would that have set him off?

Even though she was the only person or thing he had attacked so far, she couldn't honestly say that he was safe.

As she climbed back up the public right-of-way behind the hedge, the woman took the opportunity to have the talk she'd been rehearsing for some time.

Ducko, it's time you have to go. You're not happy here and we can't do this anymore.

What do you mean, I have to go? What do you mean, I'm not happy here?

Well, escaping like that.

I didn't escape. I didn't have anywhere else to land. You were hiding beneath the tree. I wanted to be by you. Really, what do you mean: not *happy* here? What have I done now?

You're potentially a dangerous bird. Nothing is the same anymore. The feral in you is boiling under your feathers. Just look at your face.

You're insulting. And that woman in the house. Monkey's bottom, indeed!

I know, that was rude. But anyway, Duckie, the man isn't going to come back until you've gone.

Ah. So that's what it's about. I hate the man. I always knew he had it in for me.

He struggled under her arm through the towel and swung his neck around to peck at her. They were at the top now, in the street. A car went past. He panicked, all bone and dragon-fire and pumping needle-claw feet dragging through the skin of her arm. She managed to unclasp the latch to the gate and contain him long enough to release him onto the steps down the garden path, where he belly-flopped down one step then another, a ball of legs and wings and towel and huff. He spun around and started for her gumboots, but she grabbed the leaf rake and held it between them.

By the front door was another pillow, one of several replica Annabels, planted there for such a situation. She managed to shuffle her way there with the rake between them, and sure enough, all his fervour was immediately directed to Annabel.

Truce. For now.

Chapter 23

HOTEL DU BACKYARD

Several mornings later, when she was releasing the duck for the day, she discovered a freshly dug tunnel leading from the lawn into the cage. Inside, the ground was scattered with feathers and maize. The duck was unsettled, quivering and side-stepping.

She'd been putting it off, but while the duck was still with her, even temporarily, it was time to do something about his night shelter. It hadn't been satisfactory for some time. He was a perching duck, as Simon had revealed. She'd found images of feral muscovies with their great clawed feet curled around branches in trees. His preference for standing all day along the deck railing or the limbs of the magnolia tree indicated that he liked to be elevated. Apart from that one branch on that tree, there were no other suitable large branches in the trees on their property.

The duck's cage came up to her thigh. There was no room for stretching upright or flapping his wings within this space that had seemed so enormous when Simon had built it for the wee duckling. The duck now had to lower his head to make his way into his bed each night. He was an old man crawling into a hole, his dreams cramped into a matchbox.

So now this latest evidence of a night-time intruder, lured by his food, forced Hannah to act.

She had to force the key into the pitted old keyhole before it would turn. The door opened stiffly and lopsidedly, one of the hinges loosely hanging from its screw in the frame. She emptied the shed, then set to with a broom, bucket and hose, working on the network of spiders' webs that looped and hung from one wall to another. When she was overtaken with a spate of fierce sneezing, the duck, outside amongst the kikuyu grass, stood erect, whinnying.

She gathered Simon's books from the shelf and took them outside onto the plastic matting she'd brought down for the purpose. Back inside, she swished soapy water across the shelves, the workbench and the bench seat beneath it. She hosed it down. She cleaned the sill and window, heaving it open onto the catch. The interior was beginning to smell almost fresh.

As the shed dried in the hot breeze, she positioned herself in the doorway, and one by one she flicked through the books to release their dust into the air. She wiped each cover with a cloth and slid them in lots into supermarket bags. University textbooks, engineering books, project notebooks. She felt a twist of sadness when she saw her husband's jottings and markings, the highlighting and underlining and diagrams that meant nothing to her. Once again she was reminded of the differences between them. But somehow they had complemented each other. He was a fastidious man; it was evident in his handwriting, small and neat with a gentle slant backwards. He was logical, with a whole world of knowledge filed away neatly inside him. She was dreamy, with everything she had ever known shoved erratically into her attic mind, the stuffing of non-descript old sacks.

Amongst papers and certificates was a letter of her own, written to Simon. It was a loving letter, contemplative, missing him. Her grandmother had just died and Hannah had been accompanying her mother on holiday. Her letter expressed concern about her mother, who, after the years of caring for her own ailing mother, was faced with the sudden emptiness in which the grief for her husband, Hannah's father, was re-visited.

Hannah paused in her reading. *Was* he her father? Did it matter? How much did *knowing* a thing change the subsequent living of a life? Or a life in retrospect? It didn't change the outcome unless a person acted upon the information.

Her mother's thinking and expression had been so woolly towards the end that the statement about Hannah's father was most likely a spasm of nonsense. Hannah asked herself why she should cling to the notion as if it had significance. She could have her DNA tested against Maggie's, but what good would that do? She had no children or grandchildren for whom she had responsibility to pass on genetic information. Whoever her father was, her branch of the family tree stopped right with her. Simon and Hannah Baker.

The final destination.

Terminus. Everybody disembark from here.

The duck had been sitting on his belly peaceably in the shade, his fluffy eyelids closed, but he perked up and waggled his tail when the woman dropped the letter onto her lap.

What's up? he said.

I've just had a thought, she said. I've always thought of you as an orphan. But your father, he's probably still alive. Do you remember him?

My father is a father amongst many fathers, he said. He didn't recognise me as his. There were many fathers, and they all had a part in the killing of my brothers and sisters, once my mother was killed so brutally.

Oh, is that so? That's awful. But you mentioned, once, something about your parents loving each other forever, if your mother had been still alive.

It was a romantic whim. I liked the idea of it. But I know more about life now. I'm grown up.

The woman thought of the pillows she had distributed around the property, and how they'd since become a replacement for the towels and her feet that he had so fiercely interacted with. His lady pillow love. His blow-up duck-doll.

Do you think about the other ducks, back at the place of your birth?

No. I just want to be with you.

That's nice, Ducko.

Are we going foraging?

I'm cleaning out your hotel. I'm trying to make you happy.

I *am* happy, he said.

I'm not sure who my father is, either.

Of course. Is anybody? he said.

Well, I was, but now I have unreasonable doubt.

Are you being riddley again? He stood up and plodded over to a dish, slurping up water then lifting his beak like a bottle into the air. Glug glug glug glug glug.

Hannah sighed and continued to dust and wipe down the books.

One of the notebooks held a collection of black-and-white photos kept together in a small plastic bag, sealed with Sellotape. She picked at the tape with her fingernail and opened the bag, shuffling the photos into her open palm.

There were photos of Simon when he was young. Younger than she'd ever known him. One of him sitting at a piano, his fingers still positioned on the keyboard, his head turned towards the camera, his mouth open in surprise. His dark hair falling around his face with a wavy Beatle fringe. Cheeks still padded with youth. Only the beginnings of facial hair. Sun streamed in through a window across the floor and a settee. A vase of daisies sat on a table, and a little white dog slept on a mat in a strip of sun.

Another of an Asian girl, laughing, sitting on the same settee, her hand outstretched towards the photographer. She looked mischievous, tiny, dressed in a fitting skirt and woollen skivvy. Her hair black and long, flicked back from her shoulders.

Another of the same girl with, presumably, her family or friends at an Asian restaurant. There were several pictures of Simon with the girl. One walking down an unidentifiable city street, hand-in-hand; one sitting on rocks with the Sydney Harbour bridge behind them; another with the two of them in a cosy embrace — she, grinning flirtatiously, on Simon's knee in a kitchen, his arms locked around her, enfolding her stomach.

The last photo was of the same girl in a hospital bed, clutching a swaddled baby. She looked exhausted. The monochromatic tones lent her face a drained, ghostly appearance, although as well there seemed to be a vacancy of expression that was almost disturbing.

And with the photos was a letter on thin, crisp paper.

Dear Simon,
I found these photos when we were going through Tuyen's belongings and I thought you might like to have them. There is no need to reply. My parents would not be happy if they knew I was writing to you. But I thought it would be better for you to think of her and everything that happened. My mother cries all the time and hardly eats. My father is angry and won't talk to anybody. They blame themselves for trusting you.
Yours sincerely,
Ron

Hannah went through the photos and the letter again and again, before placing them back in the plastic bag, apart from the rest of the books, which she continued to dust and bag, on the look-out for more revelations. Her chest felt stretched and hollow. She gathered the books and stacked them up on the cleaned shelves.

She put the duck's dish and plastic-covered cushion from his old hutch on the floor. Covered the cushion with one of his clean white towels. She placed a waterproof pillow covered with a towel on the workbench in case he wanted to sleep elevated. Replaced all the gardening implements on the hooks.

She turned around to see the duck on the top step.

What's going on? he said.

I told you. It's your new upgraded place. Five-star hotel. Come inside. Sit on your towel. You'll like it.

No, said the duck. I mean, why are you so angry? Why are you throwing everything around? What have I done now?

Nothing.

What's up?

She faced him.

Nothing is *up*, OK?

He splayed his legs, rubbing his neck over his back feathers, his crest erect. His wings starting to splay.

OK, settle down, none of that, I'm sorry I yelled.

She picked him up and sat on the step. He huffed and houghed.

I'm upset that's all. The man.

The man isn't here.

No.

So?

All these years. No babies because he said he was infertile. He said he'd had mumps when he was eighteen and that he couldn't have children. And now it looks as though he's already had a child. And never a mention. All these years. You think you know somebody. And you don't.

I told you, though. *I* told you. Remember?

You don't have to be so cocky. My God, life is weird, I tell you.

It's only as weird as you make it.

Sorry, Ducko. It's weird. Full-stop. Look at us. Are you my mother? Are you my child? Are you a duck I have to look after because you were dumped on me? Are you a duck I can't get rid of because you've eaten half my mother? Who and where is my father? Dead or alive? Where's my husband and where is his child? My brain is bursting with confusion.

That's rather dismissive of you. Perhaps we are friends merely because we like each other? Have you ever thought of *that* during your moments of in-depth amateur philosophising?

She folded her hands around his body, clamping his wings, and swivelled herself around to release him onto the scrubbed damp boards inside the shed.

Well, that's all beside the point. Welcome to your new abode. Hotel du Backyard.

The duck waddled to the cushion, his beak swaying beneath it, pecking tentatively. He then checked his bowl. He investigated the edges and corners of the shed, his tail jiggling urgently.

There's a bed on the mezzanine floor, she said. Room service some time after sunrise. I'll see you later. I have a lot of things to contemplate.

She strode up to the house and through it to the other side, through the front door and up the garden path. Through the streets towards the sea. She longed for someone to run after her reassuringly, to walk by her side, to sit alongside her on the sea wall, to casually make sense of her life. She had nothing now but a duck, and he wasn't going to follow her past the gate.

The air temperature was dropping. A corner of the sky was gathering into darkness, thick plumes of grumbling thunder. Elsewhere, the sky was teal blue.

Once at the beach, she continued past the stone wall, trudging across the sand into the mucky lagoons stranded by the low tide. The water squelching over her sandals, then lapping over her ankles. There was no one in the sea except a mother wallowing in the shallows with two kids, a boy and a girl, who were digging into the sand for pipi.

Hannah waded towards them, her arms folded deeply into her waist. She watched the children giggling as they attempted to catch the retreating tongue tips of each shellfish, squirting each other with the jet of spit as the shell clammed shut.

It must be nice having children, she said to the woman.

The mother hauled herself erect, a heave of water cascading from her. She was fat; her breasts, her hips stuffed into floral black togs. Her legs meaty, solidly earthed. Her arms as well. Her skin stretched over large cheeks, her long black hair pulled back severely from her forehead. Her eyes wary as Hannah said, It must be the best thing in the whole world. I've got a duck, but it's not the same.

That did it. One round hand grabbing a small hand, the other hand grasping another. Two children complaining as they were dragged behind their mother, looking over their shoulders at this strange dishevelled woman in all her clothes, her trousers clinging to her legs. On the sand the mother was wrapping them up in towels now, wrapping them up tight in bright parcels. She hoisted a rug and a bulging bag over her shoulder. They traipsed through the sand to a car.

For a while Hannah stood alone. All the sea, all the empty sea, all the tears. All the rumbling sky, sucking up the remaining blue, preparing to rain. All the futile days gone by, a trundler pulled behind a tramp looking for a downy hollow to lay a weary head. All the hollow straws, the short straws, the last straws. The drained cups, the empty eyes, the desiccated remains of a life that had spent its best. All the rambling shambling life that had led to this moment. Over. It had come to this. Her existence had been reduced to this unutterably monstrous loneliness.

Stupid.

A few stragglers on the beach were beginning to hurry to their cars. High above, seagulls, luminous flecks cast off by the moon, were stirring a deep purple potion borrowed from the night. And when it did rain, the whole black bowl tipped upon her, pitting the sea, drenching her immediately. She remained there, licking at the water pouring over her face, into her clothes, down her back, passively accepting the onslaught because she felt too tired and too wet to do anything else. After the first drops, the water wasn't cold. If she stayed there for long enough, the tide would rise and swallow her up, and then she wouldn't ever have to do anything again, ever. Ever ever ever.

Suddenly through the growling rain she heard a high-pitched voice.

A woman in a yellow sundress and green cardigan, under an enormous golf umbrella, her shoes nosing the water's edge, was leaning forward to call through the downpour.

Excuse me . . . excuuuse me . . . I say . . .

Hannah looked around. There was no one apart from her in the sea.

Are you needing help out there? You're getting awfully wet.

She didn't know this person who was trying to save a drowning dog without a lifeline.

The woman was kicking off her shoes, tucking her skirt up and wading unsteadily towards her. And now there was a manicured hand on Hannah's arm, coaxing movement from the statue that she'd become. Hannah looked at the smooth skin, the slim fingers with their sculptured pink nails. They would click nicely on a tabletop, she thought, and impatiently should that be the need. A substantial silver ring curled around the middle finger. The rain was catching the back of her ballooned skirt and falling onto her firm tanned calves.

Come on, dear, the woman was saying, tugging at Hannah's T-shirt. Come on now. You'll catch a chill. Here. There's enough room under this umbrella for two. Come along now.

They both sloshed through the water, Hannah following obediently, while the woman continued her banter, her cheeriness only just masking a tone of condescension.

I'm Monica. I was reading in the car; I like to come and read by the sea. I looked up to watch the front head towards us. It was tremendously dramatic. So intensely powerful and foreboding. And then I saw you out there, as if you'd come down in the rain and didn't know where you were. I thought something must be terribly wrong. Is there anyone I can ring for you, dear?

Back on the sand Hannah stepped away from the shelter of the umbrella into the pelting rain. Water cascaded through her hair and into her eyes, her mouth.

Can I take you somewhere? Let me *take* you somewhere. At least get out of this rain until it's over. Can I get you a cup of tea or coffee? Have you had lunch? Where's your car?

I'm sorry. I'm not far away. I need to walk. I'll be fine.

It was the first time she'd spoken. Her voice gave Monica a jolt, shifting her attitude. She seemed disappointed.

Hannah faced her rescuer. She saw the concerned intelligent eyes, the lipstick, the amber pendant hanging against her sun-weathered chest, the estuary of tiny wrinkles leading into her cleavage, her compassionate curiosity encapsulated under the umbrella.

She was tempted to follow this woman and blurt out the whole sorry tale. Her mother, the duck, her husband leaving her and how she missed him so dreadfully, yes she did, and even now with the discovery of his deception. And Eric, did he fit into this anywhere? If they had been sitting over a table in the warmth somewhere she might have opened all the dull little boxes of her life and pulled out the details for this stranger, then and there.

Instead she said, I'm sorry. Truly, I'm sorry. I was being stupid. I wasn't thinking. Or maybe I was thinking too much.

But you are so *wet*.

I know. I would swamp your car. Thank you, Monica. I'm fine now. And I must get back to my duck. She meant this last statement to be light-hearted, funny, but instead she saw the woman looking at her pityingly.

The rain suddenly ceased. The bowl was empty. She thanked Monica again and made her way across the sand, across the park and headed for home and a warm bath. Her clothes were sopping. She found herself missing, of all people, Toby. And, as she often did since the Christmas visit, she wondered about him, wondered how he was.

RAIN CHICK

The bowl wasn't empty. It continued to pour intermittently for the rest of the afternoon. The duck was back up on his magnolia branch, staring at her through the window as she tried to work at the table. His tail, normally a live perky thing forever poised to waggle, now drooped downward, woefully still, a conduit for the water pouring over him. It was the guttering for his leaky roof feathers. His wings resembled an arrangement of picked-over fish spines, dribbling brown juices.

A large drop formed under his belly and hung there. He looked utterly dejected, yet he wouldn't go for shelter, even though he was capable of flying down into his new shed, or the old cage, or taking refuge under the deck, where at least he would be out of the rain.

His miserable presence ate into Hannah's concentration. He'd become a reflection of herself, his demeanour mocking her. She couldn't work. She took him some corn, which he touched with his beak but couldn't or wouldn't summon the energy to eat. When she held a handful under his beak, coaxing him gently, he gave her a decisive nip, not hard but as a warning. She returned inside, sat down at her computer again.

His saturated feathers made him look thin, diminished; all that pompy roundness had been just fluff and air. She knew now that muscovy ducks, being tropical ducks from Central America, were less waterproof than most ducks, and could chill in cold wet conditions.

She was worried that he might develop pneumonia. He had pulled himself into himself and was *tolerating* the cold, the wet, the indignity.

Finally she couldn't stand it any longer. She slipped on her raincoat, grabbed a towel and went out to him once more, wrapping him up firmly as she used to when he was a duckling. She took him in her arms and brought him inside to sit on her lap. He wriggled against the towel at first, but once she was seated, he quietened. She pressed the towel into his feathers. Already it was soaked. Her coat was dripping puddles onto the floor. He grunted and poked his neck into the fuggy heated air.

There you are, Ducko, she said. That's better, isn't it?

The duck was now nudging his beak up the sleeve of her wet coat. Perhaps it *was* possible to live together harmoniously. And when he closed his white feathery eyelids, and his beak upon her hand became heavy with sleep, she was thinking, as she tucked him closer into herself, that really, she would sacrifice anything, anything at all, to make him happy.

Later she slipped into her gumboots and took him outside, still secured in the towel. By this time he was struggling against the strait-jacket, his beak swinging to peck her. She carried him to his new shed.

Inside, she released him from the towel. He landed inelegantly on his chest, but picked himself up and pecked at his bed. He stood on tiptoes and flapped his enormous wings. Yes, he liked his new house. He shimmied like a dog, a cloud of droplets spraying from his feathers. He dredged his breast and belly feathers, lifting his beak to drink from his sodden self. But when she started to shut the door, he stiffened, staring at her in disbelief.

Just until it stops raining, she assured him, and squelched her way back to the house while the rain thundered on the tin roof of his roomy dwelling.

Chapter 24

The next day the storm had cleared. She had a deadline to meet, so worked inside through the morning until she'd finished the job and couriered it away. The sense of relief she had when she'd completed a project was liberating.

She took herself into the garden. The duck was sucking at murky puddles looking for worms and grubs while Hannah picked up branches and raked leaves. She kept the rake ready in case he made a dive towards her, but since he'd had access to his multiple Annabels, their relationship had improved.

Er . . . hello there, Hannah. The hedge was dancing, wildly showering droplets. Eric's daughter emerged. Her brown hair was a tangle of dreads pulled up into a multi-tail of octopus.

Oh, hi there, Sheila. How's things with you? As usual Sheila was colourful, in her lime-green tights and two layers of long chocolate-brown singlets. Hannah noted how fresh and clear her skin was, how strong and upright she held herself within the frame of dripping leaves.

Good thanks. But I was just wanting to talk to you about Dad.

And then Rosemary was pushing through the foliage, running over to clutch her mother's green leg.

I've got a pink rabbit, she said.

The duck side-stepped up to the group.

The chicken's got a red face, she said, reaching out to him. He's shivering. His tail's wagging. He's breathing at me.

It's a duck, said Hannah. Not a chicken. But keep away from him, there's a good girl. He gets a bit pecky sometimes.

And indeed his wing feathers were flat and he was doing that sidling waddle around them.

It's OK, I'll watch her, said Sheila. No, but I was just wondering if you've noticed anything funny about Dad recently.

Hannah gripped the rake, resting the handle under her chin.

I certainly have. For one, he's hardly spoken to me for months. Ages. Something out of the blue seems to have upset him. And for another . . . She hesitated, reluctant to expose all the details of Eric's night-time escapade to his daughter. Well, for another he was gallivanting around in the garden here a while ago. Not making much sense. I can't make him out. Why? Is he funny with you, too?

Rosemary had picked up a twig and was now poking at the duck.

Honestly, please don't tease the duck. He might bite.

Sheila directed the little girl away from the agitated duck, her hand splayed across her chest.

I'd organised for him to babysit Rosemary this afternoon, but when I arrived just now he'd forgotten. He was dressed, but I swear he was in bed when I got here. And he's usually tidy, but his house is a mess. There's stuff everywhere. Clothes. Newspapers, still folded and obviously unread. Plates of half-eaten food. He was following me around the house almost suspiciously. Scary. I don't know whether it'd be safe to leave Rosemary with him. I don't know. But I thought you might be able to shed light on the situation.

Rosemary ran around her mother's leg, a tadpole darting around a frog.

I wish I could. I'm sorry to hear this, but in a way it makes more sense of what's been happening. I thought it was something to do with me or us, but . . . Perhaps he needs to see a doctor?

I suggested that, but he was quite affronted and refused point-blank. 'Whaddo I need to see a friggin doctor for?' She lowered her voice and filled it with gruff.

Hmmm, that makes it difficult.

They were interrupted by a fist banging against glass, then Eric's bedroom window opening above them.

Sheila! What's going on? What are you doing over there! His face flaming, his grey hair sprouting like hillside tussock over a fire. He disappeared inside again.

Would you like me to look after Rosemary?

Sheila hesitated. It's OK. Max is going to play with a friend after kindy, so I was just going to catch up with friends. Coffee, you know. Easily cancelled. I'll try and organise Dad and tidy up a bit. But thank you. Are you OK? You're looking tired. You've lost a lot of weight.

Oh, have I? Maybe.

And how's Simon? I haven't seen either of you for ages.

He's good. He's down in Christchurch on a contract.

Christchurch!

Yes, I know, but he's fine. He's staying with my sister and her husband. They're luckier than some.

Will he be there long?

With this earthquake, his contract has been extended. So we don't know exactly.

Rather him than me. Oh well, better get up there to Dad. Actually, perhaps you *could* look after Rose — just for half an hour, while I get the place organised a bit. If he lets me. Would that be possible?

Of course! Hannah bent down and picked up the child, settling her on her hip, guiding her legs to wrap around her back and stomach.

Is that a flower on your pocket? And look . . . pretty flowers round your trouser legs.

She was dressed in purple velvet overalls, with a pink jersey underneath. Hannah's fingers, still in the rubber gloves she used when gardening, pointed out the cuff design.

They're pink, said Rosemary, pulling a tent of rubber glove from Hannah's hand and twanging it back. Why is your skin coming off?

I'm moulting. I'm growing a new pink one underneath.

Sheila forged her way back through the hedge. Eric. She could hear him, already down on the lawn, waiting for Sheila on other side.

What in the world are you doing over there? Where's Rosemary?

And there he was exploding through the hedge, cracking branches as he surged, a wild creature from the depths, bursting through for air. His face livid and twisting, his chest foaming with fury.

What are you doing with my granddaughter? Give her back to me. This minute!

His grasping fiddling hands. And now Sheila, back.

Dad. Dad, calm down.

Rosemary wailed, her pink woolly arms extended for her mother. Both Eric and Sheila were vying to take the child from Hannah, who was stretching to pass her to Sheila. As she stepped away from Eric she caught her foot on brick garden edging. She started to topple. Snatched at a handful of Eric's shirt to regain her balance. Sheila lunged to rescue Rosemary, crashing head-on with her father, butting goats clunking temple against temple. They all fell to the ground, grunting and screeching. Hannah, still clutching Eric's shirt, pulled him on top of her as she went. Sheila, reeling from the head clash, managed to seize Rosemary before she crashed alongside Eric and Hannah. They all came to rest on the soggy lawn.

There was a moment's pause. Even Rosemary stopped her screaming, as everyone assessed the damage. Eric's face was turned away, tucked in the crook of Hannah's arm. His head smelt personal, almost rank. He needed a shower. She could see the droopy lined flesh of his ear lobe, a dark sprig of hair sprouting from the moist cave of his ear, hair that he used to keep neatly clipped. She could have lifted her hand and rested her fingers over his forehead, but she didn't. Instead she started laughing uncontrollably, her belly contorting, taking Eric bouncing alongside her. Rosemary was bawling again. Sheila lifted her head to glare at Hannah while she pacified Rosemary. They could all have been lying in the grass on a summer's day, replete after a picnic, such was their abandoned pose.

Then, the duck.

Sidling up to them, up to her, panting, his mouth open, tutting and clucking, his crimson head towering above her, tipped to view her, his black eye rimmed with scheming yellow lodged in crimson lava. She could see the sky through his nostrils. She stopped laughing and tried to pull away from Eric who, she realised, had her pinned down. The duck moved in, tentatively, piercing her with that mad eye. Edging closer, still tutting, then hesitantly pecking at her jersey, her hair.

No no, Ducko. Eric, Eric, she said. Move! But then she realised his wings weren't flat. He was anxious, concerned, but not aggressive.

Ducko, she said, I'm fine. We're all OK. She tugged herself away from beneath Eric's back. His head dropped to the grass. He snorted.

Oh, no. Sheila. Your dad. Eric. Quick.

Sheila put Rosemary down and together they linked arms to help Eric upright. His head lolled, dribble leaking from the side of his mouth.

Quick, she said to Sheila. Get a pillow and a blanket and call an ambulance.

Sheila tore through the hedge again. I meant from my place, Hannah called, but it didn't matter. She had positioned herself behind Eric's shoulders, his head on her lap. She placed her open hand through his shirt onto his chest, her palm moving across hair, across the cushy padding of flesh that had not been there eleven years ago. And beneath it, eventually she located a distant drum against his ribs.

Rosemary was starting to burrow through the hedge after her mother.

Ssssh, sweetie, Mummy's coming back. Come here and stand with Poppa.

But Rosemary continued to the other side.

And now she did run her hands over his hair, his face, sticky with cold sweat, rough with more than a day's bristle. Eric, it's all going to be all right, she told him. Whatever it is, we'll have it sorted. His face grey, his lips purple. His creamy feet standing up from his trousers, his toes knobbled and wayward, ten sparsely-bearded and blank-faced sentinels observing their master from afar. This is what happens, she thought, when musicians stop playing music. The elements holding them together collapse. Somewhere within this armour of flesh was the light-hearted person whose soul she had dived and danced into for twelve days. Or perhaps that spirit had escaped already. How many portions of ourselves constitute the whole? she wondered.

Sheila appeared with a duvet, a couple of pillows and her cell phone.

Where's Rosemary?

She followed you.

Rosemary?

She tossed the bedding to Hannah and went back through the gap to retrieve the child.

Hannah hauled Eric over onto his side on the squishy grass, eased a couple of the pillows beneath his head and arranged the duvet over the length of his clammy, chilled body. Again she wondered what had happened to the music. Like a seed under siege it might have formed a protective prickly spore and lodged in his brain. She recalled that eye connection amongst the members of his band as they played. Perhaps he was pining for his flock.

She was tucking the duvet around him on the damp grass when he opened his eyes wide and saw her there. I love you, Hannah, he murmured. The words shot through her. She squeezed his arm, and pulled the duvet up over his shoulder. You'll be OK, she whispered. But his eyes started to dart around, from the duvet, to her again, over the grass, at the duck, the towels on the clothes line, the grubby grey sky.

Where are we? he gargled. Where are we? He yanked his head up, his neck straining. What are we doing here?

You had a fall.

A fall? Whaddaya mean I had a fall? I did no such thing. Why have I got this bloody blanket over me?

Sheila returned with Rosemary hanging under her arm. She squatted by her father's head, her hand on his chest.

Dad. The ambulance is on its way.

Don't be so bloody stupid. What do I need a bloody ambulance for? I'm fine. He shoved the duvet off his shoulders and painstakingly scrambled to his feet, wobbling towards another topple. Hannah, primed to watch for falls, sprang to clutch his arm. Sheila arrived on his other side.

I'm fine, I tell you. His face draining again, and he clutched Hannah's arm. Just a bit dizzy, that's all. Goddup a bit fast.

Come and sit for a moment, while you come right.

The two women steered him towards the bottom step of the deck and plonked him down. Rosemary toddled after them. The duck waddled after her, all a-quiver, tail motoring, his mouth ajar from the excitement. Eric dropped his face in his hands, his thick fingertips circling his closed eyes, before moving to rub his forehead, his head. Then he dropped his knuckles to the deck, hoisted himself up. Slowly this time, and elbowing off attempts to stop him as he shambled his way towards the hedge.

Sheila raised her eyebrows at Hannah. What shall I do about the ambulance?

Perhaps you should cancel it. But he definitely needs to go to a doctor. He's not himself.

The duck suddenly rushed across the lawn and made a dive for one of the pillows, his beak clasping a corner and digging in, the rest of his body bearing down upon the pillow, his tail swivelling this way and that. As was his wont.

Geddoff my pillow, you dirty filthy animal! Eric ripped a leafy branch from the hedge and whacked at the duck, who stopped, legs apart, neck stiff, whinnying a high-pitched scream. Get off, I tell you!

He stooped. Snatched the pillow from under the duck's feet. You filthy vulture.

The duck attached himself to the pillow, his beak and claws digging in, wings belting.

Get off, you bugger! Eric shook the pillow at the air, its cargo with it.

Get off, you goddamned monster!

Eric, stop it — calm down! You'll make him worse.

But he gave a last violent flick and the duck was rocketed across the section, landing in a tangle of wings and legs on the stones around the pond. Hannah rushed over, but he'd righted himself and was tearing back across the lawn, his beak now stabbing at Eric's legs, grabbing the cuff of his trousers.

Ow, you bugger! You bloody bugger! Eric kicked, hard, sent him flying, but the duck was back again at the jigging legs. And now the duck's knees were bending, bouncing for lift-off, and he had Eric's face in his sights, ready to fly up at him.

No no no!

Eric gathered his anger and pulled his foot back for a bullet kick, just as the duck launched his attack. Hannah hurled herself to rescue both the duck and Eric. Her arms enfolded the duck as Eric's foot whammed into her cheek, the force of contact shooting her to the ground once more. She spun over, cringing, fearful of another blow. The duck in her arms and she curled around it. She could feel the pulsation of wings batting in vain, feet clawing at her stomach, fighting to be free. She wouldn't let go. Her cheek burning and she could taste blood. The musky musty muddy smells. Absorbing every vibration of muscle beating at her being, and she would never let go.

Rosemary was howling. And then a man's voice. Hello hello hello hello, what's going on here?

A hand on her shoulder. Two sets of legs in black trousers. A black bag placed by her head.

And she lay there curled around the feathery maniac writhing to escape.

I will never ever let anyone hurt you, Ducko, she said, as the sky spun around her and through her and into her, the whole night sky flowing into her head with tinsel stars and there they were, just the two of them now, gliding so easily, so smoothly through the stars, so many stars, and so easy to fly, she couldn't believe how pleasant, how effortless, the weightlessness, just the two of them.

CHAOS

White. All around. Dazzling white. White light. Red. Red on white. Smudged. Blood. Blood. On the pillow. Crackling crisp icy white. Pain in eye, neck, teeth. Why was she in this room?

This was their bedroom, pristine and waiting for Simon's return, and here she was bleeding on the brand-new pillow. And she was still in her dirty muddy clothes, sullying the sheets. At least, she noted, her shoes were off.

She sat up. Her head hurt. And her neck. She touched her face, her swollen cheek. Her fingers explored the pain inside her mouth. Her gums, two aching teeth. If she pressed they moved, old rocks in sand. The inside of her cheek cut.

She reached over and pulled at the curtain. Night. And in the light from her room on the deck railing the phantom figure of the duck immediately jumping to his feet, his tail winding up for waggle, his neck taut, his eye swivelling to check the moving curtain.

Night. And the duck was not in bed.

She lifted her feet across the sheets and dropped them to the floor, stood up, plonked down on the side of the bed again, dropped her head between her knees as the room fizzed. Stood up again and made her way downstairs.

The radio was blaring. She turned the lights on in the kitchen and lounge area. Papers were still scattered by her computer across the table. A loaf of bread was open on the bench, Marmite and butter alongside. It was late. She pressed her aching cheek.

And just as the music stopped, and as she made her way to turn the radio off, she heard the calamitous tones of the announcer's voice. Breaking news. A massive earthquake in Japan. A tsunami heading for New Zealand. Warning. Keep away from the beaches.

More breaking news. The world had been kicked like a football and it was breaking up and she would be tossed alone into the firmament. Outside, the spectre of the agitated duck in the gloom, the duck connected, as ducks were to all things, quivering from the vibration that was shattering the Earth into pieces. The vibration that was splitting her head in two.

She drank a glass of water and sat at her computer. Christchurch, and now Japan. Earthquake. And there it was before her, happening from afar, videos of the massive surge of water swallowing everything in its path. Buildings, ships, whole villages, bridges. The water, black, on fire. Where were the people? There were no people. How could this be happening without people?

And over and over the voice on the radio announcing the breaking news, the tsunami alert. She couldn't stand it. She switched the radio off.

She stood up, sat down, stood up and went to the window and looked at the still-pacing duck, his milky form floating backwards and forwards along the railing, an albino football tethered to the night.

Pulled again to the computer, she watched the same horrendous images over and over. And then closed the computer. She wanted to smash it.

Where was Simon? It was ludicrous that they weren't together. She sent a text. *I can't stand this destruction. What is happening to us? Is this the end of everything we have ever known?*

Then she went to her mother's bedroom, where she had been sleeping, and opened the wardrobe. No empty boxes, but she took out a cardboard box containing winter jerseys, and tipped them onto the bed. Back in the kitchen she lined the box with newspaper and a couple of old towels. She stuffed a bottle of water, a dish, and a bag of wheat into a supermarket bag.

What else? She had a quick shower. As she patted her face dry, she examined her puffy cheek in the mirror, the dark bruise from her temple and under her eye. She cleaned her teeth gingerly, swishing out a mouthful of bloodied water. She dressed in fresh clothes, grabbed the box and went out to the deck, to where the duck was huffing and houghing.

Ducko, here we go, she said with a forced jolly tone. This is it. She tucked her hand under his soft belly and he skipped as usual onto her arm, his claws pressing into her flesh.

This is it, Duckie, she repeated. She wanted to crush him to her chest, to rock him in her arms, she wanted to feel the burning rumpled skin of his face against her own burning cheek.

What time of night do you call this? he complained.

Ducko, she said. I'm sorry.

She let him down into the box at her feet on the deck. He started to thrash about, silent now, his energy reserved for survival. Her betrayal was overwhelming. She could smell his earthy odour wafting from his feathers. His fat tail shuddering as she eased her hand away. His neck flailing, his claws gouging the side of the carton, his giant wings elbowing their way through the lid as she tried to close it. The whole box was rocking as she struggled to press down the four pathetically flimsy folds of the lid, his writhing neck forcing his head through this way and that, before she finally jammed each flap down.

Inside the house, she lowered the imprisoned duck to the kitchen floor, placing a chair over the top of the box. She darted from the room to find a couple of pantyhose to tie up the box. When she returned the chair was on the floor and he was out, whining and huffing.

Bugger, she said.

She plonked herself down on the sofa, leaned over to roll up the rug, which she then kicked to the end of the room. Already he had plopped on the wooden floor. It was one of the empty watery splats, void of substance. He was starving. He started to slap around the kitchen floor. Then over to her, sidling around her legs threateningly, his wings flattened as his neck and head swooped and scooped across the floor by her feet.

Ducko, she said.

Again that pitiful whining. Was he frightened of her?

Ducko, she said, I'm sorry. The world's falling apart. I need to be with my husband. I can't stand it here anymore by myself.

He didn't answer. It was after midnight. Her head was aching. Why didn't she take him down to his shed and think again in the morning? This was ridiculous.

Then she spotted a pair of her black socks rolled together on the floor. Brilliant. She stood up again and found a pair of scissors, slicing the toe from one of the socks. Turned off the kitchen light. Now just the hall light was shining through.

Ducko, she said quietly. Come here.

He hissed vigorously as she stepped up behind him, his nostrils shooting warm sharp gusts onto her arm as she positioned herself to pick him up again. She grabbed him and flopped onto the sofa, wrestling with him as she slid the sock band over his bucking head. The battle was over.

She doubled the blindfold over his eyes while making sure to leave his beak and nostrils clear. He dropped heavily into sock-darkened induced sleep, his warm red head sitting like a trophy in her hand. When she let it go, his neck curved back into his body, an S-bend pipe, his beak resting against his chest.

His fiery defiance stilled.

Well.

She sat there. Then she moved, preparing to carry his dead-duck weight to the box. He responded by shaking his head, a convulsive quiver. Then he was still again.

Perhaps it was death throes.

She snuck back the sock to check. His eyes blinked rapidly; she could feel them under her fingers. Then he whipped his neck from the blindfold. He was awake again. He forced himself from her lap, his wings thrashing the air.

And every wispy thing in the room lifted. All the dust, papers, dead moths and flies on the window sill, her hair — all lifted in a simultaneous dance as his wings pounded the air. She had a swift insight into the nature of earthquakes, tsunamis, grief. Displacement. Something moved and everything around it was relocated. A thing moving in mud, in air, in life had an impact on every particle around it. She was familiar with the phenomenon. It was editing. A word changing affected the whole piece, the whole poem. The rest had to be reassessed and reconstructed to make allowances for the lost object.

The duck was on the floor, his big timber legs solid, splayed. Facing her.

Ducko, was all she could say.

What's going on? What are you doing to me?

Ducko. It's time. Te Awamutu. I need to take you back.

Te Awamutu! Te Awamutu! What have I done wrong?

Nothing. Nothing. Duckie, I'm sorry. You haven't done anything.

Well, why would you take me back to that terrible place?

Ducko, the whole world is falling apart. Deep beneath the earth, under the sea, something has moved and the ocean is reacting in a tremendous way.

So? What's that got to do with Te Awamutu? With us? I thought we loved each other. I thought we were going to be together forever. You *know* what happened in Te Awamutu. You know. You know what happened to my mother. You're happy for me to be dumped there, to a similar fate? You have no idea. The blood, the teeth. My mother dragged away from me. Her head jerking from those teeth, those wet gums exposed, the grass flattening in the moonlight as she disappeared. And the next night, a hawk. Another one of us scooped away. We had nowhere to hide. My uncles finished off the rest. Held under the water. Drowned. I would have been next. Once your mother is gone, the whole world is out to get you.

He was panting, his whole body vibrating, his mouth open with his ribbon of pink tongue glistening.

Duckie. Sit on my knee. Just for a minute.

No.

Please.

He glanced at the box on its side, an avalanche of towels spilling onto the floor.

I don't trust you anymore.

Hannah sighed.

What can I do? he stammered. Anything. Let me out and I'll go to bed, by myself, down through the dark in the garden and I'll go to my new fancy shed you prepared for me and I won't even ask you to close the door. Except it would be nice if you did, but you don't have to if that's the problem. But, please — don't send me away.

Ducko, there's nothing you've done wrong. It's just a simple matter of not being able to cope any more.

What do you mean, can't cope? Cope with what?

With you.

Hello? How do you have to *cope* with me? You don't have to *do* anything.

You're dependent on me.

Everyone is dependent on anybody who means anything to them. Don't I mean anything to you anymore?

Ducko, I'm tired. Look at my face. Look at it. This happened because I was trying to save your life.

Both of them flopped somehow as the kick, the slam of the foot into her cheek, took its effect again. All their gumph once again booted out of them, deflating their posturing. They eyed each other, that invisible umbilical connection still throbbing.

Then, abruptly, he changed his woeful stance, and stood erect again, his eye now harbouring a mischievous glint.

I'll eat the rest of your mother.

She'd mentioned it in passing, yes, but they hadn't openly discussed the mixing of the ashes with his feed before. His blatant remark shocked her. And he knew it. He cocked his head triumphantly.

Don't pretend you don't know what I'm talking about.

She was flummoxed. Ashamed.

I didn't know immediately, I have to say. I detected something unusual . . . And then as each day passed I started to feel a presence within me. Her. She was furious. She felt encumbered by me. She was offended by me, by my ungainly unsightly appearance, as she worded it. Yes, that's what she said! At night she entered my dreams. The battles, the wild battles we had. She was a reluctant parasite, growing into every part of my mind. The more of her I ingested, the more fierce the battles would be as she gained strength. She wanted her freedom and I was imprisoning her.

Hannah stared at him. She realised that she herself had never dreamt directly of her mother since her death.

I'm sorry, she said. I thought you'd take her flying. And, in the end, all you could manage was a bumpy ride to the bottom of the garden. She never was one for roller coasters. But as for flying, you . . . you hardly ventured beyond the fence. You are just as confined as she was, by your own perceived limitations. There's nothing to stop you, just as there was nothing to stop her.

Boundaries are boundaries, said the duck. Where did you want me to go? I've been over the fence and through the hedge. Each time you rushed after me. Your friend Eric was far from welcoming when I wandered through the hole in the hedge one afternoon. Talk about a crazy devil. And I've looked across the terrain here from the magnolia tree. Backyards and backyards. Roads and cars. So, I ask you, where? Where did you want me to take your mother? Te Awamutu?

I imagined you were going to take off each day to a distant park . . . or over the sea . . . I thought you might fly and fly and fly over all this, like migrating geese do, until you found a shimmering lake set amongst softly rolling verdant hills, where other ducks of your kind greeted you enthusiastically. I would have taken you somewhere myself, but I was always afraid for you. Dogs. Cars. You seemed to know instinctively so much about duck life, and I thought you'd just do whatever your wild self directed you to do. And I imagined you'd take my mother with you . . . I can see now I was stupid.

Yes, your mother said you had a tendency to be interfering.

What? She talked to you? About *me?* What else did she say?

Never you mind. Though she did say that you couldn't let things be. That you couldn't leave well alone. And that there was craziness in your family and that she feared for you.

Oh! *Did* she now! What a lot of poppycock. Honestly. She was the crazy one, actually.

Dead people aren't crazy. They know the truth of things. They're back in their essential nature. They have the benefit of hindsight. They have an overview of life without the encumbrance of responsibility or reaction or repercussion. They have insight that they would have given their last feather for in their lifetime. Insight that, but for their own blundering self-centredness, was available to them in life. As your mother pointed out, the whole picture is painted and you can stand back and look at the finished work.

Hannah laughed resignedly.

Well. What else do you have tucked away in your fat little globule of brain?

At that moment the duck stiffened and whinnied, his neck a tall pipe, his focus on the window. The cats had arrived, their tails flicking, out on the deck pawing at the glass. They hadn't been fed either. She got up and opened a tin, scraped the meat into their dishes, then let them in. She watched them as they devoured the food in whispering grumbling gulps, then nudged them outside again.

The cats. Who would feed the cats if she left now?

She leaned against the bench, her arms folded. The duck was still watching her, wary, his neck snaking tentatively.

Ducko, what I want to know is why you didn't discuss this before. The special mash. My mother's ashes?

She cringed as she spoke the words.

We can't reveal all our cards at once, he said slyly. Anyway, I didn't know how you'd react. It was obviously a secretive thing. Until I stopped, you never mentioned it. So I could ask you the same question. Why? So . . . now it's all out in the open and I'll stay here and eat the rest of her, OK? Deal. Then everyone will be happy. Well, your mother won't, but . . . well, sometimes you've got to take a few prisoners along the way.

Put like that, it sounded so crass. And how many other shuffling cards were out there, unrevealed? How could the night be so still and silent and heavy while the earth was splitting apart so dramatically? For a moment she had forgotten. She resisted the temptation to turn the computer on again for more news. She was overwhelmed enough as it was.

OK, then, Duckie, she said. If we're talking deals, let's start from here. If you sit on my lap, without struggling, we won't leave tonight. I know this sounds pathetic, but I just . . . I would like to hold you. It's the next best thing to a reassuring hug. And then, in the morning, if we all still exist, we'll review the situation.

The duck sighed then stretched, one leg extended behind his tail, then the other. He arched his neck and flapped his wings a couple of times, lifting on tiptoe before settling again.

Well, no stroking, he said. No patting my head or the back of my neck. No scratching under my feathers. Is that clear?

Yes, yes, yes, agreed Hannah. And then she had to add, But I always thought you liked that?

Well, you're wrong. I'm a wild animal, you seem to forget.

You used to, she persisted.

Frogs and tadpoles. Caterpillars and butterflies, was all he said.

She stood up from the sofa again. His claws clattered nervously on the floor as he crab-walked away from her.

And there's one more thing, he said.

Oh yes? Go on? What?

Did she see a sidelong smirk lurking about his beak?

I'm hungry.

Right. Of course. She went to the freezer, took out a bag of frozen corn, and tipped some of it into a bowl. Sprinkled it with water and heated it in the microwave.

Actually, Ducko, while we're thinking along those lines, I have a request as well.

Here we go. What?

She placed a newspaper in front of him on the floor and, after testing the corn for temperature, she put the bowl on the paper.

When you sit on my knee, could I place a plastic bag over your tail? Er … just in case.

He plunged his beak into his meal, eating ravenously, corn kernels flying everywhere.

When he finally stopped, she prompted him.

Ducko?

What?

He was looking for water now. She went to the deck and brought in one of his dishes. He slurped into it, lifting his head as if for a gargle.

I was asking, if you wouldn't mind, if I could place a plastic bag over your tail?

He looked at her, feigning indignation.

Oh all right, I suppose so.

She turned the light off from the hallway, fished a towel from the box, and grabbed a supermarket bag. He allowed her to scoop him up and carry him to the sofa, where she arranged the towel over her lap before sitting down, grappling awkwardly to organise his back end into the bag. He nipped her arm, tugging at a clump of flesh when she tried to cup her hand around his body.

And so, they sat there in the dark.

Just like the old days, Ducko, she said, but he was fast asleep, the tip of his beak burrowing under the edge of his wing.

HELL AND HIGH WATER

And when she closed her eyes the scenes she had viewed earlier flashed before her and it felt as though the world was going to disintegrate and they would all tumble — so slowly and free-falling in a lazy frightening way — into that abyss that had been waiting out there all along. She couldn't rid herself of the mesmerising images — the sea rearing up and stampeding, a furious animal that had finally crashed through its restraining boundary fence.

The unspoken trust holding land and sea apart, broken. The sandy ribbon of shared territory torn apart, the land ravaged. Buildings crushed into scraps, smashed into sticks.

A house floating in the sea, burning. Cars and ships and containers, and everything — devoured by the sea, until somewhere at the edge of it, the monster tired of the carnage, hung its head and sighed. The end of its breath before it had to inhale again. Then it turned back. Releasing its dead prey. And somebody, somewhere, must have cowered before its tongue and felt blessed, because there is an edge to everything, an end, and, at the brink, there is somebody standing on the other side in awe, saying look, look at this, I am blessed. I was selected to survive because I am special, because I have something to offer to the world. I was chosen for a reason.

And the Earth, squeezing open and shut. And juices seeping out of its skin. And already there was talk of possible radiation, the putrid breath from malfunctioning organs.

We are just souls that come down to Earth, and then the Earth rustles her skirts and we are flung into the heavens again.

Chapter 25

EYE FOR AN EYE

Her cell phone was ringing. She tried to extricate her head from where it was embedded in a cushion that had fallen too far behind her, over the top of the sofa. Her neck had seized. The phone. In her back pocket. And the duck, the duck. The ringing stopped, then started again. The eastern sky was streaked with blue light. She managed to lift her backside up from the couch to ease the phone from her pocket. The duck spronged from her lap onto the floor, his plastic bag billowing behind him.

Hello. Oh Simon, Simon, hi. She readjusted herself on the couch, massaging the back of her cricked neck.

Hannah, what's wrong? You sound awful. Are you ill? I've just found your text.

I've just woken up. What time is it? Her dry tongue was an interloper lurching around her mouth.

About seven. I'm sorry, normally you'd be awake.

Nothing is normal anymore.

You don't sound like you. Are you all right?

Ah . . . not really, my teeth are sore. Oh no!

The duck was dragging the bag across the floor, spilling a trail of its carefully collected contents.

What's wrong?

Oh nothing, I've just woken up, it's um, a lovely surprise to hear from you.

I received your text. Aren't you well? You sound weird.

I was sleeping in a funny position.

What's that noise? Aren't you alone?

The duck was positioning himself now, houghing with the deep guttural voice of disapproval.

Oh shucks, she said. Yes, of course I'm alone. It's just the bloomin' duck.

The duck! Oh, you're sleeping with the duck now? His voice hardened, all concern for her evaporating.

It's not like that at all.

Not like what, Hannah? You've just woken up. The duck is there. So he's finally moved into my place in the bed. I can just imagine. You'll be happy now.

Now they were severed voices in a void, drifting away from each other.

Don't be stupid, Simon. It's the first time. I'm not in bed. I was upset. Because of Japan.

Hannah, have you been drinking? You aren't making sense.

No, nothing makes sense, I agree.

Are you eating? What have you got in your mouth?

In my mouth I have almost a whole night without sleep. In my mouth I have a jumble of words cowering under my tongue. They are choking me while they blunder around trying to arrange themselves into questions for you. Big scary questions.

Hannah, perhaps this isn't the best time to speak to each other. It seems that I have rung at an inopportune moment.

I was asleep for heaven's sake.

With the duck.

Look, I've got to go. Turn on the radio. Google Japan. Are you ever coming back? How's my sister? Are we still married? Do you have any children? What are you doing with your life? Bye.

She turned the phone off, threw it across the sofa and buried her face in her hands. Her fingers carefully pressed around her temple, the puffiness under her eye, her tender cheek. She could smell the remnants of the corn she'd stirred a few hours before. Corn, and soap. Her mouth was dry. She opened her eyes. Through her fingers the light of dawn was filtering through. The duck was pecking at her toes. A busy exploratory nibbling. A tug. A yank. Ow.

Quit it! She shifted her foot, stood up, stretched. The duck backed away, straightened, whinnied. She opened the door and guided him out to the deck. He waddled to his dish and drank, his eye upon hers as she closed the door. Then she went to the sink, pouring herself a large glass of water to drink at the window, her eye upon his.

LIFE GOES ON FOR SOME

The tsunami warning for New Zealand had been down-graded to a precaution to keep away from beaches for the day, but there were new sickening images of the earthquake plummeting through the internet, mainly of the tidal wave sweeping along the east coast of northern Japan. She forced herself to turn the computer off. She couldn't help thinking of her own daily walks around the foreshore . . . what if the sea had suddenly swallowed her up? She had never doubted the safety of it, always accepted unconditionally that the boundaries between her and the sea were undisputed, with allowances in the buffer zone between high tide and low, and the occasional show of force during a storm. Beyond that, it had always been a matter of trust. That was the way of the world. The harmony resonating between every living thing, every dead thing, the dependence upon the predictability according to the nature of the beast. Otherwise, how could anyone breathe freely?

Right now, though, she was only capable of taking a couple of Panadeine and going to bed in a darkened room. But at that moment there was a knock at the door.

Sheila was standing on the doorstep, alone, her dreads and all her *joie de vivre* bundled away under what looked like a tea cosy. She clasped a hand to her open mouth.

Oh my God, she said. Look at your black eye. Oh no! I'm sorry. Dad would be mortified if he saw you.

He shouldn't be, it was an accident. Come in. Have a cup of tea.

No, I've left the kids with Andrew, but he's wanting to get some things done about the house. Thank goodness it's Saturday. I just came to collect some things for Dad. He's in hospital; they're keeping him there for tests. His blood pressure is really high for a start, but they want to look into the way he's been behaving. I've been next door having a bit of a tidy up. The house was a bomb-site. But anyway, I just wanted to see how you are. You insisted yesterday that you were all right, but you didn't seem all right to me. You wouldn't let anyone help you.

I'm fine, lied Hannah. It's all a bit of a blur after the kick, but I'm OK now. Got a shock to hear about the earthquake and tsunami in Japan, though.

Already the gigantic event that was still having repercussions across the world was relegated to a few lines of shared dismay, to be squeezed into day-to-day conversation amongst people whose lives were unaffected directly by its force.

Oh I know, said Sheila. Everyone was talking about it up at the hospital last night. Horrifying.

She paused, chewing intently at the edge of a nail. That duck of yours is a wild thing, I have to say. I don't want Rosemary or Max wandering through the hedge by themselves again. It's worse than a mad dog. Dad's legs are covered in bruises, and the doctors were wondering what they were.

Hannah's heart lurched.

Normally he's fine, she lied again. I tried to warn Eric.

Or did she? She couldn't remember. She pressed her forehead. What exactly had happened?

But anyway.

She tried a calming smile. It hurt.

I won't report it, said Sheila. But I must say that I was worried.

No, no, no, truly, he's just a stupid duck. He looks worse than he is. The red face makes him look angry. The flapping wings and everything. It's all bravado. He doesn't even have teeth.

Really? No teeth? How does it eat?

Well, he's got little ridges along the edges of his beak for filtering and also gripping worms and insects or whatever. And he eats stones and grit to help grind up food in his stomach.

She was beginning to sound like Simon.

Well, it certainly made some hefty bruises on Dad's leg.

Actually, Eric was attacking *him*.

The way I saw it, the duck was attacking Dad.

Hannah envisaged a van with a metal cage and men in boots, overalls and thick leather gloves arriving to take away her savage pet.

Sheila, I'm sorry. I am. Things got out of hand, it was all a string of events. The duck has a thing about white pillows. I'll watch him. How is Eric now? I'm glad he's getting attention. Please give him . . . please tell him I'm thinking of him.

Hopefully he'll be OK. He was supposed to be taking medication, but he never does. Either that or too much. Hopeless.

Hannah stepped forward and gave the girl a quick hug.

Keep in touch. He's a lucky man having a caring daughter, she said.

Hannah was surprised to see a flush of pink spread across Sheila's pale complexion.

Thanks, she said shyly as she turned to go. After something like this I realise I should have been more attentive. You take things for granted and then . . . Anyway, I'd better go and see how he is. Hopefully he won't have discharged himself.

They both laughed as they realised that the likelihood of escape was high.

Let's hope the food is good and the nurses are patient, said Hannah.

As she waved Sheila goodbye, a movement caught Hannah's eye. The duck had come up the side of the path from around the back, and was peering around the house. Just his red head, poking around the corner, his shiny eye watching her.

Ducko! she said. Hello! I was just coming around to see you.

His head retreated. By the time she'd taken the few steps to the corner of the house, he was nowhere in sight.

And he wasn't on the deck or in the tree. Maybe all her troubles were over. No more decisions to be made. She'd be able to ring Simon and tell him the problem between them was solved.

Even so, she continued to search the property, calling. She crawled through the hedge to Eric's place, calling, calling. Down to the rock garden in the corner where she'd lazed one balmy afternoon as Eric played his cello for her. There used to be a cultivated tangle of geraniums, daisies, iceplants and rambling roses growing there. Now those plants were struggling with the weeds attempting to strangle them all.

Oh well.

Chapter 26

ANOTHER VISITOR AND A PROPOSITION

Hi, pet. I believe this is the sanctuary for abandoned ducks? Is that correct? Here am I. Quack quack quack. Nowhere to go. Flew all the way from Christchurch. Wings are wung out. Exhausted. And they're after me. Stoats, ferrets, hawks, the lot. Rats. Can I come in? Please. Let's quack inside. Quick. I mean, quack.

Toby! What . . . ?

He arranged an expression of quizzical despair, his head tipped to let his red hair flop over his forehead, a joker's woeful pleading posture.

Oooh, your face! Is this the face that launched a thousand ships? Yep, I'd say so.

He blew a whistle of concern.

Her fingers were still clamped around the door handle, as she held the front door open for the second time that day, blinking at him on her doorstep. Black jacket over a plain black T-shirt, blue jeans and a gym bag at his feet. Again those dark shadows under his sparking eyes. His skin looking more sallow, more wan than before.

Yep, 'tis me. Toby or not Toby. That is the question. Toby, the godforsaken drake. Homeless and looking for shelter. No sex, I'm British. No, I'm not. But, just a roof. Won't be any trouble. Whaddaya say? Yes, no? Maybe so?

She opened her arms and stood on her toes to give him a hug. He stooped to allow her. How grateful she was to feel those bony shoulders, breathe in the stench of stale cigarette smoke. What sort of magic was swirling in the universe?

Is Maggie with you? she asked, knowing full well the answer.

Nup. I'm demagnetised. And sigh-man, the Good Samaritan, left far behind as well. Oh dear. They'll be looking under every leaf and I won't be there. I'll be here. But I might not be because you might give me a roasting *à l'orange* and turf me out. As you have every right to do, but I am hoping that you will not.

Yes, no, of course, she said. Come in. Actually it's so lovely to see you. She felt tears welling, her face collapsing.

Oh no, no no no . . . No blubbing please, please, please. I'm not built for emotion. I'll have to go, I'm afraid, if that's the case. He bent to pick up his bag, feigning a gesture to walk back up the path.

She grabbed a handful of jacket and playfully pulled him back in. He whirled around, and this time he wrapped his arms around her, whacking her with his bag as he did so.

Come on, he said. Let's go inside and have a nice cup of tea and you can tell me all about the thug who beat you around the face so mercilessly. And don't tell me you ran into a door.

She made the tea, watching as he paced about the deck, smoking a cigarette which he plunged into a pot plant when she called him in. At the table, he sat on the edge of his chair, his legs splayed as if ready to run. Gingernut for a gingernut, he said as they dipped gingernuts into their tea — she, tentative little edges to nibble; he, half a biscuit at a time before hanging it above his mouth just in time to catch the soggy dropping.

How's your duck? he asked.

He's . . . he's OK, I think. He's hiding actually. How's everything down in Christchurch?

That, he said, is — what do they say? — a very good question. Yes. However. Would you like to be more specific?

Oh, well, ummm . . . She nipped her biscuit. You'd probably have more idea than I would as to where to start.

The earthquakes? They suck. He suddenly turned and picked up the table with his knee, crashing it violently and noisily upon the floor. Every nerve in her body exploded.

God! You gave me a fright.

Exactly, my dear. That's what's happening every day. Sometimes small ones, sometimes big ones, in the night, during the day. And you never know whether it's going to be a big one, because we thought we'd had the big one and then when February the twenty-second happened it was more devastating, so you think there's going to be yet another bigger one. And you never know whether the container truck going past is another earthquake. You just don't know for a split second, but by then your whole body is shot with adrenaline. Anyway . . . your man Simon is down there digging us all out of the mire.

At the mention of his name, Hannah felt her stomach drop. The day was so still and quiet. Toby was a flea, and she was a jumpy cat, his host. She had questions for him, but she was concerned that, if she threw them at him too soon, he'd be frightened away. So they discussed Japan and the Earth, his work. Her eye.

You've got a little beauty there, he said. How did the other guy come out of it?

She laughed. Actually, he's in hospital.

Eeeuw, remind me not to wind you up the wrong way then. He cracked his fist into his palm. Pow, pow. Wham! But really, what happened?

She sighed. It's complicated but, basically, it was an accident. The guy next door having a bit of an episode. My face in the way of an angry foot.

He peered at her eye, grimacing. Should be OK in a day or two, he said. I killed someone once, you know.

Um, no, I didn't know that. Perhaps I shouldn't.

An old lady. I was thirteen. Coming home from football practice after school. I was kicking the ball ahead of me. I gave it an extra hard boot and it went over a low hedge. A lady with white hair and a pink cardigan was sitting at a round plastic table on a narrow verandah, writing. She had a round back. I saw the ball go straight for the back of her neck. She was sitting on one of those plastic flimsy chairs and she fell to the garden below. Grabbed the table and it went, too. In the hedge there was a wooden gate and I couldn't get the bloody latch inside the gate to open. When I finally got inside, the lady was sprawled in marigolds, sort of groaning. She had two red curlers in the top of her hair. She was looking at me.

I took the table off her, picked up my ball and walked up the wooden steps. There was a saucer on the second step, to the side. I banged and banged at the door. It had big dried bubbles in the paint. Wooden door, a sort of rusty red. An old man eventually came. Opening the door just a bit, angry when he saw me, as if he knew. He had shorts on and a green jersey with stuff spilt down the front. *Your wife fell off her chair*, I told him. *Into the garden*. He said, *Ailsa*. He went down the steps sideways, holding onto the railing with both hands. He knelt down with extreme difficulty beside her on the lawn. *Ailsa, Ailsa*, he was saying. *Ailsa*. I didn't know what to do. I stood there and then I left. I didn't even help.

He stopped. He'd been speaking quickly, hardly looking at her, his eyes far away, but now he searched her face. He took a deep breath and held it. Let go.

Well, there you go. See? Murderer.

Gosh. But she might not have died.

She did. When I passed the following week, people dressed in black were streaming in through the gate with plates of food. The old man came out and spotted me. Told everyone that I was the one who'd found her. Ailsa. There was a cockatiel hanging in a cage from a hook over the verandah. It gave a screech, a blood-curdling scream. It was trying to tell the world that I wasn't the one who'd found her but the one who'd killed her.

So no one knew?

No one. You're the first person I've told in decades. Not even Maggie. Don't know why. Why did I tell you? I don't know. Just thought of it and out it came. It has never left my head actually. The guilt. And whether she was alive when she was looking at me. Whether I was the last person in her head before she died. I never played football again.

He rubbed his arm, probing deeply into his flesh.

Well, I feel honoured that you did tell me. But it wasn't really your fault.

She wouldn't have died when she did if I hadn't kicked the ball. Maybe the next day or several years down the track. But I was the one who kicked the ball. It hit right at the base of her neck. So it was because of me that she died then. About a month later there was a FOR SALE sign outside the house. And the cage with the parrot had gone. The only consolation, if you think about it, is that she would definitely have been dead by now anyway. So there you go.

Well, Hannah said. She felt as though a tornado had suddenly passed through the house and left again.

I don't suppose, sweetie Hannah, that you have a bottle of brandy handy? Best thing in the world for after-confession trauma. And black eyes. And red eyes like myself.

She'd dribbled the last of the brandy into her Milo on the night of Eric's naked visit. She stood up, left the room and returned with a bottle of Cointreau.

She gave him tea and oranges that she brought all the way from her china cabinet, and he thanked her in his wisdom for the stone, he babbled enigmatically. Sorry Lennie, he added, watching as she poured two shot glasses of the liqueur. She passed one over to him and he upended it as she held hers to her nose, inhaling the aroma rising from a bucket of citrus left in the summer sun.

It's magical, the essence captured, she said wistfully. How a smell can transport you.

So where are you now? said Toby, pouring himself another shot.

I'm . . . she hesitated. I'm with Simon, on a picnic in the bush. We have just stopped for a break on our walk. The sun is filtering through the trees onto the rotting leaves. I'm peeling an orange, and I break it into segments, offering them to him in my palm. He takes my wrist and he eats the orange pieces, and I can feel his tongue on my palm scooping up the orange. Then he pulls me over to him and kisses me—

Enough! Enough! said Toby. A kingdom for a nuff!

I'm sorry, said Hannah, suddenly embarrassed. You did ask me, though I wasn't even thinking of it. I'm a bit at sixes and sevens today.

You always are, sweetie, of late, I believe. His upright palm slunk across the table, folded around the square bottle. He poured himself another glass. These are tiny little glasses, he said with a wry smile.

So where are *you* then? she asked.

He stared into his glass as he swirled the contents within. She could see the vulnerable peach stone held tightly in his thin throat as he tossed back yet another mouthful. Finally he lifted his wired eyes to meet hers. I'm with you, Hannah. I'm right here with you. And my wife and your husband are together in rocky old Christchurch, and here we are here, rocking in our own sweet gentle way. So what do you think of that?

Are they . . . are they having an affair?

That's a very good question. May I? he said, once again creeping his hand over to the bottle, this time pouring some into his emptied mug. Well, if you'd really like to know, I can't tell you. They're in cahoots, of course. They're an intimate knot of co-dependence. Oh, didn't they ever band together when I had a bit of a tipover . . . a little too much of whatever . . . ended up in hospital myself . . . your husband looking after my distressed wife. Extraordinarily touching. And then Feb twenty-second. I lost my job, the restaurant on the verge of collapse. Anyway, that's all beside the point, whatever the point is. What's the point?

So, they might be?

They might. My guess is no, but who knows? Simon cries a lot. Does it matter? What does it mean? A bit of earnest pacifying? They might be now. Alone and looking after each other in their respective despair. God forbid. They are so self-righteous. Sorry, sweetie, I know he's your husband, but . . .

Don't worry, just say what you think. I want to know.

Whatever for? As I say, what difference does it make? Do you love him?

Well, yes, I thought I did.

That sounds like passion *in extremis*.

No, well, yes I do. Of course I do.

Of course? Should we take these things for granted just because they have been a certain way forever? Are we able to trust the earth beneath our feet anymore? The sea lapping at our toes? Things change, Hannah.

So, do you love Maggie? she asked, sipping at the Cointreau then abruptly swilling it back, her senses exploding with citrus.

Let me tell you this. Your husband is in my house with my wife. Your husband thinks you don't love him anymore. He thinks you love a duck more than you love him. So. He's confused and needy. He's out there working like a dog, scooping up liquefaction, hauling away bricks, checking on old ladies, et cetera. The earthquake has become his duck. And Maggie is tiring of me . . . perhaps he is becoming her duck.

Is she? Is it the drugs, Toby?

Don't you start. It's all under control. More or less. If you ride a rocky terrain, sometimes you fall off your bike, right? And if people happen to be at the scene, over and over, to help clean up the blood, it gets to them. Because after a while they are always waiting for the bigger one.

He fiddled with the empty glass, then took a sip from his cup. We're all the same, Hannah. Don't you see? All of us. Every single one of us. We have our props. One day it'll be walking sticks or an old fence to lean on as we contemplate the weeds growing over the headstones.

He patted his jacket, dived into the lining, took out a packet from which he tapped a cigarette.

Ciggie break, he said, running his fingers through his hair. He stood up and opened the ranch sliders. She stayed at the table. Poured herself a second shot of Cointreau. It was already making her light-headed. She realised that she hadn't eaten at all that day. Just a gingernut, and it was way past lunchtime. She went to the fridge and opened a packet of smoked salmon not yet past its use-by date. Toasted a few slices of bread. Put the food onto a plate in the centre of the table, with a couple of small plates and a knife at each setting, sitting down just as Toby breezed smokily back inside to join her again.

Thought we'd better have a bite to eat, she said, smashing a chunk of salmon upon her toast.

Your duck, said Toby. He picked up the cigarette packet, turned it over and over on the table under his hand. He's down in the garden getting stuck into a pillow.

Oh, is that where he is? That's Annabel. Annabel has changed things between us. He used to attack me, but now he has his pillow. He'd normally be staring at me, but we had a long complex night. So he's been avoiding me.

I see, said Toby, staring piercingly at her as she slowly chewed the salmon and toast. Auntie Hannah, I do hope I've arrived in time to salvage this extremely delicate situation. You see, what I have been leading up to is this. A proposition. I could drive you and the duck down to wherever it came from. Where was it? Cambridge? Te Kuiti?

Te Awamutu.

Te Awamutu, yes. We could have a nice road trip together. So — and here I'm divulging a little secret . . . Your husband will not return home to you while that duck is still here, do you realise that? This I do know. It has been stated. So I've been thinking. Duck goes, your husband returns, and I go back to my wife. How's that? But there's no time for navel-gazing. It might even be too late. You have to choose. Duckie or hubby. It's a *Sophie's Choice* situation, I know. The excruciating dilemma. Who do you really love?

Please, Toby, don't be mean. I'm tired.

And she was. She imagined them all sitting around discussing the situation over their dratted drinks, Simon spilling out the dratted beans to whoever every-dratted-one was — Toby, Maggie and Simon, the AA meeting, the duck-widowers' anonymous therapy group. Everyone giving their two-penn'orth. And their sympathy.

Toby bit the inside of his cheek, frowning, saying nothing as he absorbed the silence. Lining up the cigarette packet with the corner of the table. He leaned down to scratch his leg.

Oh dear, he said. I didn't realise it would be such a gruelling decision. So it *is* difficult to choose between the duck and the hard place. Between your husband of twenty-something years and a duck of six months. He was right. Blimey, Hannah.

It's not so simple, said Hannah.

That's what I was saying.

There's a certain matter of my mother to consider.

I see. He leaned across the table and placed his hand over hers. Her heart swelled at the unexpected gesture of empathy, of kindness.

Hannah, my love, my dear sister-in-law. I have some terrible news for you.

She blinked. Those tears again.

What?

Your mother. Your mother . . . your mother is dead. She died nine months ago.

Hannah jumped up, scraping her chair back to hit against the wall.

For fuck's sake! Stop mocking me! Do you think I'm a simpleton? What has Simon been feeding you, for heaven's sake?

Shit, said Toby flatly. Can we start again?

You came to taunt me.

Hannah, Hannah, no. Please sit down. I thought that maybe . . . Yes you're right. I shouldn't have come. I'll find a hotel. Yep, diddlydum. Another Good Samaritan hits the dust.

He reached for the Cointreau. She grabbed it.

No. No more.

He jumped to his feet.

I beg your pardon, Auntie Hannah?

She would never ever forget that fierce blazing in his eyes as his pale spindly hand landed once again upon hers, but this time with no semblance of kindness. They ogled each other as they each grappled with the bottle across the table.

I think you've had enough.

His fingers dug into hers, his nails cutting into her skin. Her own fingers clasped around the bottle neck.

You've no idea how those particular words rile me. Those black venomous vicious sneering self-righteous words.

Sit *down*, she commanded. To her surprise he did, feeling with his bottom for the seat of the chair behind him, refusing to let go of the bottle. She dragged her own chair closer with her foot and dropped as well, the bottle now landing in the centre of the table.

She yanked her hand from beneath his. I don't want an ambulance to have to haul out yet another man from my property within a period of twenty-four hours.

The flare of anger subsided. Blew itself out. The crisp charred remains still stinging. Her heart motoring. She rubbed her hand with her thumb. He filled his cup, drank, then added the last drops from the bottle to her half-empty glass. She dropped her eyes from his, struggling to settle her breathing as she picked at an old lump of congealed food. She couldn't remember whether the table was rimu or kauri. The grain of the wood streaking past her like a river. Each line a growth ring representing a season gone. She wondered what this tree had endured in its lifetime, how many earthquakes had rattled its roots.

I'll split, he said.

No, don't. Please. I'll come down to Te Awamutu with you, if you still want to. It would be good to have company. You're right. It has to be done.

Whatever.

But not today.

No.

Tomorrow?

Fine.

I don't know what happened just then, she said.

His elbows on the table now as he massaged his head, mumbling at the table. Look, sorry, Hannah. Apologies. Up early, well, up most of the night. A lot of pacing around before I got on the plane this morning. Forgive me. I shouldn't have spoken like that. Not a good idea to fight with a drunk on a cliff-top.

His long fingers digging into his head, circling through his wavy hair. She said nothing. Watching him as random thoughts flashed through her head. How many people were still straining to pull themselves from the debris-strewn water? How many people who, just a day before, had been idly contemplating the trivia of their lives only to find themselves, right now, releasing their last breath? How controlled and peaceful and ordinary her mother's death was in comparison, lying flat in a comfortable bed as she and Simon waited together. And how many people in all the world were entwined together, at this very moment. She thought of the duck obediently sleeping on her lap all night. The whole night fighting the urge to slide her hand to rest quietly under the comfort of his wing. That was all she would have needed to complete such a strange and wondrous sense of unity with him.

Finally Toby lifted his head. Pulled his eyes open by raising his eyebrows, and gave her a forced clowny grin, his grey lips closed.

All my oomph has gone. Out the window. What were we saying?

You were making me choose between the duck and my husband. Don't misinterpret the hesitation. I miss Simon and I love him.

At that she pulled her hand up to her mouth and bit the side of her finger. Her teeth dug so deeply into the flesh, harder and harder but still she couldn't feel any pain. At least it stopped her crying.

She pushed the salmon towards him.

Eat.

He groaned. Actually, Hannah, I need to lie down. Haven't had much sleep. He took another gulp of the Cointreau and shuddered. Shit. He plunged his head into his arm and shuddered again.

OK. I'll get your bed ready.

She went to the warming cupboard and took clean sheets and pillow cases to the spare room, her mother's room, the room where she'd been sleeping the past two or three months. She could hear Toby in the bathroom, and then he was behind her, holding his bag. As she started to pull back the sheets, he stopped her.

Hannah, Hannah, Hannah. No fuss. Don't change the sheets, he mumbled. Any old gutter will do. Gravity is overwhelming me.

She looked up at him. His face looked chiselled, every bone jutting into his waxy skin. The tide was sucking out from his flesh. She stepped back to let him pass. He staggered, then dropped onto the bed and tried to shove one shoe off with the other. Exasperated because it wouldn't budge.

Here, let me do it.

She knelt on the floor and untied the laces. The shoe was long and polished. Brown with rows of indentations patterned around the toe and the edge. She tugged it away. His sock clung damply to his foot which dangled from his white leg. Then the other. This time she eased the shoe away more effectively, down from the heel and sliding it along the sole. She placed the shoes alongside each other and stood up.

There you go, she said. He continued to sit, staring ahead.

Hannah, he whispered. Look. He lifted a finger and pointed at the oval mirror hanging from the wall. She stood alongside him. He wouldn't have been happy with his reflection. He could have been an old man, shrunken, stooped, his stormy hair above hollow eyes. His bottom teeth cluttered behind his drooping mouth. And she, looking hideous with her blown-up bruised eye.

Ssssh, she said. You're burnt out, that's all. She stood between him and the mirror. Come on, lie down. He shook his head briskly and rubbed his scalp.

Come on, Toby, she coaxed.

Is she always there?

Who?

Your mother. Pointing at me.

Don't be silly, she said. It was you. You were pointing at yourself.

It was your mother. Her lips were moving but I couldn't hear. I couldn't hear her. She had something to say.

Hannah tugged the bedding from under his bottom. She hugged him. Ripples of fear shivered through his coat. He allowed her to lower his trembling bones and shrinking flesh onto the mattress, shaking the pillow before releasing his head into it. The skirt of her nightdress poked from beneath. Tiny cogs beating beneath his jaw, like the busy mandibles of a sea creature lodged under his skin. She hoisted his feet up and under the sheet. Pulled the duvet over his shoulders.

I'm cold, he whispered. Freezing. My blood is crystallising. His fingers clawing the duvet around his ears, under his chin.

She plugged in the electric blanket and switched it on.

Water, he murmured.

But when she returned with a jug of water he was asleep. She filled the glass on the bedside table and sat on the edge of the bed, staring into the mirror. Sheila was right, she *had* lost weight. She waited, closed her eyes and listened to Toby's noisy breathing, whispered and conspiratorial, like tiny faraway voices of censure. Outside in the magnolia tree, the frenetic clicking and lazy plunging whistle of a starling. A plane, filled with hundreds of people, whirring precariously across the sky. A car driving past. Another car. The world continuing about its business.

She opened her eyes again. Still there was just her own reflection framed, her eye buried in a swollen mocking wink. She stared into the mirror, at the mound of Toby under the bedclothes, at the wall behind her, at the small floral armchair sitting empty in the corner of the room. She searched for moving shadows, for shifting light. If only she could find a clue that her mother was more than just an urn — or half an urn — of ashes, buried under the bedclothes in a far corner across from Toby's sleeping body.

She bent over and kissed his impassive cheek. Lifted her hand and let it rest lightly on his cool forehead. Her blue nightdress poked from beneath the pillow. If she hadn't been afraid of disturbing him, she would have tugged it out with the other personal detritus that had gathered under and around her pillow: face cream, hair ties, a few screwed-up balls of tissue. She turned the blanket down to its lowest setting and left the room.

TELLING HIM HOW IT IS

Down in the garden, the duck was sitting peacefully on one of his pillows where she had left it beside the day lilies around the pond. He jumped up when he saw her, rushed to nibble her feet and then back to Annabel for some unabashed sex.

She sat eating another piece of toast and salmon, shifting her bottom uncomfortably over the cold damp ground. Each blade of the grass around her looked recently polished. The duck jumped from the pillow and waddled to the pond where he started his post-coital ablutions, water spraying everywhere, leaving a shattered necklace of pearly drops on the agave leaves.

Ducko?

She tossed him a crust. He ignored her.

About last night.

He dug busily into his self, his beak clamping on and swishing each feather from bottom to top, every single feather receiving his attention in an efficient matter-of-fact sort of way. He was a parent slicking the hair of all his uncomplaining children.

The mash. I've thought about it and we're not going to do that now. It's not fair on either you or my mother.

Now the uropygial gland again, now the wings. There was nothing he didn't know. All the clues imparted to him by the sensible overnight educator. If only she had such a mentor.

We're going to take you to Te Awamutu. There will be attractive white muscovy ducks there, truly gorgeous ducks there, and I'm talking about actual ducks, not drakes. And there's a pond there, a much bigger pond than here, a pond with dragonflies and frogs and bulrushes, and a sweeping lawn where you can lie with your friends in the sun, and many trees with fat curling branches where you can perch if you so desire. And natural hideouts amongst the bushes where you can shelter. There will be lots of you, and you can sleep with your furry eyelids closed because you won't have to be the only one constantly on the look-out for predators. At night you can all traipse into an enclosure protected with a high wire fence. And there'll be puddles teeming with worms, and also cicadas and crickets and cockroaches everywhere in abundance.

He stretched and spread his wings.

You might need to talk to your overnight educator about how to behave with your special white duck. Or ducks, as the case may be. Lovely moving Annabels with wings and legs. And other curly inside bits . . . that pillows don't have.

And now his head rubbing nonchalantly on his back, his crest high.

I must say, Ducko, you are looking extraordinarily handsome yourself. Your plumage is at its best. Every feather in its place, as smooth as the egg you came from. Lovely patterned pebbly grey on white. And your juicy crimson beak knobble, just ripe for the picking. You'd be the beau of any ball. The grand drake of the paddock. If I were a duck myself . . .

He cocked his head suddenly, his eye bright.

I'm going to miss you, Duckie.

He lifted his claws and furiously scratched the back of his head, then edged around the pond, away from her, cutting through the day lilies and across the lawn, where he started munching on dandelion leaves.

Well, anyway, she called. Tomorrow, OK? Don't say I didn't tell you.

VIGIL

And when night fell, after the duck was in bed in his hotel, she curled up into the armchair in the room with Toby, still clothed, because the dark held so many uncertainties. Because if the Earth burst into smithereens she did not want to be alone. Because, if the Earth stayed intact, she was frightened that Toby might be dying and she felt that, if she were there, she'd be able to prevent such a thing happening, in the way that a woman could stand at the edge of a dense forest, calling her loved ones back home.

In the small still hours of the night she woke up from her dozing to hear him groan, then shift heavily around in the bed, patting the sheets. Then the darker shape of his body rose from the gloom.

Maggs? he mumbled.

Toby, Toby. Her dislocated whispering filled the room. Maggie's not here.

What the hell! Who are you? What's going on?

Ssssh, Toby, it's me, Hannah. Sorry, sorry.

Hannah, what the fuck? What am I . . . ?

She jumped from the chair and turned on the light, to see him withering from the glare, his arm shielding his eyes.

Turn it off, turn it off.

So she did. Stood hesitantly by the door.

What's going on, Hannah? What are you doing here?

I'm sorry. I was . . . concerned about you. I'll go now.

Go? Where will you go?

To my own bed.

Where's Maggie?

In Christchurch.

Oh yeah. Of course, of course. Yeah yeah yeah. God. OK. Heck. I'd kill for a glass of water.

She moved to the drawers by his bed, feeling for the glass she'd left there earlier. Their spider fingers touched in the dark as she placed the glass in his hand.

He drank, burped loudly, and bumped the glass onto the bedside table.

Ta. Yern angel.

Then he flopped down again under the covers. Shortly afterwards she could hear that he was asleep. She refilled the glass from the jug, then dragged herself up the stairs to the pristine white bedroom that she had prepared for Simon's homecoming.

Chapter 27

A MILLION QUESTIONS FROM THE BOX

It was another two days before they managed to set off with the blindfolded duck enclosed in the cardboard box on the back seat of her car. Hannah sat with her hand resting in the box, like a child feeling for a lucky dip.

The sock over the duck's eyes had sent him into a sleepy, albeit reluctant trance. Her palm cupped under his beak seemed to soothe him. If she took her hand away he'd panic, scrabbling noisily round the box that was just big enough to contain him. It was reassuring that he trusted her enough to feel pacified by her. Nonetheless, or even because of this, she felt treacherous. This time, the operation to coerce — no . . . capture and force him into the box — was planned and neatly managed, with Toby clasping the duck's wriggling body at arm's length as she manoeuvred the sock over the head. Toby then helped by holding the box and closing the lid. She could hear workmen across the valley dismantling a house, hammering and smashing, crashing building materials into a bin. The afternoon echoed with the sound. She imagined birds in the trees nearby, and on the roof, cocking their heads accusingly. She was the cat that had finally, inevitably, pounced.

It's OK, Ducko, she whispered into the box, it's OK.

But it wasn't.

Toby drove silently. She could see the profile of his intent face as he drove, the sharp triangle of nose, his cheek drawn, his thin lips tight. How many millions of years ago since he had arrived on her doorstep, sleeping and sleeping from the evil fairy's spinning needle as creepers enveloped their house, enfolding them all into a silent pocket of breath-held time? How many millions of years since the Earth had found its boiling orbit around the sun? How many million years since ducks waddled the Earth as dinosaurs? And how many millions of ducks had arrived and left the planet since the first one? Hatched into ducklings and died amongst the teeth and slimy tongue of whatever predator? And this one, this stupid duck, this drake? Nature's miracle of perfectly designed feathering-up, and the overnight educator. What was the significance of the ridiculous regret and grief mangling her heart? In the big picture, what did anything mean?

She had rung Claire to say they were coming. And don't you think, she had cautiously suggested to Toby on the third day, that it might be a good idea to tell Maggie where you are? He had shrugged and agreed, and taken the phone she had offered into the garden. *His* phone, he'd told her, he'd deliberately left behind. She had watched him pacing below, kicking nonchalantly at stones around the pond as he spoke in low tones, his skinny back soaking up the weakening sun. And once inside, he had returned the phone to her hand without a word, slipping away to the bedroom. When she peeped later he was lying on the unmade bed with his hands behind his head. Her nightdress, she noted, was still hanging from beneath the pillow.

Everything all right? she'd asked, venturing to the end of the bed.

You could say my wife is somewhat pissed off. We'd better get that duck on the road.

His gaze had slid towards her, then back again to the blank white page of the ceiling above.

Did you know, she said to Toby as they drove, that muscovy ducks actually originated from Brazil? In the 1500s Spanish conquistadors found wild ones rounded up for food in Indian villages. And the Spanish and Portuguese took them to Europe where they became a popular table bird. Now they're established in Mexico and other parts of South America.

Encyclopaedia Brit-hannah-ca, he replied.

She lifted the lid with her free hand. Hello, Ducko. You OK? she whispered. He shifted uneasily. His beak hot. Before they left the car, when they arrived, she would enclose her fingers around a small cloud of his warm breath and place it in her pocket.

Love is a very bewildering thing, she sighed.

Auntie Hannah. Don't start. At the moment, love is rather stern and unforgiving. Once we get this duck in its right and proper place, we might be able to see things clearly.

Muscovies tend not to migrate like geese and other fowl, she added.

She had checked this as she entertained the idea of her duck returning north, landing one day unannounced in the back garden, battered and forlorn, lumbering up the steps to the deck, huffing and houghing at the window, to greet her.

THE CRUNCH

Already. Already she was missing him.

Claire was crunching her way over the stony driveway to greet them, her face now at the car window, so pleased to see them, so pleased that Hannah had finally come to her senses. Toby climbed out and stretched and lit a cigarette, jiggling from foot to foot. He'd met Claire at Christmas, and they brushed cheeks awkwardly, his cigarette held out from his arm like a smouldering wing, a light plane ready to crash. Hannah wound down the window. Hi hi hi, she'd called. Her hand still in the box that had become a cumbersome appendage, a growth that needed amputation. I'll be out in a minute. She eased her arm away. The box erupted. She pressed the lid down, covered it with a towel. Claire opened the car door. Clean brown trousers sitting loosely on her hips, earthy coloured blouse and a dark green cardigan covering her flat bottom. She was in her outdoor camouflage suit. Her grey hair flat and straight around her face as she leaned in. The air was cool, smelled sweetly of cows. Somewhere the grumbling of a tractor, and dogs barking.

Hannah refused help as she slid from the car cradling the bumping box.

Come and have a cup of tea.

The porch was cluttered with dusty macramé hangings, a forest of dangling pot plants, and a vine of kumara leaves climbing aimlessly around the walls. A river of ants wound through grime along the window sill. Boxes of shoes and gumboots, umbrellas. Stiff raincoats bound by cobwebs huddled in a corner.

Leave the box in the porch and we'll have a cuppa and scones before we introduce him around.

Oh, um, Claire, would it be all right if I kept the box with me until we take him to the . . . his hotel, or wherever it is he's going?

Hotel? That's funny, dear. Well, yes, I suppose you can, as long as he'll stay put.

So Hannah sat on the floral sofa with the worn velvet cushions and managed to drink a cup of tea with the box on her knee, choosing the smallest scone with a pond of jam in the centre of a dollop of whipped cream. The house smelt cosily of slowly cooking meat. On the mantelpiece was a framed black-and-white photo of Bob and Claire on their wedding day, the stereotypical bride and groom, tightly clasping hands as they stood on the steps of a church, their smiling faces squinting from the glare of . . . what? The sun? The realisation of their lives together, stretching interminably ahead of them? And here they are, another childless pair, surrounded by ducks. They had done better than she with their brood. And now the sun was just dipping behind a bank of trees, sending an image of glowing stripes through the venetian blinds onto the wall.

She could see Toby, who had managed to avoid the afternoon tea, pacing around the lawn, smoking another cigarette. Beyond him, behind a bed of dahlias and an electric fence, a paddock rolled down to a wooden shed under a stand of macrocarpa. And she could see white ducks and chooks casually drifting around, beneath the trees. There was a cutting that she assumed was a stream wending around the bottom of the paddock.

Indistinguishable tones of a radio came from somewhere in the house. Claire was talking to her, and a part of her was answering perfunctorily, about the weather, about the bruise fading around her eye, about Japan, and Christchurch and how was Simon (he'll be pleased the duck is coming back, dear), about whether the light was bothering her and did she want the blinds closed and, oh yes, the joke about whether they were going to have duck for dinner.

Perhaps, Hannah said, shifting the box on her knees, it might be better to take him to where he's going to sleep tonight, before it gets dark. He's getting restless.

Claire stood up, holding out her hand for Hannah's cup and saucer, noting the unfinished scone left on the plate.

And Toby, too, seems restless, Claire said with a knowing air, nodding her head towards the window. A shiny tip of tongue was trapped between her mussel lips, something sneaking its way out, forcing itself to be said. Then suddenly she stooped to Hannah who was trying to stand up without upsetting the duck in the box.

I hope, dear, that there's nothing going on between you and Toby, is there? She spoke so quietly that Hannah wondered whether she had imagined the words. It's just that you haven't kept your eyes off him all afternoon. You mean the world to Simon, you know. It would break his heart. He hasn't had an easy life, you know.

If Hannah's arms hadn't been full of box she would have swiped the woman. Well she wouldn't have, but she felt like it. She had a ridiculous thought that she was being punished for not eating the scone.

What do you mean, she said guardedly, 'hasn't had an easy life'? It's been roses, actually. We've been blessed with all the good things, to tell you the truth. Though right now, she couldn't for the life of her think of any of them.

All that baby business. Terrible for him. He's such a dear boy.

A whip of anger flicked through Hannah's chest.

Look, Claire, this duck needs to be settled before nightfall.

I thought you were arriving earlier. You said you would. Well, you said *yesterday*. We were ready for you yesterday.

I'm sorry, things don't always go to plan. She didn't tell Claire that Toby hadn't crawled out of bed until after midday today.

Well, I'm not going to be party to this. I've prepared separate bedrooms.

Hannah spun around, spinning the duck across the box, which set him scrabbling once more. She propped the box between her chin and her knee and opened the door to the porch. Down the steps and around the car to the lawn where she'd seen Toby smoking. She found him by the macrocarpas talking to Bob. Toby the city boy in his neat jacket, Bob all crazy hair and open shirt, sleeves pushed up past his elephant-trunk elbows. Grubby jeans bunched into gumboots.

Well, here she is, said Bob. A box of birds.

He moved around the box to kiss her cheek, his skin cold, his cheek plump and prickly and smelling of poisonous farm-crisp air.

So what have we got here? Let's have a look at it. He reached out to take the box from her, but she swerved away from him. Their voices and the movement caused the duck once more to shamble from side to side.

No, I'm sorry, Bob, we're not leaving him here now. Or ever.

She could feel Toby's disbelief as he searched her face.

Please, Toby, can we go now. Right now. I'm not leaving my duck here.

Just a minute, Hannah, said Toby. He took her arm firmly. Excuse us a minute, Bob.

Sure, mate, sure.

Toby led her quickly up the paddock away from Bob, the pens, the trees, the house. At the top of the rise they came to a stile, which led to another paddock. Toby climbed over and she passed the box to his open arms before she, too, clambered over. They sat down in a sunny patch of grass, the box placed between them.

Right, he said firmly, his arms folded, his hands delving under his jacket. You've really thrown a Hannah in the works. Spill. What's up?

I can't stand it, she said, and she started to cry into her hands. She was going to have a nervous breakdown, right here and now in this paddock, this very place where her duck had been born and this was where she was finally going to totally disintegrate. Then she stopped, her fury swallowing the snivelling mouse of her self-pity. All the jigsaw particles of an eggshell flying back into place. If she started now she would never ever stop. Here was not the place.

Hannah, he said, binding himself tightly with his arms across his stomach, rocking back and forth, back and forth. A stick insect in an unseen wind. It's normal that you should feel this way. I knew it wasn't going to be easy. But we have to go through with it.

She tugged the towel from the box, then opened the flaps, tipped it on its side. The duck tumbled his ungainly entrance along the cardboard catwalk into his birthplace.

We don't actually, she said.

If we don't now, when?

Never.

She pulled the duck towards her, slipping fingers along his neck, feeling his busy blinking eyes as she flipped the sock from his beak. They watched as he stood in the grass with the sun lowering itself from twig to twig in the trees above the hillside where they sat. Shadows slunk on haunches towards them and the duck stood, rigid, his mouth hanging open. His world had disappeared. To be replaced by sky and shadows and smells and grass unknown. Duckie, she said, and she reached forward, manoeuvring him onto her lap. He stayed there, houghing, his claws piercing her thighs, his neck pumping, testing this foreign air on his tongue.

We need to get him down before night falls, don't you think? said Toby.
Look, he's petrified, she said.

Hannah, he said. I can't drive back tonight. I'm knackered.

I'll drive.

You'd need to be with the duck to keep him in check. Why, what's happening? What brought this on?

She . . . honestly, you wouldn't believe her. For one, making insinuations about us. You and me. Honestly, the cheek.

He tossed his head back in a scoff.

Huh! Is that all? . . . Look, Hannah. You're stalling, grasping for reasons. Excuses. Why you shouldn't give him up. You haven't even come to the hard part yet. The withdrawal. Think of the situation. It's crazy, all that hanky panky with the pillow. Down there, under the trees, are animals of his own kind . . . he needs to be with them. It's cruel otherwise.

Look at him. He's happy with *me*.

He wants to be with you because you're his replacement flock, and we've removed him from his territory and he's traumatised. Imagine if you and I woke up to find ourselves in some desert, surrounded by creatures we'd never seen before. We'd just want to cling to each other because the situation would be so alien. Anyway, we don't have a choice. Bugger the woman thinking we're having it off with each other. Ignore it. Laugh it off. So what? It's a joke. Who cares about silly old Claire de lunatic? It means nothing.

Well, there's more.

Look, Hannah, sweetie, it will be dark soon. Think of your duck. If you *really* care for him.

He stood up and started to move down the hillside, the cardboard box and towel hanging from his fingers, bumping against his knee as he walked. She, too, scrambled to her feet. She lagged behind Toby, the duck cradled in her arms.

Ducko, she whispered. Did you hear Toby? He's right, you know. You're now going to have the opportunity to find your true self.

What rubbish, he huffed. I *am* my true self. Who else am I? Whatever other self could I be? What are you doing to me? I trusted you. I thought we were friends. I thought we loved each other. Where will you be? What is this place? It's malevolent. I'm filled with dread. Something terrible is going to happen. I know it. Don't do this to me.

She could see Bob moving in and out of the shed. Roosters and hens and ducks were making their way towards the trees where there were several coops and high wire pens, a long shelter under a corrugated-iron roof, protected on one side by a wooden wall, with wire netting on the other. The narrow stream she had spotted from the house wound its way from one end of the shelter to the other. It was here the other ducks were heading. The chooks had their own enclosed housing.

And your mother, added the duck, thinks it's atrocious. She's extremely disappointed in you. She feels betrayed by you. As do I.

There was another stile at the bottom of the paddock. Toby was waiting for her and helped her climb over.

Hannah, he said in her ear. Don't cry. Please. He pulled her to his side and kissed her head. Sssh.

She tried to wipe her wet cheeks with her shoulder. Then she lifted the duck and swept her face across that place between his wings. Into his musky earthy smell.

For heaven's sake, grunted the duck, recoiling. I *hate* it when you touch the back of my neck.

Well, called Bob, closing a gate to the henhouse. Sorted now, are we? He dug a finger into his ear, fervently, as if he might be tunnelling deeply for a thought that lay there. Well I never, he said good-heartedly as they approached. You wouldn't get any of my ducks in my arms like that.

He's feeling a bit overwhelmed, Hannah told Bob.

When I was a kid, I had a pet lamb, 'Bluebird' its name was, because it made me happy. Bob lifted his leathery hand to stroke the duck, which bit him fiercely, yanking a pyramid of skin from the back of his hand. You *do* get attached. One day I came home from school and the lamb was gone. My mother told me it'd been chosen to join a travelling circus because it was so tame. A week later a man in a van arrived to fill our freezer with neatly parcelled sausages, roasts, racks, stewing chops and so on . . . Fortunately, I didn't put two and two together. I always thought that one day the circus might come to town and that the famous Bluebird would recognise me, galloping across the ring in the middle of the show, picking me out from the audience.

His hand dived under his shirt, rubbing at his chest. Come on, he said, let's get this duck into its pen. It's one I use when I need to separate an aggressive bird from the rest, or for mothers and their chicks, or whatever.

Toby, could you please get me his pillows and towels from the car?

I didn't hear *pillow*, did I? said Bob, as Toby set off. The light of the day was quickly fading. Bob opened a high gate into a three-by-two metre stretch of dry mud surrounded by a wire-mesh fence. Hannah felt her heart sinking slowly, a dead leaf making its lonely way from a tree.

There you are, Duckie, she said brightly, as he continued to complain gruffly. Just while you get used to things.

Bob had already left a dollop of mash on a lid making do as a plate, and a scattering of pellets on the ground. In a corner was a rusty forty-four-gallon drum, overturned to form a gaping cave. How will he know, thought Hannah, that this is where he should sleep? She lowered the duck to the ground. Again that gruff grunting, as he pumped his head. Lifting his feet tentatively, as though the very ground might crack open. She could see, she knew him enough to know that, despite his apparent calm, he was petrified. Here was Toby arriving with two pillows, the plastic-covered sleeping one and Annabel. There was enough room for both in the drum. She stuffed Annabel into the back, just in case it rained in the night, and also to help compensate for the peeling scabs of rust in the walls around. The other pillow, she covered in one of the towels Toby held out for her.

Glory be, said Bob, watching in the gloom with his arms folded upon the cushion of his belly. You'll be wanting a bedside lamp next.

And yes, indeed, already the shadows were closing in. She could feel the air tightening with cold, the night creeping up her legs and sneaking its way through her hair and down her neck. The duck went to the stream and drank, the water gurgling like a brook down his throat, his eye on hers. He squirted an empty splat that soaked into the dirt, then he drank more, his beak lifting skyward as if crooning an inaudible lament for all those ducks that had been betrayed by the ones they loved and had trusted. He stopped drinking and moved away, watching her, dropping his head, bowing, bowing over and over, thank you, thank you for the good times we've had, thank you for looking after me so well, for all that cleaning of my muck and the effort to find the right food. Thank you for your company. I've made things difficult for you at times and I regret that now. Yes, regret: we laughed about that word once. It is a word I now understand. I will accept my fate with dignity, as a wiser duck.

Ducko.

She squatted and slid her open hand under his belly. He hopped onto her arm while she supported him with the other hand. The movement so familiar to both of them.

Now take me away from here, he houghed.

Duckie, I'm sorry, she whispered. I'll see you in the morning. She manoeuvred him over to the drum and into the wide ravenous mouth. He backed out, snorting. She patted the pillow. Bed, Duckie. She picked him up again, his legs paddling paddling paddling to escape, so that when she placed him inside, tail-first this time, he propelled himself back into the open.

Leave him, said a voice behind her. He'll be fine. Don't worry. He's just a duck after all.

She'd forgotten the figures, waiting, watching in the dusk. Toby and Bob. Simon. Maggie. Her mother.

She stepped back. There was a sudden burst of large wings thrashing in the branches above. Then. Then, Bob held open the gate and they filed out, Toby's fingers in the flesh of her upper arm, as they picked their way over the rumpled ground. She looked back and he was a white ghost, a blur of nothing, motionless, but she knew his eye was fixed upon her, drilling into her, as she moved away from him, until the dark enclosed him, until the dark absorbed her, until neither of them existed anymore.

Chapter 28

THE CREATION OF DISTANCE

This time, she was driving. The day was sombre. Toby next to her, drifting off to sleep, his head between the head-rest and the window.

How quickly a car can create distance between a person and a loved one, she thought. There was something unnatural about the speed of not only the actual departure but the moving away. She could feel the unravelling of that bond that had been so tightly bound in her heart spinning spinning spinning as they travelled further from him. What would he be doing now, in that pen with the drake running curiously up and down on the other side of the wire netting? And it was raining.

She'd woken up to splattering against the window, the sound of swaying trees filling the air. She had a headache. People were up and moving in the house, and the smell of coffee hung in the air. She decided she was too ill to move. If she stayed in bed, they would have to stay. She would have to stay with the duck another day. It would be better not to rush this. Toby, she was sure, would be sleeping, too.

As he was now as they drove away, away, away. The duck would be waiting for her to come back, just as he had been when she'd appeared from the house this morning, rain on her raincoat falling in loud drops from the trees. He spotted her, came scurrying to the fence to greet her. She had returned! He had survived the night and she had returned. He let her pick him up.

Ducko, she said softly. Hello.

He didn't reply, but sat calmly without scrabbling to escape as he normally had done of late. Her arms were the lifeboat, and they were going back home.

She carried him from the pen and walked about. Appealing little muscovy ducks, much daintier than the drakes, scattered away in fright. Their faces were a soft cherry pink, pretty costume eye-masks streaking from their beaks.

They passed another enclosure in which two gentle ducks with their broods of ducklings watched him nervously, emitting an uneasy purring of chirps. The same stream ran through their pen. One of the pom-poms was floating down the stream, hopping out and then skittering over the mud for half a metre to repeat the action over and over. Like a child on a slide at a playground.

Do you remember being so tiny, Ducko? Look how cute and fluffy they are. No wonder I fell in love with you.

She'd made her way over to the main covered pen, slipping and sliding over muddy clay. The rain belting down. Another female in the pen continually darted up and down alongside her mate, running outside the netting. This drake's caruncle was just a knobble at the base of its beak, just a bump compared with *her* duck's well-defined cherry.

And when he noticed the drake he struggled urgently to clamber from her arm. She set him down. He hurried unabashedly towards the drake. The drake stopped, turned and faced him, whinnying. Not the horse neigh of her duck but a refined sweet trill. Its wings were flattened, she noticed with alarm. Her duck, too, read the signal, and sidled away. The drake stepped up beside him, wings still splayed, as if marching him off the property. Both heads were pumping, tails waggling. The pace increasing. Crests flaring. Striding faster and faster, alongside each other. Finally her duck broke away, dived into a stretch of straggly weeds growing along a fence. His head thrust through a tear in the fence, but the hole wasn't large enough to let him through. The other drake was bearing down on him. Enough! Hannah scooped up her duck, shooed loudly at the aggressor, which persisted, following them, still pumping and posturing.

Bob emerged from his shed with a basket of eggs, water pooling from the end of his nose. I saw that, he said, laughing. A bit of one-upmanship going on.

It's not safe for him here, she said.

They'll settle down. Once he gets used to what he is. He's a fine specimen. Bigger than my birds, look at that caruncle. You've come at a good time. That one's just a young drake, same age as yours. The others are moulting, hiding. They have no wing feathers so they keep out of trouble. He'll be able to look after himself. See those little chicks, he said, pointing out the skittering ducklings. One day they'll be his harem. He'll be in muscovy Heaven. Don't you worry, now.

Hannah looked at her duck. And if not? she asked. What then? A travelling circus?

Come on now, we have to get up to the house. Claire will have breakfast waiting for us. Leave him in his pen.

Can I place a female in his cage with him, just to see what he'll do?

Sure, sure.

While Hannah took her duck to his pen, easing him to the ground, Bob sloshed his way into the main pen and grabbed one of the females, locking his big weathered hands around its wings to bring it into the arena.

Her duck stood, his face boiling red. His eye. On her as always.

What are you doing? he grumped. This is so embarrassing. Are you wanting to humiliate me?

Bob dropped the female into the enclosure. It was white and downy, with a triangular dash of red around nervy eyes. It hurled itself against the netting, then squeezed behind the drum in panic. Her duck ignored it. He was oblivious. This intruder was like the turtle dove, the sparrows, the blackbirds and the starlings that hung around the food dish on the deck at home. He only had eyes for Hannah. He found a puddle, slurped into it and drank. Bob opened the gate and let the female out before closing it again.

Come on, he said. Breakfast.

The wet road flying beneath them.

It was amazing, she said to Toby, how he actually recognised something about the drake as being familiar. He went up to it, to greet it, to say hello. I'm sure there was no aggression intended. He went up to it eagerly, as if at last he had an inkling as to what he was. It was a pity that the drake reacted in such an unfriendly way. He felt threatened, of course.

Ah, hmmmm, yeah, whaa? said Toby.

But the females meant nothing to him. There was no reaction at all.

And it was too wet for her to leave Annabel out. When she'd tried to explain to Bob, he looked at her with an exaggerated air of disbelief. And when she'd presented him with a pile of fresh dry towels for the bedding, he'd shaken his head.

No promises, he said, albeit kindly, taking the towels to throw onto a bench in his shed. He emerged scratching his head. But honestly, the longer we pamper him, the longer it'll be before he acclimatises.

Don't you have a hose, she'd pleaded. It's just a matter of hosing down the overnight towels in the morning, and hanging them on a tree or something to dry.

I'll do my best, he'd said, squeezing her shoulder. But, well, Annabel. If he's satisfied with . . . Annabel . . . how is he ever going to want to look for a mate?

She swerved the car off the road into a picnic area. An elderly couple was sitting at a wooden table, with a thermos and sandwiches on a spread of lunchwrap.

Toby sat up. What's up?

I'm going back, she said. I can't do this. It's not fair on him. He won't understand what's happening. Everything he knows whipped away from him.

When she'd walked away finally, he was incredulous. Each time she'd looked back, he was standing with his neck as straight as a broom, watching her go.

Toby rubbed his fingertips feverishly through his hair. Hannah, Hannah. Hannah Hannah Hannah. Hannah Hannah.

He opened the door and got out, locking his fingers and stretching his arms skyward.

She was gripping the steering wheel, observing the elderly man and woman. Such an ordinary couple, unspeaking, enveloped in habit. The woman passing a sandwich to the man. He took it without looking at her, though his fingers lingered, brushing over hers. She poured hot drink into cups. He blew into his before sipping. As they ate and drank, they both stared out across the road to the farmland that stretched beyond. How many years had they known each other? Where were they going and where had they been? She envied their sense of complacency. One day, that'll be us, she and Simon used to say about such a couple.

And Claire. Last night at the dinner table, blithely chatting as they ate stew and mashed potatoes and roast kumara. Talking about a baby. Toby sensitively trying to steer away from the topic. Toby. Who obviously knew. And she. Who didn't. But informed by the letter in the shed, she was able to pretend, and glean from bits of conversation a few more dislocated details. Something about Dennis. Simon's brother. And Tuyen, his girlfriend, Simon's girlfriend in Sydney, not long after he left school. And Tuyen, becoming pregnant — was it to Simon or Dennis? As far as she could fathom, the baby had died. Why, why had Simon never told her? Never ever in all their conversations had it come up, never ever even a mention or a hint of the girlfriend. And Toby's concerned gaze upon her indicated that he was aware that she had been excluded from the knowledge of whatever it was.

And if Toby knew, so would Maggie.

She'd attempted to bring the subject up with Toby as they drove but he deflected it. He knew nothing, he'd said. It was unfair. The more she thought about it, the more she wanted to collect the duck and take him home and live with him forever and to hell with Simon.

And here was Toby back in the car again, bringing with him a cloud of smoke.

Actually Hannah, he said, you're doing very well so far. This is the hardest part. Well, this is part of the hardest part.

You're talking as if you're an expert in leaving ducks behind.

I am in a way. I left a wife once. My first wife. We all have our obsessions and addictions. Things that aren't good for us.

What happened with your wife?

My wife. I really loved her. I was fussy, worked hard late hours as a baker. She was playful. And, so I thought, dependable, reliable, almost conventional. But we complemented each other. Lots of laughter. But then I discovered. Too playful. Affairs. Many affairs. And she wouldn't stop. One day I walked out. Literally. I hadn't even planned to. Went for a walk to think about it all and I didn't stop.

They sat for a while in silence. Hannah thought of the intensity that propelled him forward, a young man walking through the streets, each step taking him away from his laughing wife. She remembered their night-time march down to the beach a few months ago, how purposeful and fast his stride had been.

Where did you go?

I just walked. I walked through the night and into the day, along gravel roads far out into the country. Bush on one side, farmland on the other. Then I found myself by a gate. It opened to a flower-lined stone path winding to a cottage. In the garden was a wooden seat set into the bush. I lay down and slept, and when I woke up, an extraordinarily beautiful woman, Emma her name was, was standing alongside me with coffee and fresh cake. She was an artist. She invited me inside where I rang my wife to tell her I wasn't coming back. That night Emma shattered my whole compact conventional world, introduced me to the realm beyond fidelity and predictability. I discovered the insignificance of my life, but within that, the significance as well. Et cetera. The sort of thing everyone goes through in one way or another, of course. The clichéd epiphany.

Hannah wasn't sure whether she'd ever experienced any clichéd epiphany. She said, Sounds like a fairy tale. Or, more likely, drugs?

Exactly. A week or so later, Emma dropped me home. I never saw her again. My wife and I stayed together long enough to have our two babies, but the separation, when it inevitably came, was less traumatic. We're still reasonable friends. Well, more or less.

But what about the children?

Oh, you never leave children. They leave you in the end. Both of them are in London. Why do all the children of the world end up in London? But no. We shared them. Yes, no, that part wasn't ideal.

But were you sure they were yours?

No, but I loved them so much I couldn't bear to find out, just in case. It mattered but it didn't matter.

At the picnic table, the old woman was throwing crusts to sparrows, and folding up the lunch paper over and over into diminishing squares. She tipped the last drops of liquid onto the ground, then screwed the lid on the thermos.

And the other things that aren't good for you? When are you going to walk away from those?

Hannah, sweetie, haven't you noticed? Not a drop or anything since the Cointreau. Bob called me a metro wimp. No beer, no whiskey, no wine thank you very much. What are we now? Day four?

Oh. I'm sorry. I hadn't noticed. Well, I don't know what you do under the covers. But truly, Toby. That's great. But how long is it going to last?

As long as you keep away from the duck.

How could you compare caring for a duck with addiction, if that's what you're trying to say?

It depends on the intensity of the caring. Come on, Hann. Let's make tracks. One day at a time, as they say.

Hannah started the car.

The problem is not so much leaving but wondering how he's going to get along without me.

I know. You'll see things more clearly in a week or so. But give Simon some thought as well.

There's so much I still don't know about him. Like, sometimes he taps his beak into the web of his right foot between his right and middle toes. It's something very deliberate and it means something in muscovy parlance. But I have no idea what. And I don't even know his real name. When we were amongst the other ducks it mattered even more. It seemed that without a name I was just throwing him into obscurity.

What about Rumpelstiltskin? Or maybe Rumpledredskin.

Of course!

They both laughed. The old people lifted their hands in a cheery wave as she swung the car onto the road.

INTRUDERS

It was just getting dark as they made their way down to the house.

There's someone here, Hannah said, pausing on the path.

Don't be silly, said Toby.

Yes, there is. Look — lights.

We must have left them on.

No, no, we didn't. They wouldn't have been on when we left, anyway.

And the door was unlocked. They walked in. Maggie was sitting at the table with an open bottle of red wine beside her. Simon was at the bench, holding a wooden spoon. Cooking! A striped tea towel tucked down his front. Stirring onions and mushrooms. A large pot of water on the stove boiling. Salad on the table.

Wahoo, said Maggie flatly. Here come the swingers.

Simon turned around and leaned against the bench, his hands behind his hips gripping the handles of the bottom cupboard.

Hey, said Toby and moved towards Maggie, bending over to kiss her head when she didn't get up. Instead she took a swig of her wine.

Toby went to the cupboard and took a glass which he filled with water from the tap, drinking thirstily. He filled the glass again.

What have you got here? Smells good. Hmmm, pasta? Enough for four?

Hannah remained in the doorway. She and Simon looked at each other, neither moving. He was wearing a new shirt, a stylish black one, the sleeves rolled up to his elbows. His beard was shaven off, revealing lips parted slightly in an expression of helplessness and fear. What had happened to him? The skin around his mouth and jaw had a bluish hue. How long had he been away? And once again, how far away he was, and there in the middle, between them, was an island, a solid wooden island with a carefully crafted tabletop of totara. They had both been so proud of it once. And how was it that she had never been aware of the moat surrounding it, inhabited by starving unknown creatures that had been breeding there while she had been preoccupied with other things?

Hi, she called across the island.

Was that a screech of waterfowl that she had disturbed from the shallows? No, it was Maggie.

Oh, I'd forgotten, she was crooning. You two don't know each other. Simon, this is my sister, Hannah.

Hannah, he said softly. Where have you been?

We took the duck back, she told him. The duck's gone. Toby helped me. We stayed with Bob and Claire.

She bounced against the doorway, her hands clasped so tightly behind her back.

So there you are. It's done, she said.

He shrugged, one shoulder lifting to his now-exposed chin.

No excuses now, she added.

Hey, why don't I take over the cooking while you two have a talk? said Toby.

No no no, it's nearly ready, said Simon, picking up the wooden spoon from where he'd propped it on a saucer. He started to stir the food around the frying pan. Opened a jar of tomatoes and threw them in. The windows behind him were blistering from the steam. He made his way across the moat to the table, took Maggie's bottle and poured a dollop of wine into the pan. Refilled an empty glass on the bench and took the bottle back to Maggie. Hannah noticed the look that passed between them. It was too late. Her marriage was over.

So why are you here? she asked Simon.

She found herself slipping slowly down the wall to the floor, her feet dabbling in the poisonous moat. Her body was leaden. There was something from the centre of the Earth that had snared her, that was pulling her into its depths.

We thought we'd come and see how the merry couple was, interjected Maggie jauntily. We were concerned. But we realised we needn't have been. The birds had flown, but leaving all sorts of evidence of activities in their nest.

She pushed herself up from the table, went over to where Simon was cooking, resting a hand on his back as she knelt down to take a large empty saucepan from under the sink. She left the room, stepping over Hannah's legs as she went. When she returned a short time later, she stooped over to hold out the saucepan, like a magician revealing a trick. Despite herself, Hannah peered inside. Her hair ties, face cream. Her nightdress. Toby's socks, underpants.

Toby doesn't use face cream or hair ties, Maggie said. Do you, Toby? And since when have you worn blue flannelette nightdresses? She thrust the saucepan high under his nose. And I happen to know that these socks and underpants belong to my husband, don't they, Toby? Careful, they might smell.

Toby gawked at the contents. What's going on, Maggie? What is this crap? What are you talking about?

Simon flinched and turned his back.

It's not what it seems, Hannah tried to say, but the words were inaccessible, locked far away. She could hear the dry clatter of pasta pouring into the pot of boiling water, the whoosh of the water as it accepted its quarry. She turned over and crawled out of the room. She dragged herself upright and made her way from the hallway to climb the steps to their bedroom. Shoes off. Bed. She pulled the feather duvet over her head, lying with her face buried in the pillow, in the feather pillow.

The door to her room was opening. The mattress sank as somebody either sat or lay on the bed.

A weight in the centre of her back. Ballast. How many fathoms to the centre of the Earth?

Hannah.

Her name. The weight of her name. A noose around her name, hauling it in. A twisting in the tourniquet to stop the flow.

Hannah.

Someone pulling the duvet from her face. She turned over, peeped out. Toby was sitting there holding a plate of pasta on his knee.

I'm not hungry.

Of course you're not. But I had to find some excuse. Look, sit up, Hannah, please. I need you.

She hauled herself erect, her head against the wall.

What? she said.

Please come down, he said. They're both drinking. I won't be able to stop myself if you're not there. To make me. Please, Hannah.

Oh well, we'll be able to get the duck back then. So no one will have to try anymore.

I hope you're joking.

Yes, I am, she said, pushing back the bedclothes. Well, sort of.

He got up and opened a window, perched on the other side of the bed now as he lit a cigarette. He inhaled deeply before dangling his arm into the void outside.

Listen, he said. Can I just give you some advice from where I'm sitting? It's pretty audacious I know, and you can tell me to shut up, but if you could just make an effort to reach out to Simon . . .

Me? But *he* left *me!*

Yes, maybe ostensibly, but he feels that you left him quite a while ago. And you're not going to like this, but I'm going to tell you now so you don't have to hear it from Maggie, who is crowing about it, because she's angry with me. Last night they slept together— Ssssh, stop. Your stuff under the pillow, I didn't even know it was there. They put two and two together and got one. Us. Anyway, I put them right about that, but at the time they thought what the fuck, so to speak. But it didn't go very well, I gather — they discovered your mother in bed with them! I suppose she was there with me, too, was she?

God. Yes. I forgot. Oh, poor Mum. Everything was happening so quickly. I'm sorry. I was keeping her company. Where is she now?

He took another deep puff and let the smoke flow into the night.

Maggie took her down to the shed, he said. Took her to the furthest place on the property.

Oh well, that's that then. I knew it, but I'm glad it's out in the open, so I don't have to think about them anymore. It makes it easier really.

She looked around her, searching for solace, but she had bled the colour from the room. She tried to remember why she had sterilised their room so completely. In that drawer she knew his underwear was neatly folded; and the drawer below, his socks and T-shirts. She imagined the wardrobe empty of his clothes, the drawers cleaned out.

Hannah Hannah Hannah, Toby was saying. This isn't about getting the duck back. No. Please, let's not give up. But we have to do this together. They were each sleeping with Annabel because they didn't have the duck they really love.

I'm going to be sick.

No, you're not.

No, truly, I'm going to be sick. She held her hands over her mouth and retched.

No, Hannah, you're not. But his eyes sped around the room looking for a bowl just in case. Hannah found herself holding the rich bowl of pasta under her chin. She placed it back on the bedside table.

You OK? Good. Well, listen, our whole future revolves around this decision. If you embrace Simon, then Maggie and I will have a better chance, once she sees I've cleaned up for good. Honestly. It doesn't look like it, I know, but we're a good team when we're sober. You've done well by getting rid of the duck, and now you need to offer one little friendly gesture towards Simon.

I haven't *got rid of* the duck. And how many times have you cleaned up for good?

Well, sent him down to the country. With his own kind. And as for me, this time, I'm determined. I just *know* this time. This is my second marriage and I want it to work. But Hannah. Auntie sweet darling Hannah. Just try a little harder with Simon.

I don't know that I want to. And he doesn't love me. He left me. He slept with my *sister* for heaven's sake. Honestly! And all the secrets you all share and keep from me.

No, he slept with Annabel. And I *know* he loves you. The death of your mother was hard for him, too, you know. And then the earthquake . . . if you could just touch him . . . is it so difficult? Even with one fingertip at arm's length. There's a lot hanging in the balance here. We are ping-pong balls hanging in the air, and you can affect where they land. If you don't make the effort now — and it has to be now — look, this very minute . . .

Hannah had a vision of her finger stretched through space in an Alice in Wonderland sort of way, extended like a rubbery triffid, to touch Simon's sleeve, or his new vulnerable chin. And *he* was an anemone in a rock pool, inverting himself, repelled by her touch. Or would his hand close over the vine and reel her in towards him? She didn't know. She didn't know her husband anymore.

When they arrived downstairs, Toby still carrying the pasta like an offering, Maggie and Simon were clearing the table after their meal. The empty wine bottle and glasses abandoned.

Here they are! sang Maggie. Tweedle-him and Tweedle-she.

Hannah's head was pounding. For a second she thought she could hear the duck snorting outside on the deck, but it was her own choked breath.

She felt a sharp sting in the back of her arm. She yanked her arm away. Again that sharp pinprick of pain. Toby was surreptitiously pinching her. Ow, *don't*, she hissed, throwing a daggered look over her shoulder. That *hurt*. He pinched again, really hard, twisting this time. In the soft tender part at the back of her arm.

STOP IT! she yelled, stamping her foot.

Both Maggie and Simon did just that. They were burlesque dancers. Maggie in front, Simon behind, exactly the same angle, grimy plates and cutlery at the same level, mouths open, the steps halted in synch.

STOP THIS NONSENSE! she yelled, surprising herself, surprising her heart into a racing river-dance in her chest. I'm SICK of it! What are you all PLAYING at? What's happening in this house? Is it a TAKEOVER?

It was lame, she knew, but a blurt was a blurt. And it was so uncharacteristic that both Maggie and Simon stared at her, waiting for more. She caught a peripheral glimpse of Toby grinning, holding his thumb in the air, his eyes locked onto her.

She spun around and spat out the words. *Actually*, Simon. Do you think we could have a talk? In private — if you don't mind leaving my sister's side for a moment.

Toby stepped forward and took the plate and fork from Maggie's fingers. A gracious gesture. He took her hand in his. Madame, he said. May I have the pleasure?

And then they are gone, they have disappeared.

The room is silent, unbreathing, suspended.

So! Hannah says, and sees consternation trampling across her husband's face. He has a new face and it has no blood. He has new lips that have been crouching in a beard for twenty years, concealing the despondency and loneliness that have been taking refuge there. He has become old during his absence. His father had been younger than he is now when he'd had his fatal heart attack. Her own father as well. The vulnerable hearts of men. And for how long have the years have been inveigling their way into his skin, winding into crevices and fissures, splaying from the corners of his eyes? There is an intelligent kindness there, too, that she has never recognised before.

She is suddenly terrified that he might die without her. She moves across the moat towards him, and he waits now, for whatever it is. It's just a matter of sucking her feet from mud to move closer, and then she is there. Her face drops against his soft black shirt. Without turning he puts his plate on the bench behind them and she feels the warmth of his hands on her back. Every action is a gentle shift towards equilibrium. She is aware of his chin resting upon her head. Above them, in a clear black sky, the moon is rising above the magnolia tree, its sharp light glistening through the dewy glass.

Look at that moon, she says.

He turns, standing companionably beside her. He tells her that in three days' time there will be a super moon, a perigee moon, when it will be extremely close to the Earth on its elliptical orbit. 356,577 kilometres from the Earth. The average distance is 382,900 kilometres.

Perhaps that explains everything, she says.

He lifts his hand and squeezes her upper arm. It only explains why the moon will appear larger as it rises from the horizon, he replies.

He moves to the sink and turns on the tap. The water gushes onto the greasy plates. He picks at a sticky piece of mushroom.

It's nice to have you back, she says.

He looks at her, nodding, and smiles grimly. She doesn't know whether this is a normal smile for him or one for the occasion. He looks as though he might be trying to stop a sneeze.

Yes, is all he says.

Chapter 29

THE BRIDGE WITH NO EYES

The next day Maggie and Toby flew back to Christchurch. It had been decided that Toby would drive Simon's car back to Auckland to stay for a few months, away from his old contacts and the earthquakes, in order to clean himself up. Maggie was going to fly up to see him from time to time. This was to be a healing time, and Toby was on trial. They were all on trial. They were auditioning for their old parts in a tired play that was being revamped for a fresh performance.

They left in a flurry of kisses and embraces — Toby and Hannah, Simon and Maggie — on the footpath while bored blank faces stared at them from the shuttle window. Thank you, sweet Auntie Hannah, said Toby. I'll be back soon.

I'll miss you, actually, she replied. She was aware that Maggie and Simon were silent, that their hug was intense. Simon moved quickly away from Maggie, wiping the corner of his eye, looking distraught. Bloomin' heck. Maggie turned, gave her a mechanical hug and then jumped hurriedly into the van. A nice day for flying, she announced with authority to the other passengers as she hunched along the aisle.

And then they were gone. Hannah followed Simon as he opened the gate and made his way down the path. His whole demeanour was stooped and laborious. Once they were inside, the house was cold with silence. They went to the kitchen. Cup of tea? she asked, filling the jug from the tap.

That'd be good, thanks, he said. He sat heavily on the sofa and stared through the windows onto the deck.

Is something wrong?

No. No, just tired. Unaccustomed to sharing a bed. It's chilly, isn't it?

Not exactly *sharing* a bed when both of them had been hanging over the precipice of their respective ledges, the arctic floor spread far below. But she didn't mention this, didn't mention sharing a bed with the blaring void between them. As she popped teabags into their cups and poured the boiling water, she had the inclination to ask whether he still took milk, whether he wanted sugar or honey.

Despite their efforts to be conciliatory, they felt like strangers. The

Simon she knew had climbed into the van with Toby and Maggie, while an old man with an uncertain presence had stumbled into her home from the street. She had a surge of panic. Where was the normality that had carried them forward reliably through their daily lives for so many years?

She gave him his tea and he took it politely, his eyes on the cup. He was finding it hard to look at her. She wondered whether to sit next to him or whether he wanted to be alone. Shall I put on some music? she asked, standing in front of him.

If you like.

What do you feel like?

You choose. Anything.

She searched their CD collection. Bob Dylan? All the Bob Dylan they used to play when they first met. Nah. The occasion was too fragile for Dylan. Dvořák cello concerto? No, that was Eric. Old Crow Medicine Show? No, that was Eric, too. Ah . . . Leonard Cohen. Why not? 'Dance Me to the End of Love.' 'I'm Your Man.' They were both aching in the places they used to play, as Cohen pointed out so aptly.

Can we have it down a bit? he said, twisting his fingers anticlockwise in the air.

She took her tea and went outside, across the deck and down to the bottom step where she sat drinking.

Ducko, she said to the long vibrant grass. What the bloomin' heck is life all about? She could hear the kids playing next door. Later, if they were still there, she'd pop over to ask how Eric was doing, but not now.

After a while, Simon joined her. She stood up and took his arm, leading him to his shed at the bottom of the garden. She could feel his reluctance as they approached. And: Where did you find the key?

They stood in the shed together. He cast his eyes around, at his notebooks bundled into bags on the shelves. He wouldn't have any idea of the dense network of spider webs she had cleaned away, the eye-itching dust she had hosed down, as well as any evidence of the duck. Although the duck hadn't been there long, there was still an achingly subtle whiff of him lingering.

She told Simon how the duck had spent his last days here, and pointed out her mother, bundled up in a pink mohair rug, shoved there by Maggie alongside the books. He looked away. With Toby's advice in mind, she had made an effort not to make an issue of his night with Maggie. She felt cavalier and generous, with an element of guilt, considering her liaison with Eric. If there were to be confessions, the lid would have to be prised from yet another Pandora's box.

But there was one matter that she would not relinquish. She pulled down the plastic bag with the letter and photos and handed it to him.

His eyes flicked over her face but he didn't touch the bag.

Yes, he said. Well. I'm glad you know.

Along with everyone else.

I know, I know, I'm sorry. I tried to tell you. Right from the beginning. I tried but . . . I thought you'd hate me. I felt ashamed. I told Maggie after your mother's funeral. When we got drunk together. We were talking about sibling rivalry and . . . it came up.

But it was Dennis's baby? she asked, reaching to place the bag back on the shelf.

No, mine. Well, actually we never really determined. But probably mine, so far as the timing was concerned. We were young. She was my first girlfriend. Probably my only *real* one before you. Her mother was Vietnamese. Her father had been over there as a journalist. Tuyen. They escaped the war, and look what happened. That's the tragic irony. We didn't even know she was pregnant when we broke up. It was such a mess. Dennis loved her. I loved her. She had to choose and she chose him. And then, when we found she was pregnant, Dennis didn't want to have anything to do with her, so she sort of returned to me, but it felt wrong because I knew she wanted to be with him. But then the baby — a little girl — was born with no eyes, and other things were wrong, not sure what. Internal. Wouldn't feed. Two eyeless sockets, two little banana-shaped bowls lined with skin. I can still see them.

He closed his own eyes for a second, his thumb and finger pinching the bridge of his nose.

The baby died three days later. We handled it badly. Both Dennis and I kept away after she died, and my excuse was that before this had happened, Tuyen had chosen Dennis. Well, that's not altogether true, I did visit her at her home a couple of times, and took her flowers. But I was formal, polite. I had nothing to say. I didn't realise how it was affecting her. But anyway, we were young, too young to settle down. I regret it so much. I could have been more . . . compassionate. We were young but that's not an excuse. And then . . . later, a couple of months later, Tuyen jumped from a bridge.

His legs folded. He stabilised himself against the shed wall, before dropping to sit on the bench. So, there you go, he sighed, absentmindedly picking up a downy feather that had settled on a wall ledge, his fingers intent on smoothing out the explosion of fluff at its base, over and over. Hannah watched him. She loved those smokey-breath feathers. It must have flown high into the air when the duck stretched and flapped his wings, redistributing everything in the shed. Simon flicked it aside and looked up at her. She stooped to pluck up the feather as it drifted to the floor.

He told her that ever since he had told the story to Maggie, he'd been constantly reliving that period of his life. And then, the duck. Hannah's connection with it made him feel doubly distraught. He could see how her biological need to have a child had transferred itself to mothering the duck. He had robbed her of that as well.

So all this happened before the mumps?

No. My infertility was a conscious act on my part. I finally found a doctor who would give me a vasectomy. I didn't have mumps. Well I did, but they didn't make me infertile. As I said, I fully intended to tell you everything from the beginning, but every time I tried, I couldn't. So then . . . the mumps story. And then it was too late. I told myself that it wouldn't have changed anything anyway. The story had been dead for too long to unearth. But somehow Maggie and I managed to do that quite recklessly over the mix of gin and champagne on the night of your mother's funeral. But of course I didn't tell the person who needed to know. The person I had a duty to tell. And then, then I brought that duck home . . . Heaven help us — who could have guessed the feelings that *that* boiled up in the laboratory. That my up-until-then perfectly sensible wife would become infatuated with a *duck*. And for me, the duck seemed to personify my dead baby, haunting me. It was the last straw. Yet again, I felt accountable. I was the one who'd brought it to you. I've failed you in many ways.

They both sighed, Simon blowing his cheeks out like a spent trumpeter.

Oh well, said Hannah. If only the duck knew the things we attributed to him. He's woken us up a bit, that's for sure.

Simon heaved his body, the extraordinary weight of his body, up from the bench.

Well, there you go, he said once more.

She stepped down from the shed, with Simon following. The trees were filled with the chatter of birds: clucks and clicks and burbles, looped together with long sighing whistles. It sounded like a busy conference, earnest and urgent. She wondered what they were saying and whether the different species of birds were making any sense of each other. She wondered whether they noticed that the duck had disappeared since she and Toby had forced him into a box, and whether this influenced their attitude towards her. She thought of the crows that she once used as symbols for the pressure of her work. She had shot them all, turning down the last couple of contracts. She had dismissed the outside world and pulled herself away.

And now, the release of this ancient secret preserved in formalin, in a jar whose lid was so corroded that when Simon brought it out to Maggie that night, the lid had crumbled in the unscrewing. The contents had been leaking all over the place ever since.

As they made their uncertain way across the lawn towards the house, she stopped, turning to grab Simon's arm.

Listen, she said.

What?

Listen! She shook his arm excitedly. It's the duck! He's returned! He's come back to us.

Simon's face dropped with disbelief as he, too, recognised the unmistakable tones of a particular whiny sound that the duck often made. They both shifted their heads to ascertain the direction. Not the deck, not the grass. The tree. He was in the magnolia tree. But wait.

It's a tui! said Simon, and his voice couldn't hide his relief. It's mimicking the duck.

And he was right. They could just see the silhouette of a tui with its curly white beard hopping amongst the branches.

At that moment, the hedge shuddered and two little figures pushed through, followed by Sheila with her ropey fountain of hair shooting from her head.

Hi, she called. I thought I heard voices. Hey Simon, good to see you. Hannah, I thought you'd like an update about Dad. He said to thank you for the flowers and your note.

Rosemary ran towards them. Where's the chicken? she asked Hannah shyly. One eye was screwed up tightly against the sun, pulling her face into a lopsided grimace. Max was racing towards the pond.

Not chicken, she said. Duck. Muscovy duck. And he's not here.

Where is he?

He's . . . he's been taken to a circus. Where there are other ducks to play with.

Oh, that's a load off my mind, said Sheila. I was worried that if we were going to be around he might be a problem. Having seen him in action. Dad's coming home in a week or so. They're still doing some assessment and rehabilitation, but mainly it's a matter of getting his medication right. He was supposed to be taking pills regularly but he wouldn't, until he felt unwell and then he'd take a heap. So anyway, we're going to move in with him for a while. We want to buy a house, so this'll save us rent and we can keep an eye on Dad. Just for a few months or so, or a year, till he's right. Or not right, whatever the case.

There was a splash and a yelp: Max had fallen into the pond. He was sitting with the water up to his waist, jiggling with a flashing whir of orange, using his chin and jerking fingers in an attempt to restrain the flapping goldfish until it sploshed back to the water.

Did you see that! he cried to his mother as she dashed to his aid. I caught it!

His face was beaming with triumph. He climbed onto the bridge, spreading his tanned little arms proudly, his cotton shirt stuck to his body, his shorts festooned with loops of green slime.

No, cried Sheila. *Don't* jump in again. Look, you're soaking wet. Really, that pond should be fenced. Rosemary! *Rosemary*, what are you doing? Come out of that coop at once!

The chicken's gone, Rosemary announced, crawling out of the old cage still lodged on the lawn, her knees and pink dress streaked with mucky mud.

Look at you. Oh no, *look* at you!

The garden was invaded.

Simon turned and trudged up the steps to the deck. Sheila managed to gather the children together — Rosemary, grubby, on her hip, and Max, dripping, ensnared by her hand tightly over his — and they all disappeared through the hedge as the aftermath of the whirlwind was still fluttering to Earth.

Hannah stayed in the garden, listening to the birds, feeling the warmth of the autumn sun soaking into her hair. She had a sense of unease. She sieved through her mind, but whenever she felt near to hooking the source of her disquiet, it flipped away from her as adeptly as the goldfish had escaped Max's bumbling fingers.

THE HOUSE, EXPANDING AROUND THEM

Silence knitting its sticky web into every corner. They were two souls echoing off the walls, doubtful now as to how to *be* with each other. All the elements of their relationship in chaos, while each pretending that they were relieved to be home-and-hosed in the old status quo. They were wearing the same faded masks, the same tatty costumes. They danced the steps they had been practising since they first met, while each was taunted by the intolerable monotony of the tune.

THE WALNUT

When Eric was discharged from hospital a couple of weeks later, Hannah visited him formally, knocking at the front door with muffins she had baked. She was nervous. She'd chosen her clothes carefully, changing twice before deciding. Sheila let her in, shepherded her towards the kitchen. He's better than he was, she told Hannah, but he's still not quite himself.

Why, after more than a decade, was she thrown back to the time when they had talked and laughed and teased each other so freely, when he had played his cello to her in this kitchen as she fried bacon and eggs? Perhaps it was those words spontaneously released as he lay beside her in the grass by the hedge. And now he was sitting in a chair with his back to the window as she entered, his face hidden by a magazine he was reading, held up to catch the light.

Visitor, Dad, said Sheila, popping her head around the corner before she left them. He snapped down a page, and there he was, an old man, his skin too loose, and his cheeks puffs of soft pink. And the image was dispelled.

Hello, she said, placing the muffins in front of him. It's good to have you back.

He put his magazine down, and pulled his chair up to the table.

And yes, he was gruff but, thank goodness, friendly and beguilingly shy.

She sat across from him. You've been through a rough patch.

I believe I owe you an apology . . .

Not at all. I'm glad you're feeling better. She looked around the clean kitchen. All his jars of screws and small bowls of oddments, and bundles of accounts shoved behind bottles and appliances, had been tidied away. A bowl of fruit gleamed in a ray of sunlight. She noticed a single walnut amongst the feijoas, bananas, kiwifruit. Crayon and felt-pen drawings were stuck with magnets onto the fridge.

I was just thinking . . . I haven't heard your cello or the fiddle for a while.

Nah. They're gathering dust. Like everything else.

I miss the music, she told him.

Little strokes, he said.

What do you mean?

Little strokes. Little soft strokes.

Oh? She remembered how his hand had lifted through her hair, his fingers on the back of her neck.

He nodded slowly. Yep. That's what they said. Little strokes building up.

Oh. You mean, what they said in the hospital?

Thanks for the cakes, he said. She could hear the muffled thunder of kids running through the house, the squealing of voices, an eruption of wailing. The house reviving itself with the energy of young life again.

I'd better go, she said. But I just wanted to say hello. That's all.

Thank you, he said. A single tear suddenly burst from his eye and flowed down his face.

Eric, she said gently. Are you all right? What's wrong?

I'm hungry, he said.

She suggested he have an apple, or a banana, or a feijoa. What about a muffin? I'll butter one for you. Baked this morning. But he ignored her.

I'm hungry, he repeated. They don't feed you here.

He stared at her. Then he reached his hand across the table and clutched her forearm tightly, giving it a brief shake, as if to check for life. Her own eyes welled. Retrieving her arm, she stood up, stepping on a green plastic car in the process. She had to grab the table to prevent herself from skidding across the room.

Ooops, she said, and they both laughed.

Hope you had a good trip, he said, his voice unexpectedly lifting.

See you later, alligator. She blew him a kiss from the door as she left the kitchen and let herself out of the house.

DARK THOUGHTS

I'm just over half a century old, thought Hannah as she lay in the dark next to her husband.

Her mother had been seventy-nine when she died. If she lived as long, she had another twenty-eight years to fill in. All those years drifting before her as empty as a balloon. More than half the length of her life again. What would she do with the time? She couldn't think of one thing to do. She didn't have one thing left to say. Or anyone to say it to.

Simon was unmoving beside her. He was awake, his back bent away from her. He was a man lost in the snow, curled around the burning embers of a fire that was eating him inside out. She let him lie there. She was glad he was suffering. As it happened, so was she.

She slipped from the bedclothes and went downstairs, opening the ranch sliders to stand in the centre of the deck, her arms folded across her breasts for warmth. Far away from here, a large muscovy duck was huddled alone in a forty-four-gallon drum, his feathery eyelids opening and closing, opening and closing as the unfamiliar noises rustled and squeaked and sighed and mooed and barked around him. And whose eye would he look for in the daytime, now that she wasn't there? He would have no vital connection any more. No recognition. How could she have betrayed him so?

Several times she had rung, only to be assured by both Bob and Claire that he was doing well. He'd gone off his food a little the first few days, but was now eating the mash that Bob was putting out for him, and the supply of wheat she had left. As far as Annabel was concerned, she was told, there was no point, if he was to start responding to the ducks, the females. The drakes had noticed him, though, and had done a bit of pacing along the wire netting.

He'd be bereft without Annabel, she knew that. It was cruel. How could they be so cruel? It wasn't much to ask, to hose down a towel each day. They were forcing him to go cold turkey. She had looked up the term. It originally meant 'without preparation', alluding to the convenience of preparing a dish from cold cooked turkey. And then later, in the 1920s, the term was extended to the abrupt stopping of an addiction. When a heroin junkie broke the habit, the blood being drawn to the internal organs made the skin look like a cold plucked turkey. Either way, the turkey was dead, and plucked.

Her feet felt icy now and a light breeze was shifting her nightdress around her legs.

A light was switched on behind her. She could hear Simon in the toilet. She moved off the top deck and down to the bottom step, where she sat, pulling her knees up to her chin, her nightdress around her legs. Then another light filtered from the deck above, then another. Soon the whole house was flooded with light, a cruise ship coming in to port.

Hannah. Hannah! She could hear the panic winging her name across the night.

Hannah?

And then he was towering above her, his shins behind her head as he paused on the step behind. His shadow sprawled menacingly, another cut-out layer of darkness across the lawn.

Why didn't you answer me?

Because I hate you, she wanted to say.

Why are you sitting in the freezing cold?

Because you slept with my sister. Because my womb is a useless cavity stuffed with feathers. Because you made me give up my duck for nothing.

You'll catch your death. I was worried about you. Why aren't you answering me?

Because you don't love me anymore. Because you have cut me adrift into the rest of my life.

Hannah? Speak to me.

He was sitting beside her now, his bottom shunting into hers, his arm around her shoulder. Leaning around to look at her. The flat palm of his hand brushing away the tears streaking her face.

I hate you, she muttered matter-of-factly. And there, it was said, not to be unsaid, a tip-truck full of rubble pouring endlessly from her heart, the whole nasty black heap in front of them.

His arm dropped from hers, another bird shot from a high branch in a tree.

That's a pity, he said. That's a great pity. Then he added, A bloody terrible pity.

Well, what do you expect? You slept with my sister for heaven's sake. I tried to ignore it, but I can't.

Actually, and I know you won't believe me, but I didn't.

You're right. I don't believe you. And the worst thing is that you still love her.

Hannah. Listen to me.

He explained how, the night before she arrived home with Toby, he was just preparing for bed upstairs. He heard Maggie give a yelp. They were a bit drunk. He went down to find Maggie crazy with fury. Hannah's nightdress and paraphernalia from under the pillow, along with Toby's socks and underwear from the floor, were displayed in a heap on the dressing table. Simon, too, was incensed. Somehow, and he assured her hurriedly that he knew two wrongs didn't make a right, but they fell into bed together, fuelled with — he said — feelings of revenge. Simon had become aware of a lump in the bed, investigated, and emerged from under the duvet with the urn. Maggie was beside herself. She grabbed it, opened the window and threw it into the bushes below. They had little energy left for anything else and the two of them fell asleep. And they were both awakened by dreams of her mother.

Mine was so vivid, he said. She was sitting in bed between us, her arms folded, in her lacy nightdress, the one she was wearing when she died. And she was singing that old Jim Reeves song, rocking rhythmically . . . 'I Love You Most of All Because You're You'.

He dropped his chin on Hannah's shoulder.

I woke up crying, he continued. It was very bizarre. I don't know what Maggie's dream was about — she wouldn't say — but it certainly featured your mother. The dreams freaked us out. Enough for Maggie to take herself down to the garden and rescue the urn. She wrapped it up in the pink blanket, the one she gave your Mum a few Christmases ago. The next morning she took the bundle down to the shed, as you know. She insisted on being alone. She was quite upset.

That song, the one in your dream, said Hannah. Mum loved that song. We used to play Jim Reeves around the fireplace on winter nights when we were kids. Did you know that?

I'm not sure. You may have told me once.

Good old Mum, said Hannah. But if all that hadn't happened, you and Maggie would have . . .

Yes, to be honest, it was heading that way. But we didn't.

But it's the intention that counts.

Really? Is that so? Well, perhaps there is something you can explain to me, Hannah, if we're talking about counting. Hmmm?

Hannah sighed. For heaven's sake. Nothing was happening at all. I painted our room, as you know. I had a notion that I wanted to keep it clean and fresh for when, if, you came home. A symbol of new beginnings, if you like. So I'd been sleeping downstairs in the spare room, in Mum's old room. You can check, I've still got some of my clothes there. The day I was concussed, I must have forgotten, taken myself up to our bedroom automatically. I still don't remember much, actually. I bled on the new pillow. Anyway, when Toby arrived he was in a bit of state, so he collapsed into bed. All my stuff, my nightdress, was still there under the pillow. And then I forgot about it because by then I was sleeping in another nightdress. Upstairs. Believe me or not, that's how it was.

I do believe you, Hannah. Toby explained all that. But there's another thing.

Oh yes, what? she asked. He was pulling his chin to his chest, to one shoulder, to his chest, to the other shoulder. Those neck exercises.

You and Eric? Was that intentional or accidental?

Her stomach twisted. She didn't know what to say.

What do you mean? she tried.

Don't deny it, Hannah.

That was eleven years ago.

Oh, I see. If the infidelity occurs a long time ago, it doesn't count. Whether the intent was there or not, does count. Whether the act actually happens or not, doesn't count. What about the location? What about the method? All these things you have done and ought not to have done. Have you ever had unclean thoughts, Hannah?

Stop it, Simon. OK, how on earth do you know?

Oh, does this count in the final judgment as well? How I found out? Well, let me tell you. Your mother told me, bless her.

Mum? But she didn't know. No one knew. I didn't tell one soul. Not one. Only Eric and I knew . . . well, *I* didn't tell anyone.

Well, she told me. So she must have known.

When was this?

Oh, a wee while before she died. She must have been wanting to clean the slate.

I see. I see now. . . So you said something to Eric.

I quietly told him that I believed he'd had an inappropriate relationship with my wife. And when he didn't deny it, I just told him that he wasn't welcome at our house anymore. That's all. It was all very civilised.

Why didn't you say anything to me?

You were having an emotionally gruelling time as your mother went downhill. Then after she died, you were unhappy enough. As you said, and as Eric told me, it was a long time ago. I might have eventually brought it up. As I have.

They sat unspeaking for a while. Somewhere across the valley a manic babble of voices flowed from a party. All meaning was lost over the distance travelled, as words dropped out of sentences like items spilling from a suitcase. A few isolated phrases made the journey: 'but did you . . .', 'yeah but you, you . . .', 'going like the clappers . . .' Frequent explosions of laughter arrived intact. The revellers were young. She envied their easy laughter.

She thought of a university party she'd gone to with Simon in the early days, before they were married. He was somewhere else, perhaps getting a drink, while she was locked into a corner by a guy with stale breath who was zealously telling her of the declining population of Emperor penguins in the Antarctic. She remembered the closely cropped hair above his ears, the lemon shirt and tie. She was sure she could smell hairspray, but it was his breath that forced her to back further and further into the corner until she felt as though her body was angled ninety degrees in relation to her spine. Simon arrived, hovered for a while, couldn't get a word in. Hannah rolled her eyes desperately. Simon picked up the bottom of the guy's tie, dipped it well into his glass of beer and splatted it first against one cheek — 'One small slap for man' — then the other — 'and a giant slap for mankind. Now please,' he said. 'Can't you see she's not interested.'

At the time she'd found the incident alarming, but it was the first indication that Simon would rescue her should the need arise. What was that guy doing now? He felt like a creep then, confident and unsubtle as he cramped her space. Now she realised he was just a lonely buffoon, unable to read social cues. Had anyone told him about his bad breath? The population of the Emperor penguins was still declining. He was a nonentity fixed in her memory. She remembered how he'd swung around to confront Simon. There was going to be a fight. She grabbed the guy's arm and steered him out to a balcony, where people she half-knew were smoking cigarettes. Hi, she said. This is . . . sorry, what's your name? As soon as they were all engaged in conversation, she fled, back to Simon.

She shivered.

Her body was aching with cold, but she didn't want to go inside where everything would become the normal pretence again.

The way I see it is this, Simon was saying. He lifted a side of his large fleecy dressing gown to include her, wrapping it like a cloak around the two of them. We're both in our fifties. I guess if you hate me you're also telling me you want to leave me. But what I have to ask is this. What about love? I love you, Hannah. If we leave each other, we may or may not find someone else. Or we can get on with our lives and do the solitary thing, without any encumbrances. Be free. But it's not what I want. I want to be with you. I *like* being with you.

Why did you leave me, then?

You'd shut me out. And after your mother died, for different reasons, we'd both moved away from each other. I needed to think. So, when I was offered this work down in Christchurch, I thought I'd go and see what happened.

I bet it was Maggie's idea. You love her.

Hannah. I love *you*. I'd *told* you I had the possibility of a contract offered down there and I'd *asked* you to come along. Would have *preferred* you to come, but you wouldn't. I mentioned the contract to Maggie, who suggested I follow it up. As for love, well, possibly in the same way you love Toby? They're very different from us, Hannah, as you know. Maggie would never be interested in an old fuddy-duddy like me. I've come to the conclusion that I have a tendency to be boring. When they're sober or not totally drunk, they're sharp and funny and alive together. They were both kind to me. But Maggie has had some very difficult times with Toby. When he's under the influence of drugs or alcohol he can be nasty. Or worrying. But I certainly wouldn't be the one she'd be interested in, in that way.

He was talking to himself now.

You're not *that* boring, she said.

But quite, he replied.

Something inside her was splitting open. A tight membrane, tearing from end to end, to release an explosion of laughter. She managed to contain it.

Yes, she said quietly. I think you might be.

A police helicopter was moving across the sky above them. Men cocooned in a hovering machine, staring down at the world below. She wondered if they could determine the motion of the sea. But no, they'd be focused on searching for someone, like a rat in a field, cowering from a hawk.

She could jump up waving her arms, screaming. We surrender! We've stolen from each other, withheld information, done away with body parts, committed adultery. Cruelty to animals, to each other, unclean thoughts. Drugs. We're the criminals you're looking for.

But the helicopter veered off and soon was just a shudder in the distance. They were nobodies, unwanted by anybody. The party across the valley was diminishing in intensity or had moved inside. Now they were surrounded by the piping sounds of those unknown insects. Rhythmic squeaks from the rusty turning wheel of night.

One thing you might be able to answer for me, Simon, she said.

What's that?

How did I fill my time up until now? What did I do with my minutes, my weeks, my months, my years and years and years? How did I get to this actual point in time? What did I *do?* What have I *done* with my life?

He didn't answer. He clasped her closer under the big tent of his dressing gown, with the big comforting cradle of his arm. Every leaf around them was licked with light, from the hedge, from the giant feather fronds of a palm, all leaning towards them, as if waiting for an answer. Enormous shiny tongues of strelitzia hung on their every word. And now a car swishing from one edge of the night to the other.

That's a very good question, he said eventually, and I'm not sure that I can answer it.

Bugger, she said.

He shifted his buttocks uncomfortably.

Since my stay in Christchurch, I have been interrogating myself along similar lines. There was all the upheaval with you. Then the earthquake. I don't think anyone who experienced that February earthquake was left unscathed. I still have nightmares.

He shook his head, inhaled a jerky breath.

When I was there, I was around people who'd shared the experience, in however great or small a way. It was a bizarre matter of needing to have been there to be a member of the club. Everyone had their story of where they were at the time: near-misses from fridges and microwaves flying across the room, separation from loved ones, just leaving a room at that moment when a boulder crashed through the roof. After the quake, we were all in it together, helping if we could. There was something about that . . . a sense of being useful, of being part of the community. Now — and you'll think I'm mad — I feel that I'm abandoning them. The shakes are still happening and I'm up here doing nothing. I feel guilty. Alone, because at least down there everyone knows what you're going through.

So you want to go back?

No, I don't think so. I'm relieved to be out of it because it was constantly frightening. And I was an outsider anyway. I had the choice to leave or not. Some don't. But I can't help thinking about it. Ideally I'd like to be with you, as we used to be, whether we were together or not, just knowing we were there for each other.

We'll never be the same. Nothing will ever be as it used to be. My mother's dead, you've been in a tragic earthquake. She would have liked to add 'And I have met a duck', but it didn't seem appropriate. She said, Things have happened that have shifted our outlook from its axis.

She shoved herself closer to him, desperately drawing from the warmth of his body.

The thing is, he said, I think I'm nursing a terrible sense of despair.

She conjured an image of him sitting on a hilltop, rocking a grey bundle of non-descript gloom.

Simon, she said. I'm sorry. She curled her fingers around his cold knee. She could have said instead, 'You'll come right', but remembered how dismissive it felt when he'd uttered the same words a few months ago.

It sounds stupid, I know. But. That man dying in agony, alone, under a crush of rubble. What would he be thinking? All the thoughts, the stream of his consciousness that fed his whole living being, flying from him, through him, unreceived, his life leaving him. The data of his life flowing from him. And so . . . Of course you find yourself thinking of all the other people crying in pain, alone. Our lives in general have become very isolated and selfish. And then. Toby. I don't know whether you know, he so nearly died from a drug overdose. It was terribly distressing for Maggie. I think she was pleased I was there, for the little support I could offer.

Simon, she said again, hating her simplistic words. I am sorry. What can we do? Her fingertips explored the bones of his kneecap, around the rigid tendons behind and into the known flesh of his thigh, then rested there.

He pulled her closer.

That's it: I have no idea.

Actually, I don't hate you at all.

That's progress I suppose. But it feels there's a way to go.

Remember that time, she said, when we were young. When you and Roy went for a tramp in the Tararuas. I had a cold. Was happy to stay back in the hut, a fire in the potbelly, waiting for you. And you didn't return when you should have. We'd known each other for about a year. By the time I realised you were late it was pitch dark. I only had candles. I lay there, the wind and rain lashing at the windows, worrying about you. No cell phones then, of course. I started trying to imagine what life would be without you and decided that if I didn't have you, well, I may as well be dead. But when you turned up . . . Roy had twisted his ankle . . . When you walked in, I just looked up from the book I was reading, in my sleeping bag on the bunk, and said 'hi'. Grumpily. I remember so clearly how I was surprised by my own display of nonchalance. I don't know why I'm telling you this . . . God, I'm so cold, she said finally.

So am I.

I'm absolutely freezing. Let's go inside.

I don't think I can move. My hips are aching. I've turned to stone.

Me, too.

Perhaps we're dead, he said.

We could be. We seem to have all the symptoms.

Oh well, that sorts that out.

I suppose it does.

I'm glad we're together, though.

Me, too.

She took his hand and held it to her breast.

I really, really, really don't hate you, she said.

That's good, he said, unravelling himself, groaning, stretching. He helped her up and together they went inside.

Chapter 30

THE MORNING AFTER

The woman lay comfortably in the arms of her husband as the sun sluiced its way through the bedroom curtains.

What was it that had wrenched them apart, so insidiously that the distance between them had seemed insurmountable? Unbridgeable. But here they were. They must have fallen from on high, turning over and over like stones from the moon, to land neatly into the nest of each other's grasp.

She shifted to watch his face as he lay sleeping, curiously examining the corners and expression of his newly revealed lips. They were parted now and he was snoring softly.

She was waiting, patiently, for him to wake up. The night had been particularly tender, and they had both felt so grateful, and relieved, that she knew that nothing could interfere with the contentment they had found once more. It had been there all along, a misplaced recipe tucked as a marker in a book they'd been reading. A life they'd been living.

He suddenly gasped, his lips and mouth panicking, chomping on a dream-feast before it disappeared. He opened his eyes, closed them again, opened them, looked at her, and then relaxed, his face melting.

Oh. Hello, he said, smiling warmly.

Hi, she said, pressing her body more closely to his.

After a while she said, Simon?

Hmmmm?

I think it's going to be a lovely day.

It is already, he said. He stroked her hair from her face. I feel it in my bones. The walls around them were pristine white, but on the ceiling above the window, a daddy-long-legs was tremulously occupied with building its web.

I've been thinking . . . she said.

Hmmm?

Do you feel like a drive?

That sounds nice. Why not?

Do you think we could go to . . . Te Awamutu? Not to stay, just to say hello to the duck, and back again. I promise I won't ask for any more than that. We won't tell them. We'll just surprise them.

He tensed, itching his ear urgently, as if her suggestion had landed badly there. Abruptly, he turned his face to the wall. Then back again, to look at her. He was frowning now, bringing his bottom teeth over his lip to comb a moustache that didn't exist any more.

I mean if you really don't want to, we don't have to.

She waited.

Oh all right, he said with a short sigh. He kissed her forehead. OK. All right then. Why not.

SURPRISE VISIT

Claire was in her gumboots in the garden when they pulled up. She stood up, grimacing as her hands propped her back. Squinting at the car, then walking over.

Well, this is a surprise, she said, pulling off her gardening gloves, combing her fingers through her hair in a futile effort to tidy her appearance. Her hair was like the willows in the area, Hannah thought, the ends chewed level by cows reaching up for more green.

Claire gave them both a hug as they emerged from the car. Just trying to get at the weeds. They never let up. Come on in. I'll put the kettle on. I was just going to have an egg on toast. Come in. And you must take some eggs back with you. We can't get through them all ourselves. All well with you, Hannah? Lovely to see you two back together again. I don't know where Bob is. He might be at the neighbours'. Oh dear. There's a nip in the air, isn't there? Now, where did Bob say he was going? Come on then, come in.

Hannah moved towards Simon, slipped her hand into the protective glove of his own.

Actually, Claire, Simon said. She was engaged in prising her foot out of her gumboot, banging the heel at an upturned spade head buried in concrete. Once done, she yanked up the wad of green woollen socks over her pearly legs, pulled her jean legs over the top and stepped into fur-lined slippers waiting at the porch.

Actually, before we have a cuppa, Hannah was keen to see her duck. Do you mind?

No, of course, of course, of course, Hannah dear. Take yourself down. You know where it is. Are you coming in, Simon?

He caught Hannah's eye, and she shrugged.

I'll be fine, she said. In fact, she was happy to greet her duck alone. She didn't want their meeting to be compromised or sabotaged by the man, or to have the old jealousies rekindled.

As she wound her way around the side of the house, she was almost effervescing with excitement. Her feet swishing through crunchy leaves, the fragrance of autumn sweet and earthy. She loved the full range of countryside smells, so natural and evocative. She walked around the paddock and down to the macrocarpa trees where muscovy ducks were waddling, their tails propelling them along. And chooks scuffing and pecking at the ground. As she approached, some of the hens squawked, scurrying for cover, triggering a general movement away from her.

She slowed her pace. The muscovies also had their eyes on her, keeping their distance. Most of the drakes looked scruffy and she could see patches of naked wing. Moulting time, as Bob had said last time. She went to the pens where there was another brood of ducklings squeaking around their mother, as well as the larger, more gangly ones, probably the little ones she had seen a month or so ago. In the pen next door, the forty-four-gallon drum sat empty, and its pillow was pegged onto the wire netting. The lid that had held the mash was empty. Where was her duck? She wasn't aware that he had been liberated into the company of the other muscovies.

She checked the other pens, as well as the chook house, then took herself around the trees to an elevated place where she could view the pond. A couple of muscovies were puddling around the edge of the water, vacuuming up bugs with their eyes turned upwards, as her duck used to do. Bulrushes grew in the shallows, alongside clumps of flax bushes with arcing spears of spent flower heads. The surface of the pond had fraying strips of duckweed. A kingfisher launched itself from a nearby branch and flew away.

And now she found herself looking for a scattering of white feathers on the grass or floating in the water. She scanned the paddocks. She spun around, checking and re-checking the grass, the trees, the pens, the pond, the grass, trees, pens, grass trees pens pond grass. How ridiculous to feel so anxious. There would be an explanation. Perhaps she didn't recognise him. Perhaps he had adapted to his flock life so completely that he was hiding from her, fearful that she might take him away.

Down at the pond she called him, her shoes flooding in the swampy mud. A rat suddenly rocketed from beneath the flax, across the field, and disappeared down a hole.

Then she noticed in a far paddock, almost obscured by a patch of manuka, the figure of a man closing a gate. She could see him climbing into a white ute waiting on the near side. The truck started up and she could now hear it rumbling its way along a dirt track around the base of the hill, bouncing and jogging its way in her direction. As it approached she became aware of a flyaway mop of hair above the steering wheel. Bob, of course. He stopped near his shed. She hurried up to meet him, and was there to greet him impatiently as he clambered out. The door hung open from the cab like a broken wing. She kissed his sweaty fat cheek.

Claire rang me, he said. Told me you were here. Where's Simon?

Up with Claire. I was just . . . just looking for my duck. She knew by his face that something was amiss. She could feel tears collecting, in readiness.

Oh, didn't Claire tell you? Just yesterday . . .

He stopped.

What? What happened to my duck? Where is he?

Ssssh, no it's OK. He dipped his hand under his shirt, into his arm pit, beyond his arm pit, scrabbling intently for an evasive itch. I was out. I was out and someone drove to the house from the road. They do that sometimes. We've got a sign there.

He was watching her to see how she was taking it. Let's have a cup of tea.

Tell me. What have you done with my duck?

They didn't ring. They had a little boy in the back, very pale. Ill, as it turned out. They wanted a duck to take back home. They'd had one before but they'd been . . . overseas and had to let it go somewhere. A lovely family. An Indian family. They wanted another one as a pet for the little boy.

So you gave them my duck.

Well, Claire said they could choose which duck they wanted, and they selected your duck. Claire didn't realise it was your duck.

But he can be aggressive and then what'll they do? How old was the boy?

About ten or eleven, apparently. Very pale. Big brown eyes. And *really* wanting a muscovy, apparently.

Have you got their address? Did she give them Annabel? I hope she told them about Annabel. Otherwise he'll be aggressive.

No, oh no, I forgot to say. He'd become interested in another duck, a female, just one other duck actually, and they took that as well, as a pair. Possibly even to breed.

Can you give me their address? Just so I can check, that he's in a good home.

No, they came and went. They just drove in from nowhere and left. They're either from Wellington or Auckland. Or was it somewhere in Hawke's Bay? I actually have no idea where they live, to tell you the truth.

She flopped down to sit on the grass. I'm going to be sick, she said. Truly, I'm going to be sick.

Oh, said Bob. Can I get you anything?

I can't believe you would do this. In fact, I don't. This is a euphemism for the travelling circus, isn't it?

No, Hannah, don't be silly. And if I'd been here it wouldn't have happened; Claire didn't realise he was your duck. A duck is a duck so far as she's concerned. And the little boy was so happy apparently. They've got a stream on their property, they said, all fenced off. They know about muscovy ducks.

Hannah yanked at chunks of grass. In the rich black soil underneath, a worm extricated itself from view. Can you please ask Simon to come and get me, she said. Tell him I want to go home right now.

When he left, she curled up in the grass, until Simon arrived and knelt alongside her, his warm comforting hand on her shoulder.

Chapter 31

BREAD

June the third. It is the first anniversary of the death of Hannah's mother. It is also the anniversary of the simulated take-off of six men to Mars from a Moscow hangar. They have reached their destination and are on their way back, and now they are grappling with boredom.

The heater is on and Hannah is making bread. The room is filled with the same comforting smell of basic cooking that has wafted from ovens through the ages. As she breathes, she absorbs the ethereal vapours of her mother and her grandmother and great-great-great-grandmothers that have been transported through time, only to stop with her.

On the floor, by the deck windows, two children are lying on their stomachs, each with their own desk-pad, a packet of felt-pens and a box of crayons. Their mother is taking Eric to a doctor's appointment. Rosemary is drawing wavily elliptical circles, which she is attempting to colour in with her crayons. She also has a couple of sheets of stickers, and from time to time calls to Hannah to help her peel these off to place around her drawing. Max is drawing stick-figures that float randomly through his picture with arms spread like wings. He hasn't yet thought to anchor them to the ground. He has also scribbled great swirls of dense black smoke. Enemy fire.

Hannah thinks of her mother, but at the moment no specific memories are coming. She is thinking of the essence of the person she once was . . . warm and generous, kind, with a sense of humour, and a love of colour and beauty. All the usual stuff of a hastily drawn-up CV with unexplained gaps. And she is also wondering what has happened to her duck. Whether he is still alive, and whether he really managed to move from Annabel to a pretty pink-faced duck. She has forced herself to believe Bob's story because the alternative is too painful to endure. And perhaps it *is* true that he is waddling around a bubbling stream with his wife and ducklings, cared for by a pale little boy who has a passion for muscovies.

Simon flew to Christchurch a couple of days ago to collect his car. The plans for Toby to drive it up to Auckland dissolved into repeated last-minute postponements, though now it has been decided that both

Maggie and Toby will accompany Simon on this trip, to stay for a short visit. She is looking forward to seeing them. After Toby left, he and Hannah texted each other with jovial encouragement for their respective withdrawals. Gradually Toby's texts became more cynical and gloomy in content, less frequent, until they stopped altogether. Christchurch was still experiencing unnerving shakes. Meanwhile Maggie and Simon were in contact with each other as well. Simon reported that Toby had had a bit of a relapse but was now back on track.

The oven timer dings and Hannah pulls out two loaves of bread. She tips the tins upside-down and leaves them steaming on racks, two identical brown modules. She opens the window enough to let a stream of heat mingle with the nippy morning air.

For some reason a stray memory arrives unbidden through the open window. Questions from afar, from a day when Hannah was visiting her mother at Primrose Hill. A pensive little voice asking, So will I write poetry and put it in my head?

It seemed the best thing for Hannah to assure her that she would. Then she asked, Are they going to take it away on Saturday?

Only if you want them to, Mum.

Then, as Hannah was kissing her on the cheek before leaving, her mother asked, Will they look after you well when they take you away from me?

Hannah sighs. The old nostalgia is pouring back again. In a way she welcomes it, just for the day, for the occasion. She knows that it is tied up with love and she knows that it is an ephemeral thing that is beyond comprehension or control, and that one day it will find a place within her where it can rest comfortably and without pain.

As she sits on the sofa, she watches the children experimenting with shape and colour. Then she drops onto her stomach between them, takes a piece of paper, and starts to draw as well.

SALT

When you get to the beach you leave Simon and the others, and head towards the shoreline. Tiny wavelets are snapping crossly at your feet. You take both loaves from the plastic bag and roll them in the water, to make sure the crusty exterior is wet all over. Not too soggy, but damp. This is to prevent anyone nibbling at the bread.

The sky is icy blue except for suds of white cloud scattered above the brim — little lost ducks blown away from their flock. The sea is blue too, with streaks of silver. A kite-surfer is hurtling along under his bow of kite, catapulting like an escaping cricket, trampolining like a grasshopper on a bluegrass field. The beach is empty of life except for a man and his dog at the far end, and a couple marching arm-in-arm towards you. The man is throwing sticks and the dog is paddling out through the taut sea to fetch them, its ears held flat against its head. You watch the dog warily but decide it is far enough away.

You are sure that somewhere there will be a grounded cluster of seagulls all angled to the same direction, hunched up restlessly against the biting wind with their heads under their wings. There will also be a perky scout on a lamp post or in a tree, on the look-out for food. You tear off a small chunk of bread and throw it in the air. Nothing. You pick up the same piece and throw it again. You start to walk and repeat the action. There they are, two of them, the sentinels, lifting their heads; they have noticed the bread.

They rise, circling high in the sky, before landing near your feet to gobble up the food. They are making sure they get their share before their signal brings the competition. The other seagulls must be watching somewhere or have secondary scouts, because they don't come until you throw more. You are sure that there must be some remote communication between them. You throw another piece of soggy crust. The seagulls quickly snaffle it. Their beaks are sharp and red. You break off more and soon another three gulls arrive. Then there are more, and you throw more lumps of bread, which are readily devoured. You check that each piece has gone before you throw another batch.

Simon and Maggie and Toby are bunched under the shelter of pohutukawa which lean from a grassy verge over the beach. She waves to them and they saunter down. Toby's thin face pokes from a helmet of fat hood, his body padded in a blue Michelin puffer jacket. His face is purple. He is smoking. Maggie is bundled up in layers of red scarf, and a black woollen coat. Simon looks the most relaxed in his red parka and jeans. Nonetheless they are all cold and reluctant to be here. It is only because she has persuaded them to. When Simon and Toby agreed, Maggie complied. She is making an effort to be nice, Hannah notices.

She throws the bread into the wind, and suddenly the sky is teeming with gulls. Simon is informative: The large ones are black-backed gulls. Then you've got the smaller black-billed gulls with the black legs, and the red-billed gulls with the red legs. You might notice, he says, that the black- and red-billed gulls catch the bread in the air. They're accustomed to catching insects as they fly — cicadas, mosquitoes, beetles, whatever. And the big brown ones over there are the baby black-backed gulls.

She breaks the rest of the first loaf into three, and hand out the pieces. Toby extricates blanched fingers from his sleeve to take his portion. Sparse fair hairs over his hands doing a useless job of keeping him warm. Auntie Hannah, he says between clenched teeth, you are killing us. Let's find a nice warm café and have a coffee. Or, even better, a nice soul-warming red. No Toby, says Maggie, not a wine. They all dutifully toss out their bits of bread into the sand to the crazy wailing squabbling gulls.

Come on, let's walk, you say, and you start marching along the beach. The seagulls land in front of you. One of the black-backed gulls opens its throat and screams. Its gullet is a tunnel that leads to the centre of time, to the black hole of all the big questions. You throw bread from the second loaf specifically to that bird, but it's too busy complaining. The cacophony of wings and feet and beaks beats him to it. You toss another which it grabs.

You fling small chunks high into the air. All around you and above you is the whacking of wings and swishing of slicing bodies. Some of the gulls swoop cleanly by and take the bread mid-air with such beautiful precision that you do it again. You love the way they anticipate the rise and allow for the wind and take the bread in their beaks so effortlessly. You love the feeling of heaving your arms into the air to throw.

She stops. The others have dished out their bread and they are gathered in a huddle, talking. They are scrutinising something that Simon has picked up from the beach. They seem serious. Simon has his hand on Maggie's shoulder. Toby is stamping his feet in the sand.

She heads back towards them. They all look up at her, their faces pinched and stern.

Her heart sinks. Down and down.

What? she says.

Simon is the spokesman.

We know what you've done, he says to her. Maggie and Toby are standing alongside him. Maggie pressed against his arm. Toby shuffling and rubbing his hands. Flint against bone.

What?

You could have consulted with us.

What?

Maggie was just saying how your mother always wanted to come back as a seagull — so she could 'soar above the world', in her words. And it was Toby who put two and two together. That's right, isn't it?

Yes, it is.

You could have told us.

I know, I'm sorry. But you never asked . . . what we should do. And I thought, since we were all together and it was the anniversary yesterday . . . I'm sorry.

And down, how much further down, her heart. Sinking.

She turns, hurries from them, along the lonely empty windswept beach. The plastic bag with the leftover bread is whalloping her knee as she strides. The couple out walking has disappeared. The seagulls are beginning to disperse, although several are still skittering faithfully in the sand ahead of her.

Hannah! Hannah! They are surrounding her now, pressing in against her, Simon, Toby and even Maggie, their arms around each other's backs, all bustling and enclosing her as she weeps. And when she looks into their faces, they are crying, too, their eyes upon hers, alive, and laughing now. Even Maggie.

We've got you, Hannah the Spanner, says shivering Toby. No escaping.

They relax and let her go, step back. The wind whips her hair around her face. Maggie pulls her scarf tighter.

Simon moves towards her and gives her a warm reassuring hug. Then he says, We had a quick conference and we think it's a great idea. Well, not all of us at first. It's unorthodox and perhaps if you had put it to us none of us would have had the gumption to go ahead with it.

You could've told us, says Maggie.

I know, I'm sorry. But I didn't think—

Anyway, says Toby, we would like to be a part of this and we believe you have some more bread.

You delve into the bag for the remains of the second loaf, about two-thirds of it, and you hand it over to Maggie who distributes the rest. To Simon and Toby. She pauses when it comes to you. You look at each other through tears, two little girls. She steps forward and you both hug quickly, intensely. And when she gives you your share, you are both trembling so much your hands can hardly hold the bread.

And now, crying, laughing, calling into the wind, you all toss your mother to the sky. And the birds are back, some gobbling greedily and squawkily around your feet and some taking her so neatly on the wing, before soaring high into the wind. And when there is no more bread, you and Simon and Maggie and Toby all lift your eyes to the seagulls, seagulls rising higher and higher, searching for a comfortable place in the currents to watch the world below, to observe the motion of the sea far below, the salty salty sea.

ACKNOWLEDGEMENTS

With grateful thanks to Klatch for forcing me to sit down at the table to write after a period of creative void. And also to the Winnies for your friendship and support, though where was Tim when we needed him?

And I'd like to thank those people who bravely read the raw manuscript and reassured me. David White, Katie Henderson, Judy Wilford, Karen Breen, Ann Glamuzina, Mary Holm, Clem White, Xanthe White and Chris Dunn.

Thank you to the team at Random House, and especially to Harriet Allan who never gave up pestering me, thank you thank you. In my mind you were always there pulling me along.

And with deep gratitude for my ever-loving and supportive family, and to my sweet husband, David, for the astonishing depth of his love and patience, his spiritual nourishment and his bewilderingly unrelenting belief in me.

To the generous and hard-working nurses at St Andrews rest home who cared for my mother so kindly.

To the late Chico who taught me everything I know about muscovy ducks.